MEDEA

A Novel

EILISH QUIN

ATRIA BOOKS

NEW YORK   LONDON   TORONTO   SYDNEY   NEW DELHI

ATRIA
BOOKS

An Imprint of Simon & Schuster, LLC
1230 Avenue of the Americas
New York, NY 10020

First Atria Books hardcover edition February 2024

ATRIA BOOKS and colophon are trademarks of Simon & Schuster, LLC

Simon & Schuster: Celebrasting 100 Years of Publishing in 2024

For information about special discounts for bulk purchases, please contact Simon & Schuster Special Sales at 1-866-506-1949 or business@simonandschuster.com.

The Simon & Schuster Speakers Bureau can bring authors to your live event. For more information or to book an event, contact the Simon & Schuster Speakers Bureau at 1-866-248-3049 or visit our website at www.simonspeakers.com.

Interior design by Kyoko Watanabe

Manufactured in the United States of America

1   3   5   7   9   10   8   6   4   2

Library of Congress Cataloging-in-Publication Data
Names: Quin, Eilish, author.
Title: Medea / Eilish Quin.
Description: First Atria Books hardcover edition. | New York : Atria Books, 2024. |
Identifiers: LCCN 2023030982 (print) | LCCN 2023030983 (ebook) |
ISBN 9781668020760 (hardcover) | ISBN 9781668020777 (paperback) |
ISBN 9781668020784 (ebook)
Subjects: LCSH: Medea, consort of Aegeus, King of Athens (Mythological character)—Fiction. | LCGFT: Mythological fiction. | Novels.
Classification: LCC PS3617.U53596 M43 2024 (print) | LCC PS3617.U53596 (ebook) |
DDC 813/.6—dc23/eng/20230719
LC record available at https://lccn.loc.gov/2023030982
LC ebook record available at https://lccn.loc.gov/2023030983

ISBN 978-1-6680-2076-0
ISBN 978-1-6680-2078-4 (ebook)

For my mom

CONTENTS

MEDEA

CHAPTER ONE

The Naiad

Of the Oceanids, there were innumerable. My mother was the youngest, and so too lately born to be a novelty among the Titans or the Gods. By the time she emerged, lithe and childlike from the edge of the Black Sea, her pale hair stuck wetly down her back and her eyes dark and swollen with salt, she already knew what she was.

Her own mother, Tethys, possessed a maritime attractiveness. Below the surface of the water, her eyes were a murky sea green, all shadow and gloom, looming out from skin so pale it glowed with a strange bioluminescence. On the occasions that she was dredged up from her repose beneath the waves, those same eyes glittered and gleamed like molten bronze when they caught the sun. She had polished thousands of children inside of her, had sheltered and shaped them in the womb of the ocean itself. And she had nursed them on the sweet fresh water from which she drew her own powers. If she had been mortal, she might have felt her body shoring against itself, straining under the pressure of producing infant after infant. But she was a Titan, the wet nurse of the earth. And so, she gave birth to the rivers, which roared with vitality, and the streams, which moved more softly; the clouds that grew heavy with rainwater; and the springs that bubbled up from the center of the world. Such was the fertility of Tethys.

From the Titan who birthed her, my mother acquired two things. The first was a body. Miniature and without blemish, skin as smooth and transparent as sea glass. The child was anointed in oils and swaddled in strands of kelp. Tethys, wan and exhausted from labor, handed over the newborn willingly into the arms of her other daughters.

The second gift my grandmother gave before returning to her own chambers beneath the sea was a name.

Idyia. Tethys would have conveyed it in her usual manner, a manner that did not involve language, for there was no need for words among the old Gods. And then, a promise, as her womb began to reknit itself. *She will be the last of your brood.*

And so it was Idyia's sisters who whispered to the youngest the secrets of herself, explained the jagged gills that loomed like lacerations down her neck, and the webbing between her fingers and toes. Playfully they would trace, with graceful, darting fingers, the veins, which stood pronounced under the blue-green highlights of her skin. So perfectly was she suited for the sea that should she have beached herself, no mortal could possibly have confused her for a human child.

From her sisters, she understood that she was not quite a nymph, but a Naiad. They passed her among themselves, delighted by the fair hair that curled at the back of her neck.

For the children of Titans, time does not pass in the way it might for mortals. My mother spent only a matter of painful hours teething, and by the end of that first day, had gained a set of pale, pointed fangs. Her expressive eyes, initially a clouded sea green, would polish themselves in her infant sockets until they were clear gray orbs. How queer it must have been to hold her, to reconcile the supple sweetness of her newborn face with the deadly power of her muscles, the vivid sharpness of her fingernails.

From her father, Oceanus, she knew intimately of her own naturalness. He informed her in the same way he informed all his daughters, somewhere between conception and the accumulating sentience of each successive rippling impulse. She was the thing that flowed, a current that ebbed and settled itself like a compulsion. The urge that heaved against riverbanks. A shored thing. An infinite thing. She could be cut, by ship or swimmer, but never wounded. This is water's divinity.

It was known that the daughters of Tethys and Oceanus made enviable wives. Although each was distinct, all possessed a perilous beauty—

the kind of aching loveliness that drew sailors to their graves. In these daughters flowed the source of all things, and the Olympians, from on high, had ordained that they should preside over the young, nourishing and nurturing in the manner that they themselves were accustomed to. So alluring were the Oceanids that Zeus himself took some for wives.

And so when my father, Aeetes, landed upon the rocky shores of Kolchis, his eagle eyes penetrating and sharp, already surveying the land for what he could extract from it, Idyia came willingly out from the surf. It would be easier this way—if the local Naiad came to the new king's bed willingly. They already shared blood; the new king of Kolchis was Idyia's nephew, the peculiar and solitary son of her elder sister Perses. Even before his eyes fell on her and fixed upon the damp ringlets of her hair and the startling whiteness of her face, she knew what she would be to him. Even with the primordial essence of the earth and sky mixing in her veins, she was still only a woman.

■　■　■

My father built his palace at the edge of the cliffs overhanging the Black Sea. Perhaps he wanted to make his new bride feel more at home on dry land, or perhaps the construction was an homage to his own sea nymph mother. In truth, I suspect his reasons were not so straightforward or sentimental. My father, who was capable of all manner of things, from the breathtaking to the nightmarish, was naturally suspicious of every other creature he encountered. He assumed his own propensity for darkness flourished in them as well. His house, that palatial manifestation of his own power, should provoke terror in the hearts of his enemies, and kindle admiration in the breasts of his allies. A fortress straddling land and sea was militarily advantageous, aesthetically intimidating, and ideally situated for his experimentation.

But Idyia had little interest in the accommodations of mortal men. While her husband marveled at her neat ankles and luminous golden hair, she stared restlessly out of windows at the churning waters below, her yearning couched delicately on an elbow.

In the beginning, the new king refused to let her out of his sight. He had heard stories about the men foolish enough to leave their Oceanid

wives to their own devices. The pull of the sea always proved too mes-
merizing to nymphs. Neither riches nor mortal love rivaled the slow,
dark paradise beneath the surface. My father observed his new wife
closely, his golden hands never far from her throat, or the smooth skin
of her inner thigh. During the moments when he could not be with her,
he consigned her to the tent they shared while the palace grew out of
nothing, and posted guards at the entrance to keep her confined. With
Idyia trapped, he could let his frenetic mind wander over plans for
the new fortification that was growing stone by stone, or through the
churning texts of plants and herbs that were so critical to his sorcery.

In the evenings he returned to her, his keen eyes scouring her cheeks
for flush, her legs for scrapes and bruises—any sign that she had gone
out upon the beach without his permission. When he was satisfied
that she was docile and obedient, he led her to the bed. Idyia's skin was
cold to the touch, as though slightly damp with sea mist, but he did not
mind. He was a child of the sun itself, that most powerful of the Titans,
Helios, and so he glowed hot enough for the both of them.

It was known in those days that the best and only way to keep a Naiad
was to give her a child. By the time the first stones had been laid, and the
lumber set aside for furniture of the most opulent order, Idyia's stomach
had already begun to swell. And so my sister, Chalciope, was born.

Chalciope emerged from my mother's womb with damp curls the
color of soil rich with iron, and bronze skin, darker already than that of
either of her parents. My father took her gingerly into his golden palms,
appraising her as she fussed. He had wanted a boy, but he could wait.
Aeetes had always been confident, and he knew his line was assured.
For now, this child would suffice. He was pleased with her glimmering
skin and how quick she was to quiet. She might even make a favorable
match to some far-off king or demigod when she grew older and into
her looks. Idyia was confounded by the child she had sired, this strange
mix of herself and a mortal. She had known other infants, of course,
had cradled them in her long transparent arms, and blown bubbles
around their cheeks to make them laugh. But this one was quiet where
the others, her multitude of nieces and nephews, had been playful and
raucous, dark and radiant where they had been pale and softly glowing.

After the birth of my sister, it was as though my mother had passed a test. Aeetes could content himself that she would come back to him and to their child. Besides, she was more present with him on the evenings when she returned, skin frigid with chill and hair thick and glittering with salt water. And so Idyia was allowed to venture between the starkness of the sea and the opulent towers of my father's construction. Occasionally, she took Chalciope with her down beneath the surface, manipulating the currents so that a strand of air bubbles would wind around the child's face, providing her oxygen and refuge from the salt. Together, they would examine the treasures of the tides: starfish that were coarse to the touch, and anemones that sucked my sister's miniature fingers into their center, urchins that pricked her soft palms, and snails that attached themselves fondly to her legs. Chalciope was clumsy on land, but not in the sea, and so preferred the beach to anywhere else.

My sister was sweet and delicate, deprived of gills and of some of the native wildness that might have gone to her. If she scathed her knees on the uneven stones beside the beach, the wounds did not heal in a matter of moments, but lingered, ugly and vermillion and stinging under the open sky. Every bruise that appeared upon her flesh was a reminder to Idyia that her child was only semidivine. *How dreadful to beget something that would only age and die*, my mother must have thought, as she watched Chalciope wander around the newly erected palace on her fat baby legs. Death, to Idyia, seemed to go against the very laws of nature, for nature had, until that point, always been kind to her. Her daughter's mortality felt foreign and faraway, impossible to hold, and so I imagine that after a time, she ceased to think about it altogether.

For a while, at least, my mother was happy. She had a child of her own to care for, to imbue with the same wonder that she carried inside of her. Aside from the inconvenience of her husband, she was content.

It might have gone on like that, halcyon and sweet, if not for me. My mother's stomach began to swell again, the telltale signs of a body readying itself for creation. In the early months, this was not as noticeable. My mother was naturally slender, the smooth texture of her bones stood out against her indigo-toned skin, and she concealed me beneath the heavy folds of silk and lace.

Eventually, Father caught on, noticing the change in the way his wife carried herself, carefully, as though wary of damage. He observed the effulgent flush of her cheeks, the odd fire in her eyes that signaled a sacred kind of knowledge.

"You are with child," he asserted one evening, after Chalciope had been ushered away to bed. Idyia wrung the seawater from her hair, her soaked clothes clinging to her. It was not a question, because Aeetes was never uncertain.

Her eyes flicked up to his face, meeting the trenchant gaze that had always unnerved her. He shone too brightly, this husband of hers. There was too much of the sun in him for comfort. Everything he looked upon shriveled up, scalded.

"Yes, my lord," she murmured shyly. My mother had a voice that was simultaneously melodious and hissing, like waves crawling up a rocky shore.

He regarded her for a long moment, his eyes softening slightly in the candlelight. Moving forward, he took her in his arms, and pressed her cold, narrow frame against his chest.

"It will be a boy this time. An heir fit for the son of Helios." He smiled into her hair.

My mother said nothing, biting her lip, and grounding herself in the far-off sound of the surf below. Her name, *Idyia*, meant "knowing one," some intuition of her own mother, Tethys, that the last of the Oceanids would be prone to prophecy. Everything in my mother's uncanny body pointed toward another daughter. A boy would come eventually, but not now.

"I want you to stop going out in the mornings," Aeetes went on, arms tightening around her slightly. "We need to keep my heir safe, and the sea is no place for a woman in your condition. Chalciope is beginning to learn how to speak, and she should be inside, accompanied by nurses and tutors. When she comes back on your hip, her hair is a mess and she shrieks like the wind. It is unbecoming for a princess to be raised in the rough, don't you agree? No honorable man will want a savage bride."

Idyia, for her part, kept her mouth tightly closed. She knew better than to argue with my father.

CHAPTER TWO

Like a Blade to the Back

My birth was a difficult one, or so my mother would tell me in those soft hours of the early morning, before the servants collected me and Chalciope from her bed and took us to the nursery. We would lie tangled up together in between soft purple sheets my father had imported from Athens. I would awake first each morning and stare fixedly at my mother's sleeping face. I would chart the points of her eyebrows, the soft hook of her aquiline nose, and the prim rosebud mouth that opened and closed softly as she dreamed.

These were the best hours, because Father could not touch us. He had his own chambers at the opposite end of the palace, built facing the Valley of Phasis. He rose early and went out to collect herbs, a fine leather journal clasped in his arms. Sorcery, I knew, even as a child, was an all-day affair. And so we had our mother to ourselves, at least for a little while.

Then, Chalciope would stir, her face contorted in childish angst as she took in the streaming sun and stretched.

Today, I watched as her muscles flexed, revealing the secret texture of ligaments and bone.

"Tell me again, the story of how I was born," I implored Mother as she too rose gracefully from the pillows, leaning her cheek against the magnificently carved headboard.

Chalciope, always ready with a rejoinder, retorted, "No, Mama, we hear that all the time. Tell us about how you used to take me under the sea before Father put a stop to it! Tell us how you helped me to breathe underwater. Medea won't know because she's only a baby, and she wasn't even born when we used to go together!" I scowled darkly at my elder sister, and she flashed me a sly smile.

"I imagine that we have time for both," Mother soothed, her fingers slipping through my hair as though to tame it.

Chalciope was right—the story was always the same, but it thrilled and troubled me, nonetheless.

"You came early—far too early. It gave your father and me a terrible fright," my mother began, her eyes unfixing themselves. I could tell that she was more absent than usual. Later I learned that Aeetes blamed our mother for my early delivery; he assumed that she had gone out to the water against his wishes, and that the sudden surge of cold had brought on the contractions. In truth, the long days of inaction had gotten to my mother. Even with Chalciope to distract her, the inaccessible roar of the sea had mingled with her burgeoning anxiety. A perfect storm.

"Your elder sister was an easy birth," my mother went on, snapping back to the moment, her eyes flicking playfully to Chalciope, her long white fingers dancing under my sister's chin.

"That's because I'm always easy. Father says I'm the most enchanting daughter he might have asked for," Chalciope chirped proudly, glancing at me. Her statement echoed painfully inside my head, even though it was true. Chalciope was long limbed and lithe, even at seven years old, her eyes soft and demure, and her voice meek and lilting. She moved like water, a gift from our sea-nymph mother, but the resemblance stopped there. In every other way, she shone as brightly as our father, her skin tan and her once dark red hair gradually bleaching itself in the sunlight until it was a sweeter shade of flaming blond. She was everything a girl should be, and someday, as Aeetes was fond of saying, she would make a good wife and bring glory to our line.

I, on the other hand, possessed very little of my mother's maritime grace. I was pale like she was and had inherited her uncommon translucence. But I did not glow, shimmering faintly, like a light at the bottom of the sea, as she did. My hair, which was the metallic green of rust, hung in dark tangles around my face, growing impossibly fast.

With my bright red mouth and clouded gray eyes, I had the look of something sickly and unhealthy. To make matters worse, I lacked the easy charm of my sister, the molten something in her look, which drew all manner of people to her and made them love her immediately. She smelled of sweet summer breezes, and I reeked of Kolchis itself: cold, salt-stripped, and forbidding.

"Both of you are assets to this house," my mother supplied diplomatically, her eyes going vague again. "Your father and I—" She broke off, her fingers straying across her mouth, as though to stop herself from saying something. Outside, the wind howled, and pine boughs scraped against the shutters. The sun shone haphazardly through the clouds, and I shivered.

"The story, Mama," I reminded her softly, burrowing closer to her chest, watching the sense return to her.

"The winter was unusually brutal, and the contractions began in the dead of night. Your father was in his own chambers, tucked away and cloistered with his books of *Pharmakon*, and so I summoned the nurses myself to attend the birth."

"You did not tell Father that I was coming?" I inquired, though I already knew the answer. I watched her carefully for the smallest flicker of anxiety or uncertainty, but she knew better than to reveal such things to me.

"No, I had no need of him."

"Because you knew I would be a girl, and not a prince?" I pressed, again already knowing.

My mother nodded, not looking at me. She bit the edge of her lip pensively, her face as blank as a pool of water before it is disturbed. Even then, I guessed that the real reason was slightly more complicated.

"The labor dragged on for hours," she continued. "I felt as though I were being torn apart from the inside. But this was not what made the hours long. In truth, I had a knowledge of what *you were*, Medea. *Of what you would be*, even before the midwife pulled you from me." She chose her words carefully, her eyes fluttering shut briefly, as though to ward off some unpleasant sight.

"A brat, you mean." Chalciope giggled under her breath. I glowered at her. My mother gazed unseeing at my sister, before dropping her eyes to her hands, which were twisting fluidly in her lap.

"No, not that," she intoned. "It's never that clear. Prophecy comes in fragments, Chalciope, in hard rushes of feeling and sudden dread. It strikes through you like a blade to the back." She shivered, and instinctively I offered her some of my blankets. She smiled faintly at me, shaking her head.

"So what did it feel like? What did you predict about me?" I asked in a hush, not wanting to pry but feeling compelled to.

"Nothing much at all," my mother murmured, as she always did whenever I asked. "Just a feeling."

"A good feeling?" Chalciope drawled, quirking her head to the side and looking bored. A wave of nausea rose in my chest.

My mother offered a thin smile, before returning to her story.

"The truth is that I dreamed of both of you girls before you were born. Even before you had bodies of your own, you came to visit me in the evenings. Such beautiful dreams they were . . ." She trailed off, looking at the ceiling. "And that is how I knew what both of you would look like, how you would feel swaddled in my arms." Slowly the anxiety melted from my limbs as I allowed myself to imagine the incredible warmth of these fantasies.

"And you saw our brother too," my sister verified, her eyes sparkling. "The one who isn't born yet."

My mother nodded, and instinctually wrapped her arms around her stomach. Her face flashed with some unreadable emotion. I attempted to catch her eye, but she avoided my gaze.

"But how could we come to see you in dreams if we weren't even alive yet?" Chalciope laughed, her warm face lit with good humor. She had not seemed to notice our mother's change in mood.

"The Gods on high make all manner of impossible things possible." My mother's hands smoothed my hair absently, but her look remained fixed elsewhere.

"What will our brother look like?" I asked her, hoping that if I spoke, she might look at me again.

But instead she turned to Chalciope as she answered. "His skin is like the bronze of your sister's, but even brighter. He could almost rival your father with the light that spills from him. His hair, though, will be long and light as sunlight, and his eyes will be the same color as mine. And his smile is such that it will delight the world."

"What will we call him?"

"That is for your father to decide."

"You must have some idea?" my sister pushed, leaning her chin on her hands and making her eyes sweet and amenable.

"My propensity for prophecy does not extend to your father's decisions," Mother explained in a resigned monotone, and then catching sight of Chalciope's unhappy expression, she added, "But to the three of us, he will be our shining one, Phaethon."

"Phaethon," Chalciope whispered to herself in awe. "Phaethon. My brother, the Prince Phaethon. Oh, I like that, Mama. And will he be more fun to play with than Medea?" I elbowed her in her perfect ribs, and she shrieked with laughter.

"Don't be so cruel to your sister," Mother chided, looking tired although we had been awake only a few hours. "Now didn't you want to talk about our visits to the sea?"

Just then, a hard, cold knock fell upon the chamber door. It was our nurse, ready to ferry us away for a day of needlework and boredom. Chalciope was old enough, and her fingers long and deft enough, to play upon our mother's own lyre, a contraption carved from polished abalone that refracted ethereal colors on the ceiling while she fingered the strings. I was given a pan flute to finger, and no particular instruction.

"Must I go with her?" I whispered in my mother's ear, clutching her hand to my heart as Chalciope leaped from the bed, like the obedient charge she was.

Mother said nothing but stiffened beneath my fingers, and pulled away, her face backlit with something like revulsion. I felt the beginnings of tears well up in my throat. Just as quickly, the look was gone, and the kind, compassionate mother I was used to had resumed her place.

"It's only for a little while," she offered, along with a small smile. "If you behave well, perhaps tonight we can tell more stories before you fall asleep."

This promise was enough, for my mother's storytelling was unrivaled. She would whisper to us of the monsters that lurked beneath the ocean's surface, undisturbed for centuries, or that terrifying Lord of Time, Kronos, who had devoured his own children until Zeus put a stop to it.

Sometimes, she would wax poetic about the great war between the Titans and the Gods. Our father disliked this habit, because he loathed being reminded that he was of Titan stock. Even though Helios had fought for the Olympians in the conflict, and had earned himself a reputation as the best of his kind as a result, our lineage was still tainted. That we all narrowly escaped Tartarus was never far from my father's mind, and so he took special pains to keep it constantly in ours as well.

CHAPTER THREE

Witchery

In the beginning, my father was reluctant to teach me anything of his sorcery. When I asked to look over his scrolls, or to go with him when he went out to catalog plants, he would simply stare at me coldly, his coral-colored mouth thin with distaste.

"You're too young, Medea. There is no natural reason for you to entrench yourself in these things. You ought to be focusing on your embroidery, or your musicianship, or your Greek. Your coarseness proves to everyone who hears you that you have come up among a savage race. No king will ever want you for a bride if you cannot speak his language." Father was desperate for us to learn Greek. Our own native tongue, the dialect of Kolchis, was rough and uncouth—hardly respectable. It marked us as outsiders, just as our Titan blood did.

Chalciope was better at her Greek than I was, in the same way that she was better at everything. At nine years old, the once harsh iron-colored curls of her babyhood had begun to fall in softer pomegranate waves down her back, and her skin was bronze-toned, prone to shimmering in the sun. Our nurses fell over themselves to provide her with anything she might need—fresh milk, chilled in the cellars after being procured from the goats, or vivid wildflowers to weave into her hair. Her fingers moved fluidly along lyre strings, creating melodies that echoed out of the palace windows and made the gardeners in the court-yard below pause in their work, their expressions dazed and dreamy.

"Chalciope can marry a king, and I can stay with you and Mother," I offered after a moment of intense thought. "She will make a better wife than I will. And that way you can teach me about *Pharmakon*."

My father's face went, if possible, darker as I said this, his bright eyes flashing.

"It is not becoming, especially not for a girl child," he intoned roughly. I knew that this was the real reason he had denied me his knowledge. He was holding out for a proper heir to endow with the nuances and intricacies of his life's work.

"But what of Aunt Circe?" I retorted, blood thundering in my ears. "She is a woman and a witch all at once, is she not? Mother said that her knowledge rivals even yours—that she can turn grown men, burly, bearded soldiers, into writhing little animals at the flick of a wrist."

"We do not speak of her here. I've told your mother enough times to keep her mouth shut about magic she does not understand. What has she been telling you?" he snarled, rigid and taut under his cloak. These were the times my father was most dangerous, crackling and smoking with the scalding volatility of a disturbed fire.

"Nothing," I backtracked, heart hammering. "Nothing really. Just that it was she who raised you. Fed you and sung you to sleep when you were still a baby, and that she adored you utterly. And that when you grew a little older, she taught you all she knew about—"

"That's enough, Medea." His fists clenched and unclenched at his sides, his jaw working madly.

"If she really is your dearest sister, why haven't I ever met her? Mother says she lives far away on a beautiful island all alone. It must get lonely."

"I said, that's enough."

I fell silent.

I cannot say whether my father was always uncanny and strange, or if his sorceress sister made him that way. Despite my father's resistance to the subject, thoughts of Circe kept me up at night. I fell asleep imagining scenarios in my head where I would join her out upon Aeaea, that unreachable island she was condemned to. I attempted to picture what a feminine version of Aeetes might look like. Would she have my father's glowing skin, always hot to the touch? Would she have his same shrewd, calculating eyes that never missed even the tiniest detail, the slightest movement?

She would take me in her arms, and whisper to me the secrets that I had so far been deprived of. Under her tutelage, I would become a witch in my own right, more powerful than my father, more desirable than Chalciope, freer than my mother. But, of course, the days slipped into months, and I remained rooted at the palace in Kolchis, a prisoner of opulence.

There were always rumors about Circe, no matter how hard my father attempted to crush them. Some were not so pernicious—that she had spent too much time in Helios's subterranean palace and that it had warped her mind, or that she had an intense fascination with humans that bordered on the obsessive. Other tales were more insidious—that she had poisoned her husband, a prince from Kolchis, years before; that with her knowledge of the secret uses of flowering things, she had irreversibly transformed beautiful nymphs into hideous monsters. Other rumors cast Aeetes in a kind of antiquated perversion. The servants loved to whisper among themselves that before he had married Idyia, my father and Circe had been lovers. The old Gods did not possess the same distaste for familial relations that mortals did, for it was a way of keeping the bloodline pure and the power distilled, for all the good that did.

■   ■   ■

And so I determined that I would need to teach myself the intricacies of *Pharmakon*. My father departed early in the mornings, occasionally staying out for weeks at a time, always in the pursuit of forbidden and perilous knowledge. When he did return from near or far, he would be changed. Incrementally, gradually, but always darker than he had been. The kind of work he did left its mark somewhere. When he was gone, my mother would also flee, although while Aeetes went out toward the Caucasus or beyond, she would slip down into the murky depths of the Black Sea. I could not begrudge her this. After all, life on Kolchis was eerie and dull.

My sister and I were frequently left to our own devices. After our morning lessons, Chalciope meandered around the courtyards, flirting with serving boys and when there were none of those about, making conversation with slaves. She had no need for me, this much I knew. Unobserved and unbothered, I would stray farther and farther from the palace walls. In the beginning I stayed in the shadow of the towers, picking at the sweet grass that grew up around the stones. Each day, I scouted out some new and previously unexplored perch, sometimes down by the beaches, among the kelp-strewn sea caves, sometimes up on the bluffs, under the gnarled olive trees.

These adventures made my chest tight with distress—so many of our mother's stories had revolved around those who went a step too far in their wanderings, who, without meaning to, had crept beyond the realms of protection that naturally encircled them. But the rush of finding some deserted clearing in the woods, or a particularly oddly shaped piece of driftwood, was worth those fleeting nerves. Besides, my mother was not there to warn me back to the safety of my chamber.

It was here, far away from the watchful eyes of the nurses and servants, that I began my studies. From my own spying, I had caught glimpses of my father's papers and knew a little with which to begin. The art of *Pharmakon* was concerned with unlocking the secret powers of plants and flowering things. The Greek word *pharmakos* echoed around sweetly in my head, the only bit of the foreign tongue that seemed to make sense to the wildness coursing through me. I knew from my tutors that it had a double meaning: it could refer to a medicine, something to usher life back into a body and make it strong and vital again, or it could mean "poison," some substance that would send a soul directly down to those black-lit halls of the underworld. How deliciously ambiguous it all was. The thoughts of coaxing the poison from green stalks and promiscuous blooms sent terrifying thrills through me, but how exactly was one to learn which plants were benevolent, and in what amounts something could be dangerous?

Occasionally, my father would refer to the ways in which the plants he tended *spoke to him*.

A visiting king might ask how he knew what ingredients to put in a salve, or my mother might wonder aloud how my father had found the flowers for her hair, and Aeetes would respond with a sardonic half smile, "I merely asked the poppy and the aloe and the nightshade for their thoughts, how else?"

And so, in those early days, I tried speaking to the plants on my solitary forays. I asked the grass that darted up around my ankles how it was feeling, and from where it derived its sweetness. I inquired of the olive trees what they knew of their creator, that gray-eyed Goddess Athena. Of the pine trees that dappled the edge of the forest, I requested some knowledge of the properties of their sap, all to no avail.

At first, the foliage kept its secrets, whispering quietly in the cold breeze, rustling in a language only the dryads might understand. Perhaps it was a symptom of my loneliness that even though my charges did not return my friendliness, I continued to talk to them. I spent hours telling them the childish details of my life, and they listened back easily, a passive audience. Nothing was too minor or trivial for them. Occasionally I sang to them the clumsy songs of my own creation, or else the famous ones that Chalciope liked to play upon her lyre—those melodious meanderings of heroes and Gods.

Gradually, I learned to observe the leaves as they glittered in the sun, or stood out darkly against the fog that swept in from the sea. To analyze the bark that sprung up rough and heady from the earth itself. To fall into meditations on the supple flexibility of stems and stalks that bent easily under my fingers, nature's fare rendered supplicant and demure.

My father was right: the trees and blossoms were more than willing to teach any disciple who regarded them closely enough.

Every living and vibrant thing was a clue to this baffling puzzle I had been born into. Each ripening fruit, or steadily wilting sapling, encompassed a snapshot of the energy that engendered it, the mad passion that even now dwelled within its vegetable body. In my own crude scrawl, I began to take notes that were mostly just questions and passing associations. I fancied myself a miniature version of my father, conducting experiments with herbs and recording the results.

I spent hours poring over slivers of darting acanthus leaves, the rough bark of oak saplings—towering cypress trees and more modest myrtle shrubs. It was miraculous what time alone in the quiet with even the most unassuming weed could do for the mind.

I broke off pieces of juniper shrubs, crushing fragments in my palms to release their scent, exalting in the ooze of sap between my fingers. How impossible it seemed that a berry might exist external to my own body, distinct and unfathomable, yet also inevitably nurtured in the heat of the same sun that rose on me each morning—sustained with the same water that I used to quench my thirst. As I played with the lively green spines and delicate blue-frosted berries, I considered their secret meanings and uses. Why would the plant take this form? Why either those sharp, needlelike leaves, or blunt, scaled-over stalks ending in premature cones? The potent aroma and immature scaled shoots were reminiscent of mortal lungs, something I had noticed during tedious anatomy lessons with Chalciope. And so, I wondered if the juniper might be used for treatment of asthma, the clearing out of airways polluted by phlegm.

Though I was barely into my sixth year, the knowledge I derived from the plants and shrubs around me made me feel uncommonly wise. In those early days, witchcraft for me was a game of associations. The thick bark of the cypress tree reminded me of the time a laborer broke his leg. I recalled how the bone stuck out of his flesh at a terrible angle, pale and polished even where it had splintered. And this was how I came to know that the bark's peeling rinds could be soaked or chewed to strengthen the bones.

In secret, I imagined myself as a healer, sage and assiduous among the blossoms and weeds. If one of the serving girls nicked their palms while preparing dinner, I pressed fresh stalks of yarrow into their hands in secret, the bloodred blossoms ready to dress their wounds. If panic emerged in my breast from nowhere, I recited to myself the secret properties of healing herbs and imagined myself protected. When my father grew cruel and snappish in the evenings, I meditated upon the thistle, with its crown of thorns and vivid violet insides, or the acanthus, sharp and protected from any fool who might seek to unsettle it. For the first time, I had a sense of myself and my power.

I moved gradually from the familiarity of benign flora toward their more insidious counterparts. As it turned out, I had a penchant for poisons.

Oleander grew in heady bushes around the outer rim of the forest. The blooms came in a million sunset hues, some the soft color of a peach, others the vivid magenta of spilled blood. I was hypnotized by the delirious spiraling petals that emerged from the center of its flowers, by the leaves that were green and glossy in youth and then suddenly dull as the virescence ebbed. There was something of Aphrodite in the cacophony of color and sweetness, in the pale pinks and violent reds, as though all of this existed to say *love has its own edge.* When crushed with a rock, the leaves released a bitter scent that made my nostrils flare.

I learned that this bitterness made the plant unpalatable—that if I wanted to slip it into a concoction it would require the addition of honey to mask the taste. The trunk, thick and stubby, could be cut into small logs or shaved down into kindling and snuck into stores of firewood. Anything cooked over the ensuing flames would be deadly if consumed. When the secreted oil met skin, it could cause rashes and irritation.

In the back of my mind, I noted that the flowers were reminiscent of the kind that Chalciope liked to wear interspersed throughout her hair. It would not be too difficult to slip them among the other blossoms that her maids placed behind her ears and under her coronet, if she was unkind to me.

On Resemblance

Eventually my father tired of waiting for a son. I was freshly into my seventh year, and my mother was gone more often than she could be found wandering the palace corridors, or reclining in her quarters. Even when she did deign to spend the evening with us, her eyes were far away, misty and unreachable.

One day, after Chalciope and I concluded our morning lessons, I made my way down to the ground level, intending to take notes on the bougainvillea that climbed so easily along the garden walls. The hours in the stagnant air of our tutor's apartment disoriented me, as daydreams became more vivid than the lessons at hand. We had been discussing the significance of textile weaving in the Greek city-states, a topic that Chalciope found infinitely fascinating, for she had recently taken up the loom herself. Meanwhile I had drifted off into a reverie of the previous afternoon, when I stumbled upon a sea cave I had never noticed before, tucked in between the crags and the rolling surf. The walls were slick with displaced kelp, and the floor glittered with pockets of ocean water. It was an entire realm of tide pools sheltered from the worst of the elements. I wanted to remember to tell Mother when she returned from her latest deep-sea excursion. And so the minutes meandered past with devastating slowness—my eyes glazed over with waking dreams. When at last the allotted hour was up, I moved hastily toward the door.

As I snuck down the spiral staircase over the throne room, a voice beckoned me.

"Medea," my father called with his usual brusqueness from his shadowed seat. "I have need of you."

Heart drumming uneasily in my chest, I moved clumsily toward him, worried at first that I might have done something to earn his disapproval. Perhaps one of the nurses had given an unfavorable report of my embroidery, or a tutor had complained about my incessant vacantness.

"Yes, Father," I uttered, looking at my feet, hoping that whatever upbraiding I was about to receive would be swift. The silence between us stretched out uncomfortably, and eventually I raised my eyes to meet my father's. He was regarding me with his usual penetrating look, the kind that never missed a detail and that pierced to the very soul. He seemed to be debating internally about something, for every so often his angular face would flicker with a rush of quickly stifled emotion. I knew better than to vex him while his mind was occupied, and so I regarded him back, attempting to make my face as impassive as possible.

After a long moment, he rose gracefully to his feet and made a gesture with his hand for me to follow him. I hastened after him; back up the winding stairs and into the South Wing of the palace. These were my father's private quarters, and neither I nor Chalciope had free rein of them. A thousand thoughts and speculations darted through my brain like startled fish in a disturbed pond. What reason could he possibly have for bringing me here?

Eventually we reached an annex I had never seen before, a foyer at the base of the Southernmost Tower. We paused in front of a heavy oak door. My father retrieved a key from the inner pocket of his cloak, and inserted it into the lock.

"After you, daughter," he offered with a mocking smile and a flourish as the door swung open. The passageway on the other side was jet-black, darkened by shadow. There were no windows leading up the stairs.

I opened my mouth to protest, but before I could speak, he lit a candle and pressed it into my hands.

"Your eyes will adjust."

Nodding mutely, I ascended the staircase, eyes straining to see beyond the glow of warm light. The flagstones leveled out toward the top, and my father once again took the lead, unlocking a second set of double doors.

Inside was a kind of horrifying paradise. Herbs were tied from the ceiling, swaying like hanged men. Among the dried stalks and oily leaves dangled miniature models of the planets and celestial bodies. They glittered, orbiting in gentle circles reflecting the flickering light of my candle. In one corner stood an enormous desk of carved cypress, littered with scrolls that overflowed onto the floor. The flagstones in this room were covered in complicated labyrinthine rugs, the walls lined with tapestries depicting a multitude of scenes: a woman bent over a bubbling pot, her hands full of mysterious vegetation, a centaur carving a bowl from a chunk of wood in the middle of a verdant forest, a man at the top of a mountain, surveying the mess of life that extended below. An arched doorway led from this chamber to an adjoining one, and I could just make out the rows and rows of shelving crowded with faintly glowing jars and cages. One rectangular enclosure directly in my line of sight housed a pair of birds with bloodred eyes and razor-sharp bronze beaks, eyeing me hungrily despite their small size.

Noticing the direction of my gaze, Aeetes gave a slow, mirthless smirk.

"Stymphalian birds." He chuckled. "Nasty little brutes. Man-eating, and their feathers are sharp enough to pierce armor. I had to venture all the way to the little island of Aretias to catch them."

Scratching sounds and shrill whines leaked from the shadows in the corners of that neighboring room, and I wondered warily what else my father kept there.

"It is, of course, just a fraction of my menagerie," he gloated, puffing up like a peacock's frill. "I've spent decades assembling the most perilous and charming of beasts you can imagine so that they might be properly studied, and all their usefulness extracted. Some of my specimens cannot be found anywhere else in the world." My stomach sank even as a thrilling dart of anticipation ran through me. There were parts of the castle grounds that had always been strictly prohibited to me and Chalciope, by the decree of our father: specific fields left to lie fallow surrounded by tall stone walls, or what I imagined must be harmless enough clearings of wildflowers in the center of the adjacent forest. Suddenly, I understood his stubborn unwillingness to let us trespass upon those obscure spaces.

"Some creatures I have collected on the course of my journeys, while others were specially bestowed upon me by the Gods on high," he asserted casually, as though discussing the weather.

I nodded, my courage deserting me as a strange shriek erupted in the adjoining chamber. Involuntarily, I took a step forward, meaning to help whatever pitiable entity made the noise.

"What kind of creatures?" I managed at last. If Aeetes had reason to take an interest in any animal, it must be a truly terrifying one.

He made a dismissive motion with his hands.

"The things I keep indoors are mostly harmless: the brass leg of an Empousa, the severed snake's tail of a Chimera, the old teeth of a crocotta, the horns of a cerastes. Trophies, more than anything. The rest will come later. For the time being, this is where we will work. I've cleared a space for you, over here by the window. You can use any of my instruments, so long as you ask permission first," he explained in an impartial voice, turning on his heel and heading toward a shelf burdened with parchment before I could respond. I forced myself to look away from the strange creatures floating in jars, and the birds as they began to throw themselves violently against the bars of their cages. Aeetes was speaking again.

"You'll need to begin reading these. We'll start with the foundations of planetary herbalism, and then move on to more complex alchemical applications and transformations." He pushed a mountain of scrolls into my arms. I opened my mouth to speak, but no words formed.

My father, for his part, seemed not to have noticed, and he proceeded impervious to my shock. "I've seen you sneaking off during the day with your journals and jars. You're not as inconspicuous as you imagine, slipping off into the wilderness like that. I was much the same at your age, I suppose. Even though I had initially thought it unwise to induct you into this world, it seems that you're bent on breaking in whether I approve or not."

"You're going to teach me *Pharmakon*?" I breathed, still attempting to process my father's sudden change in mood.

"Yes, I am. With no heir to speak of, it seems I have no other choice but to make use of what is currently in front of me. Chalciope is a good girl, and she will make a wonderful wife and queen, but she is not predisposed to the dark arts, in the fashion that you and I are. She has no interest in the science and magic that underlies our existence, no comprehension of her own tenuous position. And so I have settled on you, Medea, my second born." He scanned me piercingly, as though reconsidering his choice.

"Thank you," I croaked, almost delirious with excitement. It was the most I could manage, given the circumstances, but my father nodded, satisfied.

"We begin now."

■   ■   ■

"The sorcerer is a transgressor, a crosser of boundaries, at once deeply entrenched in the natural order of things and simultaneously devoted to the mutations of reality on a very basic level. In the person of the witch, the line between natural and unnatural is elegantly blurred. The work we will do together is not always pleasant or savory, and mortals and Gods alike may spurn you for it."

So began Aeetes's lectures on the nature of herbal medicine. Under his guidance, I learned that in crafting plant magic, there are always astrological considerations. Vegetation derives its energy from the sun, transforming the rays of the sun into life itself. Plants are therefore an entry point for magic, representing a transfusion from the divine to the earth.

"Good witches attempt to emulate that initial act of transformation," my father explained, "and so they must be intimately aligned with the natural world at all times, no matter how uncomfortable or disturbing that might be to the human psyche. Our work is about entertaining radical connection on a scale that should be impossible, and so, of course, it will be painful."

His words made sense to me intuitively, and I took to his teachings with a fervor I had never expressed in baser subjects. That astrological magic had correspondences to earthly magic, that those faraway celestial bodies might inform the growth and power of saplings on earth, was enough to explode my worldview. If everything was connected, as my father asserted it must be, then one thing might be understood as a clue to the riddle of something else, however disparate or divergent. I realized, haltingly, that chains of relationship extended from the stars to the earth and back again. It naturally followed that the spiritual might make itself known to the observer by way of physical manifestation, if one was only brave enough to look for it.

When we were not tucked away in the Southernmost Tower, Father and I were navigating the fields and forests around the palace in search of all manner of herbs and fungi that might serve as the basis for my education. He taught me to recognize herbs with solar qualities by their aesthetic characteristics—their colors were warm and vibrant, and their petals starlike. We gathered baskets of heliotropes, those blossoms that follow Helios as he arcs his way across the sky and fold in on themselves when night falls, and crushed them with mortars and pestles. In association with the proper potions, they could enhance the development of a person's ego and wisdom—their vision and propensity for success.

Lunar herbs were more concerned with the mysterious and emotional inner workings of the self, and so were used to increase intuition in the drinker, or even promote prophecy. They could be distinguished by their succulent leaves and delicate silver blossoms, their abundance of roots and presence near water. These were the plants associated with cleansing, and so Aeetes and I began each lesson with a draft distilled from the fermented roots of star anise and mugwort.

One afternoon, as we worked alongside each other in the dirt, procuring mercurial herbs for a draft that would catalyze eloquence in the drinker, my father let out a low sigh. I had not noticed that he had paused in his movements, so caught up was I in our shared labor. But feeling his gaze on me, I shifted uncomfortably.

"What is the matter with you?" I asked, unnerved by the intensity of his glance. In the months since Aeetes had let me into his confidence, I had become more informal with him. It was strange, this love that sprang up from me, a love I did not know I could feel toward him. It was a childish, desperate admiration.

He paused, looking away after a long moment, his jaw working madly.

"You look like her, like Circe. You always have, ever since you were a little girl, but just now, elbow deep in the mud, with that look of consternation on your face, the likeness was rather frightening. You might have been her daughter and not mine."

Color flooded my cheeks, and the words died in my throat. My father had never willingly brought up his sister before.

"What happened to her?" The words tumbled out of me before I could stop them, falling with the weight of stones between us. Aeetes's face darkened and his mouth twisted in a pained scowl.

"Nothing happened to her, Medea. She merely proved to us, to all of the Gods on high, that she was exactly what we had imagined her to be from the outset. Of the things that walk this earth and are sentient, woman is the most foul, and for all of her power and ambition she was still a woman."

"I don't understand," I tried again, the faintest hint of a whine slipping into my voice. "Why is she banished to Aeaea? Why do we never speak of her?" His scowl deepened, and I sensed that this conversation was drawing to a close. For the slightest moment, something like guilt was illuminated in his face, but in an instant, it was gone again.

"We both went along the poison path, just as you are doing now. While I used what I learned to ensure a glorious kingship, she satisfied her baser urges. I suppose it was not her fault; all women are deceitful, lustful creatures, haunted by a bleak passion that does not let them up until they have entered Hades. But since she was stronger than other women, she had further to fall. Let that be a lesson to you, daughter."

Although his answers were hardly enough to build any real knowledge upon, his message was clear. He would brook no disobedience, now or ever, no matter how much he appeared to care for me. For he had loved Circe well and turned a blind eye to her in exile anyhow.

I bit my tongue, torn between wanting to ask more questions, and the need to preserve my father's mood. The rebuke still came, before I could stop myself.

"You mean that she was stronger than you," I murmured into the air between us.

For a moment, my father did not respond, and I wondered vaguely if perhaps he had not picked up on my irreverence. I lowered my head to look into the dirt as the silence stretched between us.

And then, pain. Thick and hot and electric across my jaw. I was aware of a cracking sound, the snap of my face caving in on itself. I could taste his fist in my mouth—dirt and blood and sweat mixing on my tongue. And for a moment, the world went dark.

■　■　■

When I awoke, I was alone in the clearing. It had grown darker while I was unconscious, and overhead, the first stars were beginning to litter the sky. My face throbbed painfully, and I let out a small whimper as my fingers rose to appraise the damage. My vision seemed oddly blurred, as though obscured by stars inside my own skull.

Of course, Aeetes was nowhere to be found. After he had dealt out my punishment, he probably returned to the castle. He would be tucked away in his study, warmed by the heat of a roaring fire.

If I had been the type of child who knew how to cry, I might have cried then. Under the full brightness of the moon, tears might have been a mercy.

I curled in on myself in the tall grass, breathing in the scent of the earth and the sea. So preoccupied was I with trying to force tears that I did not immediately notice the sudden silence that fell across the clearing. I did not smell the rush of heady aromas that appeared from nowhere—the metallic scent of iron, and the softer floral hints of lavender.

Across from me, a glimmer of something caught my attention: twin eyes, the color and quintessence of the moon, gleaming out from under a keen, supple brow. It was a woman coming toward me from the line of trees, glowing softly under the light of the heavens. I stumbled to my feet, heart hammering under the supernatural gravity of that gaze.

Even adorned in the fearsome armor of a man, she was more lovely than anything I had ever seen before. Beauty so intense and rigid, it was painful to gaze upon all at once. She lifted the helmet from her head, and curls, dark and luxurious, fell around her shoulders in a violent cascade. My breath caught, jagged in my throat, and I forced myself to focus on the details of her form: the olive tone of her skin, which glistened in the darkness, the toned quality of her muscles under her shift and armor, the dreadful intelligence that lurked in her gray eyes.

"I think I'm going to be sick," I told her, coloring immediately at the stupidity of my words.

Her eyebrows, thick and dark upon her brow, quirked in what might have been amusement or distaste.

"You haven't taken a draft of poison, have you, my dear? I assume your father doesn't just leave his concoctions lying around?" she inquired, looking unimpressed.

I shook my head vigorously, all attempts at crying forgotten.

"Tears do very little, I've found," she offered, voice clear and commanding. "They are a human contrivance more than anything—more manipulative affect than true catharsis. I would not expect them to come naturally to you."

It was as though she could read my mind.

I opened my mouth and then abruptly shut it again. She watched me struggle impassively, her gray eyes shifting like heavy fog.

"I know who you are," I managed at last, although the words felt as though they were dragged from me.

The Goddess did not smile. Instead, she nodded soberly.

"And I know you," she hummed softly. My stomach lurched uncomfortably, and I began to shake. That Athena should want anything to do with me implied a strangeness of fate I could not articulate.

"You need not be frightened now," she continued, taking note of my sudden paleness. "Although I am rather impressed by your cleverness. Most mortals, when confronted by divinity, assume it speaks to their essential greatness."

I shrugged, shaking my head. How could I explain to her that I was the least impressive in a family of diluted Titan blood? That I had no misapprehensions about my status in this world, as a murky girl child—ambitious, yes, but also confined.

"The favor of one Goddess might encourage the loathing of another," I said at last, looking at my feet. After a moment, a dart of cool, uncanny laughter filled the clearing.

"Very true, Medea. The interest of the Gods is often a double-edged sword. It implies, after all, no small level of responsibility. My presence here today might give you the illusion of power when really you are just as steadily bound for the black-lit halls of Hades as the rest of your breed."

I swallowed hard, my throat aching.

"We have been watching you from on high," she mused softly, taking a few steps closer. I could feel her eyes appraising me even as I stared determinedly at my hands. "Artemis found you dreadfully compelling. I imagine she might have taken you for herself if not for—" Athena broke off, her tone suddenly awkward.

"If not for what?" I prompted, heart pounding. What should a Goddess want with me?

Athena laughed again, a sound that seemed to draw the very air from my lungs and forced the wind to dissipate.

"The Huntress prefers her companions unsullied by the company of men. Naturally you might have an aversion to the masculine, for obvious reasons, but that is an aversion you will learn to put aside." She paused, and I raised my gaze to meet hers. Her face was awash with something like pity for a moment, before going hard and impenetrable again as she gestured to the bruise that was no doubt blooming across my left cheek.

"I don't want to. I hate Aeetes, and I hate it here," I whispered. A low, brutal admission. A challenge, even.

"Channel it into something productive, then. Be clever. Be thoughtful with your discontent," she returned softly, her eyes probing. "In a matter of years, you will be more powerful than you can anticipate now, and that power will need to be directed in the interest of the Gods. Do you understand?"

I was frozen to the spot, robbed of words, and so I said nothing.

The Goddess watched me carefully, smirking slightly.

"Perhaps your stubbornness will be good for him," she mused, more to herself than to me. "A hero occasionally needs humbling."

"What?" I asked, bewildered. "What hero?"

Athena merely smiled, the vast enigmatic smile of the Sphinx. The kind of smile that gave nothing away.

"Goodbye, little witch," she hummed, taking a step backward and dissolving into the shadows. I took a hesitant step after her in the ensuing silence, knowing as I moved that it was useless. Wherever she had gone, I could not hope to follow.

In her sudden absence, the birds began to sing once more, although their music was tentative and cautious now. The air seemed to crackle with electricity in the spot where she had been, and all around came the smell of iron and lavender.

CHAPTER FIVE

The Shining One

My brother arrived, as my mother had always known he would, in the heat of summer, when Kolchis was at its most pleasant, a verdant coast bathed in sunlight. Mother had been gone so frequently that I had not even known that she was with child until she appeared one morning on the beach, her eyes wide and horrified, leaving a trail of glinting golden blood in the sand. Though I was well into my ninth year, I felt myself shaking in the manner of a much younger child.

"Get your father," she moaned, her arms circling protectively around her middle. She did not need to say anything else for me to realize what was happening. Now that a boy was coming, Aeetes could be summoned. This had been what he wanted all along, after all.

Heart thrumming oddly in my ears, I scrambled up the cliff face, shouting for servants. Something about my mother's face had disturbed me. Her usual easy expression had been marred by the anguished downturn of her lips, the frantic uncertainty of her eyes. It occurred to me that perhaps she had seen something, some hint or shard of prophecy about this child that unnerved her deeply. I found Chalciope in the garden courtyard, twirling her long strawberry hair around her finger, making a serving boy blush.

"Mother is in labor on the beach," I gasped, my lungs screaming from the heat of my exertion.

Chalciope's face flickered through many emotions at once: first bemusement at my interruption, and then haughty irritation, before finally settling on something like disgust.

"Why on earth is she giving birth to the baby out of doors?" She sniffed, her cheeks flushing with color. "It's rather undignified."

"She was out," I managed, gesturing back toward the sea, which glittered on the horizon.

My sister made an impatient noise in the back of her throat, and rolled her eyes.

"Of course she was. Nothing gets between her and the water, does it?" There was a bitterness there which took me by surprise, a bitterness I was surprised to find reciprocated in my own chest. It had not occurred to me to resent my mother for her leaving. After all, I knew how unpleasant our father could be. There was nothing much for her here, besides her mortal children, and Chalciope and I were hardly prizes in the scheme of eternity. Even so, a flicker of hurt began to burn inside of me, a flame I had not realized had been scorching my insides for some time.

"Get Father," I managed roughly, shoving these thoughts aside for later.

Chalciope stared at me with something like pity, before darting off, her bright hair sparkling in the sunlight. I slipped into the cool shadow of the throne room, my throat tight and my breath frantic. At the foot of the staircase, some of the serving girls were scrubbing at the flagstones.

"Get to the beach, your mistress has need of you," I insisted raggedly. They slipped sorely from their knees, stretching out the aches in their muscles, and staring at me with startled expressions.

"Go on now," I urged, annoyed, darting past them up the stairs. From there, it was just two long corridors, and a secret passageway hidden behind an elaborate tapestry, to my chamber. I scrambled around in the drawers to my working desk impatiently, fingers trembling. Eventually, I found what I was looking for: a long narrow glass bottle, stopped up with a piece of cork. A draft to alleviate pain, distilled from milk of the poppy, and mixed with rosewater to make it go down easier. I had been saving it for the next time one of the serving boys was injured, but this would do even better.

■ ■ ■

By the time I made it back down the bluffs to the sand of the beach, my father and my sister were already there, accompanied by a flock of serving girls and the palace midwife. My mother had lowered herself down into a crouching position, and the golden blood of her kind was running freely down her thighs.

The midwife seemed to be trying to reason with her, gesticulating to a piece of soft bark that she had clasped in her hands.

"What's going on?" I called, out of breath.

"Mother won't use the witch's charms," Chalciope muttered mockingly, her eyes bright.

The midwife scowled, her worn face creasing with worry. She glanced back and forth between my mother's stony expression and my father's exhilarated one.

"Please, the baby will be coming any moment. Take some of this to hold between your teeth, and lie back."

My mother shook her head. "I'm not ready," she explained tersely, oblivious to the blood that was collecting around her ankles. Her arms wrapped convulsively around her stomach. She looked more delicate and childlike than I was accustomed to. There was a real terror in her eyes that made my heart sink in my chest.

"You will be fine, your grace. You have already done this twice before, and given your husband two beautiful daughters. This child will be a credit to you both as well, I'm sure. Please lie back." And then, gesturing for the serving girl to spread out the soft blankets on the beach, the midwife turned to me.

"Speak sense to your mother," she whispered.

I moved closer to my mother, but her eyes slid off me as though I was not even there.

"I didn't want to bring him into the world yet," she uttered haltingly, vaguely, her eyes fixed on nothing. "I thought I would have more time to prepare." She shuddered, and to my horror, tears began to leak from the corner of her eyes.

"Mother." I tried to make my voice sound soft and comforting. "It's all right, come lie down. Remember you used to tell us about our Shining One. He's finally coming. This is good news." I rubbed her arms gently, hoping to bring her back to herself.

She shook her head, her mouth gaping, a wail spilling out into the salt-laced air. While her mouth was open, Chalciope shoved some of the ceremonial bark inside, a look of distaste etched on her beautiful face.

"Idyia," my father soothed, gripping her arm and forcing her down into the pile of blankets, "do as the midwife says." His voice brooked no opposition, and his eyes flickered hotly with anticipation. At his words, my mother began to shiver.

"Aeetes," she sobbed, long and low, "we never should have borne children." My father looked startled, and his eyes sharpened with displeasure.

"Do not speak nonsense," he growled in an undertone before turning to the midwife. "What is the matter with her? I've never seen her like this. With Chalciope she did her part easily." I recalled, vaguely in the back of my mind, that he had not been present for my birth. I was a girl, and the second one at that. There had been no point. My mother began to moan, her voice mixing with the crashing of the waves like some dreadful accompaniment.

"Perhaps she's just in more pain," I offered, moving close to her, although the kind of agony my mother was feeling did not seem to be of an earthly variety. Her eyes, absent and faraway, glinted with the unbearable light of prophecy. I wondered what she was foreseeing about this child, my brother.

I yanked the stopper from my draft bottle. "Here." I pushed the rim of the bottle firmly but gently to her lips. Suddenly, her eyes snapped to meet mine. They widened with something feral, and she let out an almost animalistic snarl.

"Get away from us," she shrieked madly, pushing the bottle out of my hands so that its contents spilled into the sand. "Aeetes, keep her away. I don't want her here. I can't stand it— Not now—"

Her face collapsed in on itself and she wailed, her body writhing as a contraction rippled through her.

I fell back as though I had been slapped, numb. Chalciope looked at me with a furrowed brow, her mouth open. She seemed just as shocked as I was.

Our mother, aloof at times and certainly prone to being distant, had never acted outwardly reviled by either my sister or me, or anyone, as far as I could recall.

I realized mutely that I was shaking. The look of absolute loathing that had covered her expression seemed branded to the back of my eyelids.

A warm weight settled on my shoulders. I turned around and met my father's own impassive countenance.

"Get up to the palace, Medea," he commanded, his voice and manner dispassionate. "She'll be fine, but there's nothing you can do for her right now." My throat tightened, aching painfully to hold back a sob. I was being banished from the birth of my own brother, for no reason that I could understand.

"But I—" I began, imagining that perhaps this was all some bizarre misunderstanding, but Aeetes cut me off.

"Now, daughter. I'll send your sister with word when the prince is born." I nodded, my eyes blurring with tears. Turning on my heel, I began the long solitary trek up the cliff face, wondering what my mother could have seen in her visions to hate me so deeply.

■ ■ ■

The sun had begun to sink below the horizon, illuminating the Black Sea in molten copper and gold, before Chalciope made her appearance at the entrance to my rooms.

"They've named him Phaethon," she whispered, her cheeks pink. In spite of herself, she was not able to hold back a smile. Contentment played across her face, and the knot in my stomach began to loosen. Of course by *they* she meant Father, because it was he who had the final say.

I was too anxious to speak, so she continued.

"And Grandfather sent a gift," she whispered in an undertone, her eyes alive with awe and excitement. "A cradle for the baby—a cradle made of solid gold. Even the blankets inside glimmer and shine. I hardly knew that the Lord Helios kept up with those of us on land. If only you and I were born boys, we might have reclined in such finery during our infancy." She raised her eyebrows at me, as though to elicit a smile. But I cared about only one thing.

"And Mother?" I croaked.

Chalciope shifted, her brows drawing together slightly. "She's better than she was. I think she just needed to hold him—the baby. She wasn't herself, that's all." She shook her head, as though to dislodge some unpleasant image. The corner of her tongue protruded thoughtfully from the edge of her lips, as though she was concentrating hard on something.

I opened my mouth to ask the question that had been on my mind all afternoon, only to find that I could not articulate it. There was no way to ask what I needed to ask without sounding quite insane.

"Will she see me?" I tried.

Chalciope shook her head.

"She doesn't want any visitors just now. She's worn out, presumably."

"She looked at me like she despised me, Chalciope," I managed at last, framing it as a statement instead. Chalciope looked at me with something like pity.

"She wasn't herself," she repeated, suddenly avoiding my gaze.

"What if she saw something?" I fought back the sting of tears.

"A prophecy, you mean?" my sister whispered, fidgeting.

"Yes, exactly. A prophecy."

"She didn't say anything about a prophecy, Medea, but if she saw anything, it would have been about the new child, not you, I imagine."

I nodded mutely, not entirely convinced.

"What if—?" I halted. "What if something bad is going to happen to us?" I moaned in a rush, horrified as tears threatened to slip from the corner of my eyes. It was unthinkable that I might weep now, when my anguish was least useful. For most of my younger years, tears had been inaccessible to me. To cry was dangerous—a physical linking of my own disciplined body to a vastness of emotion I could not control. I prided myself on being able to keep my emotions in check at all times.

Crying was a form of weakness, something for little girls and the lower classes. Not for a princess and granddaughter of Helios.

"I'm sure something bad will happen," Chalciope said flatly, with uncharacteristic gloominess. "Things never go well for the semidivine, do they? Perhaps mother was right. She and father never ought to have had children, not with so much Titan blood flowing through their veins. But there's no helping that now. The Fates will have their way, and you and I and little Phaethon will just have to manage the best we are able." Despite the darkness her words carried, I felt somehow settled. She was right. The Gods may be cruel, and Kolchis savage and remote, but I could do very little about it, or so I imagined.

CHAPTER SIX

The Impossible Elder

Mother had been right to crown our brother "the Shining One," for Phaethon burned and flickered with all the heat of our father, and none of the scorch. He was the distilled essence of our bloodline, and immediately the favorite. For all of his babyhood, Mother refused to let him out of her sight. She was more protective of this new child than she had ever been with me or Chalciope, which admittedly irked me. She had even somehow managed to give up her greatest compulsion for him: after he was born, she abstained from the sea entirely. I imagine that if she thought she could get away with it without incurring our father's wrath, she might have disappeared below the waves with our baby brother, and never have returned again to the surface. But Aeetes would never have allowed it.

Mother said nothing about that day on the beach, or the strange loathing in her eyes when I had attempted to aid her through her labor. I almost convinced myself that the entire episode was something I had made up inside my head, if not for the stiffness with which she carried herself in my presence. After all, Phaethon's birth had been befuddling, and in retrospect the entire endeavor took on a kind of blurry, nightmarish quality. An uneasiness permeated my entire body, causing a tightness in my neck and shoulders. I picked compulsively at the skin around my nails, unable to stop until I had drawn blood.

When wet nurses and serving girls came to change the baby, Mother would push them away.

"I can feed him," she would explain softly. "I can help him dress." No matter how many times Chalciope attempted to explain to her that it was not proper for Idyia to be debasing herself with servants' tasks, our mother was resolute. The only times that she could bear to be parted from the infant were when our father took him from her by force.

"He is my son, Idyia, and one day he will be king of this place. You would do best to know your position," Aeetes growled, his eyes flashing, his arms outstretched to take the infant from her arms. Even when the baby cried, wailing for his mother, our father could not be dissuaded.

As Phaethon stumbled into toddlerhood, Father began ferrying him away on short expeditions to the palace gardens. I confined myself to my chamber, attempting to block out the incessant sound of his shrieking child's laugh. On some level, I had always known that with the birth of my brother, my father's need for me would be extinguished, but some part of me had longed for Aeetes to prove me wrong. I had hoped my resemblance to his faraway sister, or my precociousness, might convince him to maintain an interest in my studies and witchery. When any attention from my father failed to materialize, I grew resentful, not just of him, but also of the child who had stolen him away from me by virtue of being born a boy.

It did not help that he was the favorite of the servants as well. Even the most reticent slaves seemed to lighten when he passed, enchanted by his dimpled cheeks and soft golden curls. It was impossible to dislike a child as good and as golden as he was; even I knew this.

■ ■ ■

The days passed with agonizing slowness. Left to my own devices once more, I wandered the grounds around the palace, aimless and bored. The thought of *Pharmakon* repelled me now, as it was synonymous with my father's rejection. And so, I looked determinedly away from any plants that caught my eye. There seemed to be little point in forging my own magical path, now that Phaethon was born. What did I have to look forward to? A marriage to some far-off king was unthinkable. Spinsterhood had a certain appeal, but what were the chances

Aeetes would allow me to remain idle at our hearth when there were romantic alliances to be formed abroad?

The nights were stranger still. I spent longer and longer tangled up in bed, but never shook the sense of fatigue that clung to my muscles and weighted my eyelids. Visions came upon me in the semidarkness as I tossed and turned beneath the blankets. Usually, these shadowy phantasms were too translucent and confusing to latch on to, but occasionally the streaks of color and feeling would solidify into a face—a face so real it might have been disturbing if not for its native loveliness.

It was a boy's face, tan and assured and magnetic. Dark curls fell across his forehead, and his lips seemed the kind that smiled easily and frequently. He had blue eyes so warm and inviting I might have stared into them forever, if I had been allowed. But then the vision would be gone again, the boy all but dissolving into the dark corners of my bedchamber.

I did not bother to consider who he might be—if he even truly existed. There was something tragic in his visage, a kind of aching gravity that sucked me in. But perhaps I was simply going mad.

■   ■   ■

One evening after dinner, while Aeetes had disappeared into the staterooms to discuss business with some visiting prince, Mother appeared at my chamber door with Phaethon in tow. He gurgled happily when he saw me, his rosebud mouth splitting in a wide grin that revealed his haphazardly-toothed gums. In his innocence, he was oblivious to the treachery at work in my heart, those unwanted pangs of jealousy that tore through me each time I saw him.

"I thought you might watch him for a while," my mother said by way of an explanation, her eyes wary and clouded. She had been distant to me since the birth, not outwardly hostile, but not friendly either. Any of the gentleness in her manner had dried up, or else she was reserving it all for her youngest child.

"Oh," I muttered, taken aback. "Come in." Although I was frequently in the company of my younger brother and Mother together, Mother had never allowed me to hold him. I assumed it was because as an heir, he was more precious than normal children. I shuddered to think what Aeetes might do if something ever happened to him. It was almost too horrible to bear.

Phaethon could walk, but only clumsily, his fat baby legs jiggling with effort, his face hot and sweaty. Taking a deep breath, my mother gestured for him to come toward me.

"Go see your sister." Her eyes raked over me piercingly, as though gauging me for signs of malevolence. I shivered, wondering what had come over her, holding my arms out for Phaethon to grasp as he crossed the distance between us.

"Come here, little one," I cooed, surprised as always by the warmth contained in his miniature palm as his fingers grasped my skin. "That's it." I sighed. He lurched into my lap, cuddling close to my breast, and planting a soft, wet kiss on my shoulder.

My mother made a strange noise in the back of her throat, wringing her hands in her lap. I let my silence entice her to speak.

"Medea," she managed at last, her eyes darting from my face to Phaethon's and back again.

"Yes, Mother," I hummed softly, running a stray hand through my brother's curls. They glittered even in the low light of the candles, smooth and scented with sandalwood and rose oil.

"What do you think of him?" she uttered at last, exhaling heavily. She continued to watch me carefully, as though for signs of deception.

"I think he's perfectly charming?" I offered, confused, my voice lilting up on the last syllable so that it became a question. "He looks a bit like Chalciope but even more golden. Everyone loves him. I think you did very well, Mother." I shifted uncomfortably, unsure why my mother was behaving so oddly.

"I thought that maybe—" She broke off, her eyes darkening and then fluttering shut as her breath became less shaky. "I thought that you could spend more time with him. Take care of him. Your sister is too old to be bothered with any of this—she needs to focus on her betrothal. But you, Medea, are still young enough that you can play together. You have never much had children your own age to socialize with—"

"He's hardly my age, Mother." I giggled. "He's a baby."

My mother's face became stony and impenetrable.

"Have I told you the story of Castor and Pollux?" she asked sharply.

I shook my head, scanning my memory for a myth matching such a description.

"Listen well, then. Once there was a king of Sparta, Tyndareus. His wife, Leda, was so beautiful that Zeus himself desired to take her. One evening, after Tyndareus had left his wife's bed, Zeus entered her chambers, and accosted her. When she refused his advances, he transformed himself into a swan, a bird so beautiful and white with soft down feathers he was sure she would not turn him down again. To his surprise, Leda was loyal to her husband, and refused once more. Zeus, in the body of a swan, forced himself on her."

I clenched my eyes tightly shut to ward off the images that infiltrated my mind against my will. A flash of blood between Leda's thighs, the aftermath of so many feathers dropping to the tiled floor, the pale carnage of her face. My mother, impervious to my discomfort and horror, continued on.

"Nine months passed, and Leda gave birth to twins. One was immortal, the result of her tryst with Zeus, and he was called Pollux. The other was mortal, her husband's true son, and he was called Castor. The boys grew up and were inseparable. From their infancy they were each other's closest companion and confidant, and despite their different fathers, they were as brotherly as anyone could reasonably be expected to be. Their bond was almost supernatural, you see. Eventually, there was a battle, and Castor received a mortal wound. Pollux, realizing that his twin was going to be separated from him by the abyss of death, cried out to his father, Zeus, on high, begging the God to kill him as well. Zeus was taken aback at the idea that any immortal might willingly forfeit their infinite potentiality, the pricelessness of their expansive longevity, but he was touched by Pollux's love. And so rather than allowing either boy to die, he placed them both in the stars, among the constellations, so that they might be together forever."

She broke off, her eyes shining with emotion.

"Do you understand what I am saying to you, Medea?" she asked softly.

"I think so," I returned, unnerved by her earnestness.

"There is no love greater than that between siblings. This child is your soul mate in the way that Chalciope is as well. There will never be another of him. He will look up to you," Mother expounded. "You will be a role model to him. If Chalciope marries a faraway king, you will be the only one left to protect him. This is your sacred duty. Do you understand this? That he is your own flesh and blood and nothing can ever come between you? Not power, or wealth, or glory, or love? Do you understand me?"

I stared at my mother, mouth agape. Surely she understood the absurdity with which she was talking to me.

"I'm not going to fall in love, Mother," I huffed annoyed, blushing, and it was true. I had no interest in any of the boys my age around the palace, and they had none in me. It had always been Chalciope who drew the eye, quickened the male pulse. "And besides, what need would I have of wealth or power? Father has ensured that we are amply supplied in both of those regards, has he not?"

My mother's mouth thinned, the air gone out of her sails. She looked simultaneously resigned and defeated.

"Medea, you have to love him, you have to. He's your kin." I was caught off guard by the anguish in her words.

"I do, Mother," I assured her, horrified that she assumed I did not. Perhaps I had let too much of my resentment show on my face, during those afternoons when Aeetes would make off with him. "Of course I do. How could I not?" I continued to run my fingers through his hair as he made contented noises, his eyelids growing heavy with sleep.

My mother nodded, her jaw clenching.

"Did you see something?" I inquired at last, when I was sure the child had drifted off. Her head jerked to appraise me. The question seemed wrenched from my lips by some invisible force.

"Why would you ask that?" she deflected, so low I could hardly make out her words.

I struggled to formulate my feelings into speech. "That day at the beach—you looked so angry. I was just trying to help," I said softly, not looking at her.

I could feel her soften without meeting her gaze.

"I'm sorry, daughter," she explained. "It was the pains of labor—they took me far away from myself." She shifted in that fluid graceful way that she always moved.

"But it wasn't just that, was it?" I goaded, throat tight. I hated myself for pushing but could not seem to stop.

"Medea, you ask too much," she whispered. In that moment I knew she was keeping the truth from me.

"Please, why won't you tell me?"

For a long moment, she did not respond until finally, she sighed.

"I saw the child, that sweet boy who even now dozes fast asleep in your lap"—here, she gestured to Phaethon—"hacked apart in a dozen crude pieces. I saw my son reduced to meat," she explained at last, her voice cold and flat as an expanse.

I recalled that morning so many years ago, under the sheets with Chalciope. *Like a blade to the back*, our mother had said of prophecy, and now I knew what she meant. My blood had turned to ice in my veins, and I began to feel as though I might vomit at any moment, anything to purge myself of the words she had just spoken. This was a kind of horror I had never experienced, a kind that I did not know how to hold.

"No, that's not possible," I whimpered, shaking so hard that in my lap Phaethon began to stir.

"Don't wake him, Medea," my mother commanded. I glanced up to meet her eyes and found that they were blank and absent, somewhere else entirely.

"How does it happen?" I pressed, desperate. "How can we stop it? If you saw it, why don't we do something about it? Take him away from here or place palace guards around him at all hours?"

I did not initially ask the most important question, for something in me was loath to voice it. *Who would want to hurt him? He's only a child.*

Mother read the unspoken query in my face anyhow, for she looked away.

Somewhere in the furthest reaches of my mind, connections were being forged and burnished in a devastating heat.

"Who could ever—?" I tried at last, voice shaking.

My mother shook her head, face stoic and unreadable.

"Enough, Medea. Not even a God can change a person's fate. I imagine that if we try, we will just ensure that it happens in a more brutal and crueler method than it might have transpired otherwise."

My legs were steadily going numb under the weight of my brother, but I did not dare push him off me, not now that I knew where he was headed.

"Well, you can relinquish all hope, but I have no such intention," I spat at her as quietly as I could, my vision blurring with angry tears. How could a mother be so indifferent to the plight of her own child, especially when she outwardly seemed to love him as much as she did? I began running through types of remedies in my head, potions to cheat death and resurrect the mangled body. This must have been why I had always been interested in *Pharmakon.* Because it would be my duty to save the crown prince of Kolchis when no one else thought it could be done.

My irritation at my brother had evaporated like water under the sun, and I hated myself now for ever having entertained it. How silly and selfish I had been. How thoughtless.

My mother, for her part, simply stared at me as I clutched my brother to my chest, looking as though she was gazing at two ghosts. I shivered in my dressing gown.

She rose silently to her feet, her lips parted and her eyes unfixed.

"I think I'll go out," she hummed softly to herself, gazing out of the open window toward the sea. Something in me snapped as I realized that she meant to return to her underwater abode.

"You're just going to leave us here?" I cried, my voice sounding strangled. "Knowing what you know? You would leave us with Aeetes, without a mother's protection?"

I knew I was speaking out of turn, but I could not keep myself from lashing out. Years of abandonment had bubbled up inside of me, turning my speech venomous and my glare into fire.

She said nothing, wavering in the doorway, her face blank.

"Mother!" I shrieked, livid. Startled, Phaethon sat up in my lap, rubbing at his eyes with small fists.

"Mama?" he crooned, looking confusedly from me to her.

"You cannot tell your father any of this," Mother said at last, before turning on her heel. "He would not know what to do with any such information. He is not capable." She said these last words bitterly, her back to us. Phaethon began to cry, his arms reaching helplessly for our mother. I attempted to soothe him, my pulse thrumming in my ears.

"But he's your son!" I screamed, one last time, hoping it might get through to her.

"And you are my daughter," she returned, as though this made everything clear. In another moment she was gone, and I was left alone with a screeching child.

■　■　■

Mother made good on her promise to return to the sea, and this time it seemed the move was permanent. I spent weeks watching the shore for any sign of her, a flash of pale skin or fair hair fanning out in the current, to no avail.

The morning after her departure, I had Phaethon's golden cradle moved into my room, so that I might be the one to keep an eye on him. It took five slaves to transport it down the corridor, so heavy was the contraption. It emitted a comforting light in the corner of my chamber, a glow that permeated even the thickest of shadows.

Overnight, I took on my mother's duties and quirks, shooing the maids away when they attempted to collect him, watching the wet nurse skeptically whenever she held him in her arms to feed him. "Be careful with the crown prince," I chided, ignoring how annoying I must sound to any outside observer. They did not know, after all, what I knew.

I imagined that every stoic page I encountered in the shadowy corridors, or prettily blushing serving girl I passed in my chamber, might unknowingly harbor some insidious, secretive agenda. I tortured myself trying to read the thoughts of relative strangers as they moved through the palace, imagining what dreadful machinations they might harbor within the innermost chambers of their hearts. How foolish I had been, to believe in the good intentions of those I had imagined myself to love. No one could be trusted—not Father, or Mother, or even Chalciope.

I could not stop my father from taking Phaethon out during the day, but I could be sure that he was returned to me at night. Often, he was handed over to me, his face streaked with tears, violet bruises blooming upon the soft skin of his arms and thighs. I knew that Aeetes was careless with him on those daytime expeditions—indeed he had been rough with all of us as children, prone to shaking or striking us if we displeased him. But this was different. The idea that he could lay his hands upon so small and defenseless a child as my brother, a boy who could barely walk or speak, made my blood boil.

"You're as hysterical about him as Mother was," Chalciope would muse, shaking her head. "I never took you for the maternal type, Medea, but it would seem I was wrong." She had taken the news of our mother's departure better than I thought she would.

"You wouldn't expect a fish to live without water, would you?" she reasoned calmly during one of our joint music lessons, her fingers pausing along the strings of her lyre. I had given up learning the pan flute a long time before, and our tutor, a portly man marked by middle age and a perfectly manicured mustache, had decided to put all of his eggs firmly in Chalciope's basket. And so what was once a lesson in music comprehension became studies in musical appreciation for me.

To her credit, my sister noticed other changes in me as well.

"You're always daydreaming, little one," she uttered sardonically, her eyes squinting at me in fake appraisal. "What's going on in that sweet head of yours?"

I would merely shake my head, smiling. There was no possible way to explain to Chalciope that I was imagining combinations of herbs that might bring a mutilated body back together, to stanch the flow of blood and heal a limb that has been completely severed. There was no way to speak of the incantations I was experimenting with on frogs and vermin I found in the basement cellar of the palace. My sister had a soft stomach, and, despite her flair and feistiness, she was more fragile than she appeared. She would not take kindly to knowing what I got up to after our lessons, when Phaethon was away with father. It was hardly pretty work, but I figured my magic should start with animals and work its way up to humans. In some faraway, dimly illuminated corner of my mind, I knew that these experiments would eventually have a human body count. I would need to operate on mortal men, so that I might know how potions worked on them, before I ever tried them on my brother. The thought made my stomach heave.

But that was still a long way off. So far I could heal lacerations on amphibious creatures, but not on mammals. Their damp skin seemed amenable to these kinds of reattachments, this embodied catharsis. Many mornings I returned to my chamber, covered in blood and sweat, reeking of the animals that I had torn through and left underground. And this was to say nothing of reapplying amputated limbs.

Necromancy, I knew without ever being explicitly told, crossed a magical line, although why this was, I could not entirely grasp. I was still a child, after all, and children are rarely engrossed with the promise of their own end. Death had recently enough seemed to me a passing fancy, a problem for some later date, and so I did not investigate its nature with any rigorousness. Had it not been for Mother's vision, I might not have come to realize the terror of mortality—that loss which intertwined itself in every human form—for another few years. That my siblings and I sprung, however distantly, from the immortal power of Titans, was a further complication. In our veins ran an ancient blood, blood that had long been safeguarded against the threat of death. Though my mother could not die, my father was mortal, a trait that he bequeathed to each of his children. My body, subject to the usual mortal failings, was a queer betrayal of a long history, at once vital and doomed.

I felt my own vulnerability poignantly now, almost as intensely as I was aware of my brother's frailty. How had I not realized the extent of my own delicacy, the fragility inherent to the form I occupied on earth? The Necromancer, after all, is always weighted down by the reality of annihilation.

I began to divide my waking hours into two states. In one, I could function without utter encircling panic, my analytical mind effectively shut off for the purpose of self-preservation. This was numbness. In the second, I was brutally, vividly awake, horrifically aware of what was at stake—unable to free myself from the inevitability of Phaethon's murder. Neither state was hospitable. Both lent themselves to a kind of madness.

That Phaethon and I both encompassed infinite minds confined within finite bodies seemed to be the crux of the problem. Necromancy, at its core, was an attempt to mediate an almost insurmountable paradox, being and nonbeing held radically together, side by side.

I had the unnerving sense that I was feeling my way along a dark cave, unsure of where I was headed, or what unspeakable horrors waited for me among the stalagmites. Guesswork and uncertainty were not safe foundations upon which to build a magical practice, but I had little choice in the matter. I knew no one who might help inform my Necromancy. Even Aeetes, who was infamous for his transgressions in the name of *Pharmakon*, spurned death magic.

Sometimes, when I awoke in the middle of the night, blankets damp with sweat, I wondered about the perilous sorcery I was submerged in.

My experiments blurred the boundary between mortal and immortal, ascribing certain powers to the finite that should be reserved only for those on high. Perhaps, talking to the dead, or reviving them, infringed on the power of the Underworld, the obsidian kingdom belowground where waited Hades's seat. Or perhaps there was something even deeper and more insidious at stake, which had to do with the course of nature itself—that in resurrecting some fallen creature from the afterlife it was destined for, I was corrupting its very soul, as well as my own.

Inevitably, after hours in the semidarkness of the cellar, my nose clogged with the scent of meat and bile, I began wondering at who I was becoming. No amount of clear stream water—of sweet-smelling floral oils and burning sage, no combination of cleansing enchantments— could scourge the stains from my palms, could strip the rusty residue of dried blood from beneath my fingernails. My work marked me in ways I was not yet capable of comprehending.

I debated telling Chalciope what I knew. After all, two of us looking after Phaethon would surely help his chances. And Mother had said nothing about withholding the information from her, as she had said to do with Father. But my sister had a naivety, a sweetness I could not imagine wrecking, if only for a moment. Besides, Chalciope was more talk than anything else. Her skills had to do with beauty and social charm, not protection or healing. She would never be the witch I was. She was too prim and proper for that, and she might end up telling our father if I spilled what I knew to her. And so I kept my mouth shut, hardly paying attention during my lessons and working myself to the bone in the afternoons below the palace floors.

As our tutors droned, I would pass the minutes watching as my sister sighed and shifted, envying the loveliness of her features, and pitying the limitations of her beauty. Her mind was as sharp and facile as mine, and yet she diverted her passion into the banalities of aesthetics and civility. I hated the condescension that curled up within my breast, alienating me from her more than her teasing ever could.

In the evenings, I would sing Phaethon to sleep, and tell him the stories our mother had told me as a child, the stories she was not here to tell him herself.

And when the palace was silent, save for the sea breeze that whistled through the corridors, I would look up into the canopied ceiling of my bed and see *him*: the mystery boy who haunted my dreams. That beautiful, familiar face that appeared out of the gloom as if by some odd enchantment. I would look into his eyes as I drifted on the edge of sleep, hardly knowing anything else.

CHAPTER SEVEN

The Boy in the Sea

When our father was not out with his heir, he was attempting to forge a betrothal for his eldest daughter. Chalciope, for her part, was becoming impatient. Well into her fifteenth year, she was uncommonly beautiful, and she knew it. When she walked down the corridors, slaves and visiting dignitaries, servants and foreign princes alike, turned to watch her. She had our mother's grace and our father's fire, and a mind that was sharp and keen, if not a little restless. Many men had already asked for her hand in marriage, royals who had settled along the coast of the Black Sea in those kingdoms adjacent to ours, but they were of a brutal and savage breed. Our father, I knew, was holding out for some Greek prince—one of the kings or demigods that those on Olympus had smiled down upon—to make a match. No one else would do for a granddaughter of the sun itself.

And so when Phrixus fell from the sky, on the back of a flying ram, Father was quick to offer Chalciope up as a prize. The boy would have been only a few years older than my sister, with his smooth, youthful face and carefully sculpted muscles. Even shaky and windswept from his journey, he cut a handsome figure.

The day started out like any other on Kolchis. It was spring, and the smell of flowers on the breeze and the hot potency of fresh sap had drawn me from the cellars. *One day out beneath the sun could not hurt,* I thought, luxuriating under the open sky. My skin had grown white as marble from my time in the dark, but my diligence was beginning to pay off. I had figured out a poultice that when applied to the affected skin, could reattach bone and ligament, as long as not too much time had passed. Wrought carefully from powdered ash bark, honey, milk, and elderflower essence, the mixture was pale and sweet-smelling. One would hardly guess the work it was meant for.

I had selected my ingredients carefully, with an almost obsessive eye. One was ash, known for its liminality and resilience—that ethereal ability to root languidly in both water and earth. The first ash tree was the unexpected child of Gaia and Uranus, the latter of whom, having recently been castrated, spilled his blood across his bride and impregnated her. Ancient races of men had sprung from mountain ash, nurtured on the sugary sap concealed inside the tree's bark. Honey, of course, to enchant the tongue and rejuvenate desire. And then warm milk, the first substance to flow across mortal lips, and the libation most likely, besides wine, to tempt the dead from their wraithlike slumber. The sharp white blossoms from the elder tree, for when they are consumed raw, they harbor a latent toxicity, but when properly prepared exhibit unique healing properties. It was not enough to bring someone back from the dead, I knew, but it was something. There was also the added benefit that a pleasant cordial could be made from the leftover elderflower I had harvested and then slipped into bitter wines to make them go down easier. I began drinking longer and heavier from my cups at meals, desperate to drown out some of the intrusive machinations that haunted me even once I was aboveground.

Chalciope, as always, was in the courtyard gardens, braiding her hair in increasingly complicated designs, and soaking up the sun. I meandered down to the beach, since it was unseasonably warm. Mostly, I avoided the cliffs overlooking the sea and the rolling waves below because they reminded me of our mother. Chalciope occasionally took Phaethon down to the beach, I knew, to bathe him in the current and tempt Idyia, but she remained stubbornly absent. I'm sure this befuddled my elder sister, but she hid it well, showering Phaethon with easy smiles, and splashing him with salt water until he shrieked with mirth.

It occurred to me some time later that a fraction of my mother's propensity for prophecy had found its way to me. That was the only reason I can think of to explain why I was at the beach when Phrixus fell from the heavens, plummeting like a golden stone. Nothing but that strange gravity, which straddles the tenuous line between compulsion and knowing, could have brought me to that point.

I settled myself along the cliff's edge as though in a daze, my fingers making lazy circles in the sand. Gulls sang sweet tunes above, and the waves danced and glittered on the shore. While most days the sea looked more black than blue green, today it shimmered vibrant and lush under the sun, like a million-sided sapphire. An object on the horizon caught my eye, glinting like a second sun. I squinted to make it out. Gradually, the shape drew closer and became more defined. It looked to me at first like an impossible hybrid creature, part man and part beast, that had somehow acquired the powers of flight.

I opened my mouth to call to it, for I had never been one for subtlety. But the words died in my throat as the thing seemed to dip dangerously in altitude. Involuntarily, my hand crept to cover the lower part of my face. The thing in the sky managed to right itself for a short distance before losing its strength again, this time plummeting roughly into the current below.

Frantic, I surveyed the surf for signs of life. The fall had been a long one, and the surf was unforgiving. I considered going for help but knew by the time I reached the palace and returned with aid, it would be too late.

Without thinking, I plunged into the sea, letting out a little cry as the cold water rose above my ankles. A ways ahead, I caught a glimpse of a curled head, damp with seawater, fighting to remain afloat.

"This way!" I screamed, voice hoarse, wading into the water until it was up to my chest. My drenched clothing dragged me down, gluing me to the spot.

"Mother!" I cried, in desperation. "Mother help us!" But the waves crashed indifferently behind me, salt spewing into my face as I fought to reach the stranger in the sea. It had been foolish to imagine that she might be of help to me if our history was anything to be believed.

I cut through the ocean water, making cups with my hands that sliced into the current, propelling me forward. The waves slipped over my head, choking me, so that even when I resurfaced, I was coughing and spluttering with effort.

And then quite suddenly, I could no longer determine which way was up. My mouth opened in a silent scream as the world lost its orientation. My arms flung out fruitlessly, seeking something firm to hold, but there was only the impossibility of the sea, and the absence of air.

Mother, I thought desperately, *Mother, can't you see I'm drowning?*

Just as my vision began to go dark, an arm circled firmly around my waist, wrenching me forward. In another moment, my head was above water, my throat painfully constricted, my eyes and nose running.

"Mother!" I moaned, coughing. "I thought you had left me to die, but you found me." The arm seemed to loosen for a millisecond before tightening around me once more. As we moved toward the shore, I looked up into the clouded sky, my eyes stinging with seawater. I knew now that we would be fine, and so with a contented sigh, I let the world dissolve into blackness.

■ ■ ■

When my eyes flickered open, I was lying on the beach drenched and shivering. The sky was obscured by the head of a boy—a boy who looked almost as deathly as I felt. His face was pale and emaciated, with hunger or worry, and dark circles dipped below his warm eyes. His lips were split and chapped, but his cheekbones were angular, and his jaw was firm. There was something assured in his manner, a quality I had come to associate with the highly born.

"You were stupid coming after me," he said, running tan fingers through his sopping curls. "You could have drowned. Would have drowned, actually, if I hadn't fished you out of the surf. Who are you, and what land is this?"

I struggled to formulate my thoughts into words. It was as though the sea had infiltrated my skull, waterlogging my faculties. I coughed in his face, speckling it with spit and salt water.

He drew back, his expression equal parts disgusted and amused. "How old are you? You're barely more than a child, I expect?"

I calculated from his features, and his paternal condescension, that he must be almost twenty—nearly twice my own age.

I forced myself into an unsteady seated position, my arms trembling. All my muscles ached, even ones I did not previously know I had.

"I'm not a child," I offered at last, gazing out at the sea, which had only moments before sought to claim me for its own. "You saved me? It wasn't my mother?" I hated the whine in my voice, the liquid vulnerability that flowed through every word I spoke. I peered across the beach for signs of her, as though at any moment she might pop out from behind a rock or boulder, moving with that usual pacific grace. But it was just the boy and me stranded upon the rocks. And a little distance away, what looked like a brilliant golden beast was dragging itself along the shore, making piteous noises.

For a long moment, I lost myself in the brilliance of the animal's fur, the painful intimacy of its labored movements.

"What is that?" I asked aghast.

"A golden ram," the stranger offered, turning to look at the creature, which had stopped moving and was breathing heavily. "My mother sent it for my sister and me to fly us away from our native land." His expression had turned stony, his eyes hollow with a kind of agony I could not comprehend. I did not bother to ask about the existence of a ram that could fly, with a coat of molten gold. His mother was obviously a minor Goddess. Father would be pleased.

His look was not the kind that encouraged more questions, but I was insatiable.

"Your sister? And where is she? Did you tow her and me and the ram to shore all by yourself?" I gazed at his toned arms skeptically. Even if he was as strong as he looked, such a feat would be superhuman.

He turned to look at me, and where I expected there to be wrath in his eyes, there was only grief.

"She didn't make it," he muttered brusquely, his voice thick with tears. "She lost her grip on the creature. I suppose, in the end, she saved me. I don't know how the ram would have carried us both the distance that was required." He looked into the ruthless, blue expanse of the sky, exhaling unsteadily. He looked so miserable in that moment that

I would have done anything to ease his load. I tried to imagine what this sister of his might have looked like. Perhaps she had his quiet confidence, or the playful lilt of his mouth. But eventually my thoughts turned to Phaethon, and the parallel fate that awaited him if I failed to keep him safe. I could not imagine this boy's grief.

"I'm sorry," I whispered, placing a damp hand on his arm. "It sounds as though your journey was a long and impossible one. But you saved me, when you did not have to, and so you are welcome here." I attempted to use the voice that my father employed when talking to foreign dignitaries. I wanted this boy to know I was important in my own right, that I could offer him protection.

"Thank you, little one," he responded, not looking at me. "And where is here, exactly?"

"Kolchis," I explained, coloring slightly, thinking of how my father talked about the place as though it was inferior to the Greek city-states. "My father, Aeetes, is the king here, and the son of the great Titan Helios. And my mother is Idyia of the Oceanids."

At this he turned to appraise me once more. At first, I imagined that my ancestry might impress him, but his eyes were filled with something more trenchant than that.

"That's why you called for your mother, then," he murmured carefully, gauging my face for any reaction. "You thought that if anyone would save you it should be her."

Despite my best efforts, I could feel my bottom lip tremble incriminatingly. I glanced away, scowling.

"She's been at sea awhile, that's all. She must not have heard me," I retorted imperiously, in an attempt to hide my own horror. I hoped that he had no knowledge of Naiad existence, because if he did, he would know that my mother's kind knew of everything that transpired under the surface. How he had guessed at my feelings I could not imagine.

"Never mind that," he whispered, not altogether unkindly, and he held his hand out for me to take. "Godly parents are often busy. That doesn't mean they do not love you; it just means that their own sense of eternity clouds things. She probably saw that I was close enough to get you to shore, and so had no reason to intervene." I could sense the pity in his tone, and I bristled at it. But after a moment, I took his hand, gripping his fingers as tightly as one might grip a lifeline, which I suppose that he was.

■ ■ ■

I led the stranger up the winding path along the cliff's edge, not letting his hand fall from mine for even an instant. We had left the injured ram moaning brokenly on the rocks below.

"We can come back for it," the boy had said calmly enough, "depending on what your father wishes to do with it." I nodded, to show him that this plan was all right with me, although the idea of leaving such a lovely creature to the agony of its end, all alone, struck me as unusually cruel.

As we crept up the rocky ledges, I regarded him out of the corner of my eye. I had never seen anyone quite so beautiful, I imagined. His was the kind of beauty that inspired goose pimples to erupt in waves down my arms and legs, a kind of beauty I had never known before.

"What are you called?" I asked in a low voice, shy for the first time in my life.

"Phrixus," he returned with a slight half smile. "And what shall I call you, my friend?"

I shivered as he called me "friend," and worked hard to keep my voice level. "I'm Medea. It means 'cunning' or 'shrewd.' My mother picked my name because she could tell right away that I was too intelligent for my own good." I felt myself rambling but could not seem to stop. A blush suffused my cheeks.

Phrixus raised his eyebrows, and his lips quirked in something that might have been a smile.

As the palace came into view, I tried to imagine what it must look like from his eyes. Was it impressive compared to the structures in his land? Would he think us barbaric for our clothes, or for the accent that adorned our speech?

"I've heard tell of your father," Phrixus supplied easily as we walked, and I gazed at him furtively from the corner of my eye.

"You have?" I asked, my stomach tying itself into knots.

"His sorcery is spoken of even in faraway Boeotia, which was until now, I suppose, my home."

"Oh," I managed, not sure if this was a good thing or a dangerous one. He paused in his movement.

"They say he can do marvelous things with herbs. I've heard that one drop of Aeetes's potions can kill fifteen men ten times over. Or that he has it in his power to coax true love from a leaf, compel hatred from a single blossom. Is this true?"

I nodded, coloring. "This and more."

Phrixus's eyebrows disappeared beneath his hairline, and his lips parted in disbelief.

I thought about telling him what I could do—how I could heal wounds and reattach legs that had been severed from little animals, how I could bestow a draft on an ailing butterfly and restore it to a caterpillar. But something held me back. What if Phrixus found such knowledge uncomely in a girl, as my father said most men did? Besides, I knew my experiments were not savory to most people. While cleaning the cellar a few months before, one of the prettier serving girls had come across my disposal room, animal corpse after animal corpse, disposed of hastily and carelessly, covered in salt and quicklime and sealed off to prevent the smell of decay. I had never heard anything quite like that scream, the high, bloodcurdling terror it seemed to convey. I had been too ashamed to speak to her myself. I was often tongue-tied in the presence of older girls much more graceful and elegant than myself, and this was no exception. And so I had simply watched her skitter out of the cellars, her complexion pale and wan.

Of course the girl had reported it to her superior. I followed her up from underground to the warmth of the kitchens, observed the tremble in her limbs and the quiver of her lips as she told a senior cook what she had seen. My stomach dropped and my mouth went dry. I feared that together they might report my doings to Father. But to my surprise, the cook, a narrow woman with black eyes and long fingers, slapped the girl hard across the face.

"We do not speak ill of the house we serve," she relayed calmly, but with an edge. The girl began to wail, her face streaked with an ugly mix of grime and tears.

"But it's not natural," she sobbed. "Surely you must see that? What goes on here is an abomination. Even if they are descended from the ones on high—"

The cook cut her off. "You would do well to end your whining there, girl," she snapped in an undertone, eyes roving the room for signs of potential eavesdroppers. I snuggled more firmly against a wall, obscured from view, heart beating frantically. And somehow, that had been the end of that. Sometimes I imagined I heard the servants chattering, and then falling silent as I walked into a room. But this did not concern me. So long as my father had no knowledge of my work, I could shoulder the rest. I knew that my experiments on animals, dead and dying, crossed some sort of line. That even though magic was natural and beautiful and true in the way that so few things ever were, there was a peril to it. That perhaps, somewhere along the way, I had taken a path that should have remained untaken.

No, I reasoned, it was better to keep my machinations to myself.

Phrixus gestured for us to resume our walking, and so I bit my tongue. The sky, which had been gray and overcast, seemed pricked through with bits of blue, and I smiled. Perhaps Phrixus coming was a good thing.

■ ■ ■

Father took to Phrixus like a flame to kindling. Something about the firm set of the younger man's shoulders and the odd, frightened secrecy in his eyes seemed to evoke admiration and sympathy simultaneously. He was the kind of son he hoped Phaethon might one day grow into.

It helped too that Phrixus had the manners and rearing of a proper prince. He had slipped immediately to his knees upon entering my father's throne room, his head bowed and supplicant, his eyes not presuming to look up. A few rogue drops of water dripped from his drying curls onto the flagstone floor, and I shivered, remembering that I too was drenched.

"Father, this is—" I began, thinking to make an introduction, but before I could go any further, Aeetes broke in.

"State your name and business on my land," he extolled, in a voice that betrayed no fondness. I stared hard at him, at the flush in his cheeks and the calculating look in his eyes.

"I am the Prince Phrixus, son of King Athamas, who rules Boeotia. My mother is Nephele, the cloud nymph molded after the Goddess Hera herself. And I am here at your mercy, forsaken by my family and people, but protected by the Gods." My father nodded, his expression taut with repressed excitement.

"You are welcome here, Prince Phrixus of Boeotia, so long as you seek shelter and solace. Although Kolchis may be more remote and savage than the lands you are accustomed to, we are faithful to the principle of hospitality. Perhaps you will regale us with the story of your travels this evening over dinner. In the meantime, you are free to retire and warm yourself by the fire." At this, Aeetes jerked his chin toward one of the pages, who hurriedly gestured for Phrixus to follow him up the spiral staircase.

"Thank you, my lord." Phrixus bowed low, his eyes flickering momentarily back to my face. "And it was an exquisite honor to make your acquaintance, Medea." He winked at me and proceeded to follow the page. As soon as he was gone, my father's eyes lost their warmth and turned cold. He stared at me, boring holes in my chest.

"Do you care to explain why you are sopping wet, setting a despicable example for our guest, daughter of mine?" he barked, his fists clenching and unclenching in his lap.

"The prince fell into the sea on a golden ram, Father, and I—"

"Imagine, a nymph's daughter and you cannot even swim. You disgrace this house. Go to your chamber and try not to embarrass us any further. This prince may be very important for our family, and his connections could prove essential to any hope your sister has of advancing herself." I bit my lip until the taste of blood filled my mouth.

"Yes, Father," I managed before darting up the stairs myself, shaking, although whether from cold or melancholy, I could not discern.

■   ■   ■

I made to return to my chambers, my heart in my throat. Outside, the light was swiftly fading, and as I climbed the stairs to the floors above,

I thought again of the ram, alone and dying on the beach below. What must the creature think of Kolchis, with its rough crags and sprawling wilds? Ours was a terrible land to meet one's end. I continued in my upward trajectory, gritting my teeth against such sentimental imaginings.

In the shadowy comfort of my rooms, I reclined softly against the bed, breathing roughly, while intrusive and persistent visions of the golden ram assailed me. I imagined it contorted and glistening upon the damp sand, its eyes cast open toward the churning tide, abandoned.

Guilt penetrated me, like winter-morning cold penetrates the bones. I was a witch, was I not? And a Necromancer as well. If I did nothing, the beast would die, friendless, in the very place of my own lonely discontent.

After dinner, I decided—after the excitement of Phrixus's arrival had died down—that I would abscond to the ram's side, and work what magic I could.

■ ■ ■

I was late to the dining hall, which was uncharacteristic in our father's house. As the sky deepened with color, saturated with lavender and rose hues that melted into the back of my eyelids, I vacillated by the window. I knew that I should be heading down the spiral staircase, but I anxiously tugged at my hair, which was still stiff with dried seawater. Perhaps I ought to wash my face, to look clean and fine for our visitor, I reasoned. But something kept me rooted to the spot, tugging uselessly at my bottom lip. I had never wanted to impress anyone aside from my father before, and Aeetes was impossible to please. Some part of me wished to see what might happen if I emerged myself, grimy and shrewd and dark, as opposed to a curated version that might be more palatable. What would Phrixus think of me then? He did not have the same aching beauty as the boy in my nighttime visions, but there was something engaging about him—something soft and kind and inviting. I wanted to know him.

Eventually, I broke down and drew a basin of cold water, scrubbing my face thoroughly, and running a comb through my tangled hair until tears stung at the corners of my eyes. I felt scrubbed raw and slightly foolish as I appeared at the edge of the raised dining table, and a host of eyes fell on me, the strange second daughter of the sorcerer king.

"It seems Medea has finally decided to join us." Chalciope laughed into the tense air, breaking the silence. Her voice was tinged with affect, and I realized that she was putting on a show for the benefit of our guest, who was seated across from her. At the head of the table, my father's jaw clenched and unclenched, and his eyes directed me toward the only vacant seat.

"We meet again, princess," Phrixus murmured warmly as I blushed heavily, settling myself into a space along the bench. "You look slightly less waterlogged than when we last met, which suits you very well."

At this, Aeetes broke in, his eyes flashing at me in a warning to remain silent. "You must forgive my youngest daughter for her foolishness. I don't know how she ended up dragging you into the sea with her, but she is stupider than her sister and does not always act in a manner befitting her station." I forced a sip of wine down my throat as my entire body clenched. Father had slid into a pattern of snide remarks and cruel observances ever since Phaethon was born. It was as though he was attempting to negate everything he had taught me, every kind word he had bestowed on me during that period when there had been no proper heir.

"Actually, I am much indebted to your daughter, King Aeetes," Phrixus broke in, his eyes earnest and his mouth set grimly. "You should know that I tumbled into the ocean. The ram I had been riding was not able to continue any farther, and so she came in after me. Indeed it was her poise and stoicism which allowed us both to get to shore. After all, it was she who directed me to the beach, she who helped shoulder the burden of the ram." I tried not to let the shock show on my face as his words sank in. Without batting an eye, he was lying to his host, making me out to be the hero, when it was he who dragged me from drowning in the surf.

My father's eyes narrowed dangerously, and part of me longed to warn Phrixus not to lie—that my father had methods to determine when a man was false and that they were not always pretty.

"The princess mentioned that her mother is the Oceanid Idyia, and I imagine this is where she has inherited her maritime elegance," Phrixus went on, his eyes flickering to meet mine, his lip quirked in the ghost of a smile.

I nodded, possessed by the sudden urge to laugh hysterically. "The

Prince Phrixus is too kind." My father surveyed me sharply, as though uncertain whether to believe our tale or not. I held my breath.

"You mention a flying ram? I have never heard of such a creature. Perhaps you would care to elaborate how you came to our shores, at the mercy of Medea?" he offered at last, and I exhaled unsteadily.

Phrixus nodded, taking a sip of wine. "I was born one of two, and that is where this story begins," he started, lips pursing.

"My father, King Athamas of Boeotia, has always been beloved of the Gods, and so when it came time for him to sire an heir, they offered him one of their own to take as his wife. My mother, Nephele, was crafted by Zeus himself out of clouds in the beloved image of Hera some time ago, as part of a complicated trap, although that is another story entirely. Although she resembled the queen of the Goddesses on high, my mother's temperament was distinctly her own: she could be in equal turns flighty like the wind, tempestuous as a storm, as light and pleasurable as a breeze on a warm afternoon, and my father fell in love with her instantly. The same could not be said for my mother, for she was more the quality of cloud than mortal flesh. She stayed long enough to give birth to my twin sister, Helle, and me, and then she disappeared." Phrixus paused again, turning to look at me.

"I imagine that this house knows the power of the whims that possess nymphs—that nothing and no one is a match for their own nature, their unconquerable wildness," he added. Aeetes cleared his throat, and I hoped Phrixus would not continue along this line; it would hardly serve him.

"My father loved my mother, but he could never possess her in the way that a husband must possess a wife, and so eventually, when she had been absent from him for some years, he took a second bride. This was Ino, and she became our stepmother. In the beginning, Helle and I imagined that she liked us, or at least found us tolerable. As time passed, however, Helle would catch her shooting unkind looks in our direction, and I might hear her whispering pernicious things to our father. Of course, her lies fell on deaf ears, because King Athamas has always been a good and just man. He merely had the unfortunate fate to marry a wicked creature, a woman who had more violent potential than any of us might have foreseen.

"Ino, realizing that she would have to work much harder to get rid of my sister and me, forged a plan. She roasted every last one of the seeds that were distributed among the farmers to be sown in our fields. When harvesttime came, and the polluted seeds offered not even the thinnest sliver of vegetation, my father decided to consult the Oracle, as my stepmother knew he would. Athamas sent messengers to Delphi, seasoned men who nonetheless were fallible and fickle. Before they set out on their journey, Ino promised them riches beyond their wildest imaginings if they reported that the Oracle required a very specific sacrifice. And so when my father's messengers returned, they uttered not the true prophecy of the Pythia, but rather the rehearsed treachery of my stepmother. They lied to my father, and asserted that the famine would end only once Helle and I were sacrificed." Here, Phrixus swallowed hard, although his eyes remained cold and stony.

"Although I tried to remind my father that the Gods do not so frequently smile on human sacrifice in our own modern age, that somehow I knew Ino must be behind it all, he was not to be deterred. And so Helle and I were set upon the altar stone. Ino would have liked my father himself to wield the blade—she told him that it would look appropriate to his people—but he could not bring himself to do it. One of his advisors offered to take on the task, and so my sister and I prepared to die.

"In those moments, I imagined the world would end. My legs were unstable beneath me, and my tongue felt swollen in my mouth. Helle offered herself up first, even though I ordered her to stand behind me. She was a stubborn creature, too kind and curious for her own good." He fell silent, staring hard at his platter of meat and grape leaves. I felt my own blood turn to ice, imagining what it must be like to stand resolute at the moment of your own demise, powerless and trapped. I decided in that moment that I should never let any such thing happen to me.

"At that instant, a glimmer of something bright and warm caught my eye. I heard Helle gasp beside me, and I felt her hand fall upon my shoulder. We turned to see a ram, with a pelt that looked as though it were wrought from molten gold. Out of its back sprung a set of glorious wings, and its horns glinted menacingly in the fading light. The creature was marvelously fashioned, but I cared little for its outward beauty. The ram came upon me—upon us both—the very essence of grace. I felt a thousand things as I knelt before his glinting horns: relief and faith, sorrow and ecstasy. A breeze had crept up, softly, so softly I might not have noticed it if I were not attuned to the familiar feeling of my mother's presence. I realized then that we had only a matter of moments, that this otherworldly, graceful, impossible creature would be our only chance for escape. I helped Helle onto its back, and then hefted myself up after her. Although Ino shrieked with wrath, unable to fathom that her machinations had been foiled, not a soul rose to stop our movements. For surely, the presence of the ram was enough of a sign that we were innocent—that we never should have been placed upon the altar. As the ram shouldered us, its wings flapping madly to carry us off into the air, my father met my gaze, and his eyes were sorrier than I had ever known them to be. But Helle and I knew we would never be safe in Boeotia so long as Ino had her claws stuck into our father.

"And so we flew for many hours, high above the clouds, struggling to keep ahold on the creature that carried us. I told Helle to cling tight to me, to focus only on maintaining her position, but she was a curious creature—she had too much of our mother in her for her own good. And so, laughing with glee, she had contorted herself to look below, at the earth as it shrunk and swayed. Quite suddenly, I realized that her fingers had loosened their hold, that the beast seemed lighter. And to my horror, I witnessed my sister plummeting to the rocks below."

Silence stretched over the table, and the flicker of the fire in the hearth was the only sound that was audible. Phrixus seemed to be trying to center himself. Across from him, Chalciope had pressed a hand across her open mouth, her cheeks damp with sympathy. Only my father appeared unmoved, although he forced his face into a superficial expression of remorse.

For a moment, I imagined myself in Phrixus's place, but found the idea of losing Chalciope or Phaethon, on the very brink of salvation, too much to hold for any length of time. A dull anxiety wound through my body, until gooseflesh erupted along my skin. Even such a vibrant, tenacious thing as love is precarious, I reasoned, when housed in mortal bodies.

My experiments in the cellar were vital for precisely this reason. I would not fail my brother, no matter how distasteful my work had become.

"The rest, you already know," Phrixus continued. "The golden ram carried me, now alone for the first time in my life, far away from my home, from my father and my sister. Eventually, it began to tire under me. I could sense the labored quality of its breathing, the exhaustion building in its trembling wings. And so it was not altogether surprising when it plummeted into the sea, with me on its back. That was how Medea found, then rescued, me. Not many children have that kind of heroism in them, King Aeetes, and I feel compelled to share with you that she is a credit to your house."

My father, ever practical, merely shook his head. "And what happened to this golden ram? Where is it now? Surely even if it is no longer functional or alive, the fleece could be salvaged, and turned into something quite valuable."

"I left it on the beach. It will not stray, I know my mother, and I know the nature of her creations. If it is amenable to you, I would like to sacrifice the beast to Zeus. Once it is dead, I would like to offer the fleece to you, in thanks for the warmth of your hospitality. I am indebted to your house, and to Kolchis entirely." I shifted slightly, unnerved by how well Phrixus navigated these affairs. He had the tongue of a hero.

My father made no attempt to hide his pleasure, and a feral grin cut across his face.

"Let us raise a toast to the noble Prince Phrixus, to his fallen sister Helle, to the grace of Nephele and the Great Gods on high, the glory of Zeus, and the golden fleece, which is the treasured manifestation of grace itself," Aeetes decreed, his voice ringing out.

Everyone raised their glasses, although I noticed that Phrixus merely murmured, "To Helle," while the others went through my father's list. Where before he had been golden, illuminated in the light of his story, he seemed now to have deflated. His skin was waxen and pale, and I watched as sweat appeared along his temple.

You are like me, I thought, surprised by the toll such a performance seemed to have taken on him. *You are just as miserable and unmoored as I am.*

CHAPTER EIGHT

Khrysomallos

With dinner cleared away, and most of the court retired to their own chambers, I made haste to my room to gather supplies and change into something more amenable to the task at hand. Over my nightdress, I fastened my heaviest traveling cloak, one lined with rabbits' fur to keep out the coastal winds. In the depths of my pockets, I thrust delicate stoppered bottles of goat's milk and poppy essence beside small, carefully tied bundles of herbs—violently indigo sepal-crested aconite, mauve buds and tooth-edged leaves of vervain, and elderflower ebullient in its white blossoms.

I paused for a moment on the threshold to the corridor, biting the corner of my lip. Already, the moon would be out, and the air cold and frigid. The ram might not even be alive, since many hours had passed over dinner. And yet the idea of abandoning the creature altogether prodded thornily at me. No, it would not do to leave the ram alone. There were times, I knew, when a lack of action was as callous as outright cruelty, and this night was one of them. I forced myself forward into the shadows of the waiting stairwell, grimacing, my feet working in tight, compulsive steps. I would feel more at ease once I had left the palace behind, I reassured myself.

Even in the dark, the path along the bluffs was easy to follow. So many years of lonely forays meant that the rocks beside the shore were familiar underfoot. The stray strands of kelp, slippery with seawater, and glistening carpets of algae, which may have proved perilous to a passing interloper, I easily avoided. The crescent moon shone over everything, a thin mercurial arc.

The stars, it seemed, had been keeping vigil over the creature though I was delayed. I found the ram close to where Phrixus and I had left it in the hours before. It lay so still and silent upon the sand, that for a terrible minute I imagined that I had arrived too late—that it was dead and inaccessible. But then, I marked the shallow rise and fall of its chest, the gentle upheaval that matched the crashing of the tides a few yards down the beach.

Hardly thinking, I reached my fingers toward it, intertwining them with the lustrous yellow wool that hung thickly about its neck. Its eyes, which had been shut, flickered open. There was a trenchancy in them, but also an expansive quality that struck me. I had been wrong to assume the beast was male. I was caught momentarily in the fire of her irises, in the rich gold of their center.

"Oh," I exhaled, a little breathlessly as she stared into me. Her face was magnificently wrought. The gleaming eyes were delicately outlined in coal, matching the narrow flight of her snout, which ended in an inky, black nose. Atop her head sprouted two spiraling horns, so perfect in ratio and curvature that I imagined some supernatural force had gone into their formation. It was an entirely sympathetic face. My fingers stilled in their gentle ministrations. The ewe's mouth opened slightly, revealing the pink wetness of a tongue.

"Hello," I whispered, surprised by the gentleness she inspired, "I've come to help you." I retrieved the vials from my pockets, fingers trembling as I opened each in turn, and made to tip them backward into her gullet. She struggled softly, craning her neck away from me, her tongue working madly. I paused, uncertain of what to do. Her gestures seemed clear, however weak the journey had left her.

"You must drink," I tried again, pushing another bottle toward her. "These tinctures will alleviate some of your pain, and restore the strength to your tired muscles." I tried to speak to her as I worked, so that she might feel more at ease.

Her eyes, molten hot and steadfast, never left my face. Her mouth closed stubbornly.

"Please?" I begged, desperate now. I recalled a time, only a few years ago, when I had offered my mother entirely different elixirs on this very beach while she labored with Phaethon. The result had been much the same.

"Aren't you thirsty?" I whispered. Panic washed over me in familiar pangs. Perhaps the creature could sense that there was something wrong with me, could feel that I was untrustworthy or unlikable, as Mother had that day on the beach. Maybe she could smell the blood of so many other animals on the pale expanse of my palms.

I bowed my head, allowing the unused vials to drop into the sand, shame coursing through every part of me. Tears, unbidden, left stinging trails on my cheeks, and I shut my eyes tightly against them.

And then, a warm, damp pressure on my hand—the soft, dark nose of the ewe nuzzling close to me. I turned sharply to regard the creature; breath caught in my throat.

"Her name is Khrysomallos," came a quiet, child's voice from behind me. I jerked around roughly, my entire body tense with alarm.

A small, familiar face met mine, smiling radiantly in the moonlight.

"Phaethon!" I worked to keep my voice level. "What are you doing up and out of bed?"

"I saw you sneaking out. Why didn't you invite me?" he grumbled, looking disappointed and sour at my betrayal.

I was too stunned to upbraid him. Instead, I scanned the length of his miniature body for any obvious wounds while he continued to babble, oblivious.

"You forgot to wake me up," he mumbled into his hands, a hint of mischief alive in the happy curve of his lips.

"You might have fallen on the rocks! Or split your head and drowned," I whispered, my voice shrill and my logic overwhelmed. I felt a silly sort of frustration building up inside me that I bit back, sighing.

"You're such a naughty, naughty prince," I crooned at last, rolling my eyes.

He giggled, ducking his head, kicking sand around with his tiny feet.

"Gods above, how are you not freezing?" I continued, rushing forward to clasp him to me. He squirmed in my arms, apparently delighted by our nighttime adventure.

"We need to get you back to the palace." I sighed, frowning as I felt the thin fabric of his nightdress. Of course he had not thought to wear something warmer. Boys of his age never did.

I did not want to leave the ewe, not now when I knew how dire her condition truly was, but the bluffs at night were no place for a child.

I moved to carry him back up the cliff, eyes downcast. No sooner had I begun an unsteady trudge along the surf than Phaethon began to thrash and writhe in my arms with an unusual frenzy.

"We can't leave her," he shrieked in my ear.

I nodded, relenting and unsure what to do. As I set him in the sand he ran to the ewe's side, burying his head in her wool.

"Phaethon," I cautioned, "be careful. She's hurt."

"I know she is." He jerked his head up to look at me, his eyes wide and expressive. "She told me so."

I pursed my lips.

"What else did she tell you?" I inquired, letting out a little huff.

"Her name. Khrysomallos."

Phaethon leaned in closer to the creature, so that his ear was just beside her open mouth.

"She says thank you for the medicine," he reported, smiling up at me. "But she doesn't need it anymore. She says it won't do any good." At this his smile dropped and his eyebrows drew together in childish anguish.

"She says tomorrow she will die," he whispered, he moaned, great pools of tears appearing as if by magic in his eyes.

My throat tightened instinctually, and I reached out a hand to stroke the creature's flanks as they rose and fell.

"Perhaps not, little prince," I chided, hopeful that he would stop in his crying.

My brother snuggled even closer into the warm curve of the animal's stomach, melancholic but apparently content. His countenance was scrunched up, as though attempting very hard to make sense of some new piece of information, although how he was speaking to the beast, I had no idea.

"She says she doesn't mind the dying," he whispered after a while. "That she's going back to be with her father."

I raised my eyebrows.

"Her father?" I questioned, attempting to picture what ethereal metallic creature might have fathered this one.

"Poseidon, God of the Sea," Phaethon pronounced carefully. "Her mother is the nymph Theophane. Poseidon turned them both into rams to be together. And Theophane's grandfather," he paused, scrunching up his face once more, "is called Helios."

I continued to run my hands up and down the creature's wings as my brother spoke, as though his words did not shock me.

"Helios is our grandfather too, so that means we're almost cousins!" Phaethon shrieked, reaching to hug the ewe tightly.

I nodded, part of me skeptical, but another part, a hopeful, childlike part, alive with excitement.

The ewe looked at me with an otherworldly expression, her whole body taut with intention, as though she was trying to communicate something to me.

"Khrysomallos wants to give you something very precious," he hummed after a minute. "Is that okay?"

Not quite believing my own foolishness, I regarded her with all my concentration, my fingers absentmindedly stroking the warm wool along her shoulders.

The animal let out another compelling bleat, her eyes meeting mine with a knowing determination. I did not dare look away.

"She says you should shear a bit of her wool, now before the sun rises. That it will help you with the task at hand." He recited the last bit confusedly.

"What task does she mean?" he asked, his head quirked curiously to one side.

"Never mind that, Phaethon," I said in a hushed tone, for it felt wrong to think of Necromancy now, with him curled so close to me.

"I'm sleepy, sister." He yawned, revealing an army of miniature teeth in the darkness of his mouth. In another minute he was fast asleep, his head propped upon one of the golden legs of the ewe, his little body sheltered by one of her wings.

I let out a low exhale.

Khrysomallos raised her head slightly to look at me once more.

"I really can't save you?" I tried again in an undertone to her, so that my brother would not wake.

Her expression belied not anguish—only a radiant tranquility.

Containing my own sadness the best I could, I reached into my pocket and withdrew a dagger. Careful, so as not to hurt her, I sheared a small chunk of wool from the creature's left side.

That work at last completed, I nestled in beside Phaethon and Khrysomallos.

I would need to return with Phaethon back to the palace before dawn, but for now, we could remain like this together, under the sprawling stars, a strangely shaped extended family.

CHAPTER NINE

The Ram and the Love Draft

The following dawn, Phrixus led the men out to the beach to sacrifice the ram. Before they departed, the foreign prince appeared in the doorway to my chamber, an illicit smile on his face.

The vision of him before me was almost enough to banish the tremendous desolation of the night before. If not for the cutting of golden wool in the pocket of my nightdress, and the strange radiance I felt in my extremities, I might have imagined that my excursion beside the ram had been a melancholy dream.

"You should not be here!" I gasped, unable to repress the joy that bubbled up in me at the sight of him. "If Father catches you—" I broke off, cheeks coloring. There was no polite way to finish that sentence. Even so, his grin did not disappear. If anything, it became suddenly conspiratorial. I mirrored his expression.

"I know, but I needed to check on you. I was not lying last night when I said that I owed you a debt of gratitude. Not many girls of any age would have so courageously tumbled into the surf to save a stranger."

I blushed again, this time an even deeper shade of rose.

"You don't owe me anything," I reassured him, biting my lips. "But you are gallant to look in on me." Was I flirting? The thought was an uncomfortable one, for it seemed to go against my nature.

He shrugged; the impressive muscles of his shoulders relaxed under his tunic. How easily he moved, his good nature as bright as any beacon. This did not look like a man who had only recently lost both his sister and his birthright.

"How are you able to remain standing, beaming at me, like you do now?" I blurted out before I could stop myself. Something in his manner grew stiff, his grin slipping ever so slightly before he managed to retrieve it once more.

"I just meant that you must be burdened by an impossible sorrow," I fumbled, attempting to make up unsuccessfully for my moment of candor. "I am here if you ever wish to confide in someone."

He nodded, his face unusually sober, and his eyes piercing.

"That is very gallant of you, princess," he acknowledged in an undertone. A thrill of longing stole through me, and I quelled it. "As long as you are well, I shall take my leave of you," he concluded, offering me a charming little bow.

I nodded, smiling recklessly. My hands trembled, and so I clenched them tightly in the folds of my nightdress.

He departed gracefully down the hallway, and I watched his back recede with something like wistfulness. I hoped that Father would allow him to stay for a long time yet.

In the end, I opted to stay ensconced in my chamber, wrapped in blankets to ward off the chill of the sea fog. Chalciope joined me after her breakfast, her face shining and delirious with longing.

"He's beautiful, isn't he?" she whispered in a daze, taking a seat at my desk, and examining herself carefully in the looking glass. She shifted so that she could ascertain what her flaming hair looked like from all angles, leaning in to observe an invisible imperfection on her cheeks.

"Who?" I inquired, pretending I had no notion of whom she spoke.

"Phrixus." She sighed, her head lolling back and her eyes closing luxuriously. "He's so beautiful I could die."

I raised my eyebrows at her, and she laughed.

"You're so young, Medea. You don't understand it yet, but love makes one foolish."

"You do seem to be acting rather absurd," I affirmed, flashing a grin at her, trying not to take notice of the way my stomach dropped when she said the word *love*. I had never considered attraction, outside of how it could be cultivated and brewed. I knew how to make love potions, of course I did, but they always seemed rather unimportant. Venusian herbs—those infused with the will of Aphrodite herself, luscious and voluptuous, the type with promiscuous petals and heady blossoms—had never appealed to me.

But suddenly, I wondered why I had been so obtuse. It was as though with the arrival of our Boeotian stranger, a new world had opened up in front of me, one I had been ignoring or else blind to for the entirety of my existence. I remembered how my heart hammered in my chest when I thought of the prince, or how his arm had caught around me and dragged me from the jaws of the sea. Was this love? The thing that I had been warned about incessantly since my infancy, the thing I had resigned myself never to feel because I saw how ridiculous it made otherwise impressive figures? I shook my head to dislodge such ruminations. It would not do to entertain feelings for the man whom Aeetes planned to marry off to my sister.

"I am, aren't I." Chalciope giggled, her eyes sweet and expressive. I felt a twinge of guilt at my jealousy. Besides, Phrixus saw me only as a child. That, I knew already, intuitively, with an ache that permeated my entire being.

"No," I whispered, moving to stand behind her and running my own fingers through her hair. "I think the two of you will make a lovely couple. Has he said anything to you?"

My sister shook her head, looking slightly deflated. "We only exchanged a few words over dinner. He seemed rather preoccupied, and I imagine after the ordeal he's suffered that makes sense. But Father said he would broach the topic of a match when they slaughter the animal this afternoon." She let out a low, anxious moan. "Oh, Medea, what if he doesn't want me? What if he refuses to settle for a barbarian princess? How could he want a girl from Kolchis?"

I shushed her, taken aback by her unusual show of vulnerability. "He would be very lucky to have you," I reasoned. "Especially now that he is an exile from his native land. He is a prince in name only, and would do well to be allied with Aeetes. Besides, you are beautiful and bright and the progeny of sun and surf all at once. You will make an enviable bride—this is inevitable."

"I do not wish to be some consolation prize for his lost glory." She glowered, some of the sharpness returning to her gaze before promptly dissolving again. She stared at herself bleakly in the mirror, her reflection looking more miserable even than her true form.

"Well, tell me how you know you love him," I pushed, hoping to steer the conversation into more calming waters. I was not skilled at this kind of girlish chatter, the idle talk of feelings that seemed to come naturally to Chalciope, or the serving girls in the kitchens. After all, I never had use of it. But now seemed as good a time as any to try my hand at careful manipulations of speech, inflections of emotion, and tuts of sympathy.

"Oh, Medea, I can't explain it. He just—" She broke off, her eyes taking on a dreamy quality. For a moment I was struck by how much she resembled our mother.

"He what?" I pressed, curious.

"He sends shivers all through me. Like I've been plunged into a bath of ice water, except it's so much more pleasant. And all I can think about is when I'm going to see him again, and how to make him want me. I fell asleep imagining silly scenarios in my head, and then proceeded to dream of the soft contours of his face, the devastating angles of his eyes. I don't know what to do with myself. If he doesn't want me, I think I'll lose my mind, Medea, I really do."

"It's madness to tie so much to a man, sister," I whispered in an undertone, tucking some of her strawberry-colored hair behind her graceful ears. *Even one as comely and good as Phrixus*, I thought, coloring.

"I can't help it, though," she whined, turning to stare at me, imploring me with her eyes to understand the severity of her predicament, the depths of her feelings.

And even though her weakness chafed at me, I nodded, taking her hand, and offering her a comforting smile.

■ ■ ■

When the men returned with the golden fleece, I could tell immediately that my father was angry. I wondered vaguely what could have gone wrong in the short span of a day, when Phrixus had proved so charming the night before. My father's pages hefted the fleece between them, a glimmering, golden skin that caught the light of the sunset and refracted it brilliantly across the cove. Surely, there was no issue with the offering. I had never seen anything so radiant, besides the sun in the sky. Phaethon cooed in awe as it passed, his toddler fists reaching out as though to seize or summon the pelt to him. Tutting softly, Chalciope carried him back inside the palace.

I attempted to catch the prince's eye as he passed, but he looked distracted, his hands, blood-soaked, rubbing the back of his neck as though to ease the tension from his body.

"Medea." My father's voice cracked across the courtyard, and his wrist flicked toward the throne room. My stomach dropped. What had I done this time for him to summon me with such displeasure?

Inside the hall, my father shook seawater from his cloak and ascended the dais to his throne. He looked more than annoyed, his face masked in a scowl. There was something in his manner that hovered on the precipice of wrath, and I held in my breath.

"Did the sacrifice transpire as planned?" I began.

He shrugged dismissively.

"The ram was sacrificed to Zeus with all the required pomp and ceremony. With the marvel it performed before its death, I imagine the creature might hope to be among the stars tonight." Although his lack of empathy for the ewe sent a dull pang through me, the promise of her spirit ascending to the celestial realm was good news.

"How wonderful, Father," I intoned dutifully. "You've done very well." A silence stretched between us, potent and sour.

"The fleece is very beautiful, Father," I continued. "What shall you do with it?"

He waved his hands vaguely, as though physically dismissing my question.

"It is very lovely, indeed. I imagine all manner of princes and barbarians might wish to take it for themselves, so it will have to be specially guarded. I have a quiet place in mind. A grove that the fleece matches in splendor," he offered distractedly, before seeming to remember himself. "Not, of course, that my plans for the fleece are any business of yours, Medea." His scowl deepened.

"I apologize, Father," I intoned automatically, ignoring the wrenching in my gut. "I can be quite thoughtless. Why did you wish to speak to me?"

I was always debasing myself like this for him, making my speech palatable and my person demure.

"The Prince Phrixus has rejected my offer of Chalciope to be his bride," Aeetes said without preamble, his look smoking. "I imagine he has somehow found her lacking. I do not think that at this point your sweet sister needs to be informed, given that there is still time for the youth to change his mind." He looked at me keenly. Something in his gaze gave me pause.

I opened my mouth to inquire why he should have summoned me of all people to relay this information to. After a long moment, I recognized the set of his shoulders, the odd little grin on his face.

"Suppose I do not tell her yet?" I asked in an undertone.

Aeetes smiled and let out a dry chuckle. "Good girl. I think that once he is settled back in his chambers, you should offer our guest some refreshment. He's worked hard today, and I fear he will not drink anything I serve him. He has, I imagine, heard of my reputation, and he has just done me a slight, has he not, in refusing to wed my daughter." My stomach sank.

"What kind of refreshment?" I forced myself to speak, my voice unnaturally high.

My father paused.

"Well, the boy has had a difficult journey. I imagine his mind is not quite right, and so we cannot blame him for his initial rudeness. Perhaps you give him something sweet, to help him get over his shyness. And if that does not sit well enough with him, I'll provide a sample of my own brew." Some of the tightness in my muscles gradually began to relax as I realized Phrixus had not condemned himself to death—not yet, anyway.

"I understand," I offered carefully, attempting to keep the nervousness from my voice. "I'll take care of it."

"See that you do, daughter," my father crooned, his tone faintly mocking. "See that you do."

■ ■ ■

Back in my rooms, my hands shook so terribly I almost dropped the glass flask that I had placed on my desk. I had never hated my father before, I realized, as I bent over my drawers of herbs and scribbled out recipes on scraps of parchment—never like this. Aeetes could brew a love potion in his sleep. It had been one of the first drafts that he taught me, and yet he wanted the one that tricked Phrixus into staying with us forever to be my handiwork—my deception—for no reason other than that he liked to see me suffer. And he doubtless enjoyed the idea of a foreign prince being beguiled by the weakest, female member of our family. It would be a humiliation too terrible to be borne, I knew. Even once the draft wore off, Phrixus would not be able to abandon his marriage bed, for fear that the story might get out. I shuddered.

The fact that I had no choice echoed dully around in my head. If this did not work, Father would kill the boy. This much I knew, because Aeetes had told me this in his veiled, inconspicuous way. His subtlety was a kind of evil. I tried to recall everything I knew of Venusian concoctions.

Attempting to assuage some of the rage pounding through my chest, I thought back to a lesson with Aeetes in the woods, under a vine of dangling fuchsia.

"Before we begin with this particular branch of herbalism, Medea, you should know the dangers. Our Egyptian neighbors to the east, from whom I have gleaned all manner of magical knowledge, have only one vein of magic, which is considered truly dark, reprehensible in the way that evil is. Do you know what that vein of magic is?" My father had regarded me coolly.

"The kind that deals with the dead?" I guessed, uncertainly. "Or bringing the dead back from Hades?"

"The Egyptians do not have any comprehension of Hades—their afterlife is slightly more complicated."

"Oh. The kind that deals with monsters, then? Transformations? Like what Aunt Circe does on Aeaea?" Aeetes's face darkened, and I regretted bringing Circe up at all. For a moment I worried that he might send me back to the palace, our lesson concluded for the day. But after a long moment, he regained his usual composure and spoke once more.

"The only dark magic is love magic, Medea. Do you have any idea why that might be?"

I shook my head. "Perhaps because the Egyptians do not like being in love?" I felt stupid as I said it but could come up with no other reason.

Aeetes had thrown his head back with uncharacteristic joviality, releasing a booming laugh into the open air.

"Where you get your foolishness, I have no idea," he murmured at last, wiping at his eyes. "Love magic is dangerous because to our Near Eastern friends, of all the things in this world, love is the most powerful and compelling. To make someone fall in love against their will is tantamount to taking over their body, mind, and spirit." He paused, regarding me.

"Of course, those of us to the west understand that love is a fool's enterprise, but even so, the cultivation and annihilation of attraction is something you ought to understand. It is an expertise that you will learn to apply to your own sorcery." Perhaps Father was so condescending about love potions because he himself had never been in love, but the thought was disturbing. I attempted to push it out of my mind.

"I understand, Father. And how does one cultivate and annihilate attraction?"

"First, you must familiarize yourself with the qualities of Venusian herbs. These plants are the type that give off fragrant perfumes, which produce ripe and succulent fruits, which might be ground up for their color and applied to the female face to enhance beauty, which resemble the sexual organs and elicit an amorous response in the observer when seen or imbibed." He listed off readily, "Consider the flora that are most handsome and fertile, lush and green and vibrant, pleasing to the senses and delightful to the mind. Their flowers will be soft to the touch, and sweetly and promiscuously colored. Their fruits will make the mouth water. Is this clear?"

Emerging from my reverie, I filled a mortar and pestle with bloodred pomegranate seeds, and began to grind their sweet, tangy essence into the stone. Next came the saffron—first the bright vermillion stigma and then the rest of the flower, with its seductive violet petals. After seven minutes had passed, I dribbled a few drops of distilled essence of vervain into the paste, and crushed the flowers of a fig tree on top. Love magic, I knew, had to be more intuitive than many types of manifestation. It had to be personal, and deeply felt. And so without thinking I added a rosebud, which was my own signature, uttering the usual incantations as I worked, picturing Phrixus in my mind's eye. The thing was completed with a few stray strands of Chalciope's flaming red hair, which she had left behind, entangled in the comb on her desk.

For a moment, I considered leaving them out, and plucking a few of my own dark curls instead. I imagined what it might feel like to be loved by Phrixus. To be his wife. But just as quickly, I shut those thoughts out. Aeetes would never allow it, and I was too young to marry, and Chalciope would never forgive me.

I poured sparkling wine over the top of the glass flask, which would mask the taste. My herbs might be easily misconstrued as the dregs of the wine, and Phrixus would have no reason to suspect deception from me, the child who watched his every move like some sort of pathetic dog eager for some compliment from its master. How humiliating it was to be a woman.

■ ■ ■

I entered Phrixus's chamber with a glass in one hand and the flask containing my draft in the other. As the door swung open to allow me entry, I noted the shock in his eyes; the vague uneasiness, which seemed to melt as soon as he saw it was only me.

"And to what do I owe this honor?" he asked, offering me a half-hearted smile. Something like nausea rose in my throat at his good humor, at the kindness he showed me. *You shouldn't trust any of us.*

Nothing that comes out of this place is true, I longed to tell him, but instead I forced my lips into a smile.

"I wanted to see how the sacrifice went," I suggested, meeting his eyes to make him feel at ease. "And to bring you something to drink. You were out in the sun for a long time, and the sea air always makes me thirsty." The man's eyes darted over the flask in my hand.

"Something from your father's cellar?" he asked in what might have been a casual manner if a hint of nervousness had not seeped into his expression.

"No, I'm not allowed to go down there. I filched this wine from the kitchens, so you mustn't tell anyone, or I'll be in trouble," I lied, proffering him the glass. I hoped he might mistake my nervousness as fear of discovery, and not as a sign of my deception. After a long moment, he took the crystal in his hands, and gestured for me to fill it up to the top.

I was shocked at how level I managed to pour, at how steady my hands were despite the mess I felt inside. He raised the glass to his lips and took a sip. His eyelids fluttered shut, and I was caught in the length of those eyelashes, how they looked almost like a girl's might.

"It tastes lovely, this," he murmured, his face becoming more relaxed.

"Good," I returned, perching uneasily on the edge of an armchair. I wondered what I might say to distract him and keep him drinking.

"I think my sister, Chalciope, enjoys your company," I offered, cursing myself. I was too obvious, but he did not seem to notice.

"She is a lovely girl, and will make some man a lovely wife," he murmured, taking another long draft.

"You do not want to marry her, though?" I asked, stalling. He opened his mouth to speak, and then a cloudy expression came over him. He looked confused.

"I find myself admiring her, I suppose," he said softly, more to himself than to me. "She is more beautiful than any of the girls I bedded in Boeotia." A sick feeling seemed to grow in my stomach but I forced myself to continue.

"So why did you refuse her?" I asked, tentatively.

Phrixus jerked his face up, for the first time looking startled. In a moment, though, the dazed look had fallen once more across him,

"How did you know that? Did your father—? I suppose he must have. How fast word travels here . . ." He trailed off, a hint of wonder suffusing his tone.

After a moment, he shook his head forcibly, as though to clear some of the haze. Something like pity pierced me, but I kept my countenance indifferent.

"It's not the princess I have an issue with," he explained slowly, "so much as that I could never trust a woman after what Ino did to my father. It would be the height of folly to let any such wretched creature of the female persuasion into my bed when I know they might just be plotting against me—against my seed." He broke off, having the decency to look embarrassed. I decided to push my advantage.

"And what of Helle? Your sister?" I reasoned. "Was she so vile?"

His scowl deepened, and he looked at me blearily.

"Helle was different. Special, even. Lesser women knew it and despised her for it."

I attempted to mask the unease in my countenance, but Phrixus found it anyhow.

"Come, Medea, sit beside me." He gestured to the open seat beside him, his face regaining some of its usual sympathy.

I forced myself to approach him, each movement jerky and uncomfortable.

"I'm surprised you can even tolerate my company, given these sentiments you've so lately divulged," I quipped nervously, not fully in control of my tongue.

"Oh, princess, you misunderstand me. Of course, you don't count yet, as you're only a child, and not a woman fully formed and fledged. You aren't so vile as them, but you will be one day. You won't be able to help it." His expression darkened with some recollection, and I licked my lips.

In the silence that stretched between us, he grew bolder, his eyes tracing the lines of my shoulders and hips.

"In fact, you're getting rather close to the line." He smirked at me. That I was not even thirteen seemed of little consequence.

I wanted to shake him, to make him take back what he had said.

Tears stung at the corners of my eyes, and beneath my smile my teeth ground tightly into one another. How wrong I had been about this boy. How entirely naive, to be taken in by his easy smile and kind eyes.

In another moment, his rough hand had found my thigh, and time itself seemed to slow. He drew lazy circles along the flesh there, his mouth gaping strangely as he touched me. I prayed internally that his fingers would not go any higher, for I was not sure how to stop him if they did. How was it that I could brew potions potent enough to leave twenty men his size dead at my feet, but could not manage to push his hand away? I struggled, sluggish and outside of myself.

"You should drink up, your grace," I offered, straining to keep the terror from tainting my tongue. "You need to recuperate your strength."

He nodded, his hand removing itself to better grip the flask. I watched as he took another mouthful.

"We don't have wine this good in Boeotia." He chuckled, running a hand through his curls. "We don't have girls this good, either."

I wondered frantically if I had accidentally dropped my own hair or sweat into the concoction, my hands trembling.

"My sister, Chalciope, will be warmed to hear it. Drink more, my lord," I deflected, heart hammering. I was in danger. I never should have gone to the prince's room alone. I wondered if my father had foreseen this. If it had been in the plan all along. If my draft did not work properly, then Phrixus might deflower me, an action as binding among royalty as a marriage pact. Sweat broke out under my arms, and along my hair.

He drained the glass, his eyes trained firmly on me, as I prayed to every God I knew to keep him off me. The room felt oppressively warm, and I noticed my breath coming in shallow gasps. He suddenly appeared much bigger than he had before, more man than adolescent.

The seconds dragged by, and the dazed expression seemed to fade from the prince's eyes. His face was covered in a layer of sweat, a thin sheen that glued his tunic to his chest. He was coming back to himself. I held my breath, watching his pupils as they dilated and narrowed in rapid fluctuations.

"You'll think me rather odd, given everything I just said," he murmured softly, running a hand across his face, and blushing slightly. "But I think I would rather like to call on your sister."

I let out an unsteady exhale. "Oh, no, I don't think that's odd at all. She should be down in the garden with Phaethon, I imagine. You might be able to talk to her there before dinner." I did not trust myself to stand up, to place any weight at all on my legs, which felt like jelly. The room had begun to swim, and I wondered if I might pass out.

Was this what it felt like to die? My vision blurred and darkened, and my heart leaped erratically in my chest.

"I shall try that," he murmured, rising to his feet, smiling softly in the manner of one who has a secret. He strode past where I sat, his feet light.

I heard him pause in the doorway. "I'm sorry if I made you uncomfortable, princess, I'm not entirely certain what came over me. Will you be all right returning to your chambers unchaperoned?"

I nodded mutely without looking at him, my skin prickling horribly. As the door rustled shut behind him, I began to sob, clutching my arms to my chest and rocking manically. The last light of the day deepened into dusk, and still I could not manage to move myself from my seat. Dark magic, indeed.

CHAPTER TEN

On Mutilation

The wedding was a beautiful affair, everyone said so. Chalciope was radiant in her gown, and our grandfather Helios himself sent a coronet for her to wear, in addition to a jewel-encrusted dress that fit her perfectly. It set her curls off magnificently, and Phrixus, to his credit, or to mine, could not take his eyes off her. As I appraised my sister, adorned in all the finery that our Titan blood would allow, I wondered about my grandfather. I had never met him face-to-face, and so could not imagine what he might look like. The few stories that Aeetes told gave little away regarding his physicality—it seemed as though Helios was surrounded by such a burning, scorching light that his true form was almost obscured to mortal eyes.

To think that I was descended from such brightness felt wrong. Chalciope and Phaethon were clearly the grandchildren of Helios, but as far as I was concerned? That was less obvious.

And perhaps that was why our Titan forefather had deigned to bestow gifts on all of his grandchildren but me.

"You might pray to him," Chalciope suggested as I adjusted the dress upon her hips. With our mother gone, my sister had taken on some of her softness, a shift I both craved and bristled at. She had a way of noticing when I became withdrawn, and had an almost supernatural ability to intuit what was goading me. "Perhaps if you made an effort, he might take more of an interest in you."

I shrugged. The truth was that I was frightened of my grandfather.

That he had fathered Aeetes, a man most cruel and shrewd, did not help assuage this anxiety.

Each morning, I supplied Phrixus with more of my potion, although now I did not stay for him to drink it. Nothing, I imagined, could be worth that. After the vows were exchanged and Chalciope deflowered, I could stop, Father promised.

In the week leading up to the ceremony, I had trouble sleeping, plagued by inexplicable nightmares. Dreams of the toads I had butchered suddenly growing in size, so large that they crushed me under their slimy skin. Sometimes, the rats under my blade would wriggle, transforming into golden rams that in turn shifted into Phrixus with his hungry, loathsome eyes. Occasionally I woke up before his fingers found my flesh, and other times I did not. During the day, my vision was obscured by lethargy, and I had difficulty distinguishing whether I was awake or asleep. I ate very little during meals, and spent almost every waking hour below ground in the cellars, among the rodents and frogs.

For all of the time I spent underground, my experimentation seemed to reach a plateau. As I made careful cuts into the flesh of my charges, their squealing and gurgling rang in my ears with the potency of human screams. I wondered if I resembled Phrixus to them, if that same grasping rapaciousness in his gaze could be discerned in mine. Over and over again, I found myself pulled against my will back to that afternoon in his chamber, when I was sure my father had set me up to be ruined, when I had realized I was a pawn to the men who populated my life—another frantic animal to be exacted of its usefulness. And when I considered myself in those terms, it was too easy to sympathize with the animals in my care. I spent more afternoons than I care to admit crying softly in the dank darkness of the cellar, a wreck of what I once was.

It was foolish, I reasoned. After all, Phrixus had hardly touched me. And yet I felt entirely violated. This was how I came to know of another kind of magic—a type I had never encountered before—one that required no external substances. Time travel, more vivid than memory had any right to be, as it turned out, was entirely possible so long as a witch was terrified enough.

And so it was that as my sister tied herself to Phrixus like an ox to a yoke, I was hardly paying attention. I was everywhere and nowhere all at once: in my room the night Idyia had told me Phaethon would be severed into tiny pieces; in the prince's chamber, watching him drink a potion that would make his life a little less his own; in the shadows of the throne room as Father told me that a girl had no place learning *Pharmakon*; in the rolling blue thunder of the Black Sea as I cried out for my mother and she declined to show herself; under the covers with Chalciope, giggling as she braided my hair in tangled knots; on the bluffs overlooking the sea, wondering how I would ever make it out of this dreadful place when it was all I had ever known.

Overhead the sun beat down steadily, a final wedding gift from Helios.

At the wedding banquet, Aeetes's eyes surveyed the festivities, as sharp and eagle-like as ever. Although his face bore no trace of a smile, he looked satisfied. Chalciope gleamed, a vision in gems, and Phrixus's glance never left her lips, the sweet slope of her shoulders. Phaethon pulled at the edge of the dress I had slipped on for the celebration, his eyes wet with tears. The noise from the celebration had frightened him and no one had noticed, save me. I took him up in my arms and carried him out of the courtyard.

"Hush, sweet one," I hummed into his hair, breathing in the scent of sweat and sandalwood that adorned him perpetually. "It won't be like this forever, I promise you that. One day, Mother will come back for us and take us down below the sea with her, and everything will be beautiful and nothing will be scary." Even as I said it, I knew Aeetes would never let any such thing happen, just as I was sure our mother, for all of her dynamism and power, would never dare to oppose his will.

■　■　■

In those early days, Chalciope was happy with the match. Every one of her movements spoke to some immense, supernatural reservoir of adoration for her new husband. Her eyes lit up when he walked into a room, and her voice would take on a ridiculous lilt when she spoke of him. I had been terrified to stop making the love draft, for fear that

Phrixus might, upon regaining his sense and lucidity, collapse the fantasy she had constructed around the both of them. I found, with some measure of relief, that I could bribe a male servant or another to slip the concoctions into the kylix in his chamber. I could not bear the prospect of entering it myself, after all that had transpired.

But one morning Chalciope appeared in my chamber as I was dressing Phaethon for the day. He was grumpy that morning, his perfect little face contorted with fatigue and irritation.

"No, no, no!" he wailed, striking out at me with his miniature fists as I slipped a tunic over his head.

"Someone needs his favorite sister." Chalciope laughed, a loud, melodious sound that echoed through the room. She brushed past me and picked up our brother in her arms, swinging him around until his cries turned to giggles. I let out a little huff of exhaustion, glad for the break, if only for a moment.

"You look unwell, Medea darling," Chalciope whispered, peering more closely at me as she pressed a kiss to Phaethon's chubby cheeks. "The circles under your eyes are something dreadful."

I glowered at her. "I haven't been sleeping very well," I admitted, hoping she would drop the subject, but also, pathetically, hoping she would ask me more.

"Why not whip up one of those sleeping drafts Father takes?" she suggested. "I'm sure that would help."

"I've tried those, as well as potions to deter nightmares," I retorted harshly.

"Well, the only thing that helped my nightmares in the end was sharing a bed with Phrixus," she whispered, sharing a conspiratorial smile with me and raising her eyebrows. "It does wonders for the nerves. Once you're married, you'll sleep like baby Phaethon here." Her eyes lit up and she made a face at our brother.

"I have no intention of marrying," I shot back, annoyed. In truth, I had no desire for a man to ever look at me again.

Chalciope shook her head at me in wonder. "You say that now, but trust me, when the right man shows up you won't be able to stop yourself. Besides, how else do you expect to have children?"

"Why would anyone in their right mind want to have children?" I snapped, growing impatient with this line of inquiry. Immediately my sister went silent, pausing in her ministrations to Phaethon. I glanced up, shocked to see her eyes filling with tears.

"Chalciope, what is it?" I asked, aghast, reaching out to touch her shoulder, although the feel of her skin felt strange and unnatural under my fingers. We were no longer the loose-limbed children we had once been. Now there were secrets between us, so loathsome and dark that every gentleness I showed her felt disingenuous. I had betrayed my sister with my witchcraft, and perhaps here was the cost.

Blinking droplets of water, she placed Phaethon down carefully, before wrapping her arms carefully around her middle.

"Chalciope, what's going on?" I repeated, panic beginning to build in me.

A strange wolfish laugh tore from her throat. Grinning unnaturally like that, she almost resembled our father.

"I'm sorry, Medea," she gasped, still laughing, but pressing a hand to her mouth, as though to stop the sound. "I'm just all mixed up lately. It must be the baby." She shook her head, unable to keep the smile from her cheeks. At first I thought she was referencing Phaethon, but then I realized how her hands were positioned protectively around her middle, as though cradling it. I felt myself slide into the nearest chair.

"You're with child," I said at last, unsure why this news felt so catastrophic.

"Yes," she murmured, her eyes appraising me self-consciously. "Say something, won't you? Do you think I'll make a good mother?"

The first thought that entered my mind was one of vague anxiety. What if the abundance of love magic in Phrixus's body somehow passed to the creature growing inside my sister? Surely love magic would not harm the child, but I could not be certain.

I was so shocked I could hardly formulate words, but I forced a smile for Chalciope's sake. For she was barely past the boundary of childhood herself, even now at sixteen.

"Of course," I choked. "How could you not?"

In another moment, her arms were around me, so tight I felt slightly stifled. We so rarely touched each other in this family of ours. Occasionally our mother might brush us fondly on the cheeks, or Chalciope might smooth my hair before important events, but that was the extent of our physical closeness. In spite of my initial awkwardness, I leaned in to that hug, shutting my eyes tight and breathing hard, trying to memorize the scent of my sister, which was something like honeysuckle mixed with wild lavender.

"You're going to be amazing," I whispered again for emphasis.

■ ■ ■

As my sister polished new life within her, I redoubled my efforts below ground, graduating to larger mammals, such as rabbits and, when I could procure them, goats. With smaller animals, I was able to reattach a severed head, as long as it was done in a timely manner after the decapitation. This was a promising development, although hardly enough to celebrate.

At least with the news of Chalciope's pregnancy, I decided that I could cease drugging Phrixus with the love potion. Although he would slowly come back to himself, disoriented and confused and resentful, he would not be able to back out of this life, now that my sister was swollen with his seed. He was going to be a father, and anyway, he needed all of the support he could get if he ever planned to return and assert his claim over Boeotia—not that I imagined he had any desire to do so. But I knew my father, knew that he would stop at nothing to expand his powers and domain, and that Chalciope's husband would be seen as an extension of his own interests. When the great King Athamas died, Aeetes would be ready, staking Phrixus's claim to the throne of Boetia for him if that was what was required.

In the evenings, I would return to my room and scrub the blood from my hands and wrists. The cellars reeked of that strange metallic scent, and I imagined I must as well. It soaked into my clothes and skin so deeply that I was sure anyone who met me must be able to smell it, to guess what I was up to. And yet no one seemed to care. Once I was properly cleaned, I would collect Phaethon from my father or his nurses, then tote him around on my hip. He was getting heavier by the day, and at some point I knew I would not be able to carry him at all.

"You're going to be taller than I am, at some point," I mused, tickling the soft skin of his neck, the vulnerable area beneath his ribs. "Which is good, because we need you as big and as strong as possible for when your moment comes." I sighed heavily, trying not to let the worry show in my face, though I doubted he was of an age to understand my expression of unkempt anxiety. How delicate his body was, how frail the bones and soft the skin. How easy it would be to take up a knife and bleed the life slowly out of him. To stop myself from picturing my baby brother in his eventual carnage, I tried to imagine other things.

I longed for a friend, someone my own age who might bring a hint of joy to the relentless churn of days.

When the child could not sleep I would whisper to him the stories of his namesake, the stories our mother had told me as I drifted off to sleep so many long years ago.

"Did you know the first Phaethon was a child of Helios, just like our father, Aeetes, except his mother was the sea nymph Clymene? But from his very birth, the other nymphs accused the child of being illegitimate. Helios had told Styx, one of the Oceanids, that Phaethon was his son, and Styx had not believed him. And so to prove it, Helios swore he would grant the boy any wish he desired. Phaethon was a bright boy, and beloved by everyone, but he had an adventurous nature. He was young and terribly ambitious, and longed to be like his father in every way.

"'Let me drive your chariot, the one that pulls the sun across the sky, Father,' Phaethon demanded. Helios felt his heart sink, for he knew that Phaethon would not be strong enough for such a task.

"He begged his son to reconsider, to make a different wish, but Phaethon would not be so easily deterred. He wanted to control the great sun chariot for a single day, no more and no less, he explained. And so with a heavy heart, Helios handed over the reins to his chariot. At first, Phaethon glided euphorically through the sky, giddy with power. After a few moments, though, he began to tire, for he was not as powerful as his Titan father. The horses pulled tirelessly on the reins, and he found he could not control the course of his trajectory. The chariot veered perilously close to the earth, scorching the forests, and the tops of mountains, devastating crops and burning villages. Zeus, realizing that if he did not act swiftly, the entire earth might be destroyed, hurled one of his thunderbolts at the boy, striking him from the chariot. Phaethon fell dead, and Helios resumed the reins.

"This is why you must always be aware of your own abilities and not reach too far above what you're capable of. It is tempting to seek out glory because of the divinity that flows through our veins, but you must be cautious always, sweet boy, lest you end up like our uncle."

Phaethon, for his part, did not seem to understand the gravity of the stories I told, but they calmed me and soothed him, and so our nightly routine was not complete without them. They reminded me of our mother, an attachment I could not shake in the nearly two years since she had disappeared beneath the waves.

CHAPTER ELEVEN

Reckoning

Chalciope's son arrived in the middle of spring, as fresh and sweet as his mother had been. With his mother's red hair and bronze skin, and his father's strong nose and dark eyes, Argus, even in the heat of a tantrum, was pleasing to look at. And Phaethon, although disoriented by the addition of another child, seemed to take it in stride, cradling his nephew in his own tiny arms, enamored by the vitality of new life.

In the months since I ceased drugging Phrixus, he had become reticent and withdrawn. During the afternoons he would take long walks along the bluff, or else visit the Ares, that silent, sacred grove of trees where Aeetes hung the golden fleece. In the evenings he abstained from the dining hall, taking his meals in his room. At some point, he began to regard me shrewdly, and I knew he was piecing my deception together. When I encountered him in the corridors, his emotions warred over control of his face: equal parts wounded betrayal and abject shame. I had trapped him here on Kolchis—condemned him to the same fate I had always chafed under. The irony of our situation was almost too much to hold. Even so, I did not feel particularly bad about this; my sympathy was worn out, but I did ache for Chalciope who, swollen with child, could not figure out what she had done to make her husband hate her.

"I try very hard to be a good wife," she whispered one afternoon, a few weeks before the baby would emerge.

I nodded, preoccupied with Phaethon, who was playing with the lyre our father had commissioned especially for his impossibly small fingers. "You are, Chalciope. You're everything you should be and more."

"Then why does he treat me so? In the beginning he was so warm, so inviting. And now he is cold and indifferent. I have heard that husbands sometimes no longer find their wives attractive once they are with child but—"

I cut her off, trying not to feel sick. "That's not what it is, sister." The silence stretched out between us, and the hairs on the back of my neck began to stand on end. When I looked up to meet her gaze, her eyes were full of horror.

"Why do you sound so certain? What do you know that I do not?"

I opened my mouth and then clamped it shut once more, my cheeks coloring.

"Medea, tell me now." Her voice took on a low and dangerous quality. I opened my mouth yet again but could not summon even the slimmest of defenses. Her eyes flashed.

"Gods above," she choked. "Oh, Medea, not you. No, no, no." Her face seemed to cave in on itself. Her arms hung listlessly around her stomach.

"I'm so sorry," I insisted, finding my voice. "Father made me, he said it was the only way to make Phrixus stay. Otherwise he would have poisoned him—"

Chalciope turned to me with eyes that radiated venom. "*You* poisoned him, you wretched creature. How do you not understand that?"

I fell back against my seat as though she had struck me. From beside us, Phaethon regarded me with childish bemusement, looking back and forth between Chalciope and his lyre. His rosebud lips began to tremble, as though sensing the gravity of the situation.

"Everything you do is pernicious and unnatural," my sister shrieked, rising to her feet, swaying slightly with emotion. "No wonder Mother left us all. She knew exactly what she had created." The look on her face was all fire as she walked out of the room, crying softly. The door slammed behind her. My brother flinched.

"Chalcy is sad?" Phaethon articulated slowly, quirking his head to the side for confirmation.

I nodded, unable to speak.

...

After Argus was born, Phrixus gradually emerged from his solitude. The new child, made in his image, seemed to delight him. Although my sister had no time or patience for me, it gladdened my heart to see the two of them reconciled over the baby. In spite of everything, they might make a good match.

In no time it seemed, Chalciope's single son became four, each so closely resembling the child before that it was vaguely comical. They all possessed their mother's red hair and their father's thoughtful gaze, which made them look like old men even as children. After Argus came Phrontis. And when the two of them were hardly old enough to crawl about came Melas. Finally, in the cool aftermath of fall, Cytisorus was born, and their family was complete. Had there been a girl child, I'm sure Phrixus and Chalciope would have named her Helle, but perhaps the Gods felt uncharacteristically sorry for my brother-in-law. Bestowing four sons on him was a kind of reward for his suffering.

Somehow too Phaethon was growing into a man. His arms and legs had become long and muscled, although with none of the usual lankiness or awkwardness of youth. His skin shone brightly, unmarked by the blemishes of other boys his age, and his hair grew long around his shoulders. Throughout the palace it was whispered that my brother's fine looks were yet another gift from our grandfather. After all, neither Chalciope nor I possessed his degree of luster. He was a creature of fire, the sun distilled, but he was also gentle. It seemed that somehow he was beloved by everyone who came into contact with him. The servants would sneak him extra servings of food, rolls fresh from the oven and succulent meats skewered on sticks for him to enjoy. Slaves refused to speak poorly of him, for he was unnaturally kind. Foreign dignitaries and princes, much older than him, would follow him around the palace like dogs, desperate for some sign of favor. Even our father, who was impossible to please, was satisfied with the man his son was becoming. Over time, the bruises that sprung up like dreadful flowers along his arms and legs wherever Aeetes beat him began to sprout less often. It seemed that my brother was learning how to avoid our father's wrath.

Every other day, he pulled Phaethon from his lessons on politics and language, oration and rhetoric, to lead him away into the woods. I knew they were practicing sorcery, but for some reason, this did not goad me.

I understood my brother had no choice—he could not help being born a boy, or to a father as ruthless as ours. In the evenings he would return, smelling of sap and greenery, his eyes bright but tired. We sat in the shadows and discussed what he had learned, I marveling at his uncommon eloquence, and he asking me questions to sharpen his skills. Even if Father imagined that women had no place learning *Pharmakon*, Phaethon knew better.

At first I imagined he trusted me because I had raised him—that I, more than any other person, had been responsible for the everyday banalities of his upbringing, that I had molded him into a boy who was not a boy, not truly. This could not be, however, I knew. It was too simplistic. After all, Circe had raised Aeetes, and he still turned out a startling disappointment. Later, I realized that there was something inherent to Phaethon himself—a kind of thoughtful grace that kept him from succumbing to the baser urges of his sex.

After we went over his lessons, he told me stories he picked up from the servants or foreign kings. I would sit back and listen, eyes misty, treasuring the feeling of someone once again taking care of me.

"Medea, do you know of Arachne, the human weaver who rivaled that Great Goddess Athena herself at the loom?" he asked, his face flushed with pleasure at the thought of telling me a tale I did not know.

And so whether I was familiar with the story or not, I would shake my head, and look intrigued. There was no other soul I would play dumb for, aside from him.

"Tell me about her," I prompted, smiling.

"Well, Arachne was the mortal daughter of Idmon, and she grew up weaving tapestries. She knew the loom like the back of her hand, with an intuitive knowledge that made her a kind of prodigy in her native land. She loved the feel of the threads between her fingers, the thrill of completing row after vibrant row without a single mistake. Even as a child, her skill was universally known. Eventually, however, Arachne grew up into a young woman. And with her age came a dangerous confidence. One day, she bragged to the other women that she could weave better than Athena herself.

"Athena, not willing to take such rudeness, challenged the girl to a competition, thinking she would humiliate her for all to see. But Arachne surprised her. Arachne's hands were steady, her fingers sure, despite the strain of competing against Olympians. She wove a tapestry so beautiful that even the Goddess Athena paused, glancing over it, unable to detect a single misstep. But it is not possible to beat a Goddess, and so Arachne, unknowingly, had sealed her fate.

"In the next moment, Athena transformed her into a spider, a dark, spindly thing with hideous pincers and eight long legs.

"'There,' Athena remarked. 'Now you can weave all that you like, and no one will ever appreciate your creations. This is what your pride has brought down upon you.'"

As he finished speaking, Phaethon glanced at me from under his long lashes. He seemed to be struggling with his next words.

"What are you thinking?" I urged.

"Just that I crushed a spider underfoot, the day before. And how she might have concealed a human soul, like yours or mine. Sometimes I am baffled by the cruelty of mortals and Gods alike. This world of ours is uncommonly brutal, and I worry occasionally that I may be too soft for it."

I hushed him, shaking my head. The beginnings of panic gathering in my stomach were tempered, thankfully, by waves of fondness.

"There is no such thing as too much softness, not in a man with your power," I whispered. "It is becoming for a man to be merciful just as it is necessary for a woman to be strong. Never forget that. You are exactly what you are meant to be."

Our days passed in an easy haze, he learning sorcery from our father, and I making the daily trek beneath the palace to continue my research. In the evenings, as I stared at him, the dread would collect inside me, accumulating like clouds before a storm. My mother's prophecy was never far from my mind, but I worked hard to keep Phaethon from guessing his own fate.

Meanwhile, my brother was discovering his natural magical proclivities. Where I had been fond of herbs, Phaethon harbored a softness for all manner of animals, no matter how small or filthy. He left out bits of bread and cheese for the mice that scurried inside the palace walls and he liked to milk the goats who grazed in the pasture beyond the kitchens whenever Father was too occupied to register his son debased in such domestic acts. The animals sensed a gentleness to him, for they circled around him in droves, desperate for some scrap of his kindness. And how could I blame them? I felt as if I were following my brother from a distance, desperate to maintain his life and his favor.

Phaethon, through enchantment and elixir, learned to charm everything that lived and breathed about Kolchis. When he disappeared for hours at a time, I learned to search for him first in the forest, where I was likely to find him curled up in the muscled embrace of lions, whose backs sloped with feline grace, or tracing the long tusks of boars, who snuffled close in the dust beside him.

I tried not to think too much about what my brother might say if he knew about my work in the cellars, or about the animals I had so brutally abused in the pursuit of knowledge. He would be horrified, disturbed, even. He would never see me the same way again.

My father seemed to realize Phaethon's inclinations as well, and subsequently adapted his teachings to fit my brother's natural gifts.

One afternoon, my brother returned to my chamber pale and grim. I took in the rigid line of his spine and the labored breathing and instantly felt fear rise in my chest.

"What happened? Phaethon, are you hurt? Are you bleeding?" I raced to his side, feeling his body for signs of broken bones or lacerations.

He shook me off gently, shuddering.

"No, no, I think I'm fine, sister. Physically I am quite all right."

"What do you mean, 'physically'?" I cried, only slightly assuaged by this information. His eyes were wide and strange. They had the faraway quality of our mother's, and for an instant I longed to shake him.

"Father has procured a dragon," he explained, dragging his long hair behind his ear, his tongue flickering out along his lips.

"What?"

"A serpent, Medea, all glittering, green scales, and teeth, long and sharp and the size of daggers. Its breath smells like rotting flesh. I might have frozen when its eyes met mine. There was a reptilian, archaic power there even I had trouble warming to and—"

"A dragon?" I repeated, cutting him off. "Where did he even procure one?"

"Another gift from Grandfather. Helios apparently has a flair for flying serpents." Phaethon groaned, throwing himself down on my bed and covering his head in his hands. "Father plans to use it to guard the golden fleece. It's perfect, he says, because it never sleeps."

"How on earth have they bred the imperative to sleep out of any sentient creature?" I asked, befuddled.

"Not breeding, I imagine. Rather, some enchantment—you are familiar with Aeetes' ways." Phaethon shook his head.

I paused, trying to comprehend this new addition to our land. Our father, through his travels, had accumulated a veritable menagerie of creatures, some so fantastical that they had to be seen to be believed. Among his brood were fire-breathing oxen, serpents that spat blood, fish with the heads and front hooves of horses. Phaethon loved them all, oblivious to the risk they embodied. He fed them by hand and stroked them as they fell asleep, not caring if they burned him or cut him by accident. He spoke to them, I knew, in some fashion that had nothing to do with language, although the reaches of his compassion drove me to a terrible worry. We lived, I knew, in an age of monsters. Not all of them were beasts as obvious as dragons. Some walked among us as men.

"Tell me more, brother," I requested, settling at last in my logical brain.

"The thing is beautiful in its own way, immense and more powerful than a thousand mortal men. Smoke billows from its nostrils, and after it eats, it can emit a steady stream of fire in any direction from its maw. Its talons have the artful quality of many finely wrought blades. And then there are the wings—" He broke off, out of breath.

"A useful guard dog," I muttered dryly, and Phaethon began to laugh hysterically.

"You think, sister?" he asked in mock surprise. "I'm not sure it would be an effective means of deterring thieves, in all honesty."

I paused, thinking. "Well, if Aeetes cast some sort of enchantment on the thing to make it impervious to sleep, a different enchantment can easily break the first," I offered.

"And who out there across the whole of the Aegean has the skill and prowess necessary to work such magic?" Phaethon asked. "None but you, I, our sweet aunt Circe, and Father himself. Aeetes knows we would never subvert his will, and Circe is banished to Aeaea, so I imagine he feels that the fleece is in good hands, or talons, as it were." This was true, I knew.

"Why he cares so much about the thing, I'll never understand." Phaethon shook his head ruefully. "It's an old pelt, a morbid trophy, golden or not."

"Not so fast, brother." I raised a finger, my eyes wary, remembering my moonlight vigil beside the ram Khrysomallos, as the life drained slowly out of her. "It is a symbol—not only of our land's hospitality, but also of the Gods' grace. It is not so often that heroes encounter happy endings, but Phrixus has come close. There is something special about that."

Phaethon ducked his head in recognition. There was something hopeful in his expression, hidden under the thoughtful slope of his brow.

CHAPTER TWELVE

On Courtship

Aeetes seemed to take a heightened interest in me as the months passed, appraising me in the same manner that a sharp-eyed bird of prey might regard a soft, skittish field mouse. I would look up during meals and find his eyes trained on me, or else I would hear him murmur with my tutors when he thought I was bent over my work, oblivious to his interference. At first, his attentiveness frightened me because I assumed he was curious about my work in the cellar. If he ever truly scrutinized my habits, or noticed the intricacies of my hideous experiments, it would not take long to realize that something larger was going on.

Surely, he would want to know why I dedicated myself so wholeheartedly to such unsavory passions, and then he might reasonably find out about Phaethon. Although I possessed no warmth toward my mother, now that she had been gone for half of my adolescence, something in her final request to keep the prophecy from Aeetes stuck stubbornly in my psyche. If he found out, some terrible and unforeseen complication might arise in the saga of our family, yet another we had no need for.

Given his unusual attention, it was not surprising when a page summoned me to his chambers after dinner a few weeks after the dragon arrived.

"Medea, my youngest daughter," he began, his face contorted with something akin to pride, that could not possibly be pride. "I've been speaking with your tutors, and they are all quite impressed with you.

Your marks have been favorable, your Greek fluent. I could never have anticipated this happening so soon but I suppose the role of a father is to prepare his daughters for maturity." He offered me a smile that did not reach his eagle eyes, and my stomach sank.

"The time has come to find you a husband," he elaborated without further preamble. "A man who will bring honor to this house as is befitting its station. Obviously there are elements of your character which are less than desirable—your insidious cunning and solitary disposition stand in stark contrast to your sister's sweet nature—but very little can be done about that. I imagine we will find you a suitable match so long as we can keep your deficiencies out of the light." He paused, scowling. Words eluded me, but my silence had never bothered Aeetes.

"My primary concern is that your future husband might attempt to use your powers against me. Even though you are frail and weak by virtue of your sex, and your expertise is premature and unpolished compared to mine, you know certain things that we cannot allow you to take out of Kolchis. For this reason, I will be stripping you of your memories, all those troublesome little spars of useless knowledge that plague your infantile brain, on your wedding night. Once your husband has bedded you, and there is no going back on your betrothal, you will drink an elixir that I brew for you, and it will render you as fresh and new as a little girl. Your husband may find you simpler than he expected, but he will not be able to take back his deflowering of you. And women are simple by nature.

"You, Medea, were always an unnatural exception, far too cunning for your own good, but at last, I will be able to provide you with the peace and comforts you have doubtlessly been unconsciously craving for your entire sorry existence."

So, this was why Aeetes had allowed me to wait so long before forcing me into a match. I was an old maid, by certain standards, at twenty years old.

A coldness had settled inside me, something sharp and dangerous.

In that moment, I knew quite clearly that I wanted my father dead.

Panic made me reckless. My knowledge of *Pharmakon* had sustained me through my most impossible feelings. Witchery was the sole sustaining force intrinsic to myself that kept me afloat in an otherwise dismal reality. Without access to that portion of my being, which I knew was tethered somehow to my very soul, I should cease to exist with any trueness.

And then there was the matter of Phaethon's eventual resurrection. If I could not access my memories of Necromancy—those anguished, aching years of experimentation—he would surely perish and be gone forever. None but I had trespassed quite so far into the churning abyss of death magic, and there would be little time for anyone else to instruct themselves as I had done.

"I am not going to marry, not ever, especially not on the orders of an old and selfish fool such as yourself," I spat at him, my voice more poisonous than I had ever heard it. "You imagine me daft and malleable, but I know things that could make your head spin. Your sorcery was a crude introduction, diverting for a short period, but I surpassed it quite some time ago. If you think to drug me, to make me simple, I swear on all that you hold dear that I shall make you regret it. Any attempts you make on me will be your demise."

In an instant, and with such speed that I found I could not follow his movements, my father darted down from his throne, his hand closing around my neck. In the next moment, he shoved my skull with a brutal crack against the stone wall so hard it left my vision blurred and starry. His breath crackled with rage, the sounds of an unmanageable conflagration searing into my head. His hands were unnaturally warm; they burned my skin, and in spite of myself I cried out.

"Stupid, ungrateful child," he whispered, voice as faint as smoke. "I should have killed you for what you just said. It's the only thing to be done with a disobedient child. I know your mother told you stories about Kronos—how he devoured his children whole. I could do the same to you so easily. If I wanted to, I could destroy you utterly. I know salves that could dissolve the flesh from your bones, potions that would disassemble your body from the inside out. And I would have no qualms about it. Know your place, or lose your head. Are we clear?"

I shuddered against the wall, and something wet and sticky dripped into my eyes. I realized with horror that I was bleeding. The room began to swim.

"I'm going to have a slave escort you to your room, and tomorrow morning you will begin meeting suitors. You will be clean and desirable and demure by tomorrow at breakfast." He retracted his hand, and I slipped limply to the floor. The coolness of the stone felt soothing against my face, which was now overrun with startling wetness. Perhaps I was crying, although I could not be sure. In another moment, the strong arms of two slaves slipped around me, propping me up.

"Try to walk if you can, your grace," they whispered, struggling to support my weight as they led me down the stairs. Some of the journey to my rooms I remember, and some of it I do not. I moaned, flickering in and out of consciousness.

"She's covered in blood," one slave whispered as they led me through the bedroom door. "We don't want her staining the silk blankets. They'd be impossible to wash properly."

"Well, we can't just leave her on the floor," the other said anxiously.

"Chair," I slurred, pointing toward the wooden seat by the fire. "Easier to clean." They exchanged glances and then agreed, helping me into a sitting position.

"We ought to dress the wound," one whispered, peeling my hair back and flinching.

"Get my brother," I spoke unclearly, pale. They exchanged looks once more, as though unsure whether to listen to me.

"Send for the Prince Phaethon, now," I tried again, impatiently, and they scurried off. The room fell away into darkness.

■ ■ ■

When I came to, it was not Phaethon's face that greeted me, but Chalciope's. The room was permeated with the soft lavender light of dusk. My head rang like the inside of a great bronze bell, and I clenched my eyes tightly shut again.

"Thank the Gods, you're awake," she murmured, her hand clasping mine. I was overwhelmed by her proximity. For not since that dreadful fight in my rooms, when she realized what I had done to Phrixus, had she let herself be alone with me.

"I'm sorry, Chalciope." I began to cry, tears flowing absurdly down my cheeks, stinging my flesh. She shook her head, clasping my hand more tightly.

"Never mind that now. I'm sorry too—I never ought to have cut you off so cruelly, even if I felt wounded by you. We only have each other in the end." I was too stunned and overcome by relief to say anything rational.

"I've missed you so much," I moaned instead into her shoulder, inhaling the familiar scent of her.

"The slaves summoned Phaethon and me, and he's off in his room preparing some medicine for you as we speak. What happened? Why did father—how could he—" She broke off, her face pale.

"You know how Aeetes gets." I shrugged, triggering shooting pains down my neck.

"Well, he lashes out easily enough—he's even made you bleed a fair amount. But never like this. You look half-dead," she retorted sharply. "Mother would never have allowed that."

"Mother was too weak to stop him, even if she wanted to," I spat, crying even harder. Despite the embarrassment, I could not seem to stifle the flow of tears. Somehow I had transformed from a child who rarely shed a tear to a woman capable of sobbing, broken beside the fire.

My sister's face was troubled. I wondered, occasionally, how she managed to carry herself with such graceful detachment where our father was concerned. She knew what he was—she must, and yet she seemed to accept the inevitability of his power anyway. Perhaps that was why she had always been his favorite daughter. I could not bring myself to envy her any longer, not as she clasped my shaking fingers to her lips and shushed me.

The door opened and Phaethon emerged with a dozen different bottles.

"Drink these now," he murmured, unstopping the first glass and pressing it to my lips. I was too exhausted to protest, and drank willingly what he gave me.

"Unnaturally amenable," he muttered under his breath, catching Chalciope's eye with a worried expression. "He's hurt her worse than I anticipated."

"I'm fine," I sobbed, annoyed at myself.

"No you're not," Chalciope countered.

"But you will be, in no time," Phaethon added, giving me a small smile. "Now you'll get to see all the things I've learned about healing potions, sister."

I groaned in mock terror.

■ ■ ■

The suitors my father procured for me were old, ugly men, with even uglier tempers. Over steaming eggs and warm bread, fish stews and delicate pastries, they courted me, their eyes never truly meeting my own. They stared at the swell of my breasts, the smooth lines of my legs, the shimmer of my dark hair, drooling and obvious, and I forced smiles in their direction, more miserable than I had ever been.

Not all of them were quite so vile. A few of the kings and princes were young enough to still be comely, although I felt no stirrings of warmth or attraction toward them. So hopeless did I feel that for a time I considered brewing love potions to ensure pliability among the least unctuous of my suitors. However, I quickly dismissed the idea. Love magic was an impossibility after everything that had transpired with Phrixus. I could hardly bring myself to fathom compiling any such concoction again. Besides, I found that my native charms were enough. One king, belonging to the exiled royal family of Athens, Aegeus, was a particular favorite of mine, although my father had little time for him. He had a long, well-oiled beard and kind eyes, and he asked me questions about my studies and potion work, which was better than what anyone else might have done.

Perhaps Aegeus sensed some kindred discontent in me, for he was loose and comfortable with his words when it was just the two of us. He told me of his father, the King Pandion, and how, long before Aegeus was even born, he was driven from his homeland by usurper cousins. When the freshly landless king finally settled in Megara, he fell head over heels for the princess of that region, Pylia, who bore him four loyal sons. Pandion died as he had lived, banished from his birthright. But his sons had settled it among themselves that Athens should be returned to them, and so together, they overthrew those who had stolen away their throne.

"Do you get along with your brothers?" I asked him once, in the shade of a dozen intertwined vines, my mouth wet with wine.

Aegeus licked his lips, his eyes searing, as ever, into mine.

"There was a time when we were closer. The threat of a common enemy and the shared weight of our father's injustice kept us together. But now that our land is restored, and I am king, there is more tension. Nysus returned to Megara and rules there uncontested, but I believe that Pallas or Lycos might desire my throne for themselves. That is why I am currently in search of a wife."

"I don't understand."

"With an heir, my hold on the throne will be assured," he explained thoughtfully, sighing.

I bit back my disappointment. Of course even the most amenable of men still would see their wives only as vessels through which to procure children. Bitterness infiltrated my mouth, making my drink go sour.

Seeming to sense my displeasure, my companion paused.

"I'm sorry. That didn't come out quite as I had intended. If we were to marry—"

"Don't let Aeetes hear you talking of marriage so forwardly. He will chain you to an engagement," I cut him off, smiling darkly.

"Do you see me running away?" He smiled softly, his look gentle. Something flickered and died within my chest. Had it not been for the nauseating affair with Phrixus, I could have been fond of him. After all, I was rather good at making myself do things that I had no real desire to do. Perhaps it came from all of those hours spent belowground, cutting into animal carcasses and biting back bile. Or perhaps it came from being royal and knowing that my body was an extension of the land my family ruled. Forcing myself to fall in love should have come easily, I reasoned, or if not easily, then at least with diligent work. And yet all men repulsed me. They seemed to me to be oafs and liars, when contrasted with the shrewd intelligence of my father. And those who were intelligent were doubtless just better equipped to inflict their cruelty.

Somewhere, in the murky corners of my mind, I imagined that I was immune to romantic love.

Foolishly, I said as much to Aegeus, when it became evident his affections were not yet properly deterred.

"I am not meant to be a wife or a mother, my Lord. The necessary components intrinsic to most women are foreign to me. What you think you observe in my manner is more than likely some projection of yourself," I explained bluntly.

He shook his head. "And what, princess, do you imagine you lack?"

"Love," I returned simply, a heaviness descending on me as I said it.

I waited for him to excuse himself, to depart in thinly veiled disgust, but he stayed.

"On the contrary, Medea, I fear you love too deeply. So deeply it frightens you. For love is vulnerability—it is the opening up of the self to loss. And you have had your fair share of loves lost. Firstly, your mother, and to some more symbolic degree, your father." He paused, his expression wary. I shivered, imagining what might transpire if Aeetes caught a visiting king discussing him in such a way.

I made to shush him, blushing, but he continued, his eyes full of fire.

"Your heart is a Hydra—cut off one of its heads and two more grow from the carnage, more powerful in their affection than the last. I see how you tend to Phaethon as though he were your own child. How fondly you watch your sister in her daily tasks. When love becomes too painful to hold, you push it down, imagine it dead, when really the truth of your tenderness threatens always to arise, resurrected, to expose you."

I stood up abruptly, annoyed.

"That's enough, Aegeus," I replied imperiously. Dismissing him, I left the room, my steady gait masking my racing heart.

As I ascended the stairs to my chamber, I shook my head roughly, as though to clear it. There was no possibility of me ever making a sweet and dutiful bride. I could not imagine myself as Chalciope was now, content with only her husband for company, raising child after child, only to see them grow old and leave her behind in search of glory. Her four boys, faces still rosy and rounded with youth, younger even than Phaethon, had set off together in the previous months to seek their fortunes upon the sea. For all her attractive charm, my sister had an edge, an impossible fortitude that showed itself most in moments of immense turmoil, when she remained placid and tranquil.

The idea of becoming bound to one of these decaying, unrighteous creatures older than my father was horrible enough, but in truth, my worry was being separated from Phaethon. I would not be able to keep him safe, to administer the potions required to heal him, if my memory had been wiped, and my physical body shipped off to another land. I needed to prepare myself for the possibility that I could not save my brother alone—that someone else would need to be confided in. The questions over those weeks gradually became not *if and how*, but *when and who*. No one, it seemed to me, was sufficiently skilled or trust-worthy to work the magic that would be necessary.

■ ■ ■

The feeling that time was short drove me to work longer hours in the cellar. I had perfected my work on goats, and I could reattach limbs with ease and no risk of infection. I even successfully reapplied a head of one poor animal, and I was seeking to see if it might be replicated, but the spellwork was complex, arduous work, the kind that left my muscles sore and aching, and my tongue tied.

One morning, instead of heading down to the dining hall for hot breakfast with the suitors, or descending another level farther to the blood-soaked underground of my laboratory, I found myself wander-ing toward the beach. The feeling that led me down the cliff's face was different from the one that had guided me to the beach on the day of Phrixus's arrival. This feeling pumped hollowly through my veins, a kind of calling.

When I reached the white sand, I surveyed the waves for some sign of what had brought me to rest here, and initially nothing caught my eye. I shifted uncomfortably, removing my slippers so that my feet could luxuriate among the pale granules of crushed rock.

"Medea."

A voice called me out of my vague observations of a hermit crab scrambling along the rocks. It was a voice I never expected to hear again.

My eyes rose, hasty and desperate, to meet my mother's. She stood ankle-deep in the water, the white foam cresting around her calves. She had not aged, I realized, noting the shine of her wet blond hair, the supple, smooth quality of her skin. She gleamed like the moon, an alien thing that the ocean had given up for a while.

"Thank you for coming," she began, her eyes wary, twisting her hands, as they were prone to.

"I did not know we were meeting," I shot back, disoriented.

She shook her head at my foolishness, but did not smile. "Yes you did. You have my clairvoyance. Alone of all my children that passed to you."

"What are you doing here?" I asked finally, hating the tremble in my voice. I sounded accusatory and cold and wounded and childlike all at once.

"There is not much time," she whispered, and her words were almost swallowed by the crash of the waves. "Your father has ways of knowing when I am close. Tell me, how are your sister and brother?"

Anger coursed through me, and I felt my face color with rage. "You have no right to ask after them. You did not even appear for Chalciope's wedding—or for the births of her children—your *grandchildren*. Phaethon became a man and you were not there to guide his path. I had to do everything—" I broke off, too overcome to continue.

She nodded softly. "I know. And you performed your role admirably," she returned, voice calm. I wanted to scream, or else to shake her. I could not understand her dreadful impassiveness.

"You never told your father what I told to you, did you?" she questioned, taking a few steps forward but never leaving the sea completely.

I shook my head bitterly, biting my tongue.

"Good," she affirmed. "Medea, tonight a ship will dock along these shores."

"What? Why does that matter? What kind of ship?"

"Don't speak, Medea. Listen. The ship is carrying a hero, the son of Aeson. He will appear before your father just after the moon has risen. You must intercept him before he reaches Aeetes. Do you understand?"

I regarded her skeptically, heart pounding.

"Make him trust you. I don't care how you do this, but it must be done. He will relay his mission to you, and you will help him achieve it. You will tell no one of his plans, or yours.

"He is your only chance to escape this place," Idyia concluded, her eyes distant and melancholy. "And you, sweetest daughter, are your brother's only chance. I used to think that you were a monster, but only lately have things become clear. You must save Phaethon and yourself and not look back. Do you understand me?"

I shook my head, confused. "What do you mean you thought I was a monster?"

She paused, biting her lip. Her eyelids fluttered softly shut.

"I thought perhaps you knew, or at least suspected. You were always such a clever little girl.

"In my visions, it was you cutting your brother into pieces."

The world was suddenly shadowy, as reality split, disarranging and remaking itself rapidly. The sky and sea blurred together, and I felt myself slip to my knees. Surely my mother had made a mistake. That I could ever injure Phaethon was impossible.

She paused, her features suddenly a mix of horror and sympathy.

"Did you really not know?" she pushed, pausing. And for a moment, I wondered at myself. Perhaps I had always been aware, on some level. That I was the danger, the unnamed monster, the approaching threat. I was unnatural and ruthless. That I could land the killing blow had a certain gravity, a terrible logic. And yet I loved my brother totally. I resisted the urge to retch.

"Me? I murder him?" I asked, voice hoarse and raw. Far away someone was screaming, a terrible, animalistic sound. After an indescribable amount of time, I realized the sound was coming from me.

"No, Medea, my darling one," my mother soothed, and her cool hands gripped both sides of my face. "You simply cloak him in death. This is all I can tell you. Your fate is more complex than I could ever explain, my dear girl."

In another instant, her fingers were gone, and the heavens seemed to right themselves above me. The waves slid up along my body where I lay in the sand, and their chill settled me slightly. I knew without looking that my mother was gone, and that she would not be returning.

CHAPTER THIRTEEN

The Lookout

When I was strong enough to stand, I made my way back to the palace, my mother's words echoing hauntingly in my mind. Chalciope passed me in the corridor, asking if I wished to accompany her to the dining hall, and I shook my head.

"I'm not feeling well tonight. I think I may go to bed early."

She nodded, her eyes surveying me coolly.

"Perhaps take a sleeping draft," she hummed fondly, offering me a smile, and I nodded, stomach squirming. I had no desire to deceive her after everything.

As I climbed the stairs, I attempted simply not to feel. How strange it was, that time could go by with such arduous slowness on Kolchis, and then transpire all at once, with devastating speed. My mother had returned, looking just as pale and pretty as I had remembered her, and then disappeared again into the sea. There was a chance perhaps to escape, a chance tied to the coming hero. And the monster, the evil I had spent my entire childhood watching for, was myself.

Once I was safely ensconced in my room, I took up a position by the window, eyes glued to the coast. So far, the sea was flat and clear, brooking no trespassers. The sun would set in the next hour, I knew, and so I settled in to wait. Once I saw the ship on the horizon, I would foray once more down to the beach.

As I sat there frozen, the sea breeze blowing my hair across my face, I wondered about this hero I was intended to meet. *The son of Aeson* was all my mother had offered in preparation. I rolled my eyes at her vagueness. I do not know why I should have expected anything differently from a creature as notoriously absentminded as she.

When the speck eventually appeared where the sky met the Black Sea, I had grown slightly stiff. Slipping a cloak over my shoulders, I mentally calculated where the boat was most likely to dock, given the wind and current patterns. This was going to be an unusual evening.

■ ■ ■

I waited for him at the top of the cliffs, my cloak snapping in the wind. Overhead, the moon glinted through the clouds, casting a white light across the sea.

Come now, I thought, shifting with impatience and something like nervousness, but heavier.

A voice called to me over my shoulder, but it was not the gruff drawl of a man. I spun around, and when my eyes fell upon the woman who awaited me, the breath was knocked forcibly from my chest.

"Medea, daughter of the King Aeetes and the Oceanid Idyia," she listed, her voice high and mellifluous. I could not summon the faculties to respond, so intent was I upon internalizing her face.

Her skin was soft and flushed, and her eyes seemed to be a thousand colors at once. Her hair, which flickered madly in moonlit cascades, drifted down about her shoulders, ending at her ankles. Her lips were full and dark, her nose delicate. It occurred to me vaguely that this kind of beauty could be fatal, that perhaps it had already killed me. I slipped to my knees automatically.

Although some part of my mind acknowledged consciously that it was good and proper to treat this entity with respect, a more basic, involuntary part of my body seemed to have given out.

A part-amused, part-concerned smile flitted across her lips, and she let out a birdsong-like laugh. A shiver erupted along my spine, and as her eyes met mine I felt as though a knife had slid into my chest to the very hilt.

I must have looked incredibly foolish, slumped over before her, eyes dreamy and yearning. Unbidden, images flashed before my eyes, as I imagined what it would be like to hold her, to kiss the soft skin where her long neck met her collarbones. These thoughts were almost too much to bear. I was horrified at myself, to long for a woman—and a Goddess—in this way. As I bit my tongue, throat tight, something rigid in my psyche came loose. A mirage of faces assailed me then, and I recalled the strange fervor in my breast that could only be inspired by some of the comelier serving girls back in the palace. Of course, this queer attraction was just another manifestation of my own unnaturalness. It was not something I openly spoke of or chose to dwell on.

"Are you all right, young one? It takes time to adjust to divine presence, I understand," she elaborated, her hands making fluid gestures as she spoke.

"I-I've never felt—" I began, unsure of where I was going, but aware that my filter was gone.

"I know," she murmured. "Beauty, the kind that is true and can never be possessed, has that effect. But that's not why I'm here. I'm here because you're about to meet someone rather special." But her eyes glinted mournfully, in a way that was not altogether comforting.

I struggled to recall what had led me here, but my mind was foggy and uncouth.

She raised her eyebrows as I glanced around uncertainly, finally landing on something.

"The son of Aeson," I finally stuttered, excited to have some shred of information to give her.

The amusement in her face intensified, and she nodded. "Yes, Jason. He'll be along any minute. And I think it's going to be a love match."

I shook my head, hoping to dislodge the fog that infiltrated every thought.

"I don't understand," I moaned. "I can't fall in love with him because I'm already in love with you." I colored as the words escaped me, horrified that I had said them out loud.

"Imagine that, a mortal in love with love itself." Aphrodite laughed, some of the gentle sympathy leaving her face. "Well, think of Jason as a consolation prize, then, sweet child."

She took a step closer to me, kneeling and pulling something long and sharp from the inside of her tunic. It was an arrow, its tip coated in something oily and sweet-smelling. Before I could protest, she pricked my left arm with it, a superficial wound only. Where pain should have been there was only warmth.

"Normally, this would be under Eros's jurisdiction, but you're a special case. Hera herself took an interest in Jason, or more specifically, a distinct dislike for that usurper Pelias, and so here we are. The young hero must succeed, and he requires your aid to this end. I'm glad I caught you at such an opportune moment." She smiled fondly at me, and I shivered once more. Where the tip of the arrow had pierced me, a burning sensation began, running over my skin with a pleasant intensity I could not fight off.

"All right, child, I'm going to leave so you can collect yourself before the hero of the hour arrives. You have a very enchanting heart, and I do hope you are faithful to it," she hummed, and I was caught in the bright fullness of her lips, the softness of her tongue.

"Don't go," I begged, but she had already dissolved into mist. The pain that ensued at her absence was intense and immediate. Had it not been for the chill of the sea air keeping me lucid, I might have curled in on myself and wailed. *So this is romantic love.* I could not decide if I wanted to laugh or be violently sick, but I did know I was utterly powerless to the feeling.

Shuddering, I stumbled to my feet, breathing unsteadily. My cloak had loosened during the encounter, and I pulled it more tightly around me. So absorbed had I been in the visiting Goddess that I had not noticed the appearance of a ship on the horizon. The single sail billowed, looming like the moon across the water. The wind howled through the rocks below, sounding like the screams of lost souls. Kolchis, even for someone who had grown up calling her home, could be terrifying at night. After all, the crags overlooking the water were perilous. One misstep, and the resulting fall would finish you. The woods were winding, and populated by my father's monsters—beasts that defied imagination.

The sound of scuffling and rocks coming loose from the cliff below pulled me from my anxious wonderings. I froze, straining to determine the characteristics of the man by the sounds his body made as it attempted to grip the earth. I stared as a head appeared over the edge of the crags, and then a strong set of shoulders.

He was not beautiful, not in the way that Aphrodite had been, and this was the first thing that struck me. His eyes were blue and expansive like the sky, and they shone brightly at me even in the dark. This was the second thing I understood about him. I swallowed hard, taking note of how his dark hair fell around his shoulders, how the muscles in his arms flexed as he pulled himself onto the ground beside me. *Jason.*

I knew this man. Even though we had never met, I felt I would know him anywhere. His was the face that populated my dreams, the visage that kept me company after the rest of the world was lost to sleep.

For a moment he merely regarded me, breathing hard, still exhausted from his climb. Had he dreamed of me as well? I swiftly dismissed the silly, sentimental thought.

He waited, as though expecting me to say something, but I had no intention of giving him the satisfaction. After all, he was a trespasser in my land. And so I simply stared back, meeting his gaze squarely.

"You're bleeding," he said at last, gesturing to the wound on my arm—the one that the Goddess of love had so lately inflicted. For a long moment, I fought off the urge to laugh in his face.

"It is nothing," I remarked dismissively, shifting so that the cut would no longer be in his line of view. He opened his mouth, but then shut it again, shaking his head.

"Am I right in assuming that we have docked in Kolchis, where King Aeetes rules?" he asked at last, frowning. I heard the exhaustion in his voice, the quiet desperation that only comes with long and arduous travels. *If this is not Kolchis*, his voice seemed to say, *then I am a defeated man.*

"You are correct in that assumption," I supplied, and some of the tension left his shoulders. He glanced up at the sky, mouthing something soundlessly that might have been a prayer or a blessing. Returning his gaze to rest on me, he narrowed his eyes slightly.

"A lovely girl alone at the top of the bluffs, mysteriously wounded and distinctly terse in her replies. I sense a trap." He raised his eyebrows at me, taking a step forward. I resisted the temptation to retreat backward, clenching my fists behind my back.

"Well, at least you have some sense in that skull of yours, although why you decided to ascend the cliffs alone, without the protection and aid of your crew, I can hardly ascertain," I shot back. He seemed surprised by the irreverence in my tone.

"My crew have been steadfast and loyal, strong and resilient in the extreme, but this I must do alone," he returned somberly, taking yet another step toward me. "I seek an audience with the king here. He has something that I am in need of."

"And what exactly might that be?" I inquired. He regarded me closely; his face was conflicted, as though he was not sure whether or not I could be trusted with this information.

"You're uncommonly beautiful," he said abruptly, changing the subject, his face becoming suddenly suffused with charm. "Like a siren but more enigmatic still. What is your name?" His eyes slowly ran over my face, roving down the length of my neck and settling on my chest. I crossed my arms a bit protectively, swallowing hard. My mother's words echoed uncomfortably in my head.

Make him trust you. I don't care how you do this, but it must be done.

"That is no concern of yours. I asked you a question. What does King Aeetes have that you seek?"

A flicker of annoyance passed across the man's face, but he quickly repressed it. "The golden fleece of a flying ram," he murmured at last, and the sincerity in his voice took me by surprise. "It is a long and impossible story, but I have braved unimaginable dangers just to reach these shores, just to be speaking before you now. I am Jason, the son of Aeson, the King of Iolcus until his noble and rightful throne was usurped by my uncle Pelias. Can you take me to the king of this place? Do you know where he might be found?"

I attempted to keep my face as impassive as possible, but some of what I was feeling seemed to seep out anyway. His eyes narrowed, and he took another step forward, all but eradicating the distance between us. I had to crane my neck to look into his face.

"The King Aeetes is my father," I whispered.

He stiffened, his eyes widening, realizing his mistake. "Your father?" he hurriedly repeated. I waited for him to move back, but he did not retreat. The wind seemed to have died down as we stood toe-to-toe on the cliffs, and I could smell the scent of him: cherry and sweat and salt and rosemary.

"Yes, my father. And you should know before you foray into his clutches that regardless of what he may or may not tell you, he has no interest in handing over what you seek. Tell me, what do you know of King Aeetes?" I kept my voice low and even as I spoke. Jason, to his credit, seemed to have gotten over his initial shock.

"Not much besides what I have gleaned from some travelers off the coast of this place—the mighty sons of Phrixus, who regaled my crew with stories of their grandfather and his treasures. I presume that you are not the fair princess Chalciope—their mother," he began slowly.

I laughed. "Oh certainly not. You are thinking of my sister. But Chalciope will be pleased to hear news of her sons."

He nodded, smiling slightly. "You do not look like you have four grown sons," he murmured, ducking his head.

"They're hardly full-grown. Adolescents, perhaps," I retorted. "But this is time wasted. You must not trust my father. He is fiercely intelligent and entirely ruthless, and he has no sympathy for mortal heroes beyond what gains he can manipulate from them. Do you understand?" I said it in a rush, trying to make my tone sound as urgent as I felt.

He shook his head, his brow furrowed. "Why do you speak such words against your own father? Such treachery hardly seems logical, and if you are not Chalciope, you must be the other princess—Medea. *The shrewd one. The cunning one.*"

"Whomever you have spoken to of me has done you a grave disservice in overestimating my powers of intellect," I flung back, fluttering my eyelashes at him. "I can assure you I am merely attempting to do a stranger a good turn. Is that too much to believe?"

He scoffed, shaking his head. "Yes, actually, it is." A silence stretched out between us, and he regarded me uneasily. His face wavered between obvious attraction, the kind that made my cheeks flush, and outright skepticism.

Make him trust you. I don't care how you do this, but it must be done.

"Maybe I find you intriguing," I said at last, attempting to make my voice as low and sultry as possible. Seduction had never interested me. "Maybe I want to help you because I like you." It was a lie, and an obvious one, but a self-satisfied smile came over the man's face.

"And in return for your advice, what is it that you want from me?" he asked, his voice as smooth as silk. I shivered. It would be difficult to frame this in a way that did not paint me as desperate.

"When you sail away from here, the fleece under your arm, you will take me with you." I breathed, hardly daring to move. "You will require my help to evade whatever peril my father sets up for you, but when Aeetes discovers my treachery, I will be in danger. I must have your word that you will protect me from him with your life."

His eyebrows disappeared beneath his hairline at these words, his arms flexing as he considered my proposition.

"You would have me make you my wife?" he inquired at last, his eyes furtive. A laugh rose up in me that I immediately quelled.

"I do not much care what you call me, so long as you promise me a place on your ship, and room also for my brother, the Prince Phaethon." I paused as he digested this new information.

"Aeetes will never allow me to make off with his son and heir," Jason managed slowly, concern written in every crevice of his face.

"You will let me handle that."

He considered me for a moment, his expression searching. I forced my face to remain impassive.

"I do not imagine that my sources exaggerated your intelligence, Medea, no matter what you may say," he offered at last. There was suspicion in the way he appraised me, in the wary lines of his shoulders. I needed to secure his agreement quickly.

"Do we have a deal, Jason?" I uttered, surprised by the way he seemed to shudder as I said his name.

For a moment I feared he might turn on his heel and return to the ship, but then he nodded, squaring his stance and letting out a tight breath.

"We do, Medea. I place myself at your mercy. I can only hope that you will repay my trust not with treachery, but kindness. I shall help both you and your brother make your escape, if you can help me achieve my ends."

I nodded, offering him a sliver of a smile. In my chest, something immense and inconceivable stirred. Perhaps my sister would have called it affection, or even love, for this stranger who had appeared, offering me a way out, but I called it something far more basic than that—necessity.

CHAPTER FOURTEEN

The Three Labors

I walked with Jason as far as the palace walls, and then slinked off toward my own chamber. It would be better for Aeetes to imagine Jason had no friends here—that he had come alone on a fool's errand.

"Remember, do not drink anything he gives you. He will attempt to talk you out of what you have come for—he may offer you all manner of treasures when he hears your request, in an attempt to distract you, but if your need for the fleece is true, you must not be dissuaded." Jason nodded, his face pale underneath the evening stars. His eyes seemed to catch on the slope of my shoulders, the pale expanse of my neck. I hurriedly adjusted my cloak. It was difficult to look back at him, for even now I was having trouble adjusting to that face. The familiarity of him left me uncertain whether I was truly awake or merely dreaming.

"Do not look at me like that," I whispered, and though I had meant for it to come out as a command, there was something soft and yielding in my tone.

"Like what?"

Meeting his eyes was disorienting, so I kept my face angled toward the ground.

"Like you enjoy it," I retorted.

He began to laugh and then, noting my expression, quickly stifled it.

"You would have me seem what? Disappointed? Revolted, even?"

"That would be preferable."

"But it would also be a lie, and I try rather hard to be a man who speaks only the truth."

I scoffed. "Men like you have no notion of truth."

"Men like me?"

"Heroes," I explained bluntly. "Those who seek only their own aggrandizement, and glory, who are more concerned with their legendary legacies than with the realities of those around them, who serve as unlucky collateral. In a thousand years, stories of your greatness may still abound, while the lives and aspirations of the less charismatic mortals who served and adored you utterly drift away into obscurity, forgotten. What truth is there in that?"

"Well perhaps I'm not really a hero, then," he mused. "I have never been much interested in glory."

"If not glory, then what?" I pressed.

"Justice." The word hung in the air between us, as sharp and precise as a blade.

For a moment we simply regarded each other.

"I have never been able to discern between the gratuitousness of retribution and the righteousness of justice," I offered at last, knowing as I did so that I was being unfair in baiting him. But some bottomless, dark, rapacious part of me wanted to see his facade crack, to get to the soft and vulnerable heart underneath.

"I wonder that too, often enough," Jason admitted.

"So why travel so far on an errand you yourself are not entirely convinced of?" I goaded. The desire to leave him stripped and uncertain only seemed to rise with each passing moment.

But rather than losing his temper or storming off, his countenance lightened.

"I suppose that it's not something that can be articulated, not entirely. I *simply feel* that I must go on. I *feel* that I must claim what has been stolen from my family, robbed by means of crude violence and nefarious deception. I *feel* that it is what is right."

"Feelings can be misleading. What happens when heroes find themselves mistaken?" I urged, conscious that I was no longer speaking of his quest but my own.

"You're rather hard on me, are you not, Medea?" he asked, a note of teasing in his voice. I tried to ignore the strange fluttering in my chest that began the moment my name left his lips.

"I do not give you more than you can take, surely."

"No, but my life is not so simple or as thoroughly illustrious as you make it out to be. Every move I make is watched closely by men and Gods alike. Every flaw I might possess is rendered fatal, magnified tenfold because the success of my ventures carries such dreadful weight."

"And what are your flaws?"

He paused, considering me. And then all at once, the speech poured out of him.

"My crew tells me I can be narrow-minded in the pursuit of my goals." He appraised me before continuing. "When I want something, everything else disappears. I can be terribly stubborn, but then again so can you, by the looks of it. I currently have no country to call my own, and little to my name besides what Pelias has promised me upon my return. I am slow to trust, and slower still to love. I have little interest in scholarly pursuits. As a boy, Chiron found me easily distracted from my studies. When I become angry, I go silent, sometimes for days at a time. It makes me feel superior. Is that sufficient to satisfy your curiosity?"

"Almost. What will you do once Iolcus is yours again? When your purpose has been fulfilled and there is no more greatness to be won upon the waves or on the battlefield?"

"Perhaps we might figure that out together," he suggested.

I cleared my throat, taken aback by his words. Did he really mean to stand by me when all of this was over?

"Perhaps," I whispered noncommittally.

"Why do I feel as though nothing I've faced yet is going to come close to what happens here in Kolchis?" he remarked in an undertone, the set of his shoulders grim.

"Because your intuition is not as lacking as it looks. It will be a wonder if we all emerge from this unscathed, I imagine," I replied dryly, flashing him an impish grin. My companion shuddered, and just like that the spell was broken.

"Once he has set a task for you, or a puzzle—I'm sure he shall rely on one or the other to keep you occupied—you must come immediately to me. I know things about this place that you will not, and I alone can help you. Is this clear?"

"Of course, your grace," he spoke with a hint of mocking in his tone, and I could tell that he was already chafing under the burden of taking orders from a woman. Men were far too predictable, even those that the Gods favored.

"He may still be awake. Aeetes does not sleep in the manner of a normal man. Go to the double doors, and demand an entrance with him. They should take you to the throne room."

He shifted uncomfortably, his eyes fixed upon my lips.

"What is it?" I scanned him confusedly.

"Might I have a kiss before you send me into the lion's den?" He flashed me a careless smile as he closed in on me. His breath was hot upon my face in the shadows. This was a man used to getting what he wanted. I shook my head abruptly, but my stomach tightened, an unwanted side effect of his words. He presumed an intimacy with me I could not reciprocate so soon. Was it some sloppy attempt at charm or bravado, the effects of adrenaline or deprivation at sea, true attraction? I had no way of knowing.

"No," I imparted tersely, moving away from him. "Return to me with news of what Aeetes intends, and then we will talk." I hastily described how he might happen upon my chamber through little-used passages, to avoid being spotted. Although the disappointment of my refusal was evident in the pink tinge of his cheeks, he nodded stiffly, internalizing my directions.

I did not stick around to continue our discussion. Sliding along the garden walk toward the kitchen entrance, I pushed the door open and slid into the warmth of the foyer. No one was about at this hour, and the room was deserted. I snuck up the stairs, barely breathing until I reached the landing, the corridor, then my chamber. In the shadows, I listened to the crash of the waves outside, letting my eyes flutter shut, before pushing the doors open and shutting myself in again. The morning would bring more news, and I would need to be well rested and sharp.

I let the cloak fall to the floor, and stripped myself of the tunic and skirts underneath it. The sheets felt cold against my bare skin, but I paid them little heed. Repeatedly in my mind, a single name circulated, impossible to drive out. When I closed my eyes, it was his face that I saw. *Jason. Jason. Jason.* It was he whom I thought of as Morpheus collected me for sleep.

■ ■ ■

A soft knock came at my door a little while before dawn.

"Enter," I called, sitting up in bed and pulling the sheets more firmly around me, assuming it was one of the serving girls with fresh logs and kindling for the hearth.

When the door opened to reveal Jason, the circles under his eyes pronounced, and his look anxious and haggard, I regretted not wearing a dressing gown to bed the night before. It was startling to see him here, in my bedroom, where I had dreamed him a thousand times before. Whereas in my childhood he had been an apparition, rendered from mist, prone to dissolving into the dark shadows of my chamber, now he was all flesh.

"Jason." I breathed, anxious to regain my composure. There was little point in upbraiding him for the impropriety of his visit, not when we were plotting far more serious crimes and I had bid him to come myself. Even so, I blushed heavily, and pulled the blankets more tightly around my shoulders.

It was impossible to describe the feeling that was alive in me then, more fire than substance. There was an unbearable urge to look away, to put an end to the terrible longing that his face awoke in my breast, and yet I could not.

He stared at me, his mouth open on the verge of speech. I intervened abruptly.

"You don't look well. Did you sleep at all?"

He shook his head roughly, clenching and unclenching his fists at his side, as though to rid himself of excess energy.

"Your father has outdone himself," he murmured, his eyes dark. Their impossible blueness had taken on an electric quality, not altogether reassuring. I shifted under the covers, trying not to reveal my profound discomfort.

"You must tell me everything, but first, did anyone observe you sneaking into my chamber?" I indicated the shut door behind his back. "We should keep our association a secret for as long as we can. My father has never particularly trusted me." Again he nodded, looking around the room tentatively.

"No one saw me coming to meet you."

"You can sit." I gestured to the end of my bed before I could think better of it, and he closed the distance in an instant. It felt pleasant to have him so close, warm and luxurious, as though I were stepping out into a stream of warm sunlight. I wanted to draw him close, to ask him all the details of his existence, to divine the inner workings of his heart, to feel those burning eyes on me lit with some emotion other than suspicion. Instead, I stiffened.

"Relay to me all that has transpired since I took leave of you," I prompted. He gave a short, brutal laugh, although no real humor seeped into his expression.

"I did as you said. I appeared to the guards and demanded an audience with your father. King Aeetes allowed me inside immediately, which I found odd. Usually kings are not so relaxed with their security in the middle of the night. After I had knelt before him, he asked me what my business was in Kolchis. He recognized my name, and my family's insignia, and he had heard of the treachery with which my uncle, that ruthless fiend Pelias, had stolen my father's throne. I began to feel more at ease with him, as I relayed why exactly I had anchored my ship upon his shores."

"You never did tell me why you seek the fleece in the first place," I reminded him, irritated by his inability to tell a coherent story. His breed of hero was usually more adept at conveying the wonders and horrors of their allotted quests, at offering up the very best of themselves when they reached a new hearth. After all, the hospitality of the kings they visited depended on their credibility, their pathos. I thought back to how Phrixus had prostrated himself before my father, a vision of princely virtue, entirely sympathetic. Jason was charming and bold, to be sure, but he lacked a certain thoughtfulness that might have served him well.

"Tell me, then." I nudged him impatiently. "Hold no detail back."

"My father was the king of Iolcus, at the farthermost edge of the Black Sea. He was beloved by his people, and ruled with a steady and just temper. He might have gone on as monarch to that place in peace for many years, if not for the ruthless machinations of his scheming brother, Pelias. My uncle, tempted by the promise of power and glory, was intent upon usurping the throne for himself. After months of bloody war, he imprisoned my father underground, in the winding maze of caves just below Iolcus. From what I can ascertain, Aeson perished there, murdered by his own brother, with only the soil and darkness for company. He had no knowledge that aboveground his wife, Alcimede, was carrying their child." Here he paused, his fist clenching and unclenching by his side. His wrath, righteous and indignant, was a palpable thing.

"My mother was no fool. She had watched as one by one my father's other children were brutally murdered by the new king in his paranoia. She knew that the moment I was born, Pelias would send for me to be slaughtered as well, and so, even as she carried me with her, she contrived a plan. The women who attended her during the birth were instructed to circle around her, wailing and keening as though I had been born dead."

"Your mother sounds like a brilliant woman," I offered, and I meant it.

To my surprise, he merely shrugged. Something like sadness appeared in his look and was quickly gone again.

"I hardly know what she was. After the birth I was sent away to the foothills of Mount Pelion. There, the good centaur Chiron took me in. It was he who reared me, who taught me what a prince must be."

"You were raised by a centaur?" I breathed, taken aback. I knew from Aeetes's numerous bestiaries that those wild, hybrid creatures with the upper body of a man and the hindquarters and passions of a horse, were uncommonly uncivilized and frequently dangerous. My father liked to assert that so long as a centaur was given milk to drink instead of mead, he could keep a level head, but even the great Aeetes seemed reluctant to add one to his menagerie.

Sensing my trepidation, Jason let out a little laugh, shaking his head.

"Chiron is different from the rest of his kind. He was abandoned himself, you know, and then fostered by Apollo and Artemis. They taught him healing and archery, divination and philosophy and botany."

I raised my eyebrows, silently urging him to continue.

"By the time I had grown to manhood, my uncle for some years had ruled a land that should have been mine. As soon as I was strong enough, I returned home and demanded that he relinquish to me what was rightfully mine." Jason paused, an expression of real anger inscribed across his face.

"How incredibly foolish of you," I ventured, unimpressed. He let out a little noise of frustration.

"I can hardly believe it myself, in retrospect. How pugnacious and disturbed I must have seemed to the court in the moment of my re-appearance. I had stormed into my uncle's chambers with only a single sandal, you know. I lost the other in the churning waves of the Anaurus while helping an old woman make the crossing. I'm sure Pelias hardly knew what to think of me." He shot me a shy smile, and then his expression became cold and focused once more.

"But it needed to be done. Pelias agreed to return the crown to me on the following conditions: I must sail to Kolchis, retrieve the golden fleece, and bestow it upon him. Only once this task was completed would Pelias willingly relinquish the throne, because only then would I have proved myself to be worthy of kingship, truly my father's son. And so I agreed readily—what else was I to do? I could not refuse this quest, for if I did my honor would be tainted and no populace would willingly bow to me. Although the outlook was dire, I assembled a crew of the finest men known in all of the Mediterranean. I recruited Herakles, that strong-armed son of Zeus who can lift boulders as though they are nothing, along with his boy lover, Hylas. Orpheus too offered to join my ranks, the man with a honeyed tongue and mystifying musical skill, who once went down into the black-lit halls of Hades and returned again to the land of the living untouched. Telamon and Peleus, sturdy kings oblivious to fear, readily signed on to board my ship when they heard my sorry history. Theseus, the boy king who killed the Bull of

Minos and saved Athens from its hideous conscription, and the fear-some huntress Atalanta, who helped slay the Calydonian boar and won its hide, both answered to me. We call ourselves the Argonauts.

"Although my crew was composed of only those who possessed the most prodigious of minds and bodies, and the most impeccable of characters, we suffered greatly upon the sea. From the warm summer seduction of Lemnos, to the confusion and tragedy of Doliones, to the island of Cius, where fair Hylas fell prey to the wits of a water nymph and the good Herakles lost his mind, to the clashing stones of the Symplegades—the Argonauts proved themselves to be more than just mortals. They crafted a legacy for themselves, and crowned themselves heroes."

I wanted to interrupt him, to ask him to elaborate on each stop of his travels, but I hoped there would be time for that later. I checked my curiosity as he continued.

"I told your father of our trials and our tribulations, and of my de-sire to have his blessing when I took the fleece. He listened in silence to me speak, and when I was done, he smiled and offered me refresh-ment. I remembered that you warned me against any such offerings, and so I refused. He was not pleased, but he hid it well. From there he suggested a host of other things that I might take instead of the golden pelt: his own men to defeat Pelias by force, poisons that would send my uncle down to the Underworld for eternity where he belonged. He even offered me you, Medea." At this, he paused, surveying me from under his lashes.

Rage flared up under my skin, but I quenched it. There would come a time to punish Aeetes, but that time was not yet here.

"You declined all of these offers, I presume," I stated, shifting in bed.

"Yes, although the last was tempting, I admit," he divulged smoothly.

I rolled my eyes, annoyed. "Your usual charms will not work here, hero or not. Kolchis is not a place for them. What you need is sub-stance, not charisma, if you plan on leaving this land alive." The smile flickered and died on his face. He began speaking again, in a tone more sober than before.

"The king has said that I may have the fleece on the condition that I complete three separate tasks for him." He studied my face carefully, although for what emotion I could not discern. I nodded, stomach sinking. One task would be difficult enough, if Aeetes was orchestrating it, but three would be nearly impossible. I realized dully that I had been naive to think he might go easy on Jason, just because the Gods seemed to favor him. At least, however, Jason would not be operating alone.

"I see. And these tasks are?"

Jason shifted, his muscles straining under his tunic. His eyes, if possible, seemed to have become bluer. They were distracting to look at, not because they were beautiful, but because their lightness rendered them unnerving. How many times had I studied those same eyes in my dreams, their terrible clarity making me feel crazed in comparison? Even now that they were in front of me, I found their brightness maddening and indecipherable.

"The first of my labors involves tilling a field," Jason began. I waited for the catch. "With a pair of fire-breathing oxen under my yoke."

"Fine. The next task?"

"But how on earth do you imagine that I'll complete the first challenge? Where did your father even procure such creatures?"

I ignored him. "You were about to tell me what the second labor encompasses."

Jason pulled a green velvet pouch nervously from one of the pockets of his pants, and proffered it to me. I took it in my hands, surprised by its weight.

"I have to plant these in the earth, and handle whatever springs up. King Aeetes was vague about this one." I nodded, loosening the drawstring opening and shaking its contents into my waiting palm.

A sharp, jagged, yellowing tooth dropped from the inner folds of the pouch, and I pursed my lips. Dragon's teeth. Aeetes was playing a dangerous game.

"And the third task?" I asked, replacing the tooth back inside the pouch and pulling the strings tightly.

Jason tentatively replaced it in his pocket, staring at me with wide eyes.

"Aren't you going to tell me anything?"

"The third task. What is the third task?" I repeated, gazing out the window.

"That's what I don't understand, exactly. For the third task, I merely need to remove the fleece from the tree it hangs from and then Aeetes says it is all mine—" He broke off, uncertain. "But that doesn't sound particularly grueling."

I let out a short, low laugh. "Did my father tell you what guards the tree, hero?" I mocked, the absurdity of the entire situation striking me all at once. "Did he tell you what you would have to pass to merely touch the fleece?"

Jason shook his head, his lips pressed thinly together, his eyes shining with desperation.

"A dragon that never sleeps," I whispered, moving closer so that he drew back slightly toward the edge of my bed. "A dragon that will incinerate you the moment you step into the clearing. If that does not sound grueling to you, then you are a foolish man indeed."

"Help me, then," he urged, and to my shock, his hand found mine among the blankets, and pressed it to his chest. I swallowed hard, pulling my hand back from his grasp but instantly missing its warmth.

"I need to get ready, and then I shall prepare you," I asserted. "Meet me out on the cliffs in twenty minutes." He nodded and rose to his feet, yet in another instant, he had leaned in close, and pressed a hot kiss to my cheek.

"Thank you, princess," he murmured, before slipping out the same way he had entered. I stared dumbfounded at the door to my chamber, attempting to make sense of the strange beating of my heart.

I was not in the habit of going wide-eyed over boys, not since Phrixus had appeared however many years ago and proved himself to be a startling disappointment. Of all the men I had encountered in my life, none was particularly trustworthy or interesting, save perhaps Phaethon. Jason, it seemed, was no different. He may have been beloved of the Gods, but he did not appear to me to be exceptional. He was not shrewd like Aeetes, or amiable like Chalciope, clairvoyant like my mother, or compassionate like Phaethon. He was simply himself.

And yet my thoughts were drawn to him constantly. I was not foolish enough to imagine Aphrodite's powers were minor—no, when she cut my flesh that night on the cliffs, she was working with magic incomprehensible to my faculties. I had read of those pierced by Eros's arrows, of the passion that came over them like wildfire. A calamity so disastrous and pleasurable it drove out all rational thought. But this was not how I felt about Jason. My pull toward him was stark and practical. I thought about him because I needed to, for he was my only route out of this place. He felt necessary. Perhaps there was something wrong with me. Who else, after all, might have been struck by Aphrodite's blade and remained so cold and unfeeling?

I have always been unnatural. The thought appeared in my mind unbidden, and I shivered, pulling the blankets more tightly about my shoulders.

■ ■ ■

It took me longer than I had anticipated to ready the supplies necessary, and so when I finally appeared on the bluffs, I was nearly an hour late. Jason was crouched by the edge, looking down into the abyss of seawater and rocks below.

"My apologies," I asserted, placing a hand on his shoulder to alert him to my presence. "Your tasks required a bit of extra forethought on my part." I exhaled, closing my eyes as the wind picked up, reveling in the salt-stained air, in the frigid chill of the coast. I wondered vaguely how much longer I would wake up in this land, and be able to call it home.

"So you do have a plan?"

"Of course I do," I articulated, annoyed by the surprise in his voice. "Catch this." I tossed him the leather bag that hung from my shoulders. His reflexes were quick, and he cradled it carefully in his palms.

"What is it?"

"How you're going to survive tasks one and three," I announced.

I watched as he slid the purse open, drawing out a flat ceramic pot from the interior. He ran his fingers over the smooth terra-cotta lid, licking his lips.

"Before you go out and yoke the oxen to your plow, you must cover your entire body with this ointment. It will make your skin impervious to flames. You're lucky I keep a pot of it on me at all times, for my good brother and the unlucky slaves whom Aeetes forces to tend to his menagerie." Removing the lid reverently, Jason brought the pot to his nose and inhaled. Almost immediately, his eyes bulged and he coughed roughly.

"What's in this?" he choked.

"It's a magic balm that will keep you safe, that's all you need to know. It does not have to smell sweet so long as it keeps your skin from becoming charred beyond recognition." He nodded, looking uncomfortable.

Next, he withdrew a bottle from the leather folds of the bag. He held it up to the light, and the sun refracted through the sapphire glass in a hundred bottle-bright hues.

"And this?"

"A simple sleeping draft magnified a hundred times. You'll need to launch it into the dragon's mouth and wait a few moments for the potion to take effect. Once it's been digested, the dragon will fall into a deep sleep. You will be free to retrieve the fleece, and at that point, we will make our escape from this place."

"How am I going to get the dragon to drink this?" Jason asked, horror-struck.

"Do you really expect me to do everything for you?" I cooed, irritated. "Are you the same hero the Gods have spoken so fondly of? The same hero who has already passed through a hundred dauntless tasks? Or was that just your crew's hard work, and divine intervention, and luck?"

"Forget I asked," he commented, glowering. "But you haven't told me the plan for the second task. What exactly transpires when the dragon's teeth are planted?"

I shuddered slightly before I could stop myself. "I have never personally witnessed the teeth being seeded, but I have read about it in Aeetes's books. If someone plants a dragon's tooth in freshly tilled earth, a kind of warrior sprouts up—a warrior of the undead."

"What do you mean 'a warrior of the undead'?"

"Aeetes likes his justice to be poetic, Jason. He will think it funny that you will sow the seeds of your own destruction. Once you have dug the teeth into the ground, an army of the undead—recently resurrected corpses—will sprout up, complete with weapons. You'll be outnumbered."

"And there's no ointment or potion that you can give me, I suppose?" he questioned.

I took a deep breath and glanced around the edge of the cliffs for what I needed.

"Oh, no. I think one of these should suffice," I intoned, bending down and prying a stone from the cliff face. The rock was heavy, and my arms burned, but I turned around to face him, and proffered it.

"A rock?" Jason pronounced, regarding me as though I were insane. "You would have me bash their skulls in? They're already dead, Medea."

I forced the stone into his hand, and he weighed it carefully, confusion in every movement. "I don't understand."

"For all of their supernatural agility, these warriors no longer possess brains or wills of their own. They lack the intelligence that a more suitable opponent might have, and so they rely primarily on shock value. All you have to do, I imagine, is hurtle something heavy into their midst, and they should descend on it, utterly absorbed. From there you should be able to finish them off, no longer under the threat of being besieged by them."

Jason regarded me with his mouth slightly open in stupefaction.

"This will really work?"

"I hope so, for your sake and mine," I returned in a singsong voice.

"I don't know why I trust you," he grumbled in an undertone, running a hand through his hair and staring at me with an unnameable look.

"I'd imagine it's for the same reason that I trust you," I contended, meeting his eyes.

"And why is that?"

"Because neither of us has any choice in the matter if we want to make it out of Kolchis alive."

CHAPTER FIFTEEN

Mutilation Again

I found Phaethon in the garden, his nose buried deeply in the satin petals of a rose blossom. His eyes were shut, his mouth parted in something like ecstasy. A flicker of discomfort rippled across his expression as the soft pads of his fingers grazed a line of thorns, but small pains did not deter him. He was sweet like this, seeing beauty everywhere, and going to whatever lengths it might take to prolong the experience of it.

"Brother," I murmured gently, reluctant to pull him out of his reverie. His eyes flickered open, and I was caught for a moment in the shifting green fragments of his gaze. He resembled our mother, with his face slack and distracted, but in a moment, a sharpness had returned to his eyes that was all our father. I shivered.

"What is it, Medea? You look troubled. Have you heard news of the visitor on our shores? It seems he confronted Father this evening after dinner, appearing out of the night itself." He offered me a kind smile, and watched me for any sign of disquiet. There was no getting around the brilliance of his mind.

"Yes, that's why I need to talk to you," I began, nervous to put my plan into words. What if Phaethon chose to stay behind with Father— to become a tool of his extended cruelty and insatiable hunger?

"Go on, sister," he soothed, drawing me over to a marble bench at the edge of the pathway. "What troubles you?"

"You know what our father is," I began in a low, ambivalent voice, praying that as I said these words, they were true. "You see how he thirsts madly for knowledge, how he sees Chalciope, and me, and especially you, as an extension of his own divinity. He has been a good teacher to you, I know, but he has never really seen you, or acknowledged your autonomy." I broke off, unsure how to continue, to make him see.

His eyes surveyed me steadily, and before I could resume, he whispered, "The moment that he hit you, he made an enemy of me, Medea. Do not doubt that. What is it you need, and what is it you propose? I am your agent and your fellow conspirator, always." My heart fluttered anxiously in my chest, and I gripped his hands shakily between my own palms. It was madness, what I intended to propose, but it was the only plan I could come up with on such short notice.

"Mother came to see me, yesterday, before the hero Jason arrived. She told me that he would be our means of escape. So long as I help him achieve his ends, he will secure us passage on the *Argo*, his ship."

Phaethon looked away, his eyes dismayed. "Medea, you are resourceful, but even this you must see is impossible. Father would never consent for me to leave, even if Jason were willing to make off with you," he began slowly, his face making itself blank to conceal his disappointment.

"This is where I need you to trust me." I exhaled shakily, forcing myself to meet his eyes. "I can get you out of this place, and make a new home with you."

"Aeetes would never stop searching for me—" Phaethon groaned, looking at me helplessly. "Of all people, you must know that."

"He would if he thought you were dead," I disclosed, holding my breath.

Phaethon froze, swallowing hard. "Dead?"

"Yes. The magic required will not be easy, and it might easily go wrong. I have spent the last years perfecting my Necromancy, but there is still risk." My heart thundered in my chest. What would he think of me, now that he knew what I was—the kind of unnatural preoccupations that had been my life from the time he was a baby to now?

"Necromancy? Medea, what do you mean?" His face had gone very pale in the sunlight.

In a rush, I whispered to him of all the secrets I had kept for years, from the prophecy our mother foresaw, to my time underground, to Jason's presaged arrival.

In the end, it had been an unlikely combination of synchronicities that allowed me to weave the fraying strands of my experiments together into a single, coherent thread. The tangle of so many years of experimentation had coalesced to imbue me with an uncanny precision and expertise. But my skill alone would never have been enough to bring Phaethon back from the dead. Something external to my own desire and desperation needed to come into play—a kind of grace that transcended human capacity. This was present, I reasoned, in the wool from Khrysomallos, the soft, golden material I had been gifted as an unintended result of my brief compassion for her as she lay dying. And then there was something Aegeus had said, during our courtship, about my desire to pretend any love I felt was dead or else so deeply dormant as to be inaccessible, a sentiment and metaphorical thorn always pricking at my thoughts. For that was it surely—the missing link. Love and death were not states to be vanquished.

No, love and death were forever intertwined, and so resurrection must first and foremost be a radical expression of that most profound and repressed tenderness.

"If you have any hesitation, we can come up with something else," I forced myself to conclude as he mulled over my words. I wondered if he might loathe me for what I had just divulged, if he might even abandon me entirely.

"No," he professed slowly, "I trust you, entirely. Whatever it is you intend to do, I stand by it." I searched his glance for any hint of fear, even the slightest note of unease, and found none.

"You must be even more insane than I am," I joked, voice breaking with relief.

Phaethon rolled his eyes, a smile playing on his lips.

From there we made the logistical arrangements. Once I received word that Jason had completed his second task, but before he had triumphed over his third, Phaethon would meet me at the beach, where I would be waiting with a blade and a carpet spread out beneath my feet. The equipment necessary to complete the sorcery I had in mind, the herbs and poultices that would help my brother reassemble himself once the worst was done, would be loaded already onto the boat, ready for our getaway. When Jason appeared at the top of the cliffs, fleece in hand, I would begin the impossible task of severing my brother into little pieces. Aeetes, in pursuit, would watch me deliver blow after blow to his beloved son—he would understand the damage could not be fixed or altered, not even with his stores of knowledge and his propensity for healing magic. And of course, he would be livid. He would want me dead—his unnatural daughter who had never quite gotten over the jealousy of her younger brother. But he would not seek to bring Phaethon back because he was not fool enough for that. He would assume there was no hope. Wrapping the gory pieces of my brother up in the waiting carpet, the Argonauts would carry his corpse to the vessel, and I would follow them on board. The ship would pull up anchor, and Jason would wade out to join us, his crew welcoming him back like the hero he was.

At that point, I would begin my work on Phaethon below deck. The crew would scatter pieces of goat in the water, enchanted to look like human body parts, so that my father might assume they were his son and pursue them for burial instead of attempting to catch me. Meanwhile, I would reattach my brother's limbs, and renew his blood with sweet-smelling herbs. He would emerge stronger than he had ever been, more alive and vivacious than he had been even in his frenetic babyhood. He would have cheated death.

We did not talk about bringing Chalciope with us. She could never leave Phrixus, and Kolchis was where her children knew to find her when they returned from their own sailing journeys. When Phaethon and I boarded the *Argo*, we would do so knowing that it was unlikely we should see any of our family ever again.

■ ■ ■

That evening, dinner was a tense affair. Aeetes sat, as he always did, at the head of the table, surveying the length of the food and the faces of his guests. Jason was positioned to his right, in a place of honor. My skin crawled with the knowledge that it was a ceremonial gesture and that my father had no intention of allowing the young man to leave this place alive.

Chalciope glanced coyly between me and Jason, raising her eyebrows excitedly. She knew nothing of his business here and assumed he must be yet another suitor, one slightly more good-looking, admittedly, than the rest of them. I attempted to avoid her looks, stomach in knots as I bent over my plate. Aeetes ordered the kitchens to serve wild boar that night, and it had been served charred to perfection, a rosy apple clenched in its stationary mouth. When Jason saw the quality of its savaged skin, he blanched, and I knew he must be thinking of the oxen he would have to face in the morning. I met his glance and nodded in what I hoped was a sufficiently reassuring way. He pursed his lips and filled his plate with roasted vegetables and slices of thick, warm bread. I did not blame him for abstaining from flesh. Ever since my work began in the cellars, I too had been unable to withstand meat.

Phaethon was playing his part masterfully, smiling and joking with Aegeus as though nothing was the matter, and this night was just like any other. I watched him banter, his face lighting up with good humor. Aegeus's eyes darted every so often to look at me, the admiration plain in his features. *It will do you no good*, I wanted to say, *you may as well be courting stone.*

"The obliging Prince Jason has consented to provide us all with some entertainment tomorrow," Aeetes broke in, once he was finished with his meal. He wiped his mouth carefully with a napkin, eyes shining malevolently in the candlelight. Jason shifted as all eyes fell upon him, but he kept his expression carefully blank.

"He will be completing three tasks, none quite at the level of the labors of Herakles, but impressive nonetheless. So rarely do we here on Kolchis have the opportunity to host a hero as he proves himself for posterity, and I trust that all under my roof will join together in wishing Jason good fortune." Aeetes's lip curled as he spoke, the disdain evident in every word, as conversation broke out around the table.

"Whoever wishes to observe the youth in action should arrive at the steward's field tomorrow at dawn, for this is where the first task is set to take place." My father smiled cruelly, rising to his feet. "I must excuse myself, but I trust the festivities will continue in their usual fashion." Turning to Jason, he added, "Don't stay up too late drinking. You'll need your strength for what I have planned."

I swallowed hard as Jason flinched.

The rest of the night passed excruciatingly slowly. Once Aeetes retreated from the dining hall, question upon question was leveled at Jason from all directions. He batted them away uncertainly, his eyes coming to rest on mine every so often.

As the excitement died down, I rose inconspicuously to my feet and gestured for Jason to accompany me to the door. He was at my side in an instant.

"I shall see you tomorrow at dawn," he asserted, his hand making a foolish grab for mine. I yanked my fingers out of his reach. The momentary brush of his skin against mine had the force of a tidal wave, knocking the air from my lungs, leaving me unsure which direction was up or down.

"Don't touch me," I growled, hopeful he would take my behavior for hostility and not for what it actually was. He took a hasty step backward, but his eyes remained steadfast on my face.

"Forgive me for my impropriety, princess," he responded quietly. "I only meant to inquire where I should meet you tomorrow."

Although some part of me craved his attention, another aspect was ashamed to be thinking of anything other than the risks tomorrow would bring. I was about to betray my father and uproot the only life I had ever known. Now was not the time for romance.

"I have too much to prepare. You will face the oxen on your own. The ointment will hold so long as you apply it liberally."

"But I want you there, Medea." Again, the tidal wave, that feeling of being carried far faster than I knew how to handle as his sentiment caught me off guard. I regarded him silently, attempting to analyze his motives. "You'll manage on your own. Once word reaches me that you've completed the second task, Phaethon and I will make our way to the beach. Has your crew been readied for a swift retreat?"

He nodded, the disappointment obvious in his aspect.

"Cheer up," I murmured in his ear as the doors of the great hall closed with a soft boom behind us. "You're in good hands."

"I know," he huffed, the sincerity in his voice surprising me. "I trust you."

I froze, a little shiver running along my spine at his words.

I tried to ground myself in the warmth of his sentiment. Trust, I knew, was an easy thing to feel when you yourself were trustworthy. Those who were the first to suspect were often the first to betray. Perhaps this was an opportunity for the both of us to become better, more honorable. I wanted to believe that he would help me, and that I would help him too. How beautiful life might be, if we could leave behind the twisted, gnarled circumstances that had molded us, and could begin anew.

Jason still stood before me.

"What is it? What are you thinking?" I goaded, a dart of anxiety piercing my breast.

He let out a short chuckle and shrugged, as though in disbelief at himself.

"I'm not sure how to tell you what I want to." He paused, still smiling, although there was a sadness etched in his profile as well.

"Why don't you try?" I baited, more warmly than I meant to.

He nodded, shifting, and I marveled at the energy contained within the slope of his shoulders, the fluid strength of his arms.

"I just want you to know that you're not alone anymore, I suppose," he expelled in a rush, blushing madly. I opened my mouth, but he held up a hand to silence me. "Before you condemn me for the sentiment, which I have no doubt that you will, let me explain myself?"

I nodded tersely.

"From the moment I came upon you that night on the bluffs I knew what you were, recognized in you the same strengths and brittleness that I have always known in myself. Underneath all that impossible tenacity of yours, that potent survival instinct, which has no doubt kept you and your brother in good stead, is a raging fear. Is there not?"

I said nothing.

"We have always had to do our labors alone," he continued. "You, your sorcery, and I, my adventures. There are some things others are not able to shoulder. I want you to know, though, that as long as I am with you, you need not be afraid."

I could hardly speak, so outlandish was this proclamation.

"Good night, hero." I returned at last, annoyed by the fondness that seeped into my tone unbidden. Perhaps some of Aphrodite's love magic was making its way into my system after all.

Jason shot me a small, tentative smile. "Good night, princess."

I offered him a smile in return, feeling stupid. In a moment, he had slipped away, and I was alone in the entryway once more.

Heart pounding and hands shaking, I made as though to return to my quarters.

"Medea," a familiar voice called out from down the corridor. I froze, wondering how much might have been overheard. Taking a steadying breath, I forced my face into an expression of casual composure and turned.

"King Aegeus," I pronounced, shifting uncomfortably. "Are you well? I noticed you gazing at me this evening at dinner." I went silent then, realizing I was in danger of babbling.

He laughed uncomfortably, his hand rubbing the back of his neck.

"Was I that obvious, princess?" he asked, coloring slightly. I could not help but compare the way he addressed me to how Jason did. Where Aegeus was diminutive and respectful, Jason deployed my title as though something in it was ironic or faintly amusing, a joke that the both of us alone were somehow in on.

"Yes," I replied simply. His face was illuminated attractively under the lamplight but I was beginning to grow tired and stiff from the day's events. The anxiety of what was to come rendered me distracted and harsh.

"I wanted to ask you if—" He paused, his eyes staring into mine wistfully. "I wanted to ask a thousand things, really. Trivial, silly things that consume my every thought from the moment I wake up to the second I fall asleep. You are an enigma walking, a mystery that smiles and talks and laughs and scowls so compellingly I think at times it will be the end of me. And you keep your cards terribly close to your chest, revealing nothing. I spend my days wandering these corridors, wondering not of my lands across the sea, but about your favorite color. What is it? What kind of weather do you like best? Have you ever been in love? What is it that you fear more than anything in the world? How do you always smell so desirable—like rainwater and crushed mint and cinnamon? Do you ever intend to leave Kolchis? If I asked, would you—?"

Again he broke off.

The moment seemed to last a lifetime. I knew what subject he intended to broach with me.

"I'm so sorry, my lord, but I'm frightfully cold this evening. I feel the need to return to my chamber most urgently. Perhaps we could talk tomorrow, if that is suitable to you?" I implored as sweetly as I was able.

For a moment, the prince's face flashed with disappointment, but just as quickly, he reined in his feelings.

"Of course, Medea. I wouldn't want to prolong your discomfort."

■ ■ ■

I hardly slept that night. A chill saturated my chamber, a dampness that found its way through the cracks in the windows and gathered, pooling in the corners. The ceiling, covered in delicate frescoes, the same that had watched over me since babyhood, loomed threatening in the dark, and I tossed and turned under the layers of blankets. This would be the last night I spent here, if all went according to plan—the last night I ever spent on Kolchis.

The alternative, that lurking possibility that Aeetes would somehow find out exactly what I had planned, was unthinkable. Phaethon might survive his wrath, but I certainly would not.

When the sun finally rose, breaking over the sea cliffs with the urgency of light itself, I was awake to see it. I watched the shadows recede, the sun beginning to dapple the floor with specks of color. I pulled myself from bed. Though I would never have admitted it to his face, a part of me longed to be beside Jason as he went about his tasks, to offer him some silent support. That same shard longed for him to sit with me this morning as I brooded. I spent a moment unsure of what to wear. How should a princess dress to betray her father?

In the end, I selected one of my plainer dresses for the day, trying not to think of how by nightfall it would be covered in dried blood.

I tensed as a knock came at the door.

"Who is it?" I called, uneasy.

In swept Chalciope, her hair done up in an elaborate chignon, her face lively and intrigued. There was not a hint of tiredness in her manner as she came up behind me and surveyed the gown in my hands.

"You're not going to wear that, are you?" she commented, shock bleeding into her speech. "When the youth Jason looks up at you triumphantly, cloaked in victory from whatever Father sets up for him, surely you will want to be radiant and lovely. This dress is homely at best." I shook my head, exhausted already by this line of inquiry.

"Knowing Father, Jason will be dead before he can so much as flirt with me, sister," I hazarded, watching her face drop in disappointment.

"You're always so worried. You need to calm yourself a little, Medea," she disclosed, raising her eyebrows imperiously. "And you also need to wear something that accentuates your figure." She disappeared into my closet, humming to herself as I rolled my eyes. I supposed I had time to entertain her at least for a little while.

She reemerged with a bloodred gown, complete with an intricately embroidered corset. It was bright and gaudy, one of Chalciope's old ones that had made its way into my possession.

"You jest, sister."

"Just try it on. Humor me."

I slid the dress on over my head, not bothering to fix my hair as it tangled in the corset strings. As Chalciope offered me her mirror, and I saw myself arranged in her skirts, I realized with a pang of fondness that we did not look so unalike now. Although I had always fancied myself the awkward, unattractive one of us, we shared the same willowy frame, the angular cheekbones.

"You look beautiful!" Chalciope gasped excitedly, busying herself fixing my imperfections. "He won't be able to keep his eyes off you."

"You're just saying that because I remind you of yourself. Besides, I imagine that Jason is going to have other things on his mind," I joked vaguely, but Chalciope brushed my comment off easily.

"This is a big moment for you, little sister," Chalciope intoned, looking over at me fondly. I blushed, hating myself for all that I was omitting from her.

For a few seconds, we stared at each other in the silence of the morning until suddenly Chalciope cleared her throat, looking self-conscious.

"What?" I goaded, anxiety pooling in my stomach.

"I thought perhaps you might want a little extra luck. Something to remind you of who you are and where you came from," she offered, looking at me with an intensity I could not place. For a moment, I wondered if she might have guessed some semblance of my plan.

"Why would I need extra—?" I began, but she cut me off with a flourish, withdrawing a glittering coronet from within the folds of her cloak. The breath evacuated my throat. It was my sister's wedding coronet—the one Helios had sent to congratulate her on her nuptials.

"Because you'll want to make an impression with Jason, of course. He's special. I can just sense it. And the two of you would look so lovely together. I just want you to be happy, Medea." She smiled warmly, moving to attach the gleaming crown to my own unruly curls. I opened my mouth and shut it again abruptly, overcome.

By the time she left my room, departing belatedly to observe the end of Jason's first task, the sun had slipped low in the sky. Annoyed, I let out a small puff of air. I would need to get going, to gather the last of the supplies and meet up with Phaethon. With a last haphazard glance around my room, I slipped out the door. Soon this place would be a memory.

■ ■ ■

The walk to the beach was a somber one. Phaethon meandered beside me, peering up at the passing gulls as they cut across the sky, or glancing down at the wildflowers that grew along the bluffs. If he noticed the coronet upon my head, he did not say a word.

"What are you thinking about?" I voiced.

For a moment, I wondered if he would ignore me, but then he cleared his throat.

"I was just wondering at how lovely everything is today. The sky is blue and expansive, and below, the water churns, glimmering like a faceted gem. The birds sing sweet tunes above and the flowers tangle together at our feet. It is odd, but I feel as though I never appreciated it all until now, when I might never experience it again."

"Don't talk like that." I forced the words through my lips, horrified. "You're going to be just fine—I've done this a hundred times."

"On human men?"

I fell silent, surveying the ground.

"I trust you, Medea, but I also know that this could be it for us. And if this is where it ends for me, I want to enjoy every second of it. I want to feel the wind dart through me, the water cling to my ankles. I want to be a receptacle for all the sensations I have not felt. Do you understand?"

I nodded, my throat tight with emotion.

"I'm not going to let you die, not truly," I stated at last, fighting hard to keep tears from leaking out of my eyes.

"But if something goes wrong, and I don't make it, you must not blame yourself. I consented to this."

I scoffed. "You hardly understand what you're consenting to, brother."

"And you underestimate me, sister." I shoved him playfully, and he laughed, his golden curls flickering under the sun. I watched him move carefully down the cliff face, deftly, like a ram might. My heart clenched.

The *Argo* was docked at the edge of the cove, bobbing grimly on the tips of the waves. As Phaethon wandered closer to observe it, I began the work of spreading the carpet out underfoot. Once that was done, I slid the blade from the sheath slung around my shoulders. It was not particularly long, but it was brutal and sharp to the touch. It would make quick work of Phaethon, I knew. I shuddered, quelling the wave of nausea that rose in me. I gripped the wooden handle, breathing deeply, the sea air calming my nerves.

A hand landed lightly on my shoulder.

"You'll make it quick, won't you?" It was Phaethon, his eyes dark, and his face impassive. I noted the tremor in his voice and almost lost my nerve.

"Of course. You'll hardly feel a thing. You won't even be conscious, sweet one." I moved to brush some of his curls out of his eyes and slipped a clear bottle from the inside of my cloak.

"Drink this," I hushed. He took the glass gingerly from me, unstopping it and pausing:

"It's a sleeping draft. If you take it now, it will have time to put you to sleep before I have to do the worst of it," I imparted, my voice shaking. He nodded, and without skipping a beat, downed the contents in a single mouthful. I gripped his hands tightly as he moved to sit in the center of the carpet, his eyes already beginning to lose their focus. He swayed gently, and I caught his shoulders in my arm as he fell backward. I positioned the body carefully so that none of it was in contact with the sand.

Over my shoulder, I heard the murmurs of Jason's crew, watching me from the edge of the cove. Jason had told them that they were to help me with anything I requested, but I could feel their unease like a palpable thing.

The waves crashed upon the shore, constant and unfeeling. The gulls overhead ceased in their singing, and I clutched the blade closer to me. Jason should be here by now. By my knees, Phaethon stirred slightly and then lay still as the potion took full effect on his faculties. I tried not to look at his face.

The minutes crept by, and my heart hammered desperately in my chest. *Where is he?*

And then, quite suddenly, his head appeared over the edge of the cliffs. In another moment, the fleece, glittering and golden came into view, and my breath caught in my throat.

It had been years since I had seen it, and it brought back strange, uncertain memories of that day on the beach with Phrixus. For a moment, I froze.

"Medea!" he shouted, gesturing to begin, slipping down the rocks. I lifted the blade high above my head, breathing hard, then I looked up. Aeetes stood frozen at the edge of the crags, his mouth open in a silent scream. Without looking at Phaethon for fear I would lose my nerve, I brought the blade down with all my might. The sound of bone and muscle crunching under metal cut through the air. I heaved the blade free, from where it had fixed itself. My hands shook horribly, already slippery with my brother's blood. I paused, broken.

"Hurry," a voice broke over my shoulder, the liquid familiar voice of my mother. "You must finish the job." Could she really be here beside me, or was I merely imagining it? I nodded through my tears, and brought the blade down again. Somewhere overhead, my father fell to his knees.

How many times I brought the blade down, I cannot recall. Time seemed to stop, to slow down, to increase exponentially. The scent of blood was on everything, driving out even the heady aroma of salt. Just as my father's men began slipping down the rocks, Jason landed beside me, breathing hard.

"Help her," he screamed at the Argonauts, and after a moment of uncertainty, they plowed forward. Their eyes flickered back and forth between the blood-streaked sand, the coronet atop my head, and the golden flash of the fleece.

Somehow they understood that I wanted them to collect the pieces of Phaethon in the carpet, and they hefted him up over their shoulders. I was covered in blood by now, and shaking horribly. Jason slipped something heavy around my shoulders, and with a dull thrill I realized it was the fleece.

He steered me numbly toward the boat, and I clutched the golden pelt around me tightly, desperate for the nightmare to end.

"I killed him." I shuddered as he lifted me on board, and hefted himself up after me. Phaethon, or what was left of him, had already been placed below deck. My father's men would hit the beach in a matter of minutes I knew. The ship, with painful slowness, slid back from the cove and out into the open sea.

"And now you have to bring him back," Jason whispered into my hair, pressing a shaky kiss to my forehead. "I'll handle the rest. You get to work on the prince." I clutched the soft flesh of his palm and inhaled the sea-swept scent of him. The casualness of the kiss even more than the rocking of the boat made me clumsy on my feet. It took a moment to register the actual content of his words.

I nodded, throwing the fleece off my shoulders as though it was merely cotton.

CHAPTER SIXTEEN

Sea Legs

Sometimes when I cannot sleep now, I think about what my father must have felt as he heaved parts from the sea. How long, I wondered, must it have taken him to realize that his son was not waterlogged? That the drenched flesh the current returned to him was covered in coarse, brittle hair? That the legs his men fished out of the waves were connected to hooves? That I had committed one final insult, and deprived him of a real human body to bury? A quarter of an hour at most, I imagine. Aeetes always was perceptive. I doubt he felt true sorrow for his dead son, for anguish was simply not in his nature. I imagine that at his core, Aeetes was overcome by a cold, primitive rage.

As my father's men raided the cove for what they thought were any stray, washed-up pieces of my brother, the actual pieces of my brother were below the deck of the *Argo,* and I was bent over the galley table, organizing bottles and herbs. The crew parted around me like shy schools of fish, their eyes impossibly wide with horror as they took me in, but I had no time to feel self-conscious. There were too many of them, I thought to myself. If they pressed any closer, I would suffocate.

When I was finally alone below deck with the pieces of my brother, I let out a little sigh of relief. I had faced Aeetes on the beach, and now we were moving, by the second, farther and farther out of his grasp. Now all that mattered was Phaethon.

That night was one of the longest of my life. How I managed to keep working, to circulate what was left of my brother's blood with the finest herbs to refresh it, to reattach his mangled limbs with careful precision, and revive the rosy hue in his cheeks, I still cannot say. It was true, I had done these actions a thousand times on rats and lizards and toads, but when faced with the soft, familiar, yielding flesh of my own brother, the work was entirely different.

I cradled the most intimate parts of him in my hands and tried very hard not to feel anything except love. For love, I knew, was essential to this work. It was everything. I burned fragrant incense under his nose and twisted the wool from Khrysomallos in the thread I used to stitch and sow him back together. I massaged the stiff, clammy flesh, rubbing ointments deep into the contours of Phaethon's still and silent muscles. My fingers were sticky with the sap of elderflower, and blood, honey, and libations, and my lips went numb as I spoke incantation after incantation.

I did not cry and I did not shudder. I merely put Phaethon back together and did not halt in my ministrations until at last, he lay on the table before me, his chest straining to take its first breath. The labored breathing became gentler over the hours, and a comely flush reentered his pale cheeks. His skin did not glint in the way it had previously, and his curls did not shine with the golden light of our grandfather Helios, but he was alive, and that was enough. I could not tell if he would be beautiful, with the lacerations crossing his flesh in ragged scars.

When dawn broke, Jason appeared below deck, his eyes wide as he took in the blood-soaked compresses. We stood in the stillness, trying to ignore the reek of copper that had soaked into every board underfoot.

"Did you—?" He broke off, swallowing hard.

"It is done. If he wakes up by this evening, then we will know I have succeeded." I exhaled heavily, covering my face with my hands.

"You're covered in blood," he murmured, stepping closer. "The crew shouldn't see you like this. It will unnerve them."

"They saw me hack my own kin into pieces, Jason. I doubt very much that there is any way to make them feel at ease with me after that."

Jason nodded, pursing his lips. "Come up anyway. I'll send someone else down to look after Phaethon. You need something hot in you." He pushed, guiding me toward the stairs.

I glanced back over my shoulder at the creature behind me, the creature that had once been my own flesh and blood. Jason's gaze mirrored my own, and I watched as he regarded Phaethon as well. There was something in his look that unnerved me—something hungry.

"You should know I can never re-create the Necromancy I have just done," I lied, the words falling from my tongue automatically. "The magic was simply too draining, and the herbs I require are exclusively native to Kolchis. Besides, the only reason it worked at all was because Phaethon is semidivine. Helios is his grandfather, so he is stronger than any normal mortal." This was not strictly true, but I did not want Jason to have an actual estimation of my powers. It was better to allow some elements of my magic to remain a mystery, at least for the time being.

For a moment, the hero looked disappointed, his brow clouding with annoyance. Just as quickly, his eyes were clear once more.

"Of course, princess. What you have accomplished is impressive enough." The boat rocked beneath our feet, and a pang of loneliness soared through me.

"What have I done?" I whispered, the reality of the carnage hitting me forcefully and all at once.

"What you had to do, I imagine," Jason soothed, his arm at my back. "Come now. Let's get you some breakfast."

■   ■   ■

The crew regarded me warily that afternoon as I sat upon the deck, breathing in the sea air. They were hulking, brawny men, the kind that could snap me in half if they wanted to, and yet they gave me a wide berth. Their eyes regarded me from lengths away as though I was something venomous or volatile. They knew what I was capable of. A part of me enjoyed the space they gave, the aura of insidious intent that I seemed to exude to them. Another part of me, a softer, more vulnerable part, wanted to shake them and make them see that I was sick inside too. That I was as horrified by the events that had transpired as they were.

A part of me worried that if I looked at the men too long, some of their terror would rub off on me. I was still in shock, not quite aware of my surroundings, or of anything. The prospect of emotion felt far away, and blissfully inaccessible. With a new Phaethon under the deck, and my eyes glued to the passing sea, I could almost forget what I had just done.

When I grew braver, some of the warmth returning to my fingers and toes, I would venture glances at the deck itself. The wooden planks under my feet were a thousand shades of cherry and oak and pine, some hearty and dark, others blond and pale, all polished and tempered by the seawater that made it over the sides of the ship. Lines of oars, each many lengths long, adorned each side of the boat. Their handles were intricately carved, although worn from use, and some were ornately painted with lapis and Tyrian purple and gold. The oarsmen who wielded them had a hypnotic quality to their movements as they dipped their paddles into the water and lifted them high above their heads. Seabirds in flight sang sweet tunes, darting and diving at the slightest sign of fish. The rippling white sails caught so violently in the wind that they sounded like thunder.

Only Jason came near me, pressing a bowl of hot gruel into my hands and a roll of bread as I gasped by the railing, attempting to steady myself.

"I'm sure you are accustomed to slightly more extravagant meals, but for now this is the best I can offer you," he joked softly.

I did not respond, preferring instead to stir the contents of my bowl around with a spoon. I had no appetite. I wondered if I would ever want to eat again.

"You must think me ill-mannered, an ungallant exile who has failed to thank you properly. Perhaps I stay silent because I cannot express the force of what you've done for me. And I am not sure if I ever can." He spoke slowly, his tone thoughtful and reverent. "It would be impossible for any language to convey the depth of my gratefulness to you, or the fervency of my admiration."

His words washed over me with the startling, uncomfortable quality of freezing water, so frigid they befuddled the senses and made me think myself on fire. I found that I could not bear to look at him, to acknowledge the weight of what he said.

In truth, I had little experience with compliments.

"I am yours now," he whispered, his voice soft and husky. "Utterly. I would have you know that."

I dug my nails into the calloused flesh of my palms. My mouth opened and shut wordlessly, gaping and foolish and fishlike. How pretty those sentiments all sounded, coming out of his mouth. How drenched in decorum. It was frustrating, how despite their softness I was barely inclined to believe in them. Jason had a silver tongue, that much was achingly apparent, and I was determined to barricade myself against his loose charms.

As the silence extended between us, Jason let out a small sound from the back of his throat. He seemed to sense my inability to continue along this line of discussion and promptly changed the subject.

"What do you think of the *Argo*? She's rather impressive, isn't she?"

I ran a tongue over my lips, shifting slightly but grateful for the distraction.

"Yes, tell me about her," I suggested, attempting to sound more interested than I felt.

"The Argonauts crafted her from the trees on the summit of Mount Pelion. You've heard of it, perhaps?"

I nodded dully. "Yes, the mountain piled high by giants hoping to reach Mount Olympus."

Jason's eyebrows rose a fraction upon his forehead.

"Clever girl. Now its peak is mostly home to centaurs."

"I imagine they did not appreciate you absconding with their sacred lumber," I retorted without thinking.

The silence again descended between us.

"She took many years to construct," Jason continued, gesturing to the deck and clearing his throat awkwardly. "We knew that the *Argo* was going to be an ambitious nautical project, and that she would need to carry a crew of around fifty men. We wanted her to be sturdy, to weather all kind of tempests, but also to be beautiful. The open sea can be a lonely, desolate place, and this was going to be our home."

As I looked about, I realized that the *Argo* did have a certain warmth to it, for all of its more overt grandeur. The wooden railings were well worn, and the deck smelled sweet and salty at the same time, like leather and sweat and aging wood.

"Below deck, you might have noticed the other souvenirs from our travels. We like to think of the ship as a living catalog of all that we have seen upon our journey."

I nodded, although I had been too focused on Phaethon to examine any of the treasures he mentioned. It was impossible to ignore the fondness in Jason's voice, the barely veiled passion that he used when he spoke of his ship. And indeed, the *Argo* was uncommonly wonderful. I stared for a long moment at the hulking mast in the center of the ship, which towered above everything else. The wooden pole seemed to exert a strange, spiritual gravity, for everything revolved around it.

It struck me that the *Argo* was my home now—or at least as much of one as I could hope to have for some time yet.

"I had heard of your father's abilities long before I stepped foot on the shores of your home," he began. "I had heard that he was capable of all manner of things—unnatural things that he had learned from his nymph sister the witch Circe." He paused, staring at me to gauge my reaction.

I offered him nothing, crumbling the roll up in my hand and letting the pieces fall into the gruel. He did not seem to notice.

"When people spoke of King Aeetes and his powers, they never spoke of you, Medea. But now they will. Now they will know that the king of Kolchis has a daughter who can kill a man and just as quickly resurrect him from the dead. That the princess Medea is a Necromancer with powers far beyond those of her family."

I flinched. "No, they will not know any of that," I shot back. "I will go down in history as the monster who murdered her own blood for some man who was still a stranger to her, because no one can ever know that Phaethon is still alive. If word ever reached Kolchis, my father would not rest until he had retrieved him, and that cannot happen. Not when we have only just freed ourselves." I was shaking all over, a mess of nerves.

"You would have your legacy be that of a murderess?" Jason pressed, his face awash with shock and distaste.

"What choice do I have?" I returned, glaring at him. "Some of us do not have the luxury of being warmly remembered, not if we are going to survive in the current moment."

Jason let out a long, low breath. "You're an unusual creature."

"And what do you mean by that, son of Aeson?" He flinched as I pronounced his father's name.

"I mean that when I first met you, I imagined you a callous, ruthless, brutal thing who would stop at nothing to achieve her own ends. I thought you beautiful, but beautiful in the way that a lioness is—graceful and deft in the way that every movement signals some eventual annihilation. And now I know what you really are is selfless. Once someone earns your love, they are under your protection. That is an admirable quality in a woman, and a rare one at that. Now you are beautiful to me but for an entirely new reason."

I rolled my eyes, taking a step back from him.

"Your men won't like you warming to me," I muttered coldly. "They won't want to think their captain could fall under the spell of a kin-slayer, and a witch at that."

"I don't much care what they like or don't like," Jason hummed, closing the distance between us once more. I shivered as he brought his hand to rest just below my chin, tilting my head back.

"Don't," I insisted, more whine than anything else, as his lips landed roughly on mine. His tongue filled my mouth, hot and writhing, and his intensity startled me. He pressed me firmly against the railing, his hands moving down the length of my body, coming to rest on my waist. He pulled me tightly into him, his lips locked on mine, his breath shallow and fast. I melted under the force of his fingers, the sweet smell of rosemary that clung to his skin, and found my own mouth opening under his before I came to my senses.

"Not here," I said roughly, pushing him away, my head spinning. "I'm still covered in my brother's blood." Around us, the crew moved about conducting their usual duties, their eyes sliding off us. Jason still gripped me hard around my middle, and his eyes stared at me hungrily. A warmth I had never experienced before gathered low in my stomach.

"No, this isn't right," I murmured, leaning in to him and pressing a soft kiss to the hot skin of his neck. He went taut for a moment beneath me, but after a moment under my touch some of his muscles loosened.

"You want me to marry you first, is that it?" he asked in an undertone, his fingers surreptitiously skimming the swell of my breasts. I shivered.

I hardly knew what I wanted. Becoming his wife might afford me some protection, especially if he was to become king of Iolcus. But I was loath to tie myself so quickly to another man when I had only just escaped Aeetes.

"I don't care what you do to me. It makes little difference in the scope of things," I murmured back, eyes dull and flat. It was the truth. In the end, I had little interest in the conventions of mortal men. I would never be a man's property, a blushing, amenable bride. It was simply not in my nature. If he wanted to call me his wife, he could, so long as he knew that I was no more his than the sea owns the sky.

"Jason," a voice broke in, and I extricated myself from the young hero's arms, blushing.

"Medea, this is Telamon." Jason cleared his throat, straightening up and gesturing to the man who had interrupted us.

I bowed my head and offered him my hand. He paused for a moment, as though debating whether to take it, and I raised my eyebrows at him.

At last he took my proffered hand and kissed it. "Princess Medea of Kolchis, it is an honor to have you aboard," he managed, his expression flat and genial.

"Thank you," I whispered back, flashing him a hesitant smile, glad that he at least would not be awkward.

"The boy below deck is awake." Telamon turned to Jason as he spoke.

"Tell the lady. She is in charge of the prince's care." Jason gestured to me. Looking slightly perturbed, Telamon turned again to face me.

"I beg your pardon. The boy is awake. He attempted to speak but I told him to save his strength."

I nodded. Without wasting another moment, I clutched the bowl of gruel closer to me and hurried off in the direction of the cabin.

The scent of blood met me in the entryway, and I flinched, feeling ill.

"Medea," a voice croaked from the shadows, and I threw myself toward where Phaethon lay upon the table.

His eyes were open, and surprisingly clear and focused. One of his hands reached out to grasp my arm shakily.

"Hush now," I soothed, patting his sweat-soaked curls. "I told you I would bring you back, didn't I?"

The ghost of a smile flickered across his lips.

"You did indeed. My sister the sorceress." His eyes fluttered shut, as though overcome by a wave of exhaustion.

"You need rest and fluids." I hurried to bring him a cup of water, debating whether to mix some of the gruel in with it for sustenance.

"I don't know how you did it," Phaethon slurred from behind me.

"I don't either," I said shortly, before I could stop myself.

"Medea," he murmured again, and I turned around to appraise him. "Thank you." With a snore, he was unconscious again, and I stood there shaking in the dim light below deck. He would be all right I knew, heart pounding. But in the shadows I wondered vaguely if I would be. How could someone recover from hacking the person they loved most in the world into little pieces? I shuddered, fighting back tears. None of it mattered now anyway.

Phaethon was alive again, and Aeetes was far away in Kolchis. His magic could not touch us here.

CHAPTER SEVENTEEN

Reunion

That night, as Phaethon slumbered below deck, the waves turned harsh and frenzied. The sky, once open and cheerful, became clouded, shrouded with the beginnings of a tempest. Jason exchanged tense words with his men, and after a moment, he gestured for me to join them. Below my feet, the deck felt unstable and slippery.

"Medea, this is Argus and Peleus, my chief navigators." I nodded to each man, anxiety growing within me. Their faces were grim and slicked with seawater.

"It seems that despite all of the calculations and fair weather indicating otherwise, we are headed straight for a storm," Jason began. "Peleus seems to think that it is not a natural storm." Peleus shifted as his name was said and nodded soberly.

"You think some God is angry with us?" I inquired abruptly, the blood draining from my face.

But Peleus shook his head. "The boy, your brother, is alive. It seems to me the Gods would not punish you for the crime of not killing your own kin." He raised his eyebrows, as though daring me to object. I shrugged.

"What, then?"

"How far do you imagine your father's powers extend?" Jason articulated at last. With horror, I realized what he was insinuating.

"You think this is his work?"

"I do. He has no reason to believe your brother would survive such an assault. He may wish to punish you for your crime, and us for harboring you in the aftermath of such unnaturalness."

I contemplated his words, turning them over in my mind. "I've used most of my herbs and tinctures on Phaethon," I explained after a long moment. "I don't have what I need to stave off a storm."

Jason's face contorted with disappointment before becoming resolute again. Beside him, Argus shifted.

"If we can't stop the storm, then we will have to do our best to avoid it, even if it means going off course for a time." He sighed, watching Jason for signs of a fight. "We are near a chain of islands, according to my maps, but the closest one is not ideal for landing." He licked his lips, his eyes darting to me almost involuntarily.

"And why is that?" I interrogated.

Across the sea, the winds howled madly. The waves that besieged the boat were getting higher by the moment.

"It is Aeaea." Argus exhaled at last.

I shivered. "Circe's island," I muttered slowly.

"The witch who turns men into pigs," Jason snarled, his face flushing with rage. "We should kill her."

"I doubt very much that you would want to try," I retorted, glaring at him. "She's my aunt, and the daughter of a Titan. If we are lucky, she might recognize me and give us safe harbor until the worst of this tempest is blown back."

"We are decided, then," Argus summarized unhappily. "We chart a course for Aeaea, and the lovely Medea here does what she can to ingratiate us to the lady Circe."

I nodded, excitement in every fiber of my being. It seemed impossible that after years of wondering about her, I was going to meet the woman who had presided like a ghost over my entire life. The woman who had raised and shaped Aeetes into the monster he was, the witch who had inspired my own journey along the path of *Pharmakon*. What would she think of me? A traitor to her brother, or a sorceress modeled after her own passions?

■   ■   ■

When the *Argo* sliced into the soft white sand of Aeaea, I was the first to disembark. The island was lush and vivacious, more jungle than anything else. Mountains rose above the canopy, and the sand was soft under my feet. Once I reached the far end of the beach, I turned around and signaled to the rest of the crew to wait until my return. Taking a deep breath, I slipped beneath the cover of the trees, overcome instantly by the familiar scent of sap and greenery. The silence of the beach was lost in the roar of life that this place harbored. An enchantment must have been cast along the shore to make the island seem more inconspicuous and barren, I realized.

This was a witch's paradise—that much was obvious. All manner of plants bloomed and blossomed here, a few foreign even to me and my most elaborate imaginings. Pale purple berries hung from the trees, and moss grew wild and spidery along the trunks of trees. The rocks were covered in a vibrant layer of lichen, and the jungle came alive with the sound of insects and animals.

I slipped through the undergrowth, overcome by the potent scents of new life and decay. Following what might have been a path, or might have just been a coincidental flatness of nature, I forayed through the green, shuddering with pleasure. How beautiful it was here. How *tranquil.*

Overhead came the sound of birdsong, crisp and clear in the morning air. I shivered, continuing along until I came to a clearing. In the center was a building of no small scale, made from the smoothest polished stone and wood of so deep and pleasant a color I longed to run my fingers along it. The stone gleamed in the sun. Carved along the borders of doorways and windows were elaborate scenes, etched carefully into the cherry-colored wood. Plants grew wild around the walls, climbing up and finding purchase along the tiles of the roof, which were painted a cheerful blue. It seemed puzzling that the most feared witch of my father's generation resided here, in this charmed space.

I was so taken with my surroundings that at first I did not see her regarding me from one of the open doorways, her eyes bright and dark all at once. Her face was perfectly calm, and almost identical to my own. I stared back, enamored of this mirror image of myself. She tilted her head, and her lips parted in a kind of recognition.

I stood frozen, caught in the beam of her eyes, waiting for her to speak.

She took a fluid step forward, and the vegetation sprung up to pad her feet. I gasped, and she smiled faintly, a look of mischief in her aspect. She had the same electric aura as my father, the same hawk-ish eyes, but where his were cruel, hers were gentler somehow, more refined.

"You are not a child of Pasiphae, for I have met them, even the hideous bull she sired so many years ago. Ariadne, if I recall, had flaming red hair. And you have nothing about you that suggests Perses. Beauty is not one of my brother's gifts." She paused. "But you resemble me so intensely, I imagine that you must belong to one of my siblings. And there is a sharpness to you that speaks to something only one other child in my brood possessed. You are Aeetes's daughter, are you not?" At the mention of my father's name, her eyes became cold and impenetrable.

I nodded, my mouth dry. How long I had dreamed of meeting this woman, and now that she was before me, I could not summon up a single syllable.

"You look nothing like your mother," she noted, moving closer to observe me. "How is she?"

"Idyia?" I asked softly, stumbling over the syllables.

She looked at me. "That is your mother, isn't it?"

My cheeks burned. "She is well." I broke off, realizing that I had very little way of knowing how she was. "Well, actually, she is distant. I do not confer with her very often. None of my siblings do."

Circe made a sound in her throat to show she understood and began circling me, appraising me from all angles. "I told Aeetes that she was never long for dry land. He did not listen to me. It is almost funny to think of how obstinate he became, when as a child he was sweet and yielding." She finished her circle and stopped in front of me, barely a foot away.

"'Sweet'? My father?"

Her eyes flickered with grief, before becoming empty pools once more. "I suppose you never knew him at his best. For that, I do not envy you."

The silence that followed that pronouncement drew from me a flood of words.

"What happened between you? Why will he never speak of you?"

The agony in her look was so thorough and startling that I wished to recall my inquiry at once.

"He did not take my exile well. I imagine that for him, it was nothing short of abandonment," she offered in a voice that rang slightly higher than it had before. I was surprised by her openness, and hoped further questioning would not startle her, causing her to retreat inside herself.

"Abandonment?" The word felt foreign and nonsensical on my tongue.

"I raised my younger brother, for a time, until I was not permitted to any longer. When my father conspired with Zeus to banish me here, Aeetes transformed his rage and his grief into something far more perilous—apathy. He determined that I had elected to leave him, and as such, he rejected me. He rejected all the good in himself, all the tenderness I had planted in him too, by the end." The guilt in her tone was a palpable thing.

"But how could that be your fault?" I pressed, confusedly.

"The reasons for my exile are well documented. There was a man, Glaucus. I imagined he might love me, that men of his sort were capable of love. When I discovered that I was wrong, I turned the alleged object of his affection, the maiden Scylla, into something even he could not adore. In doing so, I revealed too much of my hand, too much of my own power. Before that, Helios had not known the extent of my abilities. After, I was too much of a threat to be left to my own devices, unguarded." I could hardly make sense of her candor. Despite the immense gravity of her words, her voice had become flat and detached.

"What did you do to her, to Scylla?" The name alone was enough to trigger gooseflesh up my arms.

"I made her a monster. Hounds sprang from her thighs and bayed incessantly, so that she would never know quiet. Her single lovely face became a hideous twelve, attached to long, snaking necks. Her teeth grew in pointed rows as though she were more shark than girl. And then I made her insatiable, so that she might never know peace."

My stomach dropped queasily. Horror was present in the shuddering of my heart, but it fell away beneath a much stronger, tenderer instinct.

"I understand you," I whispered at last, trying to pour everything I meant into those three words. Her eyes flickered with dispassionate recognition. If she was surprised to find some shard of her own darkness inside me, she did not show it.

"In your father's mind, I chose another man over him—I chose romantic love, or perhaps my desire for vengeance, over the ability to stay beside him forever. It was the great betrayal of his life, but that is all done now." She straightened, her eyes liquid. "So tell me, what are you called, daughter of Aeetes?"

There, I longed to argue with her, to tell her that not all of Aeetes's cruelty could possibly be because of her, but instead, I bit my tongue.

"I am Medea," I began, breaking off as her eyebrows rose.

"The witch," she said simply.

I stared at her openmouthed.

"Your mother visited me after you were born." Circe smiled. "She revealed to me some of what she had foreseen in regards to you—some of her visions were less than savory, and fell under my purview, it would seem. As the resident witch in the family, she naturally sought comfort from me." She watched me carefully. "She loved you very much. She was very concerned about your future. Tell me, did she end up giving you any other siblings? You had an older brother, didn't you?"

I shook my head, dumbfounded. "You mean Chalciope. She's the eldest of us. And when I was a ways along, Mother and Father had Phaethon—the only son. He is the youngest."

My aunt nodded. "And where are they now? Why are you here? I assume some calamity has brought you to these shores. You're lucky I did not begin the preparations to turn those sailors you arrived with into pigs. I considered it, you know. But then, when you appeared, looking so very much like me, I knew I wanted to give you a chance to explain." Her gaze lingered thoughtfully on the dark green of my hair, the pale translucence of my skin. Despite being told my entire life that I resembled her, I could not seem to see it myself. Her hair had a virescent quality, yes, but it flowed full and glossy in enviable waves down her back. Where my own eyes were a stormy gray, hers were hawkish and yellow. Her countenance was sharp; to look at her was to be cut through. I wondered if I might inspire the same intensity, if my own look had the potential to wound.

I bowed, shaking. "Thank you."

"A witch never grovels," she shot back, eyes glinting. "Now tell me why you are here. And tell me what you know. I do not often receive company."

She led me inside her dwelling, which was warm and comfortable and smelled of wildflowers and salt. She gestured for me to sit at the edge of a large circular table, and I obliged, glancing around at the tapestries that hung on the walls, all intricate and beautiful and familiar.

"My father has ones by the same artist," I murmured, excitedly pointing. She threw back her head and laughed.

"He kept them, then? I wove them for him when he was only a child, to adorn his bedroom in Helios's palace beneath the sea." She smiled faintly at the memory. It occurred to me that signs of my aunt had been everywhere on Kolchis, if I had only been clever enough to discover them.

She gestured for me to begin, and so I told her everything—of growing up under Aeetes's scrutiny, of how my mother gradually slinked back into the sea, of how I came to teach myself *Pharmakon,* of how eventually my father took an interest in me, of how Phaethon was born and that put an end to my lessons, of the prophecy that my mother revealed to me before she disappeared, of how I spent the next years polishing my Necromancy, of Aphrodite's visit, Jason's arrival, and, finally, of my impossible plan. When I finished she regarded me closely, with something like appreciation in her face.

"You brought him back from the dead," she repeated, stringing the words together carefully, as though each was a bead she wanted to look more carefully at.

"Yes, I did."

"That is not done, Medea," she whispered in an undertone.

"Well, it was the only way I could think of—" I attempted to explain, but she interrupted me.

"That's not what I mean. Hades does not take kindly to being robbed of his subjects. And whether or not Phaethon emerged from the Underworld, that does not change the fact that you landed the blows that killed him. These kinds of things leave a mark. This kind of magic is heavy indeed. I do not know of many who have ever attempted it, even among the Gods or Titans."

I squirmed at her words, suddenly afraid. "Surely you have—?"

"No," she returned simply. "I have never. I have done other things, cast other spells and concocted other potions, which may be worse—I cannot say. But I have never done that."

I blanched.

"Do not fear, child. What's done is done. But you and the boy Jason will need to be cleansed. And you should be married. The Gods may take mercy on you if they presume that you acted madly out of love."

I hesitated, and her eyes raked over me.

"What if I do not love him?" I tried to sound casual and convincing, but the thunder of my heartbeat gave away, if only to myself, that this was a lie.

"Why not ask your real question?" she inquired patiently. I licked my lips.

"What if I am not meant to be a wife?" I said it so quietly she was forced to step closer to hear me.

To my surprise, her eyes flashed with mischief.

"Then you will doubtless find a way to free yourself from your marital bonds when the time is right." She uttered this with the smallest and most brazen of smiles upon her lips.

I agreed mutely.

"Bring him here, to the clearing, and come alone. The rest I will do for you."

■   ■   ■

Jason was not eager to foray into Circe's jungle. His muscles were tense under my fingers as I guided him toward the gap in the trees where I knew her home to be.

"What exactly does she intend to do to us?" he chanced in an undertone, looking around furtively.

"She will cleanse us, with herbs and oils and salts, which is more generous than we deserve. She had never met me before in her life, and still she offers us her aid. You must show her your appreciation," I counseled him softly. "And then, when we are sufficiently cleansed, she will marry us."

I said the last sentence in a rush, hoping he would not touch upon it, but he froze along the path, his eyes darting to me.

"Marriage?"

"Yes, she thinks it may encourage clemency on the part of the Gods," I elaborated, blushing, unable to meet his eyes.

"Good," he remarked, a smile splitting across his face. His hand reached out and tangled with mine, and something warm exploded in my chest.

"You think it good to marry a savage, a witch, a kin-slayer?" I whispered as he pulled me close under the trees.

"I think it is the only thing that makes sense," he whispered into my hair. I shivered as his hands traced the skin of my arms.

"We need to get on, we cannot keep her waiting," I blurted out, disentangling myself from his embrace.

Some part of me had hoped that Jason would resist the impending union so that I would not have to. I thought about my mother, stripped of her freedoms and wildness by my father, forced to bear him child after child until a proper heir emerged. Would Jason expect the same of me? Should I have warned him perhaps that motherhood had never been meant for me—that being a wife would not come naturally? For all the casual disregard with which I had treated our relationship up until this point, a part of me genuinely called out to him, even longed for him. It was dangerous to build a marriage on pragmatism, but perhaps an even more perilous pursuit to build it on love.

The house emerged from out of the jungle, as I knew it would, and Circe was in the front garden waiting for us.

"Shall we begin?" she suggested, addressing me. She did not bother to look at Jason. I nodded with more vehemence than I felt.

"Take a seat." Circe gestured to a circle drawn in candle wax upon the ground. I shivered, but moved forward, heart pounding. Beside me, Jason followed suit, his fingers grazing the fabric of my cloak as though to pull me closer.

After the incantation had been said, and sage applied in smoking layers to the air we inhaled, after stones, the names of which I could not have recited, were placed upon the exposed skin of our bodies, and after salt water was poured carefully over our heads, the thing was done.

In another moment, Circe had whispered the necessary marriage rites over us, her palms hot on my shoulders as she drew me into Jason's arms.

"Is that all?" Jason asked, surprised. I shifted. Circe acted as though she had not heard him, and I smiled. I imagined he was not used to being treated like nothing.

"Perhaps you and I might encounter each other again," I divulged as we stood to exit the clearing later.

"Perhaps," Circe disclosed, although her eyes did not seem particularly hopeful. "But even if we do not, I am glad that now I have met you." The words were simple, but they sent a bolt of pleasure through me. Somehow I had always dreamed that this very conversation might transpire, and now here I was, on Aeaea. I felt more heartened by her presence than by my new husband's, and for a moment I wished that Phaethon and I might stay forever on the island.

As we began to leave, Circe called out impassively, "You should consummate your marriage before you return to sea. Make sure that your bond is strong." I froze, but Jason's hands found their way to my lower back, propelling me forward. The house was soon out of sight, and I was alone with my new husband. My skin prickled under his gaze, and coloring hotly, I hastened in the direction of our ship.

We made it perhaps a mile before Jason's hands found my waist, pulling me back against him. For a long moment he simply held me like that, against his chest, with both of us breathing shallowly. Without turning me around to face him, he began to pull my skirts up. My breath came in low, uncertain exhales as he pushed me to the ground.

"Jason—" I could manage only his name as his fingers slipped and entered the most secret parts of me. Then he had drawn his hand away, and I ached, missing the pressure of him. And then he was filling me, and I could not stop myself from crying out, which only seemed to make him more frantic. He became wild, and I lost myself in the feel of his skin, in the steady rhythm of our connection. Under my palms, the jungle floor was soft and yielding. Overhead the birds sang, and I disappeared into a strange pool of ecstasy.

■ ■ ■

The aftermath was vibrant and melancholy. Perhaps there was something in the air itself on Aeaea, or in the water that caressed the shores, or the plants that erupted lushly under our bodies. The colors were more intense, the feelings impossible to hold. I lay with my back to Jason's chest, ensconced in the warmth of his arms. His hands drifted aimlessly through my hair, and I did my best to remain perfectly still—to match my own unsteady exhales to the easy patterns of his breathing. A lizard darted playfully among the bushes, its black eyes fixed upon mine.

"You're quiet," Jason offered into the heat between us. I found that no matter how much I might have wanted to, I could not speak. Gently but firmly, Jason turned me toward him so that we were face-to-face. I tried and failed to meet his eyes. They were too blue here in the island shade.

"I've upset you?" he tried again, pulling me close. Unnameable emotions slipped through the cracks made by our union. I felt so much, so intensely; I was not sure whether I could force it all back down again, once this moment ended. Instead, I nestled against him so that the world around us was lost in the darkness of his skin, the fresh scent of his sweat. His proximity was a double-edged sword, at once soothing me and causing me unease. Surely, I ought to feel happy, or, at the very least, some semblance of belonging or rightness or peace now that we were bonded.

As we lay together, intertwined, one of his arms slipped upward, away from my shoulders. I missed its presence immediately but bit my tongue.

"Look, Medea. Isn't it beautiful?" he spoke under his breath, bringing my attention to his fist. In his palm was a delicate white flower, so soft and fragrant and familiar that some of the sadness dissipated. Thousands of the blossoms hung over our heads, billowing softly in the breeze.

"Jasmine," I affirmed. "On Kolchis I would use it to brew tea."

"Nothing more nefarious than that?" He chuckled, tucking it softly behind my ear.

"No, but I suppose you could use it in anything. A rather disarming lunar herb."

"Like you, then," he said lightly.

"What do you mean?"

"I find you disarming, if that were not obvious."

I swallowed anxiously, hiding my dismay behind a smile.

CHAPTER EIGHTEEN

Of Sirens and Snakebites

The walk back to the ship was a quiet one. I kept a few paces ahead of Jason, attempting to digest the events that had taken place in the past two days. I had become a murderer, a Necromancer, a niece, and a wife all in the span of what felt like a few moments.

The storm would have abated now, I knew, with Jason and I wed and the ship safely hidden from Aeetes's prying eyes. Even so, as the sails came into view, and the sprawling deck swayed upon the sea, I did not feel quite ready to leave Aeaea. How nice it would be to spend another night here, to bathe under the moon somewhere Aeetes would never think to look for me. I was now an exile. In the same manner that Circe was a prisoner of this place, I was now chained to the Argonauts, however unsavory a reality that seemed.

"What are you thinking about?" came my new husband's voice from behind me as we stood in the shadow of the ship. My stomach lurched as I frantically searched my thoughts for some innocuous enough detail to give him—to put his mind at ease.

"Just about how peaceful it is here, I suppose," I managed at last. This was not exactly a lie, given the terrible, untouched beauty of the island, but it was an omission. Then again, how was I to explain the sense of wrongness I felt about our union, the doubts that crowded my head without an end in sight? Jason would not be able to quiet my own sense of impending doom. It would be better not to trouble him.

"You look so far away," he pronounced softly. "Even less present than you seemed on Kolchis, and I did not know that was possible. I thought you might be happy to be free of that place." He broke off, observing me.

"I am," I insisted, voice cracking.

"What darkness pursues you, then?"

To my horror, hot tears sprung up in the corners of my eyes, spilling across my face without warning. I turned my face away abruptly, thanking the Gods for the dark, virescent curtain of hair that veiled my expression.

"Oh, Medea," he exhaled, his voice pained and comforting all at once.

Before I could move away, Jason's arms were around me, firm and steadfast and warm. I stifled the sob that rose in me.

"I hardly know you, and I've given you everything," I cried into his shoulder, shuddering with the enormity of what had transpired in just a few days.

"I intend to honor that vulnerability, princess." He sighed into my hair. "As you have honored me."

■ ■ ■

When we came abreast of the boat, Jason gave me a leg up so that I could pull myself up over the side. Peleus waited for us on the deck, his eyes shining.

"You were gone longer than we expected. We were about to send a search party out to find you," he claimed. His voice was dry, but there was a mischievous glint in his eyes. Could he know what Jason and I had done? The thought was slightly mortifying.

"We were caught up, but the witch has cleansed us with herbs and seawater," Jason imparted, his eyes flickering to mine with the lazy knowledge of our marriage.

"I'm going to check on my brother," I insisted after a moment, unable to bear the tension that permeated the air as Peleus's gaze rested on the mess of my hair, and the untidiness of my dress.

Below deck, Phaethon was doing a bit better. He could sit up on his own now, and was taking a long drink of water from a calfskin pouch when I entered.

"You're finally back." He smiled, gesturing me over. "I was worried. How was our aunt?"

"She's simultaneously everything and nothing like I imagined." I sighed. "And she looks exactly like me." I gestured up and down my body for emphasis.

"So there are two of you! Aeetes must have been terrified when you were born and he noticed the resemblance." Phaethon laughed gingerly, clutching at his stomach. His wounds may have been healing with supernatural speed, but they were still evident. I was struck by the shadows that seemed to cling to his skin ever since I had reassembled him—perhaps some trick of the light, or perhaps some visual evidence of his brush with death. I shivered before I could stop myself, recalling the expression on Circe's face when she learned the extent of my Necromancy. Had I erred in bringing a mortal back from the dead, no matter how dear that mortal was to me?

"You must promise me something, Phaethon," I said suddenly.

"Anything, sister." He looked up at me with his guileless eyes. "Unless you expect me to help you improve at the lyre. I'm afraid that is beyond even my immense skill." It was a poor attempt at humor, and we both knew it.

"Promise that we will never break apart like she and our father did," I whispered in a quiet voice. The thought had been at the back of my mind since Aeaea had been settled upon as a destination.

"We could never," Phaethon soothed.

"But I killed you." I groaned, tears forming in the corners of my eyes. "I killed you, and Circe says that leaves its mark somewhere."

"You did," Phaethon considered, before adding in his usual sensible tone, "but then you brought me back. You proved yourself to be more powerful than anyone could have ever anticipated, and I am honored to watch you learn and grow."

Touched, I knelt down and gripped his hand in mine. Words momentarily escaped me as I clutched him, this boy I loved more than life itself.

"Medea, do you know why I agreed to this insane plan in the first place?" he hummed softly.

"You wanted to be free of Father, free of the confines of brutal Kolchis. Just like me," I returned automatically. In truth, I had been too relieved that he was willing to leave to analyze his reasons more deeply than that.

He laughed softly, shaking his head.

"For someone so brilliant, you're terribly dense sometimes," he began, raising his eyebrows. "I agreed to die and be born again because that was the only way I could stay with you."

"Everything I do is for you as well," I admitted shakily, embarrassed at the sudden emotions that coursed through me.

"I know, sister. I'm well aware." He smiled sadly at me, as though possessed of some tragic knowledge I had no access to. I hated that look, and so I determined to change the subject.

"Jason and I are married," I whispered, raising my eyebrows conspiratorially.

"What?" Phaethon's face was all shock. "When?"

"On Aeaea. Circe performed the rites," I explained, blushing. Phaethon lay back upon the table, his mouth slack.

"I never imagined that you would marry," he expressed slowly.

"Neither did I." I wrung my hands in my lap.

"You love him?" Phaethon asked, peering at me with his inquisitive eyes.

I recalled how Aphrodite's arrow had pierced my skin only a few nights before, a superficial wound, but surely sufficient.

"I do not think I am not capable of love," I replied, closing my eyes tightly so that Phaethon would not see my dishonesty. Even as I denied the feeling, I was plumbing the depths of my interiority for some sign that the unknown sensation in my chest could be just that—love.

"You do not *think*?" my brother pressed, letting out a low chuckle.

"Well, I dwell primarily in abstraction. You know this. I am hardly embodied enough to recognize love when it strikes, but perhaps this is as close as I can get to feeling something like it."

He nodded, finally satisfied with my answer.

Overhead, I heard a frenzy of boots running over the deck. Phaethon shot me an alarmed look.

"The Argonauts are not usually this active," he vocalized, attempting to sit up once more, but I pushed him roughly back into a horizontal position.

"You rest, and I will go back up and find out what exactly is going on," I insisted roughly, getting nimbly to my feet.

Above deck once more, the crew was a flurry of movement. My eyes searched for Jason, but finding him occupied with Peleus and Argus, I approached Telamon, who was tying knots to hold a few stray chests in place.

"What's happening?"

Telamon regarded me with a slightly contemptuous expression that melted, after a moment, into resignation.

"We're on track to sail directly through the Sirens," he imparted in his soft, gravelly voice. "Peleus must have made some kind of miscalculation regarding the stars, and now we have no choice but to continue on. Your father's storm is blocking the only other available course, unless we want to sail back toward Aeaea."

"The Sirens?" I repeated, feeling suddenly hollow. "Surely not."

"Unfortunately, I have no reason to lie to you, your grace. You should get below deck, not that in the end it will make any difference. I imagine Sirens enjoy the meat of drowned princesses just as much as the meat of lonely sailors."

I brushed past him, annoyed.

"Jason," I called, gesturing him over. "We're going to hit the Sirens?" A note of desperation slipped into my voice. When I was a child, Idyia had told stories of those creatures, with the fair, alluring heads of women, and the bodies and talons of birds. Their voices were such that when they sung, no mortal could resist their call. As far as I knew, not a soul had ever survived an encounter with their breed.

"Yes," Jason admitted, looking more panicked than I had ever seen him. "But we have a chance." I waited for him to elaborate, but he merely pointed toward a blond man perched at the helm of the craft. The man was lithe and angular, and his thin face was impossibly melancholic. In his fingers he clutched a lyre, more beautiful than any that our music tutors ever procured for Chalciope on Kolchis. I realized with a start that of all the men on the ship, this one had never attracted my notice, so small and unassuming was he.

"Orpheus." Jason uttered the name like one might a prayer. "He has an otherworldly voice, but his true gift is those nimble fingers of his. When he plays the lyre, the world stops and listens, the birds fall silent, and the chimes shrink back in shame. There is no mortal creature like him."

"I don't understand," I questioned. "He's so small. What chance would he have against so many—?"

"He might be able to drown their Siren song out with his own melody," he explained, his voice anxious. The idea seemed far-fetched to me, but I kept my thoughts to myself, moving past my husband to approach the boy.

After sensing my presence, he glanced up into my face, his sky-blue eyes wide and languid.

"You are Medea." It was not a question, but I nodded anyway. His voice was sweet and mellifluous, high and honey-like as a girl's might be.

"Jason says you can stop the Sirens," I began slowly, watching his face for signs of unease, but Orpheus merely shrugged.

"Perhaps."

We sat quietly together as the crew moved frantically about us, shouting orders and readying the ship for contact.

"You look young to be such a skilled player. My sister is very good at the lyre, but she's older than you, I would imagine. How did you learn?"

"I taught myself." He shrugged again, his eyes sliding from mine as he looked at the sea, blank and impassive. "Music has always come naturally to me."

"What a gift," I managed, beginning to feel awkward in the presence of such terseness, and yet for all of his quietness, Orpheus was not rude or abrupt. He reminded me a little of my mother—absent and far away. He was missing something, just as she had missed the sea.

Ahead, a blur of cliffs loomed out of the fog, and I swallowed hard.

"You're nervous?" He turned to look at me, his face still impossible to read.

"Yes, a little. I've heard very dark things about this place indeed."

"Do not be afraid, dear one," he uttered softly under his breath, his fingers hovering above the strings of his lyre, but never striking them. "The worst that can come to you is death, and of this life's torments, death is nothing."

I stared at him, uncertain. "So what is?" I asked, intrigued.

"What is what?" he returned distractedly, wetting his lips and staring up into the clouds.

"What is the worst torment?"

At this, Orpheus smiled a cold, feral smile. Instantly, chills erupted on the back of my neck. Where before he had been beautiful, radiant with youth and promise, he was now transformed into something sharp and perilous. He looked at me, his eyes narrowing slightly.

"I misjudged you, Medea," he hummed in that unnatural tone of his, his smile slipping. "I assumed, from how you hacked the young prince apart, that you were a stranger to love. But that is not the case, is it?" He quirked his head to observe me from behind his blond curls. The fog around the ship was growing thicker now, and the men seemed to be moving slower.

"I don't understand." I played coy, uncomfortable.

"The worst torment is the loss of love," Orpheus explained, playing a single note upon his lyre that sliced through the air and cut me to the quick. His finger flitted, as though to play another note, but I hurried to stop him. That one had been enough. The unnerving note continued to echo through me.

"Who did you lose?" I asked.

The rocks were terribly close now, and Orpheus shook his head.

"I think it is time to play." He offered me a thin smile, one that was not as animalistic as his previous. I shivered as the melody began. His fingers blurred upon the strings, so quick and deft were they in their movements. All other sound slowly faded: the roar of the waves and the crashing of the surf on the rocks, the shouts of the crew.

Then Orpheus began to sing.

The curious thing was that although when he spoke it seemed Orpheus was merely stringing words together, when he sang his voice, honeyed and polished, rang with a richness that was unrivaled by any mortal. I watched in awe as he sang, his fingers darting impossibly fast over the lyre strings. The Argonauts paused in their ministrations, half of them transfixed by Orpheus, and the others staring in horror over the edge of the boat. After a moment, I felt brave enough to follow their glances, and nearly screamed.

The Sirens were beautiful above the waist, with long, rippling hair and eyes so bright and lovely that I myself unconsciously took a step forward. Their mouths were cast open in song, but I could not make out what exactly they sung of, so powerful was the voice of Orpheus. Dense, dark feathers layered their legs, and their claws were immense. Bits of flesh dangled between their talons and were strewn across the rocks that they perched on, and in a few spots, bones gleamed where they had been dropped, picked clean.

Afraid that I might be sick, I glanced back toward Orpheus, attempting to focus on the words he sang. After a moment, I closed my eyes, letting the music become my vision.

> She was lovelier than the stars above,
> And there were flowers in her hair,
> Never since her have I been so mad in love
> For she was my water, my earth, my air.
> The day we were to marry
> She walked the river with her feet bare,
> The bouquet she sweetly carried,
> But still danger lurked for her there.
> A serpent hid among the weeds
> Its reptilian eyes prepared to strike
> And when those fangs had done the deed
> So ended my fair one's life.
>
> I held her on the river's edge
> My heart as cold as stone.
> I begged her to return like she'd said
> But I sang to flesh and bone.
> I determined then and there

To follow her below
I'd follow the flowers that dropped from her hair
Where no new life can grow
I played my lyre to the rocks
Until they split wide apart
I searched the Underworld hoping to
Persuade the God who had acquired my heart.
Hades was not so convinced
But Persephone understood
She promised my love back to me
If one task to complete I could

And so I stalked back up the way I came
Singing on my lyre,
Trying not to turn around
But terrified that the stakes were dire.

And so one moment passed and two
And I glanced behind my back
And my love was cast down all black and blue
Before I could carry her back.

When Orpheus let his lyre fall gently from his hands, the quiet that ensued was almost unbearable. I watched as his eyes became once again distant and unperturbed.

The rocks were gliding away behind us, and soon they, and the Sirens, would be a distant memory, but in this instant, the world itself felt broken.

"I'm sorry," I whispered, clasping his hand, my heart aching for him. He surveyed me impassively.

"Do not be sorry until you have made the mistakes that I have, Medea. You will have time enough to suffer." His gaze made me stiffen. It was a strange type of seeing, and I registered that I knew it well. I realized with horror that he reminded me of my mother—both possessed the same uncanny breed of clairvoyance.

I opened my mouth to speak, but all my words had dried up.

"You should go below deck, and be with your brother. He is probably worried about you. Besides, someone in your condition needs to be careful and conserve their strength."

His eyes flickered to my stomach. I swallowed hard.

"My condition?"

He nodded. "Yes, but you would have eventually sensed it too, princess. After all, you possess your mother's gift, even if it is a fraction of it." Orpheus smiled, but no humor reached his eyes. "How lucky you are, to have two of them growing inside of you." I felt a surge of acrid bile rise in my throat.

"I'm going to be sick," I muttered.

"That would be only natural," he acknowledged softly, turning his gaze back to his lyre, apparently done speaking to me.

There Are Monsters
Everywhere

I could not eat or drink for days, so wretched did I feel. Whether it was the unsteady tumbling of the ocean beneath our intrepid ship, or the new life growing inside of me, I could not discern. All I knew during that period was that my heart ached. Orpheus's thinly veiled hints made sleep impossible, and in the darkness below deck, I replayed them in my mind.

You will have time enough to suffer.

I knew intuitively that I was not meant to be a mother. The idea was laughable, absurd. Somehow it had not occurred to me, on that hazy, lust-stained afternoon on Aeaea, that there would be any consequences to lying with Jason. The marriage needed to be consummated, yes, but surely I had been born barren. Part of me, from my youngest remembrances, assumed that I was sterile, so unnatural and foreign did the proposition of motherhood feel to me.

There was no one to ask for advice. Idyia had been gone for most of my adolescence, and in the years before she fled Kolchis she had been vacant or else full of a faraway sorrow. Aeetes, meanwhile, had preferred to vacillate between outright cruelty and calculating condescension. How, growing up as I had, was I ever to be expected to be trusted with children of my own? The labors and perils I had forced Phaethon to undergo were evidence of that. Surely, I was doomed to repeat the behaviors of one or the other of my parents, damaging my children, just as I had been damaged. The prospect was a potent kind of torture.

I did not tell Jason of my knowledge—something held me back. Phaethon, however, guessed almost immediately with his usual intuition.

One afternoon when he was well enough to venture above deck, we had taken a seat toward the prow of the ship, and he had reclined, letting his head fall sleepily into my lap. As he looked up into my face, I ran my fingers through his curls, in the manner our mother once did when we were children. They had not regained their golden luster since his death, but he was alive, and that was enough, even if some of his fire had been diluted in his revival.

"There's something eating at you," he observed, his eyes wide and searching. I shifted uncomfortably, hoping he would forget about it if I changed the subject.

"Your scars are healing nicely," I prattled on, my eyes compulsively tracing one of the white, spidery lines that ran across his biceps.

"They are, so tell me what it is that has made you so quiet and withdrawn, sister." A command, not a question.

"You should know better than to tell me what to do, Phaethon," I threatened, my hackles rising. He raised his hands in deference and had the good grace to look embarrassed.

"I just want to know how I can help."

"I don't know if you can." I covered my face, horrified at the sting of tears forming.

One of his broad hands settled comfortingly on my shoulder. As the quiet stretched out, I began to regain control of my tear ducts.

"I'm with child," I said at last, still not looking at him. I felt his sudden intake of breath beside me.

"You're going to be a mother," Phaethon stated at last, his voice surprised. "Does Jason know of your condition?"

"No, and I'm not sure that I want him to know yet. We are nearing Iolcus, and he has enough to contemplate without this on his shoulders." In my mind's eye, I saw Phaethon's eyebrows rising.

"Since when do you care about the feelings of some man?"

I shifted, caught out.

"Well, perhaps I do not trust him with this yet," I admitted finally. "Perhaps this is something I wish to keep for myself. He is not king as of now. Presently, he is an exile. His children might be in peril in this land he seeks to return to."

My brother acknowledged the truth of this with a grumble.

After another moment, he spoke again. "You said 'children,' plural."

Annoyed, I realized my mistake. "Orpheus believes there will be twins." Phaethon took this in stride.

"Yes, I've heard he has something of the Oracle about him, poor boy."

I tilted my head back to observe the sky, which was uncharacteristically cloudless.

"I'm going to be an uncle," Phaethon mused after a moment, a smile slipping across his face. "Imagine that."

"Chalciope already made you one four times over." I rolled my eyes, annoyed by his irreverence. How could he not feel the peril of my situation?

"Yes, but you have always been my favorite sister, and so these babies will be my favorite nieces or nephews." He said it easily, plainly, as though it was nothing.

"You don't mean that," I tutted, but secretly I was pleased.

"Do you think that I should be allowed to be there when they are born?" my brother asked quietly, in a voice that was shy and uncertain.

I glanced over at him, surprised. "Of course, why wouldn't you be allowed? You're the one living person I love best in this world."

"Because"—Phaethon paused, as though unable to land upon the correct words—"because I am not natural. I have lived and died, and been resurrected in the manner of some fabulous supernatural being. I am a kind of abomination. I should not sit here in front of you, laughing and talking and loving and thinking and imagining the future, and yet I am. I do not know if children should be exposed—"

I cut him off abruptly with panic swirling in my stomach. "You are more natural than anyone I have ever met. Even dead and resurrected you are warmer than any boy or man has a right to be. Don't talk of such things."

Despite the conviction of my words, he shook his head. Something in his expression gave me pause.

"What are you keeping from me?" I inquired softly, dread pooling in my chest.

"Did you know there are rats aboard this ship?" he parried abruptly, not looking at me.

"I would imagine so, Phaethon. But what has that to do with our current conversation?"

He paused, shuddering. "They won't let me touch them or stroke them. They will not sniff the crumbs I leave for them to feast on below deck. They do not come near me at all."

"I don't understand, brother," I offered slowly, although I was beginning to.

"Before, animals flocked to me, and I found such comfort in them. Now they flee from me. They can sense my wrongness," he expelled in a rush.

For a long minute we simply sat together, charting this new revelation.

"I'm so sorry, Phaethon—" I began at last, but he cut me off.

"I just want you to know that though I am grateful for everything you have done for me, I also understand that I am divided from you now, from all living creatures who walk this earth and know not the endless embrace of death, whether we want to acknowledge it or not."

"What makes you think that no one else feels death so viscerally?" I retorted before I could stop myself. Phaethon regarded me with furrowed brow, suddenly concerned.

"What do you mean?" he pressed inquisitively.

"Only that ever since my earliest recollections I have felt like an impostor—an absence parading as substance—a void pretending to be a human being, who ended up in this very body by coincidence or perhaps cosmic mistake. I have never felt real in the way that other people are—in the way that you and Chalciope and Mother are. In the way these children I carry inside me have a right to be. And yet I am polishing life inside of myself—this is, you understand, the most impossible magical feat I have ever had to perform. Bringing you back from the dead was nothing because you had so much life to begin with. But me, the impossibility of my own dreadful nothingness being enough to sustain two new lives—that is not done—it is not logical." I broke off, breathing hard.

Phaethon watched me but did not speak, and feeling compelled, I resumed my speech.

"As a child I was always so jealous of you and Chalciope, for the connections you made and the feelings you harbored in your breasts while I went about cold and unfeeling and connected to nothing. Even Mother knew, from the outset, that there was something wrong with me, that I was not like her other children—that I would be a danger to all of you. Father alone understands because he is a void too, only pronounced a thousand times, his vacuity exacerbated by divinity, by his proximity to the sun itself."

Phaethon gently patted my shoulder again as I shook violently beside him.

"I think, sister, that you underestimate yourself," he murmured, his concern in every syllable.

I scoffed. "Phaethon, I've had long enough to think about this, I imagine."

But he smiled. It was infuriating to see. "You would not be able to be the witch that you are if what you said was true."

"And what makes you say that?"

"Witchcraft relies on the connection among all things, the intrinsic links that tie us all together. And as far as voids go, I would imagine that all of us are mostly made up of space—although whether or not that qualifies as emptiness is another matter."

I leaned in to him, the tenseness in my muscles evaporating, the frenetic energy that forked me through gradually slipping away.

"Perhaps," Phaethon added, "existence itself is merely the recognition that *being* exists alongside *nonbeing*. Paradox is the mightiest and most impossible thing to hold, and yet we do it. You are not evil or unnatural for viewing something from all of its sides, in all of its complexity."

■ ■ ■

The sea stretched out in all directions, a thousand hues of aching sapphire and cobalt. How different these waters were from the ones I had known on the beaches of Kolchis, which were frigid and dark and inhospitable. And so I spent hours out upon the ship's deck watching the expanse, as unsettled as seawater.

Occasionally, faces would appear from beneath the waves, flickering countenances that would dissolve as suddenly as they had appeared. They stared back at me with a kind of vague recognition. Perhaps the Oceanids of this place could sense I was descended from one of their own, or perhaps they did not care.

"We've set a course for Crete," a voice intoned softly from behind me as I leaned against the ship's railings one afternoon. I turned, surprised to find that it was Telamon who had spoken. Despite the proximity that came with sharing a vessel, we avoided each other, and he had never sought me out individually before. I simply assumed that for all his outward civility, he was just as averse to me as the other sailors.

He must have registered my surprise, because he let out a little puff of air, and offered me a soft smile.

"I'm sorry if I startled you, princess," he added quickly. "Some of the other men tell me I tend to approach too softly. It can be a skill on the battlefield, but a fright to my friends."

I nodded, wondering if he considered me one of his friends. Surely, he was not so misguided as that.

"What exists for us in Crete?" I asked, attempting to be pleasant.

Telamon shifted, biting his lip.

"A place to dock and rest awhile, assuming we can get past the island's guardian, Talos. From there, it should be a straight course to Iolcus."

He stared out at the sea, and for a moment I felt as though I was interrupting him, and not the other way around.

"I have an aunt in Crete. Queen Pasiphae, my father's elder sister. And she has children—my cousins, I suppose," I remembered after a moment of awkwardness.

Immediately after the words had escaped me, I wished that I could take them back. Shards of conversations resurfaced in my memories, those whispers and rumors from my childhood that were so horrible that even my mother, master storyteller that she was, refused to speak of them. Most of what I knew of my extended family, I had found out from the servants, who were more indiscriminate about their prattle.

The worst stories concerned my youngest boy cousin on Crete, a child called Asterion. His name meant "Starry One," which might have been beautiful if not for the circumstances of his birth, which most of the Aegean seemed to know in lurid detail.

My aunt's husband was the King Minos, a much beloved son of Zeus. When the Sea God, Poseidon, sent a snow-white bull to Crete as a symbol of divine favor, the expectation was that Minos would promptly sacrifice the beast, as proof of his devotion. But Minos was overcome with greed, and so he determined to keep the creature for himself. Poseidon, not one to be outdone, placed a curse upon the queen, making her fall madly in love with the bull. And so it was that Asterion was conceived, part man and part animal.

The story went that the subsequent birth nearly tore Pasiphae apart. And that after the child was born, it had an insatiable taste for human flesh.

The world would come to know my cousin as the Minotaur, or "the Bull of Minos," an ironic translation that no doubt humiliated my uncle to no small end.

"Oh yes, I've heard about them." Telamon let out a heavy sigh, still not looking at me.

I swallowed hard. "I suppose it does not surprise you that I am related by blood to a monster."

"There are monsters everywhere." Telamon shrugged. "Some have the heads of animals, and others wear human faces." I let his words linger in the warm air around us.

"Why are you being so kind to me?" I managed at last. "Surely you think me unnatural. You've seen me hack my own kin into pieces."

Telamon froze, his expression stony and impenetrable.

"You would prefer it if I ostracized you?"

I shook my head, staring at him keenly, so that he knew I had no intention of letting the subject drop. For a moment, he seemed to chew his tongue, as though wrestling with his next words.

"You're not the only kin-slayer aboard the *Argo*," he offered, finally turning to face me. "The difference is that some of us did not bother to bring our brothers back."

My mouth went dry as the full weight of his words washed over me. His eyes were remote and inaccessible.

"What?" I questioned, disbelieving.

"Mine was called Phocus, and he was young and glorious and beautiful—our father's favorite. I was stupid with envy."

"You killed him?" I whispered tentatively.

"I threw my father's discus directly at his perfect little skull and crushed it into a thousand pieces."

I could not think of a response that would suffice, no matter how much I tried, and so I gave him nothing.

"You don't have to say anything," Telamon continued, as though reading my mind. "I am accustomed to silence. It's the worst when I'm all alone in the nighttime. But I thought my loss might assuage your conscience. There are worse crimes than the ones you have committed. If members of our crew resent you, it is simply because you are a woman, an intelligent one at that, and they expect women to be softer, and more nurturing. But in the end, there is not one among us who is innocent."

I nodded, my throat tight.

"I'm sorry," I uttered at last, face flushed with color. "I know what it is to land the killing blow."

The older man nodded, shrugging again.

"Prepare yourself for Crete, princess. We may well need your help when we arrive onshore. I'm sure Jason will explain," he expounded brusquely. It was as though the entire conversation had never occurred. I nodded mutely, heart thundering as I watched the sailor stride off heavily down the deck.

■ ■ ■

"Did Telamon tell you about Talos yet?" Jason asked, his breath hot upon my neck. His fingers, hot and firm, had found their way beneath my tunic and settled upon the soft skin of my waist. It was one of the first times we were completely alone below deck since the marriage had been consummated. My breath hitched and I fought to keep my voice level.

"Not really. He only mentioned that he was the guardian of Crete. Are you going to tell me the rest perhaps?"

Jason paused, as though he had not heard my words. "You're so stiff with me, Medea," he murmured at last into my hair, his front pressing into my back, his hands running wherever he wished.

"Am I?" I inquired coyly, glad that he could not see my face.

"Yes, you are. Even when there's no one else around to see us. And it's driving me mad," he continued, his voice rough. "I can't stop thinking about that day on the island. About how lucky it was to be bonded to you—to be so briefly intertwined with you, even though you are the most mysterious, independent creature I have ever encountered. It frightens me to think I might never know you fully or possess the brutal extent of your mind."

I blushed as his hands continued their ministrations. For a moment I was overcome with the memories and sensations we had shared together under the dense jungle foliage, just the two of us. My heart fluttered annoyingly in my chest, and I worked hard to maintain a clear head.

I was surprised by the breathless quality of his voice, the shaking of his fingers. It was strange, his desperation for me. I wondered for the first time if perhaps he had been struck by Aphrodite's arrow as well.

"I lie awake at night just thinking of you," he admitted suddenly, his voice quiet and reverent.

I was too stunned to speak. He went on, his cheeks suffused with color.

"And when sleep finally comes for me, I dream about the lushness of your tangled hair, green as springtime itself, or else your eyes, softer than fog and keener than steel—your neat ankles, the whole willowy elegance of you. In these dreams I can't tell if I want to crush you in my palms or kiss you until I waste away." He shook his head in wonder.

I shifted, leaning in to his arms, allowing my eyes to flicker shut. Around us came the sounds of footsteps on the deck above, the creaking of the ship upon the sea. As much as I tried, I could not feel at peace pressed against him, there in the darkness, and so I opened my eyes again. Desire pulsed, hot and certain in the shadows, and I was unsure what to do with it.

"Tell me about Talos," I requested at last, hoping that a new topic of conversation would distract us both.

A flicker of disappointment appeared in Jason's gaze, but he quickly stifled it and cleared his throat. I turned to peer up at him.

"No one, so far as I can ascertain, is entirely certain about his origins. He has traversed the shores of Crete for as long as I can remember, warding off any enemy ships that might attempt to run ashore."

"And how exactly does he do that?" I pushed, licking my lips.

"He possesses a superhuman strength. Some sailors who have miraculously survived their encounters with him have reported that he appears to be rendered out of bronze, or some other metal—perhaps he could be some cruel invention of Hephaestus. No one has ever been able to get close enough to know for sure. In any case, he can lift boulders the size of a house and lob them into the sea with fearful accuracy. He's sent hundreds of fine men to their watery deaths. It is believed that he cannot be killed."

"A man made of bronze?" I repeated, attempting to imagine what such a creation might look like and failing miserably.

Jason nodded, his expression tight with worry.

"And there's no way to avoid passing by Crete?"

"Unfortunately not." From overhead came the muffled sounds of sailors shouting.

"So what exactly is our plan?" I bridged at last.

When his eyes met mine, his look was so coldly ambitious that for a moment I felt unbalanced.

"I am hoping that perhaps you might be able to aid us. Such a monstrosity should not be free to wander the isle, inspiring terror in every passerby. Surely you can agree with that?"

I shrugged, torn. "It sounds as though he predates all of us. Perhaps we should simply let him be."

A look of contempt and irritation washed across Jason's face. I trembled at the thought that I had been the cause of his sudden, apparent unhappiness.

"So you'd have me abandon my quest, my birthright, as though it were nothing, just so some giant can continue in his native savagery?" he suggested darkly, venom dripping from every word. His hands tightened uncomfortably around my wrists, and I swallowed hard. The comparison was unsaid but obvious: one barbarian recognizes another.

It was impossible to ignore the inadequacy that washed over me then, the sense of a prophecy being fulfilled. After all, Aeetes had always warned me of this. *What king would want a savage bride?*

"That's not what I meant," I uttered under my breath, but Jason's grip did not loosen. He leaned in.

"Are you going to aid us, or have I perhaps made a grave mistake in trusting you, Medea?" he whispered in my ear, so mournfully that I shivered.

"I shall see what I can do," I managed at last, feeling hollow. The animosity evacuated Jason's face with such speed that I thought I might have imagined it had been there at all. He released me, and placed a soft kiss upon my brow, so tender that my head began to spin.

"I'm sorry." He shook his head violently, as though to drive the residual anger from it, "I'm sorry. I don't know what came over me. I've not been myself for some time now—I have not been the man I want to be. You have helped me enough already, and yet I pressure you still for more. It is not what you deserve." He looked so penitent that a portion of the anxiety in me eased.

The way he caved in on himself then, the remorseful curve of his shoulders—they bid me to take him in my arms.

"No, I understand," I mumbled into his tunic, breathing in the smell of him: the desperate stench of sweat and seawater, and underneath it all, blood.

And it was true—I did understand. There was a darkness native to both of us, a terrible grasping void that swallowed all it encountered. And part of me was thankful someone else in the whole sprawling universe was capable of being just as latently brutal as I could be—

someone I might be entirely true to and candid with because there would be no need for judgment. He and I were the same, in a cruel, perverted fashion.

"How can you understand?" he rasped in my ear.

"Because you and I are made of the same shadows, crafted from identical alchemical absence. You know me, in all my unsavoriness, and I know you. And we stand together anyway."

His grip tightened around me.

"We are more than our darkness, Medea. You are a witch, and I am a king—an ineffable combination. Together we can bring a new brightness to the world. What is holding you back, even now, from acknowledging the power at your core, from fleeing your native prison? Kolchis is far behind us."

I shrugged.

"You are more confident than I am, perhaps." I chewed the inside of my cheeks. "I've seen what ambition does to men—my father chief among them—and I have no interest in replicating that depravity." For a moment, his eyes flickered with understanding. A rush surged through me then, at the prospect of being known like this, by an outsider.

"I am not Aeetes, and neither are you," he returned simply. I nodded, feeling small and awed and far away.

He took a step backward, a grin splitting across his expression.

"I've told the men to provide you with whatever assistance you might require. We should come into range of the giant sometime after dark," he rattled off, turning his back on me to return above deck. In a moment, he was gone.

As soon as I was alone again, I reached for the nearest bucket and retched violently into it. Bile, hot and acidic, wound its way up my throat and through my sinuses. There had been a terrifying moment where Jason resembled my father. I did not have the energy to consider what this meant. Perhaps the dynamic between Aeetes and me was doomed to play out again and again, for as long as I was alive. Or perhaps all men were simply doomed to harbor something hard and malicious inside of them.

I shook my head to dislodge any stray thoughts. This was not the time to be overcome by sentiment. There would not be many hours left to deal with Talos, and so I would have to begin at once.

■   ■   ■

Telamon personally brought the materials I had requested to where I crouched at the helm of the ship, just as twilight stole softly across the horizon.

Beneath my feet were a few thin cotton blankets, enough to keep me warm while I slept. Phaethon was positioned at my side, his face a mask.

"A dagger cast in bronze for the princess. It belongs to Peleus, and he's rather protective of his weapons, so be careful with it," Telamon warned, his smile dry.

I nodded, clutching the warm metal in my palms, as he also proffered the incense, oils, and sleep draft I had asked him to retrieve from my stores.

"This isn't a sound idea," came Phaethon's voice in my ear, soft but persistent. "You're playing with a magic that predates us by centuries, maybe millennia."

"I know. That's why I'm not going in person."

"Dreams can be dangerous too, Medea."

I tried not to let the truth in his words frighten me. Didn't he understand that I had no choice? That our very position on the *Argo* was precarious? One wrong move, and Jason could leave us empty-handed at the nearest port.

"Have a little faith, brother," I reassured, attempting to sound slightly more confident than I felt. "Besides, I have you to keep an eye on my material body. At the first sign of trouble, you can simply rouse me."

"We don't know what Talos is capable of. What if I don't wake you quickly enough?" His look turned perturbed.

"I trust you, utterly," I replied firmly, pressing my hand to his chest and feeling the outlines of scars there.

"I left my home for you," he pushed. "If you die, or worse, what was the point?" The worry in his words threatened the facade of tranquility I was attempting to evoke.

"Pass me the sleeping draft now, Phaethon. And remember the incantations," I hummed, as though I could not hear him. For a moment, I wondered if he might refuse. His countenance had taken on a stormy disposition. But at last, he picked up the bottle and passed it into my outstretched hands.

"What did you even put in there?" he asked in an undertone, although there was no need. The other men were giving us a wide berth, as though somehow my witchcraft might be contagious.

"The usual—valerian root and essence of chamomile," I rattled off as I took the first sip. Phaethon pursed his lips as I chugged what remained in the bottle.

My understanding of sleep magic was limited to what little I had ascertained from poring over Aeetes's scrolls during the brief period I was allowed in his confidence. Though I experimented with dreaming occasionally, mostly to stave off nightmares on Kolchis, transforming chaotic terrors into curated night escapades, what I planned now was a good deal more complicated.

The liquid went down easily enough, and so I reclined back against the deck, pulling the blankets up around my neck to ward off the cold ocean breeze.

Overhead, the stars seemed to blur. My limbs tingled with a strange numbness, and I let out a pleased, little groan.

"Where do you want the dagger?" my brother asked faintly, as though from a great distance.

"On my chest," I slurred, enjoying the pleasant sense of weightlessness overcoming me. As Phaethon began to chant, I relaxed into the sweet sound of his voice. His words ran into one another, and after a while I could not make them out.

As I drifted off, I attempted to meditate on the way that the warmth from the bronze permeated through the rough cloth. The blade shuddered with each beat of my heart.

CHAPTER TWENTY

The Last of the Brazen Men

Iwoke surrounded by sand and seawater. Overhead, the moon was a sliver, darting in and out of the clouds. For a long, uncomfortable moment, I felt disoriented, unable to place where or when I was. These shores looked nothing like the beaches of Kolchis.

Panic rose in my throat—an electric kind of fear that abated somewhat as sensation returned to my limbs.

Gradually, I registered the feeling of something heavy clasped in my hands: the dagger from the ship. I let out a little moan as I remembered why I was here and forced myself into a sitting position.

Talos.

The night air was heavy with cold, and my head pounded as I dripped upon the edge of the surf. The horizon was awash in stars. It might have been beautiful if the excursion were marginally less dangerous. I rose unsteadily to my feet, chills breaking out across my skin.

The beach seemed to be deserted. Jagged cliffs sprung up from the sand, and kelp tangled upon stray stones, but the only sounds were the gentle crash of the waves and the whistle of the wind. Could I have dreamed myself onto the wrong island?

I glanced uncertainly out to sea, wondering for the first time how I was going to return to the ship. I would not wake naturally for some time—the sleeping draft would make sure of that, and Phaethon would have no reason to rouse me.

A voice called out from behind.

"What are you?" I didn't expect this voice to belong to a giant, for it was soft and smooth and sweet as nectar.

I jerked around, heart hammering, expecting the flicker of bronze. But I was still alone on the shore, with the cliffs encircling me.

"Who's there?" I called tentatively, my throat constricting.

No response came, and I struggled to keep my emotions in check.

"What are you?" came the voice again, from the direction of the crags, and I froze.

I squinted. The darkness of the stones could conceal all manner of predators in the dark. I searched frantically for the shape or outline of something resembling a man, and finding nothing, realized I needed to stall.

"I am Medea," I said back, voice low. "A mortal, daughter of the Oceanid Idyia and King Aeetes of Kolchis, niece of the enchantress Circe."

"*Enchantress* seems a clever euphemism for *witch*."

I opened my mouth to speak and shut it again.

"You are also a witch, are you not?" he pressed.

I shivered. "Yes, I am. How did you guess?"

A low chuckle reverberated from the stones.

"I did not hear you approach. Indeed, I might not have even sensed you if the night had not been a silent and placid one. Humans find it very difficult to slip past me, no matter how lithe or nimble they might believe themselves to be. Therefore, you must not be an ordinary human."

I nodded, tightening slightly as the breeze picked up. "I transported myself to the island of Crete through dream magic. It's rather uncomplicated really, but very few people can do it," I provided, lips loose.

"So, you're not really here."

"Well, I am but I'm not. My material body is elsewhere, although I can still be wounded here, with you." I could not fathom why I felt the need to reveal this vulnerability to a creature indistinguishable from the shadows. But my tongue seemed to have a mind of its own. In dreams, I knew, reflexes were slower and misgivings less urgent. And this was something of a perilous, lucid dream.

"What exactly does the visiting witch desire?" The voice was sardonic.

"To talk." I returned to the night air. Somehow, I knew that this was the only answer I could give. The dagger seared white-hot against the skin of my palm as I gripped it behind my back, and I ignored it. Diplomacy was preferable to outright violence.

A face emerged from among the boulders, a face so beautiful that my breath caught in my throat. His eyes were queer and mercurial, like liquid silver constantly altering its own shape. And his face, despite being the same eroded pallor of the stones, shone brightly, as though lit from within. A second later the head was followed by shoulders, thick and muscular and shining; a torso as coarse as the cliffs themselves; and two thick trunks that might have been legs. Before long, the whole of the creature's body was free of the cliff. Despite his overwhelming size, the giant moved gracefully upon the earth, like a dancer might. If we stood next to each other, I would have to crane my neck upward to look into his face.

I wanted to cower at the sight of him—although whether it was his beauty or the raw power contained in his person, I could not say. But Phaethon had been right; there was an ancient magic at work here I could not begin to comprehend.

"Talos." The name was ripped from me and carried away by the breeze.

The giant nodded. One massive bronze hand reached tentatively into the distance between us, and I flinched. The fingers retreated almost immediately.

"You are young to be a witch," he said at last, his eyes tranquil.

"And you are very old," I retorted automatically, immediately horrified by my reckless words. Talos could strike me dead upon the beach, but he simply tilted his head back and laughed.

"I am," he acknowledged, eyes glinting merrily in the faint moonlight. "Almost as old as this island itself."

"How did you come to be here?" I asked curiously, momentarily ignoring the purpose of my excursion.

"You haven't heard the rumors, traveler? That I was wrought by the Great Craftsman himself, that God of the forges, Hephaestus? That I was meant to be an automaton fit for those on high? That eventually I was gifted to King Minos to keep his land free from nefarious interlopers?" Something in his tone was scornful. I realized with a thrill that he was testing me.

But I was never easily deterred. I drew back my shoulders. "I do not deal in rumors," I replied. "Where did you really come from?"

For a moment, the giant appeared pleased but then he frowned, the corners of his mouth drawn down in disappointment.

"In truth, I hardly remember myself," he admitted slowly, moving to sit on the sand a few yards away from me. His weight made the ground tremble. I considered what it would be like to have no clear origin. Perhaps it was a kind of blessing, to have no tie to the past besides that which existed, written indelibly upon the body.

"You must recall something," I insisted, my anxiety fading away by the second. "After all, there's a reason you guard these shores, is there not?"

"I guard this island because it is what I have always done," he said softly. "Once there were more of us, but now it is only me. We sprang, fully fledged, from the Ash Trees across Crete—incarnations of the soil itself. I cannot cast my mind backward beyond when we all took human form; reality began for me as a collective consciousness—an army of Brazen Men. An army reduced now to one. I imagine you understand that in your own way." His eyes flicked down to meet mine. I was caught in the shifting silver of his eyes.

"What do you mean?"

"You know what it is to be alone, unmoored, with only yourself for company. That was why I did not smash your body into particles the second I found you on the beach. I recognized you."

"I'm not alone. I have a brother." I knew I sounded agitated. For some reason, it did not occur to me to evoke Jason, though he was my husband, or the twins taking shape inside of me, though they would be my children. Only Phaethon seemed to count in this strange in-between place.

Talos regarded me softly, his eyes only slightly duller than the moon overhead.

"I do not see him beside you now, little witch." He shrugged, face as impassive as ever.

"He did not want me to come here," I admitted, coloring slightly. "He said it was dangerous. But he's waiting for me with my material body."

"He was right. This is no place for a mortal on her own."

I was growing annoyed now. My skin, drying from the seawater, itched, and my fingers were slightly numb with cold.

"I am not just some mortal girl," I shot back. "I am more powerful than he is. I do what no one else is willing to do."

"Perhaps there is a reason no one else will do those things, little witch."

I scowled.

"Offer me an alternative," I challenged. "To what I have had to become to survive. To sustain those around me." Despair, cold and thick, lodged itself in my gut. I was inevitably myself—the result of so many lonely hours on Kolchis, tearing into animals and avoiding prophecies. If I was fated to be isolated by my own power and lack of magical inhibitions, so be it.

"I cannot. I fear we exist in different categories of experience. The urge toward survival or annihilation, which is so vital in you, is secondary to me. While you attempt desperately to maintain yourself, I simply am. Since I cannot perish in the manner of your kind, I cannot pass judgment on the exigencies of your situation. The mortal condition is such that you are all divorced from your divinity and imagine yourself finite. I am under no such illusions."

I turned the word *annihilation* over and over in my head like a compulsion.

"So, what would you have me do with my loneliness?" I asked, hardly registering the words, and the admission they encompassed. That he was right stung—but I did feel lonely and doomed and vacuous.

"There will always be the black-lit halls of Hades," Talos mused, not unkindly. "There is company and solace to be found among ghosts, or so I am told."

I felt myself deflate under his gaze.

"What are you suggesting?" I asked, listless.

"Only that at least you know with certainty where you are headed in the end, and that such knowledge brings peace."

"So, I should take comfort in the fact that one day I will be dead and buried?"

"Something like that." He smiled without humor. "There is a special kind of agony that comes with immortality."

I paused, looking into his weathered, well-sculpted face.

"And you cannot die." It was more of a statement than a question.

Talos shook his head, gesturing toward his ankle, which glowed with a strange, molten light.

"It seems very unlikely," he permitted dryly. "Given that it has not happened yet."

"But you could be killed? Oblivion is possible?" I could not be sure why I was pushing him. All I registered was a slow, swelling rage inside me.

"In my body flows golden ichor, the blood of the Gods. As long as it circulates through me, I shall remain here, as I am," he explained.

I watched the warm, yellow light shimmer and reflect along his calf, winding up through his thigh and toward his heart. I was so caught in that meandering brightness that I hardly noticed the change in my companion's expression, or the stiffness that came over him as we sat together under the sharp curving moon.

The giant's liquid eyes were glued to the horizon, and as I followed the line of his vision my heart sank. For it was the sails of the *Argo* that were waiting there, billowing beneath the stars.

"Talos," I warned, my voice urgent as his massive hands automatically began to search out boulders along the sand. "That is the ship where my body lies."

The last of the Brazen Men turned to appraise me, his face a mask of disappointment.

"It is too close to these shores," he murmured. "What good is a guardian who lets intruders in?"

I shut my eyes, feeling the wind graze my cheeks as horror coursed through me. The ship had appeared too soon. If I had a few more moments undisturbed with the giant, perhaps I might have been able to talk him out of his suspicion. After all, the Argonauts would do him no harm. We were only meant to be passing through.

"Please," I tried. "If you sink it—" I broke off, unable to continue.

"If I sink it, you will die," he finished for me. He truly sounded regretful. "But you must understand that I cannot allow any bark to land here, no matter how disarming her inhabitants."

Jason's threats from that morning echoed in my head with dizzying clarity.

Are you going to aid us, or have I perhaps made a grave mistake in trusting you, Medea?

In my hand the bronze dagger seemed to pulse with latent energy. It would be easy—too easy—to make a lunge for the creature's leg and hack at the artery flowing through its ankle.

I took a step forward upon unstable feet. And then another.

Are you going to aid us, or have I perhaps made a grave mistake in trusting you, Medea?

The giant was only a yard or so from me now. I moved again, clumsy like a child, as Talos palmed stones the size of a small dwelling.

I lifted the blade high above my head, resisting the urge to be sick.

Are you going to aid us, or have I perhaps made a grave mistake in trusting you, Medea?

How many millennia had Talos stood here, guarding the island? Who was I to remove him from his native soil?

The dagger gleamed menacingly in the moonlight, and for a moment I was struck still, paralyzed.

I shivered, poised to strike. That was all that Talos required, and as his uncanny eyes fell upon me, they flashed with pity. A witch was no match for him.

He moved easily out of range, but I brought the blade down in a perilous arc nonetheless, accepting as I did so that it would be useless.

Perhaps Jason had made a mistake. And Phaethon. Everyone who had ever made the error of loving me.

The moon curved ruthlessly overhead. The giant took a steadying step backward.

I knew then that I must act. I shut my eyes and began to whisper low, desperate incantations. Though I was versed in Necromancy and planetary herbalism, never had I attempted to goad the earth itself beneath me into action. That ancient magic I had long assumed was my father's alone. I cried out to the stones along the water's edge, the cliffs that rose sharply overhead. I sang to the particles of sand and the fragmented shells beneath my feet. The air wavered with energy, and the ground buckled jerkily along the coast.

I watched blearily as his strange body moved, his foot catching upon a stone that seemed to erupt from nowhere only a few paces away. The carnage was brief and immediate.

The vein along his calf split open, and molten ichor spewed out from the wound. A scream rose in my throat.

In a second, the tremendous length of him had come crashing down to the surf, the whole island quaking as he fell. His blood covered everything, seeping into the ocean in a thousand violent hues.

"Talos," I gasped, taking a step forward and then collapsing to my knees. The giant groaned into the sand and then lay still.

"Talos," I whispered again, for surely, he could not be dead—not like this. My magic was such that I did not even need to raise a hand to my defense. Words were enough. The vein had torn, because I had begged the rocks themselves to inflict the damage that they could—to betray a creature as ancient as themselves.

Talos never would have fallen if I had not appeared beside him tonight on the beach. He might have gone on traversing the shores for another thousand years.

The dagger fell limply from my hand, and with it my vision dissolved.

■   ■   ■

I came to, shivering in Phaethon's arms. Around us, the other sailors watched with wide, unnerved eyes.

"What happened? Are you all right? You're not hurt? We could hear the thing collapse from all these leagues away—it created such impossible waves," he declared frantically in my ear.

He brushed the hair back from my face, his fingers sweaty and trembling. I could not speak, so I only nodded.

"No broken bones?" Phaethon continued, his hands searching beneath the blankets for any obvious wounds.

I shook my head. Beside us, the bronze dagger fell to the deck of the ship with a sickening thud.

"I think I killed him," I whispered, tears leaking unbidden from my eyes. "I didn't mean to. He was going for the boulders, and I couldn't figure out how to stop him. It was like I made the earth itself move." I choked on my own tongue as I explained.

Around us the various crew members began to part.

"Give her to me," came Jason's voice, taut with excitement. "She is my bride."

Phaethon's grip tightened. "It's okay," I muttered, and only then did he release me and stagger back, allowing Jason to take his place.

"Oh Gods, Medea," he exhaled into my hair, pulling me against him. He shook as he clutched me, wracked by silent sobs.

"Why are you crying?" I murmured so only he could hear.

"I thought that perhaps I'd sent you to your death. The second you went under I was sure I would never hold you properly again. And then you took so long returning. You might have died for me."

I couldn't return the force of his embrace. I should have been pleased that Jason had been worried, for that meant he cared, didn't it? But I could not focus on the implications of that sentiment. Just as I could not unsee the torrents of flaming blood and the exsanguinated giant who towered over me just minutes before.

Revulsion, unexpected and unwelcome, rose like a tide, and I shut my eyes against it.

"I love you," he said as I floated indifferent in a haze of pain. "I love you. I love you."

I wished he would stop.

CHAPTER TWENTY-ONE

The Daughters of Pelias

It took us another month to reach the shores of Iolcus, by which time the slightest hint of a bump was forming along my middle. I knew that Jason would find out eventually, and so I spent my days avoiding him, pretending to fuss over Phaethon. I could not bear to look at my husband in the sunlight, and so I kept my eyes on the damp wood of the deck or else the rolling mist of the clouds.

In the evenings, when Jason would lead me to the cabin we shared, the only solitary sleeping space on the whole boat, we existed together in the dark. Somehow, in the shadows, the strange loathing toward him after the death of Talos melted away. He did not bother to light candles before he took me up desperately in his arms. It might have been hours that we lay together in the darkness of the hold, simply clutching each other with mad intensity.

"I'm frightened, Medea," he would admit as I ran my fingers through his hair, or across the scarred skin of his chest.

"As am I," I would return quietly. He would clutch me against him then, with pleasant urgency. There was something comforting about being needed by him, to ward off the worst of his nightmares or re-assure him that his journeying served a purpose. And for my part, I craved him with a desperation I had never experienced before.

Occasionally, even when the sun was out, I would watch him from the corner of my eye, fixating on the broad span of his shoulders, the sharp line of his jaw. And when I could take it no longer, I tossed my dark hair over one shoulder, regarding him through hooded eyes. He would freeze in whatever he was doing, usually talking to one of the Argonauts, and his eyes would appraise me hungrily. As though taking no notice, I would rise to my feet, then disappear into the hold. He would follow. All there was to do at that point was wait.

In a matter of minutes, he would slink below deck, locking the door behind him, and his mouth would swallow my sounds as we moved, intertwined.

It was one such afternoon, when Jason lay beside me, his chest warm under my hand, that the call was sounded from above: land had been spotted at last. Quickly we dressed, and I smoothed my hair so that it fell in elegant cascades down my shoulders. Jason stared at me for a long moment, as though debating whether to join his crew, or stay with me forever. His eyes were hollow, sinking things.

"You need to address them," I whispered, moving forward to place a hand on his arm. "They have come all this way with you, some of them losing companions in the process, so that you might return to these very shores victorious, once again a king of your rightful land. Show them how much you appreciate them."

But Jason merely stared at me, shaking his head.

"I appreciate *you,* Medea," he murmured, looking at me with an intensity that made me uncomfortable.

"There's something you should know." I paused, weighing my words carefully.

"What?" The alarm in his face was almost comical.

"In a matter of months you will be a father," I admitted in a rush, bringing his hand to rest on the almost imperceptible swell of my stomach.

He looked dumbfounded for a moment, and then his face was split wide with glee. I had never known him to look so happy and untroubled. The smile that appeared transformed the entirety of his face, making him look years younger.

"A child?"

"Two, if the resident oracle is to be believed."

"Two," Jason repeated, apparently overcome.

"You are claiming this land, your rightful land, not only for yourself and for me, but also for the heirs that are growing between the two of us," I murmured simply, regarding him closely, to be sure he understood. "There is no room for failure or error, do you understand?"

He swallowed hard, but nodded, gripping me tightly as I spoke.

"I do."

"Then get above deck and prepare the Argonauts to dock. I have a feeling that Pelias, contrary to what he may have said previously, will not be eager to part with a kingdom, fleece or not."

■ ■ ■

Running ashore at Iolcus was a somber affair. It was as though the entire city held its breath, ready for some spark to set off a conflagration. The Argonauts regarded the dry land suspiciously, as though it was contaminated by the king who presided over it, which in a way, I suppose it was.

It was only once I had disembarked from the *Argo* that I realized how wrong land felt underfoot. A frenetic energy had been winding its way through my body since I had staggered on board this ship—a madness or mania that seeped in through the salty sea air and ran rampant inside my heart. I could not seem to discern who or what I was anymore. A murderess and a mother, a Necromancer and a kin-slayer. The incoherence of it all echoed cruelly about my skull. Perhaps Talos had been right and all there was to look forward to, in the end, was Hades.

A sudden, sharp movement in my abdomen nearly made me lose my balance. The sensation was more startling than painful, somehow foreign and familiar at once.

Phaethon was at my side in an instant.

"What is it?" he whispered, alarmed.

"Nothing. Just one of the babies kicking, I imagine." I breathed, horrified at this evidence of life swirling inside of me.

A little smile darted across his face, and I looked away. Now was not the time for mirth.

I steadied myself in the earth, breathing deeply, hoping to absorb some sense of the strange land we were about to enter. Around us, the hills sloped pleasantly, awash with the verdant green of sprawling vegetation. Wind rustled through the branches of olive trees. The sand and stones along the beach gave way to sweet-smelling shrubbery as the altitude rose. The place itself might have seemed cheerier than Kolchis, if only our mission here was not nearly so dire.

King Pelias sent his emissaries to escort us to the palace directly from the dock. Lookouts positioned around the city's shore had recognized the *Argo*'s sails and raised the alarm. There would be no time to prepare, to consider our strategy. My skin tingled uneasily under the hot summer sun and the luxurious blue sky. It was beautiful out, but oppressively warm, the kind of weather that lent itself to irritation and hostility. Despite the sun, Jason was moving about the streets with the fleece draped over his shoulders, a symbol, I knew, of his accomplishment. I tried to imagine how Pelias might receive his nephew, but I knew in my heart that it would not be a sweet and cathartic homecoming.

As we walked the stone streets, past flowing fountains, and handsome, well-maintained temples, I realized this was Jason's native land, the place that called out to him through all of his travels—his home—the initial site of his pain and the seat of his duty. And perhaps not too long from now, Iolcus would also belong to our children, if Pelias honored his word.

I was familiar with the mythology of Pelias, and knew that his history was a dark and winding one. His mother, Tyro, was already married with three grown sons when Poseidon himself took her to bed underneath the sea. A God's seed is potent, and so nine months later came the twins Neleus and Pelias. After the birth, Sidero, Tyro's stepmother, drove her adopted daughter to the edge of madness. Tyro was so distraught that she left her children out upon a mountaintop to die of exposure. The Gods, taking pity on the infants, sent a herdsman out upon the crags to find them. He raised them as his own until they were old enough to go in search of their true parentage. Once they found Tyro, they learned of Sidero's brutality, and made up their minds to kill her. Pelias pursued the desperate woman to Hera's temple, which should have been a sanctuary. Despite the laws against bloodshed in a sacred place, Pelias slaughtered her upon Hera's alter, thus incurring the wrath of the Goddess herself.

But Pelias's trail of ruthlessness did not end there. The young son of the Sea God turned on his own brothers, exiling even Neleus. Aeson, the king of Iolcus and Pelias's own half brother, attempted to stand up to him but found his own powers lacking. After a short period of imprisonment, Jason's father was murdered, and Jason exiled. The usurper, now assured of his reign, went on to have many children of his own.

As we entered the throne room, Jason stiffened. I followed the line of his gaze to where an aging man sat, hunched slightly at the shoulders in the center of a grand, gold-plated dais.

"Uncle," he called coldly, his face contorting as he took the knee. The other Argonauts followed suit. I said nothing and bowed to no one. The hairs on the back of my neck stood on end. There was nothing about this king that reminded me of Aeetes—where my father had been sharp-eyed and cunning, his face usually blank until the last possible moment, Pelias was soft and languid. His eyes were green, and deceptively gentle. He had something of the sea about him.

"Beloved nephew," Pelias called, gesturing for Jason to rise. "How long has it been since you left these shores on your wild journey, abandoning us here on Iolcus for the glories of the open ocean?" I shivered. This felt like some elaborate trap.

"Long enough," Jason returned, dislodging the fleece from his shoulders and displaying it for his uncle to see with a flourish. "And I have returned with the fleece." His eyes burned with rage, an impossible fire that made me uneasy, when contrasted with Pelias's amenable charm.

"I can see that." Pelias's eyes glistened with what might have been merriment if the situation was any different.

"Having done all that you requested, I am here to claim the throne that should be rightfully mine. I have fulfilled my end of the bargain, partaking in a perilous quest, and now it is time for you to fulfill yours." Jason squared his shoulders as Pelias shifted on his throne. The old king gave a soft chuckle, glancing at his fingernails, as though they were incredibly interesting.

"Oh, Jason. You're so much like your father. Always quick to act, and slow to think. If I recall, we had a very different conversation before you set out upon your little trip."

"Oh?" Jason questioned, his voice barbed and dangerous. The room crackled with electricity, but Pelias seemed immune to it.

"Yes, I think you must have misunderstood me. I should not be surprised at all by your confusion. After all, you're still a young man, eager to earn your share of glory. But I never *promised* you the throne. The idea itself is laughable, I'm afraid. You are still far too young and inexperienced to rule this land, nephew, and I'm sure, on some level, you must know that yourself." Under his armor, Jason's muscles flexed, his jaw tense. I placed a careful hand on his arm to steady him.

Pelias resumed his speech, as though unaware of his nephew's rage. "I am, however, deeply honored by your tribute to this land, and can assure you the fleece will be kept somewhere safe. Before you return to your travels, of which I'm sure there will be many, you are welcome to stay a night here with us. We shall hold a banquet in your honor, and my daughters, the Peliades, shall attend to you themselves. It is the least we can do to thank you for your brave and selfless service to this land that your father once ruled, the same land I now preside over in his noble place."

The old king raised his eyebrows, and gestured for one of his pages to retrieve the fleece from Jason. But the younger man was taut with anger, and he gripped the pelt securely. The rigid set of his shoulders, all power and restraint, did little to hide the hurt coursing through him. The impotence of his situation filled me with a surge of white-hot rage.

"Do not be foolish, Jason," Pelias murmured in an undertone. "I have waited a long time for the fleece. It is said to have all manner of healing powers, and I am an old man. Come now, obey your uncle and ease his pain." A sickly smile slipped over the king's haggard, wrinkled face.

When Jason made no move to relinquish the fleece, Pelias's eyes flickered and his voice dropped to a low whisper.

"At least little Promachus had the decency and good breeding to know when his time was up. He was a better nephew all around—

drained his cup of bull's blood obediently and died as bravely as he could beside your mother." The king's eyes twinkled, ripe with good humor. A weight had appeared in the pit of my stomach.

The snarl that issued from Jason's lips was ferocious.

Who was Promachus? I looked swiftly to Jason for some explanation, but he was overcome with wrath, his logical faculties unreachable.

"You have no right to speak of my brother, fiend," Jason shouted, his face an unattractive shade of maroon.

"Shall we talk of Alcimede, then?" he mused, chuckling. "Your mother, at least, was a beauty, all charm and loveliness. It was obvious why Aeson adored her. Such a pity that she killed herself as well. Devastating, even." He paused, letting the words hang in the air.

"She would never have taken her own life if you had not forced her hand, murderer," my husband retorted. Jason seemed to be struggling for breath, his knuckles white upon the golden wool of the fleece. Pelias continued in his speech casually, as though he could not sense the rage emanating off the other man. I knew somewhere in the back of my mind that Jason was moments from snapping. If he took up arms against Pelias here, outright, we would be hurled from the gates.

"Unfortunate really, that the cravenly brother who abandoned his family to die is the one who would seek to prop himself now upon their throne. There is no accounting for justice." As he delivered this last line, his eyes sharp and disdainful, he looked so much like Aeetes that I felt the urge to retch. The unrelenting madness inside of me had reached a fever pitch. I could barely feel my body as I slipped free of the Argonauts and approached the throne.

Gods help me, I thought over the roaring in my ears. The room swum, the air thick and unreal.

I stepped forward, bowing my head, as though in submission. "King Pelias, if it pleases you, Jason will hand over the fleece immediately. But you should know that it does not have the powers of which you speak." I was careful to keep my eyes upon my slippers. From beside me, Jason stiffened, but he made no move to interfere.

"And who is this?" Pelias asked, his voice tinged with the first notes of irritation.

"I am Medea, princess of Kolchis, daughter of Aeetes, and niece to the witch Circe. I myself am skilled in the magical arts, which is why Jason has brought me to your shores, in the hope that I might help." I fought to keep my voice pleasant and demure. Pelias paused, but as soon as he spoke, I could tell I had caught his interest.

"And why does my nephew associate with a witch? Does he seek to curse me, an old man and his only kin for miles?"

I shook my head. "If it pleases the king, I can explain everything. But you must send your men away. What I wish to offer you is access to a new and secret art. One that I guard most closely. If it suits you, the two of us might speak alone." I held my breath, and after a long moment, the king acquiesced. A collective inhale stole across the room, and murmurings began.

My legs had taken on the quality of jelly, and I fought to remain standing. Pelias gestured for his guards to disperse. Jason and Phaethon shot me twin glances filled with alarm as they were led from the throne room.

"Come before me and speak, then, witch." The king watched me approach with his odd, languid eyes.

I raised my head and regarded him carefully, hoping that I looked innocent and compelling, as his men filed out of the doors.

"I am the pride of a magical family," I began once we were alone together. "My father, the sorcerer Aeetes, taught me everything from love potions to poisons, healing balms to herbs that induce hallucinations. Jason explained, upon his arrival in my land, that his uncle, the great king of Iolcus, was ailing. My father, eager to improve relations with Thessaly, sent me with the offer to rejuvenate you if you would be so willing." The story was tenuous, I knew, but I continued. "In return, of course, he would require a form of payment, but we can discuss that later."

The old king's eyes narrowed, and for the first time he looked truly dangerous. "Why would I trust a witch with my health, especially one in the company of my traitorous nephew? Do you know how he has tried to rob me of my seat since he came of age? Has he told you that?"

I nodded and answered somberly, "I understand your concerns, which is why I have brought along proof of my powers."

"Proof?" he sneered, though he had leaned forward. He was curious. I pressed my advantage.

"Might my brother, Phaethon, join us?" I asked quietly, attempting to appear as shy and helpless as possible.

"Your brother?"

"Yes, my lord."

Pelias nodded, tersely, obviously impatient.

"Summon him, if you must," he allowed. I darted from the room, heart pounding. There would be no time to brief my brother, but he was smart enough to follow my lead.

Once he had joined us, Phaethon caught my eye, and carefully arranged his face into a mask as he stepped forward.

"This is my brother, the crown prince of Kolchis. A few months ago, he was dead, chopped up into dozens of pieces." The omissions from my story were almost comical, but I did my best to ignore them. Pelias's face remained indifferent, betraying nothing, and so I continued.

"The Argonauts, those brave men who helped steer Jason back to these shores with your fleece in hand, those men whose honor is impeccable, will vouch for this. They saw him, minced up like a meat pie. In the span of a night, I reassembled him, and brought him back to life stronger than he had been, with the use of my expertise and witchery. And I can do the same now for you, in exchange for favorable trade relations with my home." I was careful not to reveal my true connection with Jason.

I pointed to the pale scars that crisscrossed Phaethon's skin, the only signs of where he had been split apart under my blade. "He is as strong—stronger even—as the day he was born. I have herbs that when mixed with the blood, can render an old man, such as yourself, youthful and vital once more. Your aches and pains, the impossible annoyances of age, will be a distant memory, and you shall be able to rule this land for a hundred years." I broke off, breathing hard, unsure if the man would be grasping enough to fall for my deception.

"You brought this boy back from the dead?" Pelias voiced slowly.

"I did. And believe me when I say that this is one of my lesser powers." He leaned back tentatively in his throne, his arms crossed.

"How, exactly, would you make me young once more?" he finally articulated slowly, his eyes still suspicious. I smiled, knowing then that he was as much of a fool as any man.

"I will require the aid of your daughters, and the use of one of your royal bath chambers," I listed easily. "The transformation, to be effective, must be instigated by a family member who shares your blood and loves you completely. That is the only way it will work." This, at least, was the truth, and why for all of the agony I carried now, I had needed to be the one to murder Phaethon.

"Fine," Pelias conceded at last, to my immense surprise.

"So, you agree?" I asked before I could stop myself.

A sly smile slipped across the old king's lips as he glanced between Phaethon and me.

"Of course. So long as you can provide me with a demonstration first. Your brother is a pretty prop, but I will want to see the process in exact detail. Perhaps you might do it on an animal first, to prove to me that you are gifted in the way you claim."

I let out a little exhale, relieved. An exhibition of my Necromancy would be easy enough to arrange. I had done it a hundred times over, in Kolchis.

"As you wish, my lord. Have your soldiers provide me with a cauldron and some sort of creature—any sort—and I will show you what I can do."

■   ■   ■

In the end, Pelias settled upon a ram so elderly and stooped that his hooves dragged upon the flagstones. Despite his obvious age, the animal's horns were glorious, curved in perfect symmetry with one another. It would be pleasing work to restore such a creature to his youth, I thought to myself. It was impossible not to think of the golden ram of my childhood, Khrysomallos. Something in the tranquil, steadfastness of his gaze struck me as the same, and I wondered if perhaps the ram had been reborn.

"Hold him down, so that he's facing away from me." I gestured to Phaethon, who had taken up the role of magician's assistant. It was only the three of us and the quivering ram together in the throne room, because I could not take the chance that one of the guards might discuss my powers. Word could easily spread to Aeetes that Phaethon was alive and well, and that was a risk I could not justify taking.

Beside us, a large bronze cauldron bubbled ominously in the center of the floor, already stocked with precious herbs to ease the transformation. I could smell the acidic, earthy pungency of the concoction inside; it was not a pleasant aroma, but it had a certain potency that rendered it captivating.

Phaethon's hands shook as he gripped the ram's horns, and with a pang of shame, I realized just how much I was requiring of him. Not so long ago, I had been poised over him with a twin blade, ready to deliver the killing blow.

"Are you all right, brother?" I asked in an undertone, attempting to stifle the distress in my tone.

He nodded easily enough, but I noticed that his jaw was clenched, his breathing uneven. I would need to be quick, to spare him worse anguish.

Without another word, I slung my blade down across the animal's throat, letting loose a wave of red and the unbearable smell of fresh blood. Phaethon gagged slightly but held tightly to the creature as it shuddered in his arms.

He shook as we hoisted the ram over our shoulders and carried it toward the cauldron.

"Steady," I reminded him softly, hoping he could keep himself together until the display was concluded. He grunted in answer.

A moment later, the carcass was slipping into the boiling water with a sobering hiss. The flesh was drenched in a matter of seconds, blood mixing with the hazy potion of my own devising. I swallowed the bile that rose in my throat and began the incantations.

The minutes trickled by, and I spoke in a ceaseless chant. Beside me, Phaethon stood stiff and resolute, more statue than human. The weight of Pelias's eyes was almost overwhelming, even with my back to him. Still, the entire procedure was far easier than my work on Phaethon had been. The ram's body was not nearly as damaged, for one, and for another, I was more used to working on animal subjects.

And then, quite suddenly, the horns reared from the water, splattering droplets across the walls. A head appeared, steaming from the liquid, and my breath caught in my throat. Where the ram's eyes had previously been white and clouded with cataracts, now they were yellow and gleaming like molten gold. The fur, damp as though from afterbirth, was glossy and new, a thousand shades of radiant chestnut. Phaethon jerked backward slightly, gripping my arm.

The ram, eager to test out its newly rejuvenated limbs, sprung easily from the cauldron, then landed somewhat clumsily upon the flagstones. It shook itself, drops of potion landing across my hands and robes.

Despite his new strength, the animal seemed fragile somehow, vulnerable like a newborn.

Without thinking, I began to walk toward the creature, to make certain that he was all right. But the ram, as though sensing what I was, took a stumbling step away and let out a strange bleating cry. Its eyes flashed with an emotion beyond fear, and I halted in my steps.

Behind me, Pelias was clapping in a slow, measured rhythm.

"We shall dine handsomely tonight," Pelias said, his voice overflowing with condescension, contempt, and thinly veiled curiosity. "My chefs will butcher and prepare this very animal. And then this evening, when the time is right, I shall gather my daughters in such a place, and you will make me young again."

I closed my eyes. That the ram would not live, after everything else we had witnessed, should hardly have stricken me the way it did. But all I could imagine were those keen, golden eyes, renewed after so many years. And all for what?

I would take a special joy, I knew, in what was to come.

With a flick of his hand, the old king dismissed us from the throne room, and as we exited, Jason was suddenly at my side.

"Medea, what are you doing?"

"Retrieving your throne, and ensuring our family is safe, Jason, since you are not in a position to do it yourself. Do you take issue with that?" I glanced up into his face, annoyed by the fear that I found there.

"What is it?" I pushed. "Do you want your children to grow up as exiles, or kings?"

Jason swallowed hard, his voice shaking as at last he spoke. "Do what you need to do."

"Good." I nodded, intertwining my fingers through his for a fleeting moment before I pulled myself away. "Your uncle will be dead by sunrise."

■ ■ ■

After a tense dinner, Pelias assembled his ten daughters in the bath chamber. I regarded them closely as they filed in, one by one, in a parade of silks and seams. All of them were beautiful, with bronze skin and dark charcoal-colored hair that cascaded down their backs in waves. Their eyes had the same nautical quality that their father's did, but their eyelashes were thick and full, and their lips sultry. The oldest looked to be about Jason's age, and the youngest was a child of maybe twelve. She was the last to enter, and she shot me a furtive, curious glance as she came to stand beside her sisters.

I gestured for Pelias to take a seat in the marble tub in the center of the chamber, which was already filled with steaming water, and perfumed with rose oil. Perhaps it was the humidity, or perhaps the ragged fear inside me, but I felt as though my vision was strangely affected, at once misty and devastatingly queer. I had only ever felt like this while in the presence of Aeetes, and I wondered suddenly if he, by some strange magic, had found a way to be here in the room with me. I could not breathe properly.

"Tell me, your grace, which of your daughters you favor above all the rest," I declared shakily as he cast off the robes from his body. Naked, he looked even more frail and pathetic than before. His hunch was more pronounced, and his ribs stood out, pronounced against his liver-spotted skin. His beard quivered with cold.

The wrongness of the scene was undeniable. I wondered for the first time what exactly I was doing, perched shakily upon the tiles. It seemed that the entire evening was a strange fever dream, and that I had only just woken up to find myself here, poised on the edge of some unspeakable dread.

"I do not have a favorite," he asserted. "I love them all equally. They

are my joy." He gave the youngest a soft smile as he spoke, and she returned it sweetly. I nodded, waiting for him to lower himself into the
floral-scented water.

"In that case, they shall take turns," I explained, drawing a long
carving knife from the folds of my cloak. Pelias's eyes narrowed, and
he stiffened in the water, so that it rippled about his precarious frame.

"Come now, your grace," I soothed, allowing a hint of irritation to
enter my voice. "You saw my brother's scars. Surely you understood that
this was part of the ritual. Each of your daughters will cut you open,
so that you bleed into the water. Once you have been drained nearly to
the point of death, I shall circulate this blood with herbs, and say the
necessary binding incantations. Once the blood is replaced, and you are
healed, you will be a man reborn. Unless, of course, it frightens you." I
goaded him with a placid smile that he did not return.

"Fine, then," he muttered. "Get on with it."

I gestured for the eldest of the Peliades to step forward. She paused,
her face uncertain and ragged with worry.

"Alcestis," Pelias demanded from the tub. "Do as she bids you." The
girl swallowed hard, coloring as she moved to stand before me. I handed
her the knife and offered her what I hoped was a reassuring glance.

"Cut him here," I whispered, drawing a line with my finger down
the length of my left inner arm to demonstrate. She shuddered, shutting her eyes tight. For a moment, I wondered if she might refuse, but
then she opened her eyes again, suddenly resolute.

She knelt skillfully beside the tub, looking down at her father with
warmth before gently raising his arm up to the light, and slicing it open.
Pelias cried in pain, and for a moment I wondered if he might slap her,
but instead he merely squeezed her hand.

I watched the sudden redness make delicate tendrils in the water
and was momentarily transported back to the shores of Crete. The
vermillion lifeblood of the king was a far cry from the golden ichor of
the giant, but the feelings it inspired were the same.

Surely it was not too late to stop this.

I hesitated, and in the ensuing silence the girls tittered nervously,
shifting in their silks.

A sudden jolt in my stomach, the soft kick of infant feet, as solid and real as anything, brought me back to myself. I would be a mother in a matter of months, and my children would require the security of a kingdom. We would never be out of harm's way so long as Pelias was alive.

I gestured for the next girl to take her sister's place.

"Hurry, Pelopia," one of the middle girls chided, pushing her sister forward. "Let's get this over with. It's terribly morbid."

One by one the daughters of Pelias delivered their lacerations until the man sat nearly unresponsive in the bath, the water dyed a terrible shade of crimson.

With each gash, something broke and eased inside me. An impossible mania had been kindled with the first sign of blood, and there was no way to quench it. Meanwhile, the distinctive features of Pelias's face had begun to blur, and in flashes it was my own father, bleeding out inside the bath, and not the king of Iolcus. They were of a similar age, and their voices carried the same ruthless cruelty I had grown to despise. A violence to one was a violence to both in my fragmented mind. I hardly knew where or when I was.

Soon, there was only the last child. Tears slid silently down her cheeks as she watched her sisters take their turns beside their father. She began to shudder.

"Come now, little one," I purred, offering her the knife, but she shook her head, burying her face in her hands.

"You must do this if you want your father to wake up. Be a good girl and take the knife," I hummed quietly, moving to stroke her face. She jerked away from me, her eyes wild with terror.

"Why are you always such trouble?" one of the older girls accused, glowering and bloodstained. "You're wasting time." In another moment, the older girl crossed the room and took the knife from my hand. She moved snakelike to her sister's side, pulling the younger girl up by the wrist, and forcing the blade into her hands as the child shrieked and writhed. Forcing the child to stand beside the bath, the elder sister guided the knife down across Pelias's throat.

The child screamed as a shower of blood splattered across her face.

"There, it's done. You make a fuss of nothing," the elder girl spat. I watched as she let the girl go, and the child fell hard upon her knees, sobbing.

"Thank you, princesses," I broke in, my heart thundering in my chest. "That was the last part of the process that I will require your assistance for, so you are all free to go. I shall return the king to you in the morning." The girls filed out, all save for the youngest, who did not seem to be able to raise herself off the floor.

I knelt beside her as the door closed with a delicate click.

"You made us kill him," she sobbed into her hands. Her dark hair was matted with tears and blood, and her face was flushed from crying. I might have lied to her, but denying her a truth she already knew seemed like an unnecessary cruelty.

"I did," I replied simply, watching her in her grief.

"You're not really going to bring him back," she accused, her voice shaking. "You were never going to, were you?" Her eyes bored into my own, the weight of her childish fury pronounced. In that moment, I looked at her and saw myself, as I had been at her age. The resulting pain of that recognition was sharp and trenchant.

"You at least are smarter than the rest of your sisters," I tried, reaching out to tuck a long dark strand of hair behind her ear. She shied away from my touch and began to retch upon the floor. The unpleasant aroma of vomit joined the sharp scent of copper.

When she was done heaving, she turned once more to look at me.

"It doesn't matter, you know. The boy Jason will never be king. Not now that he has helped kill my father by means of such vile trickery." With a strange lightness in my chest, I realized there was some truth to this. I thought back to the fear on Jason's face as I presented myself to his uncle.

Had this been what he was worried about—that his new bride would alienate him from his subjects forever? I shivered.

"I'm so sorry," I whispered at last, unsure what exactly had possessed me to speak. Even if Pelias deserved to die, this child had earned no part in it. "You alone refused to betray your father. You had to be forced to cut him. This is something to pride yourself in going forward," I rambled.

The girl shook her head, and made the symbol of the claw striking outward from her chest. I knew that this was a gesture to drive off evil, and that the evil was I.

The door clicked open, and Jason appeared in the doorway, his face alarmed. When he saw the body in the tub, his mouth opened and closed in horror.

"Medea, what have you done?" he cried, slipping to his knees. "Bring him back. I thought you meant to weaken him." His eyes roved my face desperately, and I felt the white-hot tug of annoyance. Regardless of what Jason said, he had known full well what I had intended. I had told him, after all. In the corner, the girl child pulled herself up against the wall, staring at the both of us with hatred and fear.

"I cannot bring him back," I said. This was the truth, I had none of the usual herbs that I would need for such a resurrection, having spent them on the ram. By the time I procured them, it would be too late.

At this, the child let out a long, mournful cry, more animal than human. She sounded uncannily like the ram Phaethon and I had slaughtered just a few hours earlier.

My husband paced the floor, his eyes wild and unrecognizable.

"Be silent," he barked at the child, his face a mask of animosity. But the youngest daughter of Pelias could not halt her despair.

"Be silent," he screamed again, a vein bulging grotesquely in his neck.

Before I could register what was happening, Jason drew his sword and charged at her, bringing the blade down across her throat. For a moment the three of us balanced frozen in our separate roles, before she fell heavily to the floor.

I watched her bleed out, her own life mixing with the vermillion stains of her father's. Jason breathed hard. I could not speak; I could hardly dare to breathe. Her body twitched for a moment, then she lay still. The quiet that stretched out in the aftermath was unbearable.

So this was the man I had married.

The man whose children I sheltered within myself, protected and molded with my own body. Nausea overtook me. The entire scene lacked reality. The air around us swirled and blackened with nightmarish surreality.

"What—?" I managed at last, heart thudding dully in my chest as I regarded the girl's lifeless eyes. I could not bring myself to look at Jason.

"I'm not— I didn't mean to— I just— She was making too much noise. Would have sounded the alarm. We have to get out of this place now," my husband retorted, although his eyes looked uncertain. His hands were unsteady, and his face was more frazzled than I had ever seen it, as though he could not quite comprehend his actions. His murder.

What madness had taken hold of us both tonight?

Jason moved toward the door, poised helplessly upon the threshold, as though paralyzed.

"She did nothing to you," I croaked, struggling to keep the room from spinning. Jason had just murdered a child, a girl barely old enough to marry. Entirely innocent.

The confusion in his face turned suddenly to rage. "And Pelias did nothing to you, if I recall. Neither, as a matter of fact, did your beloved brother, but you did not hesitate to cut him into chunks." His voice acquired an edge—a cold, calculating dimension that reminded me of my father's. But that could not be—for I had left my father on Kolchis, and then killed him just now in the bath. The night air shimmered, stars floating across my vision. It occurred to me, as I shivered upon the marble floor, that I had never considered what might transpire after Pelias had been banished to Hades. The critical thing had been to get him out of the way, to clear a path for Jason's ascension. But now the old king was dead, and we were still exiles. Jason would be blamed for the murder, even though I had been so careful to ensure he was absent from the scene. I resisted the urge to retch.

"Get up, we need to get back to the ship." His cruelty struck me to the bone, rendered him unrecognizable. I slipped heavily to my feet, damp with blood and bathwater.

The heavy fall of footsteps echoed from down the corridor as Jason pushed me through the bath chamber door and into the night.

CHAPTER TWENTY-TWO

Morning Sickness

The tumbling of the *Argo* upon the sea did little to help with the upheaval already at work inside of me. I could not stand to be in Jason's company in the days after we fled Iolcus, and yet simultaneously, his physical nearness was the only balm, the only serenity I could find in the aftermath. When I thought of him, the tangled curls that slipped along the steep edge of his forehead, the cunning mirth of his eyes, the image was enough to make me retch. In the same moment, I would long to be beside him, only satiated by the familiar scent of his skin, the crooked length of his smile. A sense of him was everywhere upon the ship, and elsewhere too. I saw traces of his passion in the flow of the ocean current, his mystery in the dense overlay of the morning fog. And escape was impossible now, with Jason's children growing and taking form within my womb. He invaded me in ways I had not known I could be invaded.

In the pale light of so many stagnant afternoons, the unwanted flicker of a thought seared through me. If only I had loved him a little less, had given less of myself over for him to hold and know. Perhaps then, his haunting would not be so potent, so permeating. But perhaps that was all love was in the end, a mutual haunting.

"What happened with Pelias?" Phaethon had asked me when we were alone early the next morning, taking watch and enduring the unforgiving heat while the Argonauts were busy with their tasks.

I shook my head.

"You can tell me. I would never love you less," he insisted, expression blazing.

"I know," I returned quietly, a shell of myself. "But it is not your love I fear losing. I trust that you will always be beside me."

"Who, then? Jason? You imagine that he will not forgive you?"

How could I explain that the events in Iolcus had stripped me of everything I had known to be true about myself? That I no longer loved, or even much liked, the creature I was becoming? I could not be sure who or what I was anymore, with so much blood spilled in my wake.

"Please, sister? You have to talk about this. Otherwise, you shall never feel any better about what transpired."

"Perhaps I do not deserve to feel better, Phaethon."

"Nonsense," he said. "You've experienced a terrifying ordeal, and healing from violence of that magnitude takes time. But you will heal, Medea."

"I sometimes feel as though I'm standing on the precipice of some immense void. A kind of madness. I worry I might go over the edge. That all the time I'm moving nearer and nearer to it, and that when I do fall, I'll take everyone who matters with me," I supplied carefully, my words flat.

"You won't fall over the edge, sister. And you mustn't believe so, even for a minute."

"How do you know?" I pressed, my voice sounding small and childlike. I thought for the thousandth time of the youngest daughter of Pelias, the mask of terror on her face as she bled out on the bathroom floor. I would be forever recalling her face.

My brother pulled me into his arms. "Because I shall make sure of it," he promised into my hair. In that moment, I could almost believe he was right.

■ ■ ■

If the rest of the crew resented me for their hasty expulsion from Iolcus, they had the good sense to keep it to themselves. Perhaps they, like my brother, did not initially understand the specifics around Jason's sudden necessity to flee.

When Phaethon was indisposed, I found myself drawn to Telamon. The weathered lines of his face and the stoniness with which he carried himself could not disguise the kindness in his expression, in the movement of his hands. I could not imagine him using those fingers to carry out the brutal and violent deed he had told me of, no matter how much I tried. There was no use attempting to reconcile the stoic quality of his soul now with the bleak history he left behind. In those weeks after Pelias, he was simply Telamon, my friend.

For the most part, I simply observed him silently as he worked, fastening knots, or working the oars. Between us, there was no need for idle chatter. The tranquil silence that extended out from him provided a kind of peace that I could not find elsewhere on the *Argo*.

One evening, as the stars began to appear overhead through the clouds, I voiced something that had troubled me ever since the disaster on Iolcus.

"My children," I began, uncertain how to proceed.

He nodded mutely, watching me from behind his cool gray eyes.

"They are going to be born at sea, aren't they?"

He dipped his head once more, his countenance impassive.

I sighed, picking at the corners of my fingernails.

"They will have no solid place to call home," I hinted at last. "No kingdom, and no place to land."

Telamon considered me thoughtfully for a time, before shrugging.

"Leto, much beloved mother of divinities, gave birth to the twins Apollo and Artemis balanced upon the bough of an olive tree," he mused raising his eyebrows. "If bark is enough for the glorious children of Zeus, I imagine it will be hospitable to your brood as well." He tapped the deck of the *Argo* with his foot as he spoke, the smallest hint of a smile evident upon his crooked mouth.

A sweet euphoria came over me then, only for a moment, as I gazed at the man across from me.

"Your children will have the *Argo*, and more importantly, they will have an entire crew at their disposal, my lady," Telamon reminded me, his eyes glinting softly in the moonlight.

CHAPTER TWENTY-THREE

Of Stones and Seashells

The twins arrived in the heat of summer, when the *Argo* was caught in the middle of the Black Sea. They resembled their father in all ways, but one: their eyes were blue like his, but sharp and hawkish like mine. Their hair was soft and golden, and their skin had the quality of warm dough before it was baked in the hearth, impossibly smooth and sweet-smelling. Despite my initial misgivings about motherhood, I had no such doubts about the two of them.

I had been plagued by worry in the final months leading up to the birth, afraid that my body would somehow reject the twins before they were born. Less obvious was my anxiety about being a mother in the event the infants did survive. What if they loathed me immediately, shying away from my touch? Or worse yet, what if I managed to hurt them somehow when they were so small and vulnerable and frail? But the labor was an easy one, thanks to Phaethon, who used his own knowledge of sorcery to ease them into the world as gently as one could possibly expect to begin existence, in the rocking below deck of a narrow ship. And it was he, not Jason, who took them in his arms and held them against his chest before handing them over to me.

"What shall we name them?" I whispered into the humid air of the hold, exhausted and worn out from pushing.

"I've always liked Eriopis for a girl," Phaethon suggested, looking embarrassed. I smiled despite myself. Eriopis meant "she with the lovely hair." The idea of naming my daughter something so light and carefree felt almost decadent.

"She does have beautiful hair like her aunt Chalciope," I agreed. The little girl's curls were a shimmering strawberry blond, and the elegant lines of her profile ensnared me immediately. He smiled at me softly, and we both nodded.

"We must assume that they will have an easier life than ours. Now you name the boy." He indicated the smaller of the two children in my arms.

I glanced down at him, at his pouting magenta lips and soft, damp curls. He radiated light, for all of his smallness.

"Pheres," I murmured. "That's his name. I've just decided it." As if to show he had heard me, the child opened his mouth in a tremendous yawn. I was caught in the perfection of that miniature face, so transfixed that I hardly had a moment to worry about prophecy. A part of me feared that I might experience visions like my own mother had, the kind that would torture and devastate our family for another generation.

But my brother's delight pulled me from my mind's abyss. "There we have it, then." Phaethon smiled, offering his finger to the girl child. "Eriopis and Pheres, the fairest babies born at sea in some time, I'd imagine." He grinned at me, and despite my secret misgivings, I felt myself grinning back.

■   ■   ■

The first weeks with the children were complicated by the bizarre sensations of abject grief that tore through me from time to time, without warning. Who or what I was grieving, I could not say. It seemed, now, that there were simply too many dead to count. But still, any discontent felt wrong, given the wonders I had only lately given birth to. Guiltily, I ignored the searing fire under my skin, the ice that trickled through my veins, and I did my best to be a good mother.

The only member of the *Argo* who seemed to understand was Orpheus. Whenever I clutched the children tightly to my breast, breathing hard, driven mad by their wailing, he would materialize silently, arms outstretched.

"Let me hold one. Perhaps the girl?" he suggested kindly one evening. Although in the beginning I might have resisted, these days I knew better. Relinquishing Eriopis with a swift kiss, I watched as he cradled her close to his heart, humming delicate melodies that instantly put her at ease. In a matter of seconds, the wailing ceased, replaced by endearing coos and gasps.

His singing released something in me as well, although I could not ever think to name it consciously. Where once I had found the notes that tumbled from him unnerving and slightly terrifying, I now looked forward to them, craved them as much as men craved power.

"How will I manage without you when we dock?" I asked him one evening. The night was calm, and the babies slept soundlessly in our arms.

"By then you will be strong enough to sing to them yourself," he replied simply, flashing me that queer smile of his.

"Not like you," I argued, and it was true. No living creature could sing as he did.

"No, not like me." He shrugged. "I imagine you will sing exactly like yourself. As you are meant to. And your babies will love you for it."

In my arms Pheres woke up. He began tugging stubbornly at his own hair and then crying sharply at the pain. He had not yet realized the complexities of his new body. I giggled, despite myself.

"Music is what comes after the worst is done. It is the thing that heals," Orpheus confided softly.

It occurred to me, as Orpheus resumed his melody, that the crew of the *Argo* had become family in the short span of time we had sailed together. Some of the agony inside me lifted, replaced instead with a burgeoning hope.

■　■　■

Jason was different after Iolcus. Perhaps it had to do with guilt, at having lost his father's throne once again. Or perhaps it had to do with me, his witch of a wife. As we neared Korinth, he spent more time above deck with his crew. He no longer wasted the evenings away with me. Although he claimed our children as his, he did it with a kind of reserve that unnerved me. He would hold them only as long as they were still and sweet. The moment one began to cry, he would promptly return him or her to my arms and depart once more.

For my own part, I was glad to see less of him. Some evenings I would wake in a cold sweat, awoken from dreams of the little girl, the youngest of the Peliades, as all the blood in her small body emptied itself out upon the marble floor. Or else I would dream of the quality of his ice-blue eyes directly after the killing, when they were cold and unfeeling. What kind of man, my heart shuddered, could kill a child so easily, and then move forward like it was nothing—as though it was somehow justified by his own frustrations?

One evening, I cornered Jason below deck, after the children were asleep.

"What if we are only bound together by our own propensities for evil? We both have spilled our fair share of blood. That leaves its mark somewhere. And love—real love—cannot be built on such darkness," I began, biting my lip.

He ignored me, moving to catalog supplies in the darkness of the hold.

"I can't stop thinking about it," I told him, trying not to sound desperate. "She was only a child. Now that we have a daughter of our own, surely you—"

"The darkness comes from you, Medea. None of it would have been necessary if you hadn't made such a mess of things with Pelias. His blood is on your hands, as is that little girl's."

I shook my head. "No, that isn't so. She did not have to die."

"I do not have to listen to a kin-slaying witch discuss ethics with me," he growled, and I took a step back as though struck. His brutal words fell like heavy blows, and I was not prepared to stave them off.

"You know I am not a kin-slayer," I shot back, attempting to reassert some degree of reality over the proceedings, but Jason let out a short, caustic laugh.

"But no one else does, do they, my love? Your father imagines that you chopped the young Phaethon into pieces, and the Argonauts will swear that you did as well. It may be true that you brought him back, but as you said yourself, your legacy will never be cleansed, not truly. You will go through this life a traitor and a murderess, and you are lucky to have one with a character such as mine, lofty and noble, to support you in all of your depravity. And if for one moment you forget yourself—and decide that you are anything but lucky—I can say whatever I wish about you, and the great men of this world will listen." He broke off, breathing hard.

Every part of me turned cold and afraid. "Not so long ago you told me that you feared never truly knowing me. But I think now that it is you who is unknowable," I managed to say.

My husband shrugged, his face a mask.

"I am glad you will never be king," I admitted, my words so quiet that I doubted Jason could hear them.

In another second, his hands were around my neck, squeezing the air from my lungs. I coughed, clawing at his knuckles as my vision began to cloud. Just as quickly as his hands had encircled my neck, they drew themselves back. He retreated, slamming the door to the hold behind him, leaving me in darkness. I shuddered, limp and ragged upon the ground, sick to my stomach.

Underfoot, the deck creaked with the push and pull of the waves. Even then, life was still peaceful, in a way.

■ ■ ■

Within an hour of having docked at Korinth, Jason absconded to meet the king of the city, hoping to make him amenable to our cause. What exactly that cause was, I could not say, but I was glad to feel solid earth once again under my feet.

The children had spent their babyhood upon the deck of a ship, and so their plump, toddler legs were unused to the steadiness of the ground. They stumbled across the beach, enamored with the texture and consistency of sand, surprised to find that a whole world existed outside of the open ocean. As Phaethon skipped stones for the amusement of Eriopis, I helped Pheres collect fragments of shells, and shards of pottery so polished by the waves that they had lost their sharpness. He cooed at the treasures we piled up together, gripping them carefully in his meaty palms. And so for a few days, we were happy, spending hours upon the beach, returning to the *Argo* only in the evenings to eat and sleep. The skies were clear, and the air sweet with the scent of wildflowers.

Somehow, here in Korinth, Kolchis and its horrors seemed very far away. I found that I could speak freely of what had transpired on our travels at sea, or of Aeetes and his abuses.

"You seem renewed," Phaethon suggested on that first day as we reclined on the hot sand. "Did you take some potion or brew?"

"No, not at all," I fired back, more relaxed than I had felt in a long time.

Turning to Eriopis, I pointed to the crashing waves.

"Idyia," I pronounced slowly for her. "That is where your grand-mother dwells." The girl child giggled, watching the surf animatedly. "One day you shall meet her." I kissed into her soft red-blond curls.

Phaethon smiled lightly but said nothing. Beside him, Pheres traced the outlines of my brother's scars with childlike precision.

■ ■ ■

When people asked about Phaethon—who he was or why he had such a peculiar appearance—I simply explained that he was foreign, a tutor hired to look after the children once they were old enough to begin their education. In a way this was true—I intended for me and Phae-thon to teach the twins together, so that they might be sorcerers in the same manner that we were. The street vendors of Korinth were warm, engaging people, who offered the children samples from their stalls free of charge, and pinched at their cheeks. I imagined, for the first time, the possibility of beginning a life here, of settling and creating a safe home.

Other villagers crowded excitedly about the *Argo*, jostling to get closer to the heroes they had long heard stories about. Eriopis and Pheres drew delighted exclamations from other visiting Korinthian mothers, while I only watched, content to be invisible.

"Did you really travel past the Sirens?" a little boy with wide dark eyes asked Telamon, who seemed uncomfortable with all the attention.

"Aye." He glowered sharply.

"Was it terribly frightening?" the boy pressed, vibrating with excitement. "Were they hauntingly beautiful?"

"Go ask him about it, boy. He's the one who kept them at bay." Telamon shrugged, gesturing to Orpheus, who was besieged by his own new Korinthian acquaintances.

"Him?" The child gasped. "But he's not nearly as big as you!"

I stifled a laugh.

The city seemed to receive us with open arms.

Old women were quick to draw me into hugs when we first met, their wrinkled faces splitting in hospitable smiles that eased my suspicious heart. The village children took turns vying to hold the twins, and even Phaethon found himself drawn into long conversations with fishermen by the docks, who wished to hear about how he had acquired his scars. That they left those conversations disappointed with my brother's vagueness hardly mattered.

The natives of Korinth did not know me for what I was. To them I seemed like just another dutiful wife and doting mother. Perhaps I had a strange gravity about me, or a shrewdness, but this could be forgotten with the remarkable Argonauts beside me or one of the twins pulling at the hem of my dress.

When at last Jason returned after nearly a week, he seemed a new man. Time with the royal family of Korinth had done him well. His skin was sweet-smelling and tan, his muscles thick and strong, his hair as luscious as I had ever seen it.

For a glittering, nostalgic moment, I was thrust backward in time and space to that first instance I had ever glimpsed him, out among the bluffs in Kolchis. A wary fondness infiltrated my unaccustomed heart. Jason, however imperfect he might be, had a certain hold over me, one I could not reasonably disregard.

"Tell me everything." I embraced him, forcing myself to ignore the chills that erupted along my spine as he took me in his familiar arms.

"At first," he explained with less of his usual antagonism, "the king, Kreon, was not particularly excited at the prospect of allowing us refuge, given the bloodshed that seems to follow us. But he allowed me to spend a few evenings under his roof, and I used my time wisely, divulging parts of our story here and there with excellent dramatic timing."

I held my breath, nodding.

"And?"

"And he has finally agreed to extend us protection. We are to stay here in Korinth for as long as we desire." His face split into an easy smile, the first I had seen in some months. His usual sober weariness had all but evaporated.

Some of the tension left me then, and some of the madness too. I found myself grinning back, almost disbelieving.

"So we have a home," I whispered, my fingers covering my mouth.

"We have a home," Jason verified, his eyes soft and warm and apologetic. "A safe place for us and the children to start again, Gods willing." He paused, staring intently at me.

My hands rose involuntarily to my throat, where only weeks before he had gripped tightly and nearly squeezed the life from me. I felt ill, but only slightly, and perhaps it was from latent seasickness.

"I want to make amends," he insisted, "for everything. This is my chance to be an honorable husband to you—and a good father to Eriopis and Pheres. Returning to Iolcus, to the place that held such impossible pain and turmoil for me, nearly drove me out of my mind. But that's not who I am, not really. You know that, don't you?"

A strange dislocation rose in me then, so that I hardly knew which way was up. The air felt thick and suffocating below deck, but I found myself nodding, from outside of my body. When he said it like that, how could I possibly disagree?

CHAPTER TWENTY-FOUR

Humming

In the following weeks, we moved from the *Argo* into a comfortably furnished home on the sea's edge. It was not the palace that Jason might have pictured for himself in his daydreams, the spiral staircases and well-worn corridors of the castle in Iolcus, but it would do. There was a charming room for Phaethon, and a nursery for the children adjacent to my own chamber.

For my part, I never loved a place more. The rooms were pleasantly domed and airy, with plenty of windows to let the light in. The floors were swept clean, and the beds made each morning by a maid we employed from inside the city's center. In the heart of the space was an outdoor courtyard, complete with a fountain fed by one of Korinth's many natural springs and carefully kept herbs. There was room too, along the outside periphery of the house, for me to begin cultivating my own garden. Phaethon and I spent hours bickering happily about which seeds to sow in the space allotted to us.

My heart was less gladdened to take leave of the Argonauts. Telamon, in an unusual display of tenderness, pressed a kiss each to the forehead of the twins at our farewell. Turning away from the others, he embraced me in his veiny, muscled arms, letting loose a sad exclamation in a tongue I could not make sense of.

"I'm so very glad to have met you," I whispered into his shoulder, refusing to let myself cry.

"I feel the same way, princess," he choked out, voice gruff. In another moment, he had disentangled himself and absconded once more below deck.

Orpheus was the last to send me on my way. His eyes, blue and bright, seemed even paler than usual. He accompanied me and my brother to the very edge of the dock, something in his manner distracted.

"Be careful, little one," he murmured, bending low and speaking so softly that only I could hear. I smiled to myself at his eccentricity. He was hardly a man himself, and yet he imagined me young. Perhaps that was some side effect of the prophecy swirling inside him.

"Only if you are as well," I returned. One corner of his red lips curved upward into a slightly disconcerting half smile.

"Goodbye, then," he hummed, swaying on the balls of his feet. He watched us as we made our way into the waiting sand, hardly blinking.

■ ■ ■

In those early days, Jason and I were never far from each other's side. If he took leave of us, it was only early in the mornings, to visit the merchants along the dock, seeking news of the outside world.

"We are strangers to this land," he explained one evening over supper, as though it was not intimately known to me. "That makes us vulnerable. The more friends we have here, the harder it will be to drive us out." I nodded quietly into my soup. Creating allies never seemed to be an issue for Jason. He was naturally charming in a way I could never hope to emulate. Women and men both took to him easily, with wide, appreciative eyes and honeyed tongues. I did not mind it, so long as he was in an amiable mood when he returned home.

"You are far more charismatic than you think," he would maintain when I refused to accompany him, preferring the cool confines of my new home to the bustle outside. "You won me over, didn't you?"

I did not bother to argue with him. I had never spoken of the night along the bluffs with Aphrodite, but I knew enough to suspect that my relationship with Jason, however compelling and personal it might feel, was the result of some larger divine plan. I was alluring to him because I had to be. Because it was ordained.

And yet my heart would beat strangely when his fingers moved to push a strand of hair behind my ear. So striking was his presence to me, that a single meeting of our gazes was like a blade to the chest. I found it difficult to breathe when I thought too deeply about him. When he was away from me, I felt uneven and clumsy, as though missing a part of myself. This was nothing like the steady bond that existed between Phaethon and me, or the endless, expansive peace that sprung up when I considered the children. This was an obsessive, feverish love. The kind of love that drove the sufferer steadily toward some edge or precipice. The kind of love with no bottom in sight. A desperate, harrowing affection that I could not disentangle on an analytical level, or strip from the traitorous muscles of my body. I needed very little in the way of human contact to survive. As long as Jason stood by me, and the children were healthy, and Phaethon was safe from the scavenging eyes of our father, I was content.

"You are so beautiful and clever, Medea. Why not use those attributes to ingratiate yourself here?" he proposed again and again, as I receded more and more into myself.

And to some extent he was right. For all the awkwardness that hung about me in my youth, I now possessed a strange, hard-won beauty. Though I might feel unlovable and reticent by virtue of the things I had done, my strangeness was not overt. Especially now, with a dashing husband by my side, and two attractive children clutching about my skirts. I felt as if I were engaging in some elaborate game of play-pretend, acting as though I were anything but extraordinary for the sake of my new Korinthian audience. But perhaps this was a small price to pay for normalcy.

■ ■ ■

Those happy autumnal months passed with unnerving speed. Phaethon and I tended to our herbs and vines, urging fruits and flowers from them with our usual skill. Eriopis toddled around excitedly after us, her dainty feet leaving soft marks in the obliging earth. Her brother was more reserved, preferring to watch the action from the shade of the porch. From time to time, the children would confer among themselves, passing seed pods and twigs back and forth in some bizarre bartering game neither Phaethon nor I could decipher.

The air steadily grew colder, although winter kept its distance. While our neighbors struggled to grow food in the burgeoning cold, we maintained a steady supply.

In the mornings, before the little ones rose, I liked to sit beside the open window of my bedchamber, letting the air blow across my face. I imagined the wind might have journeyed all the way from the clouded towers of the palace in Kolchis—that it contained the energies of my faraway home.

On one such morning, after Jason had departed in the direction of the docks and as the children still slumbered in the next room, I was couched upon the windowsill, glancing outward at the rocks along the sea. A dryness had descended in the nighttime, and my lips and the skin of my hands were chapped. Despite the city's proximity to the sea, Korinth received very little rainfall. I would need to make a salve for all of us once Phaethon awoke.

A strange humming interrupted the morning quiet, a buzzing, frantic sound. I searched the sky for the source of the noise as rosy-fingered dawn went about her usual ministrations. An insect hurtled close to my face, and I flinched, drawing back. The thing, which was small and dark and quivering, dropped suddenly, twitching upon the sill, and then lay still. I held my breath, taken aback as I shifted to examine it.

Akrída. The locust. Coming upon such a sizable insect was unusual for this time of year, although sometimes I knew of crickets that occasioned parts of the scrubland throughout the Aegean.

Without thinking, I blew lightly upon the creature's limp form, regarding the delicate lines of its exoskeleton. Its wings fluttered, the vast spheres of its eyes reflecting me, glassy and wide.

"Where did you come from, little one?" I murmured. The thing merely twitched, as though in pain.

"You're dying," I acknowledged. A terrible droning had started up once more in my ears, though there were no other bugs around to blame. The sound intensified, and I shut my eyes against it, gritting my teeth.

Stop. Stop. Stop, I commanded myself, annoyed.

When I could take it no longer, I forced my eyes open once more. The locust shuddered upon the sill, still in the process of ceasing.

Unable to stop myself, I brought the flat expanse of my palm down upon its body.

The humming ceased with a dull crunch.

CHAPTER TWENTY-FIVE

On Scarcity

Jason was spending longer periods away from home, sometimes being gone from sunrise to dusk, appearing only after I had cleared dinner away for the evening. When he was away, the roar would intensify in my ears with impossible fervor. I investigated every nook and corner of the house, searching for locusts that might be lurking, but found none. The chaos of it was rooted in my own psyche, I knew, but I had no idea how to stop it.

And so I waited, tight and anxious, for Jason to come back to me in the nighttime. I was convinced that he alone could undo some of the tension in my limbs, the tangles of intrusive thoughts in my mind.

"I'm sorry I've been so distracted," he would whisper, pressing a kiss to my forehead when he returned, his voice soft and careless.

Or else, "Some of the men and I went drinking and I lost track of time telling them the old stories." And his eyes would glint excitedly with wine and recollection. In those instances, I had no desire to corrupt his mood.

One evening, he appeared on the threshold, face unnaturally sober.

"There are rumors of famines in the surrounding areas. *Akrída* appearing from nowhere to blight the crops," he explained slowly. "With winter on the horizon, and no rain to speak of, the land seems poised on the edge of peril."

I shuddered, unnerved by the prospect. The idea that vegetation might not be readily available, for food or *Pharmakon*, was enough to instill in me a sense of dread.

For what was a witch without her magic?

"I noticed a locust the other day," I confessed automatically, before attempting to block the memory out.

Jason raised his eyebrows at me.

"If there are not enough resources, we'll have to move on again. Go in search of some more hospitable place." He swallowed hard, a muscle working in his jaw. My stomach dropped.

I could not fathom setting off again on some ship, for however long it took to find shelter. Life was just beginning to make sense here, to settle into a comfortable rhythm of sweet domesticity—and with that sense of roots came a peace I had never known before.

"I don't want to leave," I elucidated, aware of the whine in my voice.

Jason's eyes narrowed slightly, and he let out a caustic laugh.

"Obviously, princess." He scowled, his temper now foul.

So taken aback was I by my husband's unhappiness that I did not hear Phaethon approach through the doorway leading out into the courtyard.

"What is this about leaving?" he asked, eyes deceptively serene.

Jason bristled at Phaethon's interruption. My husband and my brother had never been entirely comfortable with each other.

"I'm going out again," he growled, not bothering to look at me as he stormed out of the house.

The cherrywood door slammed behind him, sending tremors through the walls. For a moment, Phaethon and I froze, waiting to see if the children would wake.

"Our resident hero seems to be in a good mood," Phaethon observed at last, his lip curling.

"Don't," I retorted, my eyes swimming with tears. I could not seem to find a balance with Jason, no matter how much I tried. His moods were volatile and shifting. At the first sign of inconvenience, he turned on me.

"I'm sorry, Medea," my brother breathed, moving to put a steadying hand on my shoulder. "I shouldn't jest."

"We may have to depart from Korinth," I explained dully, through the fog in my head. "Jason thinks there will be a famine."

Phaethon nodded, his face placid as ever.

"You don't seem surprised," I pushed, biting my lip.

"In the market, the cost of produce has been increasing steadily. There is less to choose from. I might have attributed it to the coming winter, if not for—" He broke off abruptly, swallowing.

"What?" Dread ignited in my stomach at his caginess.

"It's nothing, sister," Phaethon lied, shifting on the balls of his feet, not meeting my eyes.

"Do not deceive me," I threatened. Nothing felt real, and I realized I was somehow outside of my body—a dissociation that was becoming more and more prevalent.

He looked sadly at me.

"There is death in the air," he acknowledged simply, his eyes unnaturally keen. "It clings to the stalls of vendors and the stones along the docks. I can feel it. I always feel it—or I have ever since you brought me back—but it's different here. Heavier." He paused, watching my face for a reaction.

Of course death pervaded here. For it would follow me anywhere. The air was thick with floating stars, and my brother went in and out of focus.

"Medea?" Phaethon prompted, suddenly concerned. "Are you feeling all right?"

I nodded, taking an unsteady step backward. The stars seemed to coalesce, and the room teetered toward blackness.

The next thing I knew, the world was dark.

■ ■ ■

Jason did not return for breakfast the next morning. Each time the wind picked up outside, my body flinched. Phaethon watched my movements with uncertainty from the nearest doorway.

"You should be in bed," he insisted, the worry evident in his tone. "I've never seen you faint like that, out of nowhere."

"It wasn't out of nowhere." I retrieved four red clay bowls from the shelves, intending to fill them with porridge. My fingers felt unnaturally heavy—thick and clumsy.

Two of the vessels slipped from my grasp, shattering upon the neat floor.

I cursed, retreating backward against the wall as Phaethon moved to recover the shards.

"To bed with you, sister," he submitted, his eyes dark. "I'll make sure the children eat."

I nodded, my throat seeming to close in on itself as I padded gently in the direction of my chamber.

My brain was filled with mist, my thoughts difficult to identify or hold. One truth was certain, though, throughout the chaos: if I wished to earn Jason's favor back, if I wished to stay here, safe with Phaethon and my children, the famine would have to be averted. I doubted our relationship could survive another move if I did not succeed.

■ ■ ■

Before Korinthos was Korinth, it was called Ephyra, after the native sea nymph who first dwelled there. There were nymphs, I knew, surveying the city at all times, multiple in every fountain and well and freshwater spring. Though they were not immortal, they had the life span of ten phoenixes, or so the old legend went. And yet they did not make themselves known to me as I set off from my house in the direction of the Acrocorinth a fortnight after my fainting spell.

In a matter of days, the situation had gone from negligible to dire. The influx of produce from the surrounding countryside had all but evaporated, and the locusts descended across the region in waves, many times a day.

At the marketplace beside the docks, fewer and fewer stalls remained open, and the vendors who did appear attempted to sell the saddest fruits at an exorbitant rate. Even Phaethon and I found it difficult to coax vegetation from the earth, something we had never had trouble with before.

"This isn't sustainable, sister," he pointed out daily, whenever the children were out of earshot. "If the soil yields nothing, we must move on."

But that was impossible for me to accept. I devised my own plans, some absurd, some less so. Spells that might coax water from below the earth, incantations to make the plants produce more than they currently were. Indeed, I spent a few long nights speaking to the earth itself, as though to usher water from it, unsuccessfully. From what I could ascertain, Korinth was built upon a layer of limestone, so porous it made water magic difficult. And this was to say nothing of the locusts. I had never attempted to cast a spell with such a far-reaching scope.

The answer came to me unexpectedly one morning as I brushed twigs out of Eriopis's hair. Her face glowed with its usual radiance and luster, and her eyes darted playfully about, tracing the trajectory of stray locusts as they hovered outside. She was too young to see them for what they were.

She babbled with her infant tongue, her fingers reaching to tangle in the fabric of my dress. I felt uncomfortably powerful as I held her close. Her happiness depended on me. Her livelihood was indelibly intertwined with my influence. How intimidating it was to have such a stake in another living creature. I shuddered, unnerved. Perhaps this was something like what the Gods felt on Olympus as they regarded the mortals below.

I remembered the divinities who had appeared to me in my youth when I needed them most fearfully: Athena first, and later, Aphrodite. How their forms, uncommonly beautiful, had contained an urgent knowing, a desperation despite the promise of eternity. Or was I simply attributing my own exigency to them?

I thought about Talos.

There is a special kind of agony that comes with immortality, he had told me in a candid moment. Before I killed him.

Perhaps all existence was agony. Or at the very least, sublime discomfort.

Perhaps those on high suffered for the things we did here on earth.

And there was the answer.

I would appeal to the Gods. One God, in particular.

■ ■ ■

The trek was a long and lonely one, made worse by the dryness and cold that permeated the air. A looming, mountainous spot that brushed the sky, the Acrocorinth was the primary cult site for the surrounding areas. It offered views down into the sapphire Gulf of Korinth and was covered with green scrub that clung to my ankles. The farther I drifted from the city, the better I felt. The air smelled sweet out upon the rocks, rather than salty. I drank it in deliriously, glad that for once the strange humming in my ears had abated, if only for a moment.

I slipped past the outworks toward the Northeast Gate, my throat raw and painful with the effort of ascending to such an elevation. My destination was just past the western summit.

The Sanctuary of Demeter and Persephone was lovely and still. I paused in the doorway, beneath an arch of stones, gazing into the dim light. As my eyes adjusted to the shadows, I could make out Korinthian pottery, lovingly thrown and lavishly painted, peppered about the chamber. Plaques and votive offerings adorned the walls. Herbs and flowers hung from the ceiling, perfuming the air with a fresh, clarifying scent. Unlike the city below, this place still felt alive.

In the silence, I knelt upon the floor and bowed my head. Images flickered softly in the darkness behind my eyelids: sprawling fields of grain, golden and swirling in the breeze—orchards weighed down by the burden of fruit—sprouts appearing easily from out of the soil, the impulse toward life and the beautiful impossible to conceal for too long underground.

I must have stayed there, in the dust, beneath the stones, for hours. My legs grew numb, and my back ached from the stance of supplication, but I kept my mind on my meditations.

I waited, breath bated, for Demeter to appear, knowing as I did so that the odds were slim.

The minutes crept by until I no longer had any perception of time. Outside the wind roared. On previous occasions, Goddesses had appeared to me because it was amenable to them. I had never tried to summon one on my own time.

At last, I rose unsteadily to my feet, light-headed with hunger and thirst. I would need to return to the house before nightfall to check on the children, otherwise I might have stayed until dawn.

I slipped from the sanctuary, disappointed in myself.

Overhead, the sun glinted glumly through the clouds.

I watched the horizon blearily as my eyes adjusted to the brightness, worn out and defeated. Perhaps Phaethon was right, and it was time to move on.

It was then that a face appeared from between the bushes, lovely and pointed and distinctly inhuman. Something in the eyes made me think of my mother, although the resemblance stopped there. My breath caught in my throat.

"The Goddess Demeter does not see mortals this time of year, as a general rule," the creature offered, eyes expressive and clear in the daylight. As though to reinforce her words, a frigid wind slipped across the crags, chilling me to the bone.

"She is grieving her daughter," I returned, more statement than question.

The nymph nodded slowly. "It is not a wound that heals cleanly—the separation from one's children," she hummed into the space between us.

"I understand."

The nymph rose from the brush, her long torso and legs appearing from the plants themselves.

"I heard your prayers. They were thoughtful," she offered as though in consolation. Her face was soft with pity.

I swallowed hard.

"I have nowhere else to turn."

"You smell like you hail from elsewhere," she asserted suddenly. I colored slightly, wondering what sort of odors might cling to me, despite the distance between myself and my native land.

"Indeed. I was once a princess of Kolchis," I divulged.

"It is admirable to pray for a land that is not your own," she whispered to herself, "a land filled with strangers who might turn on you at any point."

A hollowness permeated my chest at her words, but I kept my face indifferent.

"This place is my home now."

The nymph shrugged, her long golden hair cascading down across the marble slopes of her shoulders.

"Perhaps I could help you," she said quietly, her eyes narrowed. There was something feline and predatory in her elegance, and I knew to tread carefully. "No one has bestowed the proper reverence on my sisters or I in some time," she mused lightly, her voice deceptively casual. "At this point I imagine that the only thing that would do is blood magic."

Her eyes flashed, and I nodded slowly.

"You require a sacrifice," I inferred.

She quirked her head incrementally to the side, a small smile playing upon her lips.

"Is that something you can stomach?" she baited.

I stifled a laugh. If this nymph had any idea of the blood that already coated my hands, she did not show it.

"I imagine so," I granted.

"Come tomorrow, then. Bring a blade. We will take care of the rest," she relayed.

As I wound my way back down the hill toward the city, I wondered if I had trusted the nymph too easily. Blood sacrifices were becoming rarer as the age advanced, most Gods preferring other, less violent libations. Perhaps she had another motive in drawing my ruthlessness out. But my doubts were weak in comparison to the strange tranquility that filled my limbs, a kind of otherworldly knowing that my labors were in accordance with some higher will.

■ ■ ■

That night, I cornered Jason in our bedroom. His mood had not improved in the days following our previous argument, and I was anxious to make amends.

"I have a plan to avert the famine," I tried as he pulled the tunic roughly over his head.

"Of course you do." He scowled. "I wonder who is going to have to perish to pull this one off."

Ignoring the drop in my stomach his words evoked, I continued.

"You've been gone lately," I broached. "Phaethon seemed to think that you've been visiting the court of King Kreon."

Jason shrugged noncommittally.

"Have you been?"

"So what if I have? I thought you might appreciate me ingratiating our family to the ruling class," he rebuked, annoyed.

Something in me shriveled up under his tone.

"I do, Jason. I only asked to make conversation," I insisted, embarrassed.

"You have an odd way of showing it—always complaining, as if I have a choice."

Any kind words I might have planned to say died in my throat. I knew as he threw himself onto our bed that this night would be a long one.

"I'm leaving again in the morning," he admitted in the dark. "I may be gone awhile."

"All right. I trust you," I lied as he lay stiffly beside me.

■   ■   ■

When I returned to the Acrocorinth the next day, a knife tucked into my cloak, the nymph was already waiting for me. Her eyes were the same halcyon blue as the open sky, and her lips were the pleasant pink of rosebuds. Her legs seemed to sprout from the earth of this place itself.

From a satchel, I withdrew two amphoras: one filled with milk, and the other with oil. Nymphs, I knew, did not appreciate wine offerings.

"This was not necessary, but my sisters will appreciate it," she acknowledged softly, her voice like velvet.

"I wanted to make a good impression," I explained. "I am grateful for your help."

"Follow me," she interrupted, uninterested in my explanation. Slowly, she led me up the mountain back toward the sanctuary.

"This is where I take leave of you," she submitted, face impassive.

In another moment, she had disappeared into the earth itself, the grasses along the footpath shivering to accommodate her.

I waited in the ensuing silence, the knife clutched in my fingers. Who exactly would be providing the blood for the sacrifice? Was I meant to bring the blade down across my own flesh?

Suddenly, a crisp snapping sound, as of twigs underfoot, caught my attention.

I glanced about in the direction of the noise, my eyes falling upon the soft contours of a pelt. Two eyes, wide and yellow, glistened. I was caught in the darkness of the nose, the delicate pinkness of its maw, the straining spires of its horns.

It was a ram, meandering about the stones. Although it looked natural enough in stature and manner, there was something extraordinary about it. Where the bristles of its coat should have been coarse, the fur was soft and glossy. A glowing emanated from its chest, white-hot and pulsing.

I wondered how I was supposed to catch the thing, for its legs were muscular and sturdy. He could easily outrun me if he so desired. After all, his hooves were made for the uneven cliffs and my own feet were sore from the journey up the mountain.

No, the ram would be impossible to overcome.

"Hello," I whispered into the air between us, heart thundering in my ears. I was transported to my childhood in Kolchis, to that night on the beach with Khrysomallos. This ram had the same determined, ethereal gaze.

To my horror, the creature pawed the earth and then began to move toward me. His eyes, filled with impossible radiance, locked on mine as he closed the distance. I brandished the blade without thinking—some strange attempt at honesty, but the ram did not seem to see it or care. The creature bowed its head, only stopping its movements when it was a few inches from where I stood.

I thought of Pelias then—of the ram I had killed and brought to life once more in front of him, not so long ago. I already knew that there would be no such hope of resurrection for the creature in front of me.

In my hand, the knife trembled.

I reached out to grip the animal's chin, expecting some kind of fight. But there was none.

The eyes watched me with a kind of unbearable knowing, and yet they were serene.

What magic was this?

With my other hand, I brought the blade down across its throat.

Blood, hot and immediate, poured across my feet, staining my skirts and spraying my face.

I was transported again, this time back to the cellar rooms of Kolchis, to those years of my childhood where I spent hours cutting into flesh, dismembering bone. But those animals always trembled and contorted in on themselves, anything to escape me. The ram in my arms put up no such struggle.

My eyes blurring with tears, I consecrated the twitching length of the animal to the Lemnian Nymphs, and to the Goddess Demeter.

As I retreated down the mountain, a crackle of thunder echoed in the distance. I paused as a few stray droplets of rain darted down upon my parched face, no doubt mixing with the blood already dried there.

CHAPTER TWENTY-SIX

Exile Again

When Jason failed to return after nearly a fortnight, Phaethon began to worry.

"What could possibly be keeping him detained with King Kreon? I don't like this. It feels off," he remarked one evening when we were sheltered together in the house. I kept my face impartial, despite my own nerves.

"I do not much care what he does any longer," I lied, reluctant to admit the ache that had started up in me at his absence. The rain had not let up for several days following the slaughter of the ram, and the locusts had moved on to some other port town. That was all I had the energy to be concerned about.

"Perhaps you should," Phaethon mused, his eyes glinting in the candlelight. "Jason has proved himself to be dangerous, and I fear that we may have made an enemy out of him." I appreciated his use of *we*, but I could not bring myself to agree.

"I don't want to think about men anymore, Phaethon," I murmured, closing my eyes. "First Father, now Jason. When will I be free of them?"

Phaethon's hand sought out mine and gave it a light squeeze.

"And now I'm a real murderer. Before Pelias, I killed you, but I brought you back. There was Talos, but his slaughter came out of necessity. Now there is a king in Hades because of me. I never imagined things would turn out quite like this."

"You are also a mother, Medea," Phaethon insisted. "And a damn good witch. You are not just the one thing."

I nodded, suddenly exhausted.

"I may retire to my chamber," I whispered, "and try to get a bit of sleep before the children wake up."

Phaethon nodded, turning to extinguish the candles along the mantelpiece so that we were submerged in darkness. In the ensuing blackness, I might have been anywhere—back home in Kolchis, or below deck on the *Argo*. But really, I was here in Korinth. An outsider forever.

■ ■ ■

The next morning, Eriopis rose early, even for her. She appeared beside my bed, her features still rosy from dreaming.

"Can't sleep, Mama," she said excitedly. It was impossible to refuse her anything, so sweet and effulgent was her smile. I forced myself out of bed, still exhausted from my conversation with Phaethon the night before.

"Where's Pheres, sweet one?" I questioned her as I arranged my hair in a knot for the day.

Eriopis shrugged, nonplussed.

"Why don't we go check on him?" I encouraged, rubbing the residual sleep from my eyes. She nodded excitedly and pelted off down the corridor toward the nursery.

"Hush, you'll wake your uncle," I called as quietly as I could, to no avail.

Somehow, despite the rampage of her small feet upon the freshly swept floor, Pheres continued to sleep restfully enough.

"Pheres is always dreaming," Eriopis said out loud, making no effort to be quiet. "Maybe you should have another baby for me to play with." As though sensing he was being talked about, her brother stirred, his eyes blinking blearily as he attempted to take in the room.

"I think the two of you are more than enough to contend with for now. Let's not pressure your dear mother," came Phaethon's genial voice from the doorway.

I smiled exasperatedly at him. "You don't have to get up yet, I'll take care of breakfast."

"And miss a bit of extra time with my favorite children?" He shook his head, laughing. "Not a chance."

As he led the children forward, out of their room, I was struck by how simple this was—how good and easy. I hoped life would stay the same for a bit longer.

■ ■ ■

It was not Jason who returned, but a page of the king of Korinth. He carried a sealed letter from my husband that he demanded I open in his presence.

"I don't understand," I explained as the man proffered the missive expectantly. "Where is he? Why hasn't he come himself?" But the page only shook his head, his eyes full of something like pity.

The letter was brief and sent a stab of fear through me.

Princess,

The Admirable King Kreon has extended to me his kindest hospitality, and after many nights under his roof, I have entered an engagement with his daughter, the princess of Korinth. She is called Glauce and she is loveliness and grace personified. We are to be married in the coming weeks, and so I am sending you this letter to inform you of an end to our previous arrangement.

Your companionship during these years together has been useful, and I wish you the best of luck securing some place for yourself outside of this city.

Please give Eriopis and Pheres my love. Tell them of the greatness of their father and the nobleness of his heart—for they had no say in the woman that their mother became, and I therefore bear them no ill will or blame. That they are illegitimate is also through no fault of their own. It is for this reason that I shall collect them directly and provide for them here once you have departed. They will be siblings to royalty, and that is the best life they might reasonably expect.

Perhaps if our marriage had been officiated by someone with the

true and uncorrupted power to join man and wife together, things
might have been different, but as it is, I have no use for a savage
bride, now that a legitimate one has made herself ready for me.

Jason

Numbly, I let the letter slip between the clumsy pads of my fingers. Somewhere, perhaps very far away, the king's messenger was asking me if I understood the correspondence. I nodded, feeling faint.

Glauce. I turned the name over and over in my mind, like a polished stone. Was it possible that I hated her? Could it be that I blamed her for Jason's sudden absence? I probed inside myself for some hint of feeling but found only pity. She was nothing, just another pretty piece in Jason's game. A girl ripe for the taking, as I had been.

I could not begin to think of my heart, which was shattered and fragmented now beyond repair, and so my thoughts turned to practical matters. If this letter was to be believed, it rendered the children illegitimate. For a moment, I struggled to breathe. Where would we go? I could never return to Kolchis, I knew, for Aeetes would kill me the moment I stepped upon the beach. Iolcus was equally hostile, and now we were no longer welcome in Korinth. It seemed incredibly cruel that I might be banished from the land I had so lately saved from scarcity and starvation. Down on the beach, Eriopis shrieked with laughter, splashing Pheres and Phaethon with ocean water, her blond curls glimmering in the sun.

If she stayed here, she would be well cared for, but always second-class. But if I took her and her brother with me, their lives were effectively over. What would her life be then, as the bastard child of a witch mother? And Pheres, for all his boyish charm, was just as poorly set up.

You will have time enough to suffer. The words Orpheus spoke as we cleared the Sirens reasserted themselves in my mind, and I could no longer hold back the dread.

CHAPTER TWENTY-SEVEN

The Family Dragons

In the end, I wrote three letters. How I managed this—with the unbearable droning noise echoing about my skull, and the strange dissociation that permeated my body, rendering me feverish and clumsy—I cannot say. Madness had been kindled in my mind somewhere along my long journey, and now it was too late to put it out. I was burning alive, only no one could see it yet.

The first letter, I addressed angrily to Jason in the palace at Korinth, refusing him access to the children. They were mine, more so than they would ever be his, and they would grow up knowing nothing of him. This letter, I promptly tore up and scattered in the ocean. It served no purpose besides giving language to the rage that wound its way white-hot and scorching inside of me.

The second letter, I placed in the hands of the page. It was cordial and kind, the sort of simpering prose that a foolish man might read and believe. It arranged for Jason to collect the children the following day by the docks. I then asked the messenger to provide the princess of Korinth with a wedding present so that there would be no hard feelings for the difficulties that existed in our complicated triangle. Relief broke across the man's face, and he agreed to take whatever it was to her directly, at the same time as he delivered my letter to Jason. And so, with the second letter, I proffered a box containing a lovely white dress scattered with lace flowers, one that I had bought from a street vendor some days before. Wrapped inside the dress was an uncommonly jeweled coronet—the very one that Helios had bestowed upon my sister, and that she in turn had given to me.

"Tell the fair princess that I have enchanted this garment and the crown so that whoever wears them will bear only sons. Her fertility will be assured," I explained, and he nodded readily, amazed.

My throat was tight with pity—for Jason's new bride and for myself. As the box slipped from my shaking fingers, I wondered at my ruthlessness. Surely, this was not who I was. *Not really.*

I watched the page scurry off. When I closed my eyes, a smattering of faces flickered across my vision. *Phaethon. Talos. Pelias. The little girl, his daughter. The ram, with its wide yellow eyes.*

What would it be like to add another to their ranks? To carry another face inside me, the very image of my guilt, forever?

The third and final letter was addressed to Athens.

I recalled the naive fervor with which King Aegeus had pursued me in my youth back in Kolchis, how he longed to make me his wife. It seemed an incredibly futile attempt, but I was running out of options.

When I whispered that night to Phaethon of my plan, his eyebrows shot up into his hairline.

"Jason will never let you leave with the children," he responded immediately. "And he is the future king of Korinth. How exactly do you intend to leave these shores without the passage and protection of some other king? It could take months to hear from Aegeus."

"I have methods." I brushed off his concern, pursing my lips. It was an absurd plan, but perhaps it would work.

In truth, I had no way of knowing whether there was any hope of success, and the stakes were impossibly high. As I attempted to close my eyes, my mind flashed with spars of rumor, the fruit of intrusive stories brought across the ocean to Korinth only a month or so before. A visiting fisherman had told Jason of that demigod Herakles, who in a moment of madness had butchered his wife and children. Herakles, who was once my husband's companion on the *Argo*. Perhaps there was no limit to what men were capable of, even toward those they were supposed to adore. But was I any better?

Hours later, when Phaethon's breathing evened out in the predictable rhythm of sleep, I prayed under my breath to my grandfather, the radiant Titan Helios. Never before had I attempted to make contact with him, and I was not entirely sure how to do it properly. I whispered to him of my father—his son—and of my aunt Circe. I told him of fair Phaethon, who had once shone brightly with the Titan's own blood, and of the twins who slept curled up beside me. His great-grandchildren. I whispered about my magic, about my fierce love, about my impossible fear. I whispered finally of my dire need for him.

I did not expect any sign that he had heard me.

■ ■ ■

The next morning, I went out early in search of herbs, knowing I should assemble double the amount I usually required. Some I procured on the cliffs overlooking Korinth, and others I could buy from the city's vendors. By the time I returned to the house, it was nearly midday. Jason would be arriving soon.

Dully, I realized that I had used all of Khrysomallos's wool on Phaethon. My own skills, it seemed, would have to be enough to carry us through this latest challenge.

Attempting to still my shaking hands, I called out for Phaethon and the children. It was easy enough to convince the little ones to spend a day beside the water. And I hoped my brother would go along with my plans, if only for the sake of keeping me sane.

"What are you going to do, sister?" came his voice in my ear as we wandered down to the beach.

"I have neither the strength nor the desire to discuss our circumstances, Phaethon. Can we not simply have a single day to ourselves under the sun?"

After a long moment he nodded, his expression tight and wary.

For a while, the children danced upon the shore. I watched them through slitted eyes, my heart pounding in my throat.

■ ■ ■

And then the moment came.

My brother emerged onto the sand, carrying one child in each arm, his face split in a smile that did not meet his eyes. He was playing pretend, I knew, for the benefit of Eriopis and Pheres; he did not want to part with them, did not want Jason to take them away.

As their innocent, trusting eyes fell on me, their faces erupted in identical smiles, and my heart ached.

"Jason will be coming to collect them soon, and I need your help," I explained slowly, looking up into his eyes. He watched with concern as tears collected in my own. I hastily forced the emotion down again.

"What are you—?"

I was laying out the herbs I would need along the ground, and after a moment Phaethon seemed to realize what they implied. He led the children away along the beach, encouraging them to play in the sand. When he approached me, his face had paled.

"Medea, no," he protested, looking frantic. "Not this. It is too risky. Their bodies are so small, so underdeveloped. So many things could go wrong."

"You doubt my abilities?" I retorted, doing my best to look enraged instead of worried. He shook his head and ran his fingers through his hair.

"They are children. Your children," he emphasized, speaking slowly as though I was a child myself.

"I can give them something to induce sleep, as I did once with you. They will not feel the sting of death if you help me." I gestured to two identical stoppered bottles with sleeping draft propped up in the sand.

"They are your children—" He broke off, clutching absently at his own throat as though he was having trouble finding his breath.

"They are young enough yet that they may not remember all of this when they grow older," I reasoned softly, not even believing my own words.

"The body remembers, sister."

I shrugged, feigning indifference.

"This is madness, Medea, surely you can see that. Besides, Jason knows of your proficiency in Necromancy. He will simply force you to bring them back."

I shook my head.

"I told him once, long ago, that I was not capable of any more acts of resurrection—that my magic only worked on you because you were the grandchild of Helios."

Phaethon looked unconvinced.

"He needs to pay for what he has done to us," I continued, anxious now. "I want him to feel a fraction of the anguish he has forced upon me."

"What you have planned will destroy him," he retorted, face pained. I forced back a smile. If Phaethon noticed even a hint of pleasure at that outcome, he would refuse me on the spot.

"I need you to hold them still, while they fall asleep, brother, otherwise I won't be able to do it," I articulated, not looking at him. His silence was damning, and I squirmed, beginning to panic.

"Please, brother. If you don't help me, I don't know what we will do." Now I began to cry, honest and heavy tears, which stung my cheeks.

Phaethon's face went through a thousand different emotions, each less bearable than the last.

"This is madness," he repeated once more. The strain in his voice almost broke me.

"You will need to hold them still," I whispered. "For what if one or the other of them wakes or will not drink?"

"And if I refuse?" he asked at last.

"Then I shall never forgive you."

After a long moment he nodded, gritting his teeth. "Gods help me," he muttered softly, turning around to call the children to him.

■ ■ ■

I worked in the shadow of the ships as the sun rose to its zenith. Sweat collected on the back of my neck as blood smeared across my palms. Phaethon was silent beside me, his whole body trembling. The children had fallen silent a long time before, and now there was only the sound of our own breaths mingling. I did not allow myself to contemplate what Eriopis and Pheres would look like when I was done with them. I did not allow myself to think at all.

■ ■ ■

When Jason appeared at the end of the deserted dock, his face contorted with rage, his entire body heaving and twitching, I knew that the first part of my plan had worked.

"Medea!" he screamed, tears falling down his cheeks as though he was a child and not a man. "Show yourself, you most vile and despicable of creatures!"

Beside me, Phaethon gripped my upper arm, attempting to restrain me. "Why does he look so angry? He hasn't even seen the children yet."

I turned to look at him blankly. "Because I have just murdered his new wife."

I pushed the two bundles we had readied into his arms, trying not to notice how crimson liquid dripped sickeningly from both.

"What?" Phaethon gasped.

"The dress I sent along as a wedding present was soaked in poison—a particularly nasty one, the kind that might dissolve the skin right off the wearer."

I imagined the childlike, pretty face of Jason's bride, melting like limestone in the rain. Perhaps she doused herself in water to extinguish some of the pain as the acid magic in the dress ripped her body apart, for all the good that would do. Her death would have been a hideous one, but I needed to be sure she was unsalvageable.

Phaethon stared at me in disbelief.

"I don't understand," he murmured. "Why?"

"So that Jason never becomes king." The answer was simple and ruthless, and I shivered at the impassiveness in my voice as I said it. This world would not benefit from another Aeetes, and that was my justification.

"But she did nothing," Phaethon argued, his face pale and waxen.

"She would be complicit in his rise to power. We cannot afford to have another man on the throne like him—like our father," I growled. "Besides, it's too late. She's dead by now, I'm sure."

Phaethon trembled beside me in the shadows, his face a mess of emotion.

I glanced up, directly into the heat of the sun, and noticed a speck far up in the sky. Smiling to myself, I turned once more to look at Jason, knowing this would need to be timed perfectly. I stepped confidently from the shadows of the ship so that I knew he could see me.

"Husband," I called in a high clear voice. "What brings you here in such a violent mood?" I pulled my eyebrows together innocently, making my lips pouty and my eyes naive.

He turned toward me reeling, his face scarlet.

"You wretch," he snarled, moving toward me. "I will kill you for this." I glanced once more at the sky, as the speck moved slightly closer.

Before Jason could take another step, I brandished what I held in my arms.

"O Gods, no, Medea," he whispered, the fury drained out of him. Now there was only terror. His eyes were fixed on the severed heads of our twins, which dangled from my fingers by the ends of their blond curls. I myself could not look at them, for fear that I would be sick.

Behind me, Phaethon let out a long, low moan.

"How could you let her do this?" Jason asked, his voice raw. Here he looked at my brother, his eyes working madly. He dropped to his knees in the surf, seawater spilling across his legs. "They are children."

After a moment, he gazed at me once more. A thousand emotions flickered across his face. A strange, terrible satisfaction ignited inside of me as I watched him crumble and attempt unsuccessfully to rebuild himself. He would never be able to recover from this, I knew.

He staggered toward me, his eyes bulging from his head. How I had ever found that face handsome, I could not now conceive of. I realized with a thrill that he meant to kill me.

"What is your plan, sister?" Phaethon called out to me anxiously. "We have nowhere to run."

And as usual, he was right. We were trapped by Jason and the citizens of Korinth on the one side, and the sea on the other. Once, I might have cast myself into the waves, trusting in my mother to ferry us off to some safe harbor, but now I knew better. Jason continued to move toward us, foaming at the mouth like a rabid dog.

The answer appeared out of the ether like a bolt of lightning in the form of Chalciope's words to me forever ago:

"You might pray to him," my sister had suggested innocently, on the

occasion of her wedding to Phrixus. *"Perhaps if you made an effort, he might take more of an interest in you."*

And so I shut my eyes tightly and prayed again as I had the night before.

As I mouthed my entreaties, the whole world seemed to go silent, suspended on its axis.

Grandfather, I whispered to the sun itself, *help me. Please.*

"You monster. You bitch," Jason screamed into the daylight as a shadow passed overhead. He did not notice the change in the light, so focused was he on my face.

"You must bring them back, Medea. You must!"

But I only shook my head. "You know that's not possible, *husband*. I told you I would not be able to do it again. Even my powers have their limits." In that moment, thunder crackled across the sky, despite the clearness of the afternoon. It was as though the Gods on high were agreeing with me, as if the heavens itself had reached a judgment on the fate of my children before I could even begin the work of resurrecting them.

The blood in my veins turned to ice. Had I taken my sorcery too far—beyond the limits of what those on Olympus would allow? The idea was too horrifying to acknowledge, and I worked to banish these thoughts.

Phaethon let out a strangled gasp as a chariot landed in the sand beside us, nearly crushing Jason, who scrambled out of the way at the last possible moment.

"Get aboard, now." I nudged Phaethon onto the gleaming chariot. His eyes were caught on the hulking forms that pulled the vehicle: two immense, glittering dragons. Their scales were of a color nearly impossible to describe—one moment they might be the dark, sharp green of cypress boughs, and then the next, a shimmering gold, depending entirely on the angle of the sun through the clouds. Their eyes flashed as they appraised us, but I knew intrinsically that they would do me no harm.

"How?" Phaethon asked in an undertone, stumbling forward to help me up beside him.

"A gift from our grandfather, I'd imagine," I offered, declining to elaborate. Phaethon stared at me in awe.

"You are more like Aeetes than I could have ever imagined," he murmured at last, turning to look away. Although his words cut me to the quick, I did not let myself dwell on them.

Then the ground was slipping away far below us, and Jason's screams dissolved into the roar of the wind. Phaethon gripped the bundles in his straining arms so tightly I had to pry them away from him.

"You can navigate, brother," I dictated, gesturing to the reins. "And I am going to put my children back together. We need to head toward Athens."

Under my palms, the flesh of my children still warm, I began to weave life back into what I had so lately destroyed.

CHAPTER TWENTY-EIGHT

Unsalvageable

It would be impossible for me to relay the events of that arduous flight, so focused was I on the carnage strewn across the floor of the chariot. While Phaethon gripped the reins, steering us through the clouds, I knelt, trembling over body parts, my clothes stained with drying blood.

Repeatedly, I reminded myself that this should be easy, efficient work—after all, I had done it before, more times than I could count. That my own brother was standing, alive and vivacious, next to me was evidence that my Necromancy was powerful. But my hands trembled terribly, and my vision blurred with tears. I stumbled in my various incantations. The herbs set aside to rejuvenate the lifeblood of my children were crumbled, dry, and unusable beneath my fingertips.

As I worked over the flaming strawberry curls of my daughter, I slipped in and out of time, in and out of my body. I was a child again, brushing Chalciope's long, glossy hair out of her eyes. Just as quickly I was on my knees, here in this chariot, gripping a severed thigh thousands of feet above the ground. Instead of a comb, I now clutched at medicine bottles.

It was difficult to stay rooted beside my children in the chariot. I was cast back, again and again with devastating clarity, to the most banal of moments. Eriopis mouthing her first words, the way her bright eyes lit up as she struggled to expel the word *Mama*—how strangely gratifying that had been. I was on the stone tiles of the courtyard in Korinth as Pheres toddled clumsily after butterflies and crickets. He never attempted to catch them, to crush them in his tiny palms. Instead, he liked to watch them, with childish wonder in every movement. He was so much like Phaethon in that regard, almost instinctually gentle.

No, no, no. Please work. Please wake up.

All sense of control vanished. Perhaps Phaethon had been right when he suggested the twins were too young to sustain this kind of trauma and return to life unscathed. Or could it be that Phaethon was sturdier than they were by virtue of his proximity to Titan blood? After all, Eriopis and Pheres were fractionally less of Helios than he was.

My fingers were slippery with their blood, and the smell was overwhelming and hideous. I attempted to breathe through my mouth, with little luck. As the minutes went by, the task seemed more and more impossible. Had Phaethon's resurrection been quite so grueling? I could no longer recall.

Even so, I reattached their limbs with excruciating care, despite the waves of nausea that rolled through me every other minute. I watched for the fluttering of an eye, for the shuddering rise and fall of their chests.

"Wake up now, wake up," I cooed under my breath. I caressed their waxen, pale cheeks, pressing gentle kisses to their crimson-stained foreheads.

As the hours passed, Eriopis and Pheres—or what was left of my children—grew cold to the touch.

I began to sob. Futile, stupid, animalistic sounds.

"What's happening, Medea?" Phaethon roared over the wind. I could picture the horror of his expression, but I did not have time to look at him. I tried again and again, until the light began to fade.

"We have to land," Phaethon's voice reached me over the gales. "It's getting dark." I did not bother to argue with him, to insist that we make a direct course for Athens. I was not capable of language.

I clutched my children's dreadful, reassembled bodies as we crashed toward the ground.

■ ■ ■

In the aftermath of the landing, Phaethon wrenched the children from my shaking arms.

I watched listlessly as he tried his own futile forms of magic—his sober, aghast attempts to restore them to the land of the living. Despite his entreaties and salves, they remained motionless under the stars. From somewhere in the distance came a terrible keening, and I realized that the cries were my own.

"Phaethon," I whispered, tears slipping down my face, "it's not working. Why isn't it working?"

But he did not spare me a response. His face was silver in the moonlight, nightmarish in its earnestness.

With harrowing clarity, I realized that I had been right about the thunderclap. The Gods on high could not allow a mere mortal to transgress again and again, forever testing the universe itself. I was an affront to nature, and my children had paid the price.

■ ■ ■

I did not sleep at all in the darkness, and neither did my brother. We sat together in silence as the dragons paced beside the chariot, eager to take off into the sky once more.

The children lay a few yards away, silent and unsalvageable. I had covered their faces with my traveling cloak so that I would not have to see their eyes reflect the lights in the heavens above.

And so when the sun finally rose, dreadful in its unaffected consistency, we were both awake to see it. The horizon was awash in a hundred pastel colors, but their beauty could not touch me. Nothing would ever seem beautiful again. The rest of my life would be a wasteland, an expanse of emptiness, characterized by an absence so immense it could not even be conceived of.

"Where are we?" I managed at last, surprised at the roughness of my voice. My throat was still raw and painful from my cries the night before.

"Just outside of Thebes, if my calculations mean anything," he responded, his voice flat and emotionless.

"Thebes," I repeated flatly, as though the name meant anything to me.

"Land of the Sphinx, sister," Phaethon supplied automatically. "I

read about it once with Father. The creature is believed to hail origi-
nally from Ethiopia, but now it guards the city gates, allowing no one
entry unless they answer its riddle."

The reference to Aeetes broke something in me.

We lapsed into silence again.

"There are monsters everywhere," I muttered, fighting the urge to
vomit all over myself. The words were familiar, but I could not place
where I had heard them before. All I knew was that they were true.

Phaethon said nothing.

I began to laugh hysterically then, a wolfish, low giggle that seemed
to swallow me up and never end.

■ ■ ■

Phaethon roughly shook me awake a few hours later, when the moon
hung low in the sky. The ground was hard and spartan beneath me,
and overhead the stars shone too brightly. The twin dragons, all fluid
lines of dark and silver, gnashed at their reins, their scales shimmering
brightly in the moonlight.

Was I dreaming?

In another minute, though, the horror of our circumstances rushed
back. My throat constricted; I found it impossible to breathe. A shrill,
tense whine slipped from between my lips, and the tears started again.

"We should prepare to fly to Athens," my brother said at last, his
eyes locked on the horizon so that he would not have to see me.

CHAPTER TWENTY-NINE

The Oath

We arrived in Athens before word spread of what I had done. And so, when the chariot landed in the olive tree–lined courtyard leading into Aegeus's palace, the king, and my old admirer, invited us inside without qualm. That each of us bore the bloodied body of a child in our arms, still garish from reassembly, was not too beyond the pale. Phaethon had urged me to bury them in Thebes, before we made off again, but I could not leave them. The idea of the earth swallowing my children was unfathomable.

"They stay with me," I asserted simply, despite his incredulous, pitying looks.

Aegeus's eyes, as green and alert as they had been when he was still a young man, were glued uncomprehendingly to my own. My own glance passed blearily along the coarse hairs of his graying, well-oiled beard, no longer as dark or shining as it had once been.

"How utterly monstrous. Who are they?" he inquired, his look fatherly and mournful.

No words seemed apt.

Phaethon intervened smoothly, noting my unfit state.

"They are Medea's," he murmured. "And they were gravely injured getting here. We attempted to heal them—my sister's powers are formidable as you know, but we could not." He broke off before any emotion could seep through. Though he lied for me, he would still not meet my eyes.

Aegeus bowed his head. A rush of resentment filled me then, at his show of sorrow. He did not know them—not like me or Phaethon.

"How terrible," he uttered softly, turning to address me. "Though this will not assuage your loss, I promise that your children will receive a proper burial here."

I ought to have groveled before him then, to offer my thanks, but I could not. The king of Athens cleared his throat, gesturing for several nearby pages to relieve us of our burdens.

When one reached to remove Pheres from my arms, I screeched, clawing at the page's face so roughly that I drew blood. He jerked backward, his face awash with surprise.

Phaethon's hand landed upon my shoulder.

"Let them take him," he whispered softly into my hair. "There's nothing else we can do for him now."

I sobbed, shaking my head, pulling the body more firmly against me.

In the end, it took four separate men to wrench my son from me. I screamed hysterically under the midday sun. Phaethon's hands were locked on my wrists. "Please," my brother insisted in my ear, his voice desperate and lost.

All at once, the fight went out of me, and I deflated. His voice—there was no affection left for me, not now.

Aegeus watched the scene play out with his lips pursed.

He did not bother to ask who their father was, for which I was grateful.

His eyes glanced concernedly at my brother, noting that some of his light had been diminished, and that his skin was now covered in a thousand healed scars. I realized, with a jolt, that Aegeus had taken my brother's apparent resurrection with bizarre grace. He had been present on Kolchis, after all, when I hacked Phaethon to pieces. It would have been inevitable that news of my betrayal would make its way throughout the palace. Phaethon brushed off his inquiries easily.

"The journey that brought us here was fraught with peril, my friend."

"Well," Aegeus finally said. "I shall have the servants lead you up to your rooms, where you will be able to freshen up. Is there anything that you have need of?" He was a charitable host, even in the heat of his curiosity.

I let a page lead us to our chambers. I did not care where we were going. I was haunted by a future that could never be, now that my children were gone.

Phaethon kept close to me as we trudged the rest of the way through the courtyard. It was arrestingly beautiful, and even in my despair, I took small comforts in the stretching blue drapery of the sky above, and the cleverly placed tiles, each square a different gleaming color, below our feet. A reflecting pool ran through the center of the outdoor space, clear and glistening and cool. Around the water's edge grew all manner of herbs and flowers, each more striking than the last. The walls of Aegeus's palace were adorned with decadent pastel frescoes. Winged creatures stood beside men in sparkling armor, and golden-colored lions prowled silently along miniature lapis rivers. In some places delicately painted birds stared down from the ceilings, or lizards glanced curiously up from the floor.

We passed the rest of the day cloistered away in a bedroom, me staring listlessly out of the window, and Phaethon pacing anxiously along the length of the carpet, his eyes troubled.

"Once he knows what you have done, he shall not let us stay here. And then where will we go, Medea?" he asked plaintively.

I shook my head, not bothering to answer.

From out of the window, I watched as the sun set on Athens. It was as though the day was setting on me as well.

■ ■ ■

Since our arrival, I had taken to talking to myself, something I had never done before.

"You need to focus, witch," I asserted under my breath, though I was alone in the dark. "Aegeus's goodwill is not infinite. At some point his generosity will come to an end, and we will be in peril once more."

I stifled a laugh at my own absurd thoughts. The future was meaningless. We were past the point of no return. All there was for us now was death.

"Medea," a different, sweeter part of me insisted, "I know it feels like the world has ended, but it has not. You are still here, and Phaethon is as well. You will get through this together, but you need a plan."

"Leave me alone!" I snapped. I reached for an amphora of wine, which had been left upon the dresser. As the luxurious purple liquid slipped across my tongue, it tasted of blood.

■ ■ ■

My mind was at work constructing a new plan, one that would ensure us safe harbor here for as long as we should need it.

That evening before dinner, I left Phaethon curled up asleep in our chamber. In the late afternoon he had begun to stir, sweat thick upon his clammy skin, his fingers twitching from some nightmare.

"I should deal with Aegeus alone," I considered out loud. A few feet away, my brother shifted again, but did not awaken entirely.

On the threshold, I allowed myself a moment to imagine what might have been, if the twins had survived.

Pheres slumbered on the bed. Phaethon was now awake, exhausted but comfortable beside the warmth of the fireplace. He held a sleepy Eriopis gingerly in his arms, rocking her back and forth gently, singing a lullaby to them both. I told him I would be back soon, and he smiled contentedly at me.

■ ■ ■

The layout of the palace was fairly intuitive, with all corridors leading back to common areas. Elaborate tapestries adorned the walls, so intricately woven even I made note of them in my wearied state. I moved, with weighted feet, toward the dining hall, where I supposed Aegeus would be.

It was not long before I arrived at a set of impressive double doors. The table was set elaborately, each plate, goblet, and knife perfectly polished. This meant, I hoped, that Aegeus was interested in impressing us. That he was eager, still, to win my affection.

He sat patiently at the head of the table, and he only rose as I entered. "I'm glad you decided to join me for dinner," he offered into the silence, his face unbearably compassionate. I might have hit him, for no reason other than my own sense of insanity.

A waiting page pulled out a seat for me, and I slipped into it. Aegeus attempted a little smile and gestured to the various platters set before us.

"Before we eat, friend, I have a deal to offer you," I began, appraising him as he lifted the first spoonful of soup to his lips. He paused, then dropped the spoon back into its bowl.

"Of course, princess." He smiled carefully at me, his eyes keen but unclouded by suspicion. I flinched. Jason had often addressed me with that title.

"I will tell you of what has brought me here to you in due course. More than that, I will supply you with herbs, poultices, and potions— any that you might require. I would serve as your own personal witch for as long as you might have need of my services. This I offer you freely, because I have adored you since you first courted me back in my native land of Kolchis."

He looked faintly taken aback by this pronouncement. "I had no idea you harbored any such fondness for me, Medea," he admitted slowly, a blush suffusing his cheeks. "Indeed, I thought that Phaethon seemed to like me better than you did. You were always off, in your own world. You had no eyes for me."

"Perhaps I hid it well," I mused, not looking at him. He regarded me for a long moment, and then shook his head.

"I doubt that, somehow," he eventually replied.

I swallowed hard. Playing nice was more difficult than I had antici- pated. "What, then, do you want from me, in exchange for refuge?" I spat.

"Medea, I require nothing from you," he said incredulously. "Noth- ing, that is, that can be forcibly taken. I have long pined for an heir, and I feel that pain most poignantly now as I age. If you would be in- terested, I would make you my wife in an instant."

I scoffed in disbelief, before I could restrain myself. "Your wife?" I repeated when I had recovered some semblance of composure.

"Yes. Is that so hard to believe?"

I paused and drank from the wine set before me. "Sometimes I think about what you said, when the two of us were still together in Kolchis,"

I began slowly, unsure how I might explain myself. "When you called my heart a Hydra. When you said that every time one head was lost another two would appear in its place."

Aegeus raised his eyebrows, urging me to continue.

"I fear the beast is dead now, each neck scorched and cauterized. There is nothing good left." I had forgotten that my goal was to win him over, to make him adore me again. Instead, I was confessing to him.

The king sighed. "The heart is never vanquished, Medea." I regarded my soup silently as he continued. "You already know, surely, that I have burned for you. This has not changed, in the many years since I have seen you. And my offer to make you queen of Athens, so long as you are still unmarried, stands." He smiled.

I tried not to react to the word *unmarried*. He could not possibly know of my past.

"Whether you make me your wife or not," I broke in, attempting to frame what I needed in the best possible light, "is not of consequence to me. But I do require your word that Phaethon and I are safe here, for as long as we require sanctuary."

Aegeus's eyes narrowed slightly. "Why would you not assume that this is already the case? My home is yours. Your father, Aeetes, was incredibly hospitable to me during my travels, and I have no intention of—"

"You must swear it," I whispered, interrupting him. He paused, and a strange silence descended upon the table. For a moment, I thought that he would refuse, but then he bowed his head.

"What shall I swear on, princess?"

"The earth and sun, on the Old Gods, and on this city that you rule." I broke off, watching him carefully.

"On these things I swear," he promised, without a moment of hesitation.

"No matter what you may hear in the coming months?"

"No matter what I shall hear, you are safe. Now tell me what all of this is about. It seems I have much to be caught up on."

The victory of the moment was tempered by my own self-loathing. My children had not been dead forty-eight hours and I was already on to my next scheme.

Taking a deep breath, the anxiety gradually ebbing from me, I began my tale.

Aegeus, to his credit, listened carefully. If he felt some disgust or wrath toward me, he hid it well. As the story twisted and turned, he simply nodded, his profile guarded and thoughtful. As I spoke, he rubbed the back of his neck in slow, soothing movements.

When at last I fell silent, the king rose slowly to his feet. I waited for him to make some decree, to upbraid me, to say anything at all. Instead, he moved carefully along the length of the table, hands outstretched so as not to startle me. In another moment, he brought me into his arms.

I knew then that Athens had been the correct choice of destination—that its king was as good as his word.

■　■　■

"It is done," I called into the dark, shutting the chamber door behind me.

From the shadows, Phaethon jerked awake. "What do you mean?" he asked slowly, rising unsteadily from the blankets. I could hardly look at the scars that adorned his torso.

"We are safe here," I replied, limp and exhausted.

"How did you convince him?" he inquired in a flat tone. I knew it would be a long while before the raw wound between us would heal, and I resigned myself to it.

"He made me an oath before I told him any of what brought us here. You will be provided for. And I am to be his wife," I concluded, attempting to sound less distraught than I felt.

Phaethon said nothing, standing up and stalking to the other end of the room.

"What else was I to do?" I uttered at last, unnerved by his silence.

"I cannot say."

The quiet resumed, save for the gentle buzz of insects outside the open windows. Overhead, the moon shone down upon the courtyard with cool indifference, almost unaware of its own loveliness.

I held my breath until I could no longer stand it. "I'm sorry, brother." I looked down at my feet. "I am sorry I forced you to do something that I never should have asked of you in the first place." The silence stretched on, and part of me fragmented under it. "If I could undo everything—"

"The rift between us might not ever heal entirely, but I am still here with you," Phaethon expressed at last, turning finally to meet my eyes. "You are my sister, after all. I am only adjusting to the ways in which you are your own person, I suppose. Different from how I idealized you. Different from the limits of my comprehension." His face appeared unmoored and lost. The desperation rose in me like a wave, smothering everything else in its path.

"No, Phaethon. Don't speak like that. I am exactly as you imagine. I just made mistakes. I'm sorry, I—"

He shook his head, raising a hand to halt my speech.

The quiet enveloped us both. A sob rose in me then, and I beat it back.

"Medea, there is nothing you could do that would alienate me from you. I love you always, eternally. This I promise." He stared at me then, with his wise, mournful eyes.

"We are going to be all right? We will survive this?" I questioned. My relief in that moment was palpable.

"Yes, of course we are," he returned, but something in his voice gave me pause.

"You're lying," I accused without thinking, stricken.

"I am not the lying kind, sister," he reminded me, although his expression was rendered almost unknowable to me.

"But how could you ever forgive me, now?" I shuddered. "Everywhere I go, death follows." Pelias and Talos. The littlest of the Peliades, and now my own children. For the first time, I allowed myself to imagine Jason's bride, alight with joy on the day of her wedding, burned alive by my spite and rage. Glauce was innocent enough, armed with only whatever palatable, simpering story Jason had told to her, and still, I had killed her.

Phaethon paused, intent upon the moon that loomed above the courtyard outside.

"Grace," he said at last, as though the single word was clarification enough.

"I don't understand," I moaned, wiping the rogue tears from my eyes.

"I forgive you as an act of grace, against my own will. There is no alternative, because we only have each other. Forgiveness is like love—it is not something that can be controlled or rationed out. It exists or it does not."

I allowed his words to sink into my guilt-stained mind. Perhaps it was not the explanation I wanted to hear, but it would do. For a moment, we gazed at each other.

"Enough, Medea," he murmured gently. "You need sleep." His voice sounded like our mother's.

Numbly, body heavy with fatigue, I crawled into the bed beside him. He adjusted to make room for me, gently pulling some of the blankets up around my face as I shivered. There was no need to speak.

Eriopis and Pheres were there, everywhere in the air around us.

And in the delicate haze of my approaching dreams, there was another child too—a baby yet to come.

Idyia had been right about me in the end; prophecy was as much a part of who I was as anything else.

Surrounded by the silk hangings, the air perfumed by the scent of myrrh and olive trees, I flickered between waking and sleeping, loss and love breaking over me in waves.

Medus

My son sits hunched over a lyre, his face screwed up in concentration. His fingers are already deft like his aunt's at just ten years old, though he has never met her and likely never will. He has my looks—the shrewd, cautious face and faintly green hair. His eyes are wide and yellow, like an animal's. But he acts uncannily like his father. Every move he makes is gentle and full of love.

From the outset, Aegeus required an heir, and so I gave him one—but just the one. I do not think my body could have managed another, after everything.

Phaethon and I decided, on the eve of the baby's birth, that he would not learn *Pharmakon*. There would be no need, I hoped. He was, as far as we knew, the only son Aegeus had ever sired. He had no competition for the throne of Athens. Selfishly, I desired for him to grow up as normally as possible.

Aegeus told me that I should be the one to name him, and so I did. *Medus.* Because the moment he was born descended sweet and thick like honey, whereas time before had been bitter. It was delirious, that sweetness, but sobering too. That he was vivid and alive in spite of so much carnage—that his smile would never know the horrors of what had come before. His presence was a view into another life, one impossibly rich and full.

I cannot keep my eyes off him, even for a moment.

He places the lyre upon the nearest bureau, his eyes darting up to meet mine. The music is extinguished, but it will begin again the moment he wishes it to.

"I made you a gift," he says shyly, his cheeks going red. I brush the patina-tinged curls back from his face.

"Oh?" I ask, pretending to be taken aback. Children are never so furtive as they imagine themselves to be. Then again, neither are adults.

"It's a special potion, to help with your nightmares," he explains knowingly, reaching into a pocket in his trousers and drawing out a small, stoppered bottle.

He deposits it excitedly in my lap as I attempt to hide my real surprise.

"Do you like it, Mama?" he asks anxiously, tugging at the corner of his tunic.

"I do. What did you find to put in it?"

"Well, at first I wasn't sure, but then the flowers told me. There's chamomile and honey and wine and peppermint oil and poppy extract."

For a moment, I cannot speak.

"The flowers told you?" I say at last, almost frightened.

"Oh yes. Sometimes they offer me little clues." He smiles animatedly at me.

Phaethon watches us from the doorway, his face a mask. For a moment our eyes meet, my stomach tying itself into knots.

And then my brother dips his head, his gaze so steadying and sure that some of my burgeoning terror abates. A smile appears along his lips, and I find myself returning it, despite everything.

Because his look is plain and undeniable:

This child is not his grandfather.

I nod back, before turning to grin at Medus.

"You're such a magical, clever boy," I hum into his hair, pulling him close. He smells of citrus and cloves and olive oil, and for a moment I am content.

He lets out a squeal of laughter, pressing a slightly wet kiss to my cheek.

"Witchery must run in the family," Phaethon whispers, taking a seat beside me, so quietly that the child will not hear.

Together we watch as Medus resumes his position upon the stool with the lyre, his whole being intent upon his music.

Author's Note

When I was a child, my mother would, having tucked my younger brother and me into bed, set about reading to us from a well-worn children's book of the Greek myths. I fell in love with those accounts swiftly, sensing in their glossy pages and vivid illustrations something of the hidden nature and shadowy infrastructure of all stories. Although I imagine that the intention of these nighttime readings was that our eyes might grow heavy with childish sleepiness, the fervor and intensity of the chronicles harbored inside those pages were not the kind to inspire repose. In all reality, the events of that long-ago time were so shocking as to require censorship. My brother and I might be denied the specifics of, for instance, how Prometheus had his liver torn out day after day for the crime of having given humanity fire. Instead, my mother amended, the Titan had simply been put in a rather long time-out.

I imagine, now, as I consider the manuscript before me, that I am doing something of a similar sort. Delicately taking up the glittering spars and trenchant barbs of an ancient story and presenting them reverently, and perhaps a little anxiously, in my own style.

Any modern portrayal of Medea presents an interesting challenge.

She commands a thousand associations and identities within the strange terrain of her semidivine body—she is at once the archetypal femme fatale, a mother, a sorcerer, a sister, a murderess, a daughter, a kin-slayer, a wife. Some of these characterizations might superficially seem at odds with one another, a notion that is only subsumed into her complexity. She is savior and Siren contained in a single, bewitching person.

The Medea who scandalized antiquity is indelibly intertwined with social constructions of gender and sexuality, perilously tangled with historical conceptualizations of psychology and the divine, and even caught up in the interface between the perceived barbarity of foreign cultures and the sophisticated, erudite, and decidedly patriarchal civilization that was Ancient Greece. She has emerged as a condensed symbol of nefarious womanhood and a perpetual outsider, mediating a strange dichotomy between her native wildness and the chaos of the natural world and the carefully constrained and familiar realm of the domestic.

So many aspects of Medea's person and interiority inspire empathy—from her difficult position as a girl child coming of age in a society that cared little for the rights and autonomy of women, to the tragedy and trauma of the events that ultimately populated her life. Her resolve, always present, is more than admirable—it is supernatural. And yet certain crimes, particularly those involving the murder of her own children, are difficult to reconcile.

Indeed, cultural depictions of Medea from the classical period offer a fascinating glimpse into that uncertainty.

The Medea of the *Argonautica* is a striking, sympathetic creature, characterized primarily by the sheer fervency of her ardor for Jason. Her knowledge of witchery, while impressive, is considered a mastery to be manipulated by the Olympians on high and a resource to be extracted by Jason and the Argonauts.

Apollonius of Rhodes spends much of Book III of his *Argonautica* foreshadowing the appearance of the obscure Kolchian princess before finally permitting Jason to encounter her as he wanders from room to room in Aeetes's palace. At this moment, Eros draws back his bow and sends the full potency of his arrow into Medea's heart, so that "sudden muteness gripped her spirit / . . . Anguish / quickened her heart and panted in her breast, / and she could think of him [Jason], him only, nothing / but him, as sweet affliction drained her soul" (Apollonius, *Jason and the Argonauts*, A. Poochigian [trans.] and B. Acosta-Hughes [ed.], [Penguin Classics, 2014], pp. 378–81). There is a certain insidious melancholy in the implication of these lines, wherein Medea's first instinct, when overcome by romantic love, is to silence. As a woman doomed to the conventions of antiquity and love for a man, she is, before all else, stripped of her articulation and her autonomy. She is not the agent of her own heart. From the outset, she is deprived of control. Medea's passion, instrumentalized by the Gods, is transformed from a kind of madness into a weapon of deadly precision.

Apollonius is more concerned with depicting Jason's labors alongside the Argonauts and the sagas that accompanied that crew's heroic effort to retrieve the golden fleece than with Medea's own experience. She is an important but peripheral love interest, a character defined in relation to her ability to help or harm a dashing young hero on his adventures. Even so, upon being alerted to Medea's prodigious skill for the first time and told in no uncertain terms to seek her aid, Apollonius's Jason is quick to qualify his faith in the girl with the dismissal, "if we entrust our homecoming to women, / our hopes are very pitiful indeed" (Poochigian, pp. 646–47). Even the granddaughter of a Titan, a genius deft and skilled in the preparation of herbs and the weaving of enchantments, a priestess of Hecate, is reduced, however misguidedly, to the banalities of her sex. By the end of the *Argonautica*, readers have gleaned a contradictory vision of the witch: she is at once cunning in intellect and powerful in her knowledge of herbalism and also utterly desperate, overwhelmed by the onslaught of her sudden love for Jason and poorly equipped when it comes to committing any acts of actual bloodshed.

Euripides' *Medea*, conversely, begins sometime after Apollonius's *Argonautica* has drawn to a close, once Jason and Medea have settled in Corinth with their children, although the play is undeniably invested in the history that precedes it.

Euripides' decision to place Medea herself at the heart of the tragedy, showcasing her interiority, however uncomplimentary over those of the men who surround her, is in itself a radical reorientation. It is this very reconfiguration that allows Euripides' Medea to speak those striking, irresistible lines like, "Surely of all creatures that have life and will, we women / Are the most wretched. When for an extravagant sum, / We have bought a husband, we must then accept him as / Possessor of our body. This is to aggravate / wrong with wrong. Then the great question: will the / man / We get be bad or good? For women divorce is not respectable; to repel the man, not possible" (Euripides, *Medea: And Other Plays*, P. Vellacott [trans.], [Penguin Classics, 1963], p. 24). The Medea who has come to settle in Corinth, though always flashing and formidable, is no longer the young girl who left Kolchis.

Even so, tension abounds as a result of the protagonist's definitive otherness. For Euripides, the native savagery of Medea, who is so volatile and brutal in her intensity, stands in flagrant opposition to the order and civility of the Greek city-state. Her mere presence in Corinth is a destabilizing force. Perhaps, femininity, together with foreignness, functioned in Ancient Greece as they do in the contemporary period, under fairly consistent policing, encompassing a kind of embodied, unspoken relational threat to innumerable societal structures that any hierarchical society might depend on. The instability suggested in the person of Medea is rendered exponentially more perilous by her position as a mother, and therefore, as a vessel of futurity for not only her own lineage but also the values of the Greek city-state.

One might go so far as to read her dissolving union with Jason as an allegory for the incompatibility of two vastly divergent ways of life—the barbarian at the whim of immense feeling, and the civilized, so confined as to be unfeeling. Similarly, the eventual murder of her own progeny might be construed as a rather extreme parable on the difficulties of ensuring that independent, intelligent women properly submit to their husbands. Ineffective wives breed ineffective mothers, posing an almost unmentionable peril to the nuclear family model.

Motherhood, it seems, is never simple.

At last, we come to the elephant in the room. Medea's story is in part so captivating because it represents a kind of horror almost too arduous to hold with any coherence: the murder of children.

I think it is important to remember that Medea was not the first tragic hero to slaughter her children in their infancy, even if she is the most maligned for her transgressions. Herakles, that famed and beloved son of Zeus, renowned for his strength, killed the children he shared with Megara after sustaining a searing, complete kind of madness sent by Hera, queen of the Gods. Tantalus, that wealthy king of Sipylus, murdered his son Pelops and cut him into pieces, serving him to the Gods on high as a kind of perverse test of their discerning palates. Agamemnon, through distressing guile, lured his daughter Iphigenia to the site of her sacrifice to Artemis, before landing the killing blows himself to ensure favorable winds on the Achaean's route to Troy. And Kronos himself made the altogether alarming decision to swallow eleven of his Olympian children one by one as they were born to stop any one of them from overthrowing him, although of course, they all ended up surviving.

I do not know if the work before you exists as a defense of its protagonist. I do not know if certain annihilations can be defended. I possess only the knowledge of my own feelings about Medea, feelings that range from steadfast admiration to breathless unease to rueful recognition. As her agent, I have no choice but to trust her fully, although even if it was not so, I still think I should.

The story I have attempted to tell is one that has been polished in the minds and mouths of much more skilled and eloquent composers. I have crafted it, then, not to copy or detract from its original tellings, but rather to explode it. In this novel, I propose that Medea is not simply misunderstood—for that would be overly simplistic—but that she is, in all her complexity, a product of the impossibility from which she emerges. My *Medea* is superficially interested in feminist reimaginings of a classical text, but more than that it is concerned with monstrosity in an age and setting where monsters existed everywhere.

Even so, the book is not my own. Writing is as much an unconscious process as a conscious one—the lyrical turns of phrase and unintended poetics that emerge on the blackened page are a kind of unexpected topography of the deepest parts of ourselves. At the risk of veering too heavily into the esoteric, I would argue that especially when paying homage to the most ancient of narratives, one is opening up oneself to a kind of possession, yielding discoveries of a strange and magical quality. Like most works of the artistic persuasion, I like to imagine that, though it was shaped by my own faculties and linguistic quirks, the story itself, and the end result, came about through channeling that which was external to my own conscious mind—that is to say, Medea herself.

■ ■ ■

The subject of historical magic is not one I undertook casually. I imagine there are many witches, academics, and occultists of all persuasions who have a different experience with the types of sorcery described in the novel, because magic is, in my admittedly narrow experience, deeply personal in both practice and theory.

As such, Medea's experiences with witchcraft in the novel are not necessarily meant to be pedantic, or an objective assertion of correct magical practice. Rather, the preceding manuscript represents a sort of alchemical fusion, which at once attempts to honor ancient practices and rituals as well as the context out of which they emerged and convey them in such a way that they felt true to my own intuition and philosophy. In a sense, the writing of *Medea* was my own clumsy attempt at necromancy—the resurrection of an ancient story, which never really perished in the first place, all guided of course by the personage for whom the piece is named.

Medea's early encounters with witchcraft in this story are informed first and foremost by her own intuition in correspondence with the natural world (specifically the plants that she strives to understand, communicate with, and take solace in), and secondly by the expertise of her father, the sorcerer Aeetes (who himself we might reasonably assume to have been informed by his elder sister the witch Circe). In this regard, sorcery is a family affair, and as such, it parallels a certain degree of intoxicating beauty, attachment, and dysfunction. Put another way, Medea's magic is undivorceable from the context out of which it arises—plants curl vividly under her fingertips, and the dead are bidden to rise again because they sense in equal parts in her a propensity for creation and destruction. There is a peculiar intersection between trauma and magic, transcendence, and psychosis that even the most diligent student of psychology or earnest disciple of spirituality might find difficult to parse.

I would add here, before too much detail is gone into regarding witchery, that there is some pressure in the modern world, perhaps unconsciously, to label magic as real or unreal—a tension between belief and skepticism. Though such a reduction is pleasing in an ironic, aesthetic sense, it does not apply to the practices described in this book. We live in an interesting age, one that is both beguiling and banal because it promises, like each that preceded it, perhaps disingenuously, to be more advanced than what came before. We might imagine ourselves, as modern people, as being very far away from the magic of earlier ages. It is beneficial from time to time to suspend that urge. The idea that the scientific method and archaic forms of magical practice might be mutually exclusive is, of course, an entirely uncreative one. True intelligence rarely lies in exclusion, but flourishes in broader connections, in the application of one discovery to the next.

As Medea becomes aware of her inherent abilities, she begins to take an interest in *Pharmakon*, those practices that served as the basis for her father's abilities as a sorcerer. As though aware of its own poeticism, the word *pharmakon* might be translated from the Ancient Greek to mean simultaneously "remedy" or "poison." For anyone interested in plant magic, etymology itself seems to cry, *"The stakes are high!"* However, the ambiguity of the discipline endears itself immediately to Medea's nature, which is never wanting in the paradoxical or obscure itself. Her studies of the properties of plants parallels her development as a distinct self, her own mind becoming as lush and vivacious and contradictory and potent and precarious and queerly beautiful as the herbs she adores.

At the core of Medea's practice is the belief that all things in nature are connected, from the sun in the sky to the seed germinating in the soil. Everything physical, then, is a manifestation of the intangible, of the transcendent, and as such might be interpreted as a sign or microcosm of something more expansive. This mystical epicenter of belief and ritual is informed, like much of the novel itself, from a multitude of sources. I was lucky enough to draw from poignant sources in my representations of magic, and not all of them were necessarily Ancient Greek in origin. For Medea's brewing of love potions, I drew from the ancient Egyptian premise that the only dark magic is love magic. In describing the philosophy of planetary herbalism, I drew on the concept of the Elizabethan chain of being, in which the divine is considered connected to the lowliest worm through the secret processes of this life. In Medea's discussions of correspondences, of one thing being a clue or signpost to another, perhaps divine thing, I relied on my knowledge of Sufism.

To formulate the descriptions and theories behind Medea's usage of *Pharmakon*, I relied heavily on my own knowledge of botany, classical artistic symbolism, and contemporary practices of planetary herbalism in addition to my own intuitive feelings. Subsequently, the poultices and potions derived in the novel are informed by multiple sources that I shall elaborate upon now. Over time, I found that Medea's witchery made more intuitive sense to me as I submerged myself deeper and deeper into not only her story but also these distinct disciplines. For a deeper understanding of planetary herbalism, the insights and offerings of Catland Books, specifically the expertise supplied by Melissa Jayne Madara, proved invaluable. For a beginner's exploration of the symbology behind all manner of vegetation and a sampling of the stories associated with flowering things, I applaud Jean-Michel Othoniel's informative and aesthetic *The Secret Language of Flowers*. For a more academic examination of the occult in Ancient Greece and Rome with accompanying primary source materials on everything from alchemy to divination, Georg Luck's second edition of *Arcana Mundi: Magic and the Occult in the Greek and Roman Worlds* offers abundant commentary. And for a slightly fanciful, poetic take on the botanical sciences, one need look no further than Dale Pendell's *Pharmako/Poeia: Plant Powers, Poisons, and Herbcraft*.

Of course, the best information to be gleaned on the subject of herbalism always comes from the plants themselves. I say in the novel that plants have a supernatural manner of "talking to" or communicating with Medea and her family members, and this is something I believe to be true generally. A good witch must and foremost learn to communicate with foliage through the mediation of her own intuition. In Oscar Wilde's *The Picture of Dorian Gray*, there is a scene in which Dorian plunges his nose into the heady bud of a flower, and as he is overcome, the omnipresent Lord Henry asserts, "That is one of the great secrets of life—to cure the soul by means of the senses and the senses by means of the soul." I imagine that there is something of witchery in such a sentiment.

Following her submergence in planetary herbalism, Medea is compelled to undertake the study of a related but drastically more perilous subject: necromancy. Necromancy in Ancient Greece was traditionally less focused on the notion of resurrection and more concerned with the communion between the living and the dead. The means by which some form of communication might be established by a living party for the benefit of conversing with a deceased person were somewhat complicated. In Homer's *Odyssey*, for instance, Odysseus is able to consult with the shade of the blind seer Tiresias only after following a complex ritual involving the digging and filling of a pit with milk, honey, the blood of sacrificial animal(s), and libations. Conversely, in the myth of Orpheus and Eurydice, the shattered bridegroom can enter the underworld and converse with Hades himself on the merits of his voice and lyre-playing abilities alone. To some extent, the procedures and magical rites described in this tome are the accumulation of hybrids of existing dramatizations and my own creative choices.

It was incumbent upon me to present Medea's experimentation with necromancy in such a way that would not strike readers as overly gratuitous or violent. For that reason, the details of the physical acts she is forced to carry out are relayed with less detail than the philosophy behind them. Even so, there were occasions where certain instances of death or mutilation struck me as distressing and may also engender such feelings in a sympathetic reader. All that I can say for the defense of their continued inclusion is that I have attempted to keep unnecessary bloodshed to a minimum, and that what has been allowed to remain in the current manuscript serves an important narrative purpose. The depictions of necromancy in the novel not only offer insight into Medea's ability to force herself to carry out tasks most averse to her, to overrule the inclinations and hesitations of her own body, but also to press at the boundaries of her propensity for ruthlessness. What follows, then, is my trauma-informed attempt to honor Medea's experience and also build a vivid and evocative world that feels true to myself as a storyteller.

I shall close with the following disclaimer: the mythology of Ancient Greece is vast and varied—so much so that certain narrative versions contradict others of the same subject. I have attempted to remain as true as possible to elements of the stories that are so well loved by so many while also allowing for creative agency and divergent lines of logic and action among certain characters. Certain "reductions" have been implemented for the sake of clarity. For instance, Medea's brother, whose given name was Absyrtus, but whose nickname, "Phaethon," came about from his outshining the other boys of his age, is referred to simply as Phaethon. Additionally, there have been times when I have been forced to choose between different accounts of the same story or family lineage. The example that springs now to mind is the existence of a plethora of accounts of Medea's childhood that name Asterodeia and not Idyia as the mother of Phaethon, making him Medea's half brother. I hope that these liberties I have taken with the historical material might be inoffensive to readers who are familiar with divergent accounts.

Acknowledgments

I have been miraculously surrounded by some of the most resilient, tenacious, empathetic, and intelligent people who could be expected to exist, and more than that, I have had the extraordinary good fortune to love and be loved by them.

This book would be nothing if not for the protagonist who helms her—a woman who painted the walls of antiquity red with passion and rage and labor—Medea herself. Navigating my relationship with her has been a queer, heady experience built on trust and wariness, curiosity, and mutual understanding. I am honored that she entrusted even a fragment of her story to me to polish and proffer forth on her behalf.

Thank you to my mom, twice orphaned and always kind, whose heart of gold never ceases to amaze me. It would be impossible to articulate how much you mean to me, to count every night you stayed up with me to finish a school project, or talked me through moments of intense anxiety, or made me a steaming mug of good black tea. Somehow, you never doubted my ability to write, or forced me to take some alternative practical path despite the risk and uncertainty others attributed to my dreams. I love you infinitely!

To my brother, Ben, my Gemini twin. I loved growing up with you—the good parts: completing motherboard missions, telling each other stories before bed, building monster traps—and the bad: switching between homes and forcing you to wake up five million times in the night whenever you bonked your head. You have grown into the most honorable, philosophical, infuriating, kind, pepper-obsessed man I have ever met—but what did we expect? You were always the coolest child.

To my wonderful girlfriend and archival consultant, Hailey Marie Wolovetz, who is as clever and ethereal as she is breathtakingly beautiful and resourceful. I'm so lucky to have you to explore the world with, from googling eels, to looking for Ogopogo, to debating whether mermaids lay eggs. Meeting you felt delightfully fated and loving you has been terribly easy. I have a hard time trusting anyone, as you know, but with you I have always felt safe and held, which is a blessing beyond description.

To my mortal enemy, court astrologer, and only friend in all of Los Angeles, Leka Gopal. I'll buy you a Fiji when this is published, probably, if you're lucky. Also, Hearhers says you haven't visited her at her illustrious Swiss boarding school in over seven months, which isn't great, if we're being honest.

To my ex-roommate and fanfiction recommender extraordinaire, Elizabeth Chyn. Thank you for showing me *Voltron* and being so cool since the literal first grade.

To my first literary collaborators, the brilliant Sam and Anna Griffith.

To my demanding but ruthlessly efficient ice-skating coach, Little Ben (Evgeni) Griffith.

To my cat, Suni, who owns my heart. To Vinnie (my muse), Patchie (who reminds me to have boundaries), Zip Zop (my contentment), BK (my ethics instructor), Biddle (equal parts sweetness and strength), and Mabel (who keeps me on my toes). To my sweet pups, Mushi and Berry.

To my dad, who told me stories of his own invention before bed each night and continues to weave tales even now that my brother and I are grown. I treasure our memories of searching for ladybug nests and rockhounding.

To my brilliant agent, Jessica Spitz, who took a chance on my debut manuscript and seemed to understand it in a way that was almost supernaturally intuitive. Her ability to navigate the publishing world with wit, patience, and diplomacy should be studied by academics for years to come.

To Suzannah Ball, James Munro, Carolina Beltran, and the rest of the team at WME who were so supportive in a process that was entirely new and foreign to me.

To my phenomenal editor, Loan Le, who thoughtfully devoted herself to making this novel the best it could be. Her prowess at video editing cannot be overstated.

To Elizabeth Hitti, whose diligence, speed, and preexisting knowledge of mythology were unmatched.

To the gorgeous team at Atria, specifically Paige Lytle, Shelby Pumphrey, Lacee Burr, Dayna Johnson, Holly Rice, Katie Rizzo, Nicole Bond, Shelly Perron, and Kyoko Watanabe for their care and enthusiasm with my debut novel. To Kelli McAdams and Jimmy Iacobelli for their work on the astounding and breathtaking cover (a cover, I will note, that apparently made all of Atria gasp when they first glimpsed it).

To Melissa Jayne Madara and the crew at Catland for granting me a foundation in planetary herbalism and methodically answering my many questions.

To my favorite cinema directors, Delaney Posey, Wyatt and Wayde Sellers, Jackson and Johnny Weghorst.

To Ludim Galdamez, who is kind, wise, and strong. Thank you for being there without fail every Monday since I was small.

To the visionary hosts of CageFest! and Passover, Carol Glazer, Rachael Sevilla, and Guy—and I suppose, at a distance, Nicolas Cage.

To Nancy Cronin, for the lifts to the train station and steady encouragement always.

To Karen Miller and Kaete Elliot, for keeping me mostly sane and my mind expansive.

To the teachers, professors, graduate-student instructors, and mentors who have been so instrumental in encouraging my self-confidence and scope of knowledge and passion—Grace Lavery, Monique Saenz Wilshire, Jenna Coughlin, and Ashwak Hauter.

To Reece Clark, the definition of a Renaissance man and king of my heart.

To Sasha Roeske, for serenading me with such luxurious chicken *à la Sasha* on weekdays that she can be forgiven for not naming her firstborn Alfonso or Granola. To Lorena Lara Vacaflor, who was always so gentle from the time she first met me at CEC. Thank you both for being so patient with me before my frontal lobe was fully developed.

To my DI associates, and the foremost experts on paleo-biological perspectives in all of North America, Madeleine Woodward, John Griffith, Lisa McNulty, and Remi Nichols.

To my friends old and new: Athalee Aguilar, Nate Goodwin, Andrew Sattler, Emily Colon, Ruby Guzalowski, Joy Benjauthrit, Ethan Angold, Monica Song, Neena Mohan, Margo Oka, Ani Sarkissian, Taline Balian, Savannah and Frank Mournighan, David Larson, Maddi Ghatak, Diya Chaudhuri, Stacy Kim, Erin Gould, Iain Filkins, Anthi Sklavenitis, Sabrina Holguin, Amber Erwin, Gerry Carson, and Cass and River Hall.

To my author and poet besties, Hannah McKelson, Jett Elijah, Sonia Del Rivo, Mr. Max, and Jessica Webb. To my internet lovelies, Isabella Viega, Krista Watson, Valentina Lunasanta, Airidescence, and Charlie Mendoza.

To my effervescent exes (because I am doubtless a lesbian stereotype), Brianna Vega, Zhena Morillo, Megan Tetrick, and Vanessa Lopez.

To my spiritual advisor and first babysitter, Roger Dahl.

To Carol Victor for accompanying me through the Oakland nighttime and being a spectacular honorary aunt. To Kristi Keller, a wonderful hiking companion. To Michelle Sherman, of secret-gate lore.

To Ioanna, Makis, and Christos Sklavenitis, for inviting my mother to Greece so many years ago and starting a love affair with the mythology that sprung from there.

To the man who single-handedly got me through precalculus, Jihwan Kim.

To the dedicated group of moms who let me intrude on so many soirees: Jenny Pippard, Susanna Griffith, Nina Ries, and Lori Oliwenstein.

To the shrewd young creative minds that startle and inspire me, specifically Selena, Rey, Sara, Forrest, Caroline, Abhay, Frankie, Anaya, Arjun, Lily, Emilie, Mikaela, and Stella.

To my uncle Ted, who could never once throw me in the ocean if he tried. I win.

To my amazing extended family all over the United States, from Kern County to Anchorage.

To Anne, Milt, Zelma Lou, George, Eleanor, and Bill.

Eilish Quin is a queer writer and artist based in the bustle and glamour of Los Angeles. She enjoys conversing with plants, watching British crime dramas, photographing lizards, rereading gothic novels, and staring aimlessly into tempestuous bodies of water. *Medea* is her first novel. Follow her on Twitter @eilish_quin or on Instagram @eilishquin for writing updates or pictures of her various cats.